ICEFIRE

JUDITH & GARFIELD REEVES-STEVENS

POCKET BOOKS
New York   London   Toronto   Sydney   Tokyo   Singapore

POCKET BOOKS, a division of Simon & Schuster Inc.
1230 Avenue of the Americas, New York, NY 10020

Copyright © 1998 by Softwind, Inc.

ISBN: 0-671-01402-1

First Pocket Books hardcover printing July 1998

10 9 8 7 6 5 4 3 2 1

POCKET and colophon are registered trademarks of
Simon & Schuster Inc.

Printed in the U.S.A.

For Murray Kingsburgh.
A great brother-in-law
who knows far too much about
cold wet weather.

Those who use fire to assist their attacks are intelligent.
Those who use inundations are powerful.

Sun Tzu, *The Art of War*

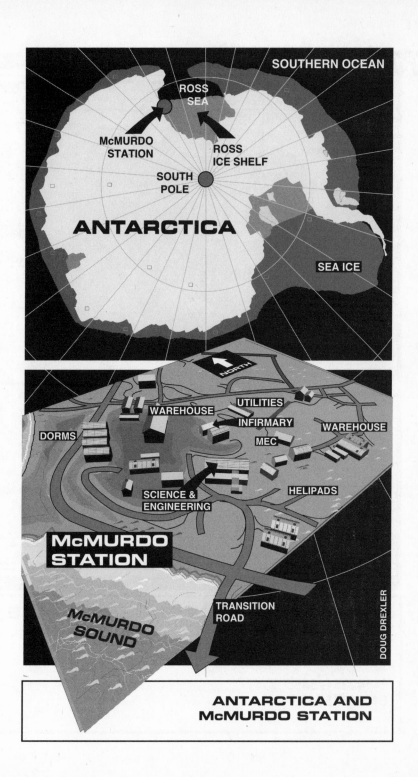

ANTARCTICA AND
McMURDO STATION

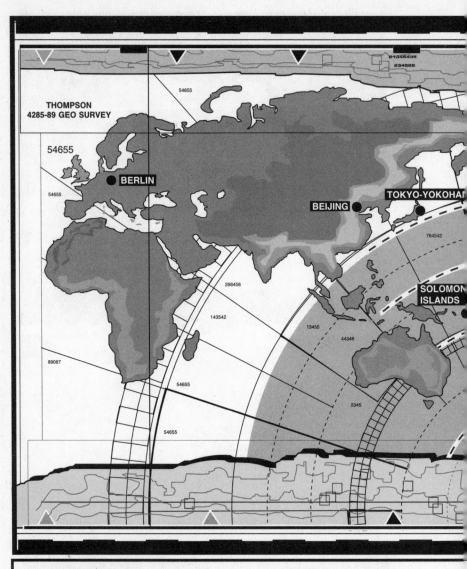

THOMPSON
4285-89 GEO SURVEY

54655

54655

BERLIN

54655

BEIJING

TOKYO-YOKOHA

764542

266456

143542

13455

44346

SOLOMON
ISLANDS

89087

54655

2345

54655

ICEFIRE DETONATION SEQUENCE
NOVEMBER 24-27

3454235425455
64536645643

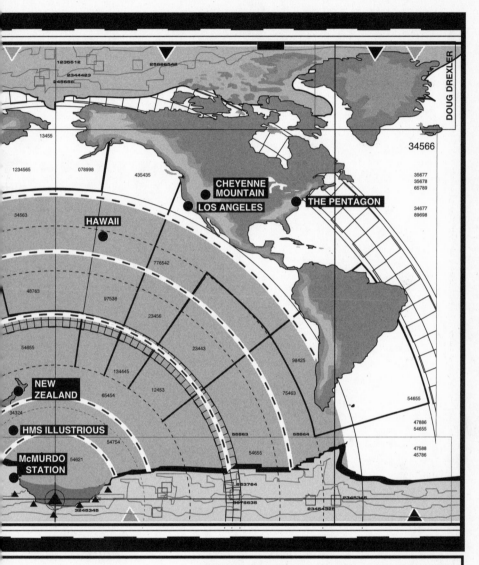

DOUG DREXLER

HMS ILLUSTRIOUS - EVENT PLUS 03 HOURS
NEW ZEALAND - EVENT PLUS 10 HOURS
SOLOMON ISLANDS - EVENT PLUS 23 HOURS
HAWAII - EVENT PLUS 35 HOURS
TOKYO-YOKOHAMA - EVENT PLUS 38 HOURS
LOS ANGELES - EVENT PLUS 40 HOURS

7726-TGS

EVENT MINUS 7 HOURS

As it had for more than ten million years, the Ice waited, stable, unchanging.

Each passage of the Earth around the sun brought long months in which the southern pole faced only stars and the dark of space, and as the snows fell in those desolate winters, they did not melt.

In time, the Ice grew, until seventy percent of the world's fresh water, and ninety percent of the world's ice, was locked in its embrace, captured by temperatures colder than those that extinguished the life from the sister planet, Mars. In places, the Ice was more than three miles thick.

At times, driven by the cycles of the sun's output and the slowly changing angle of the Earth, the Ice surged across the planet, growing out beyond its bounds, embracing other lands, forever changing the landscape and the life-forms that evolved there.

At times, the Ice retreated, melted by the warming currents of the oceans that surrounded it.

Usually, it was a slow and rhythmic dance.

Then the humans came, and like the Ice they surged across the planet, forever changing its landscape and the life-forms that evolved there. In time, they found the Ice.

They sailed there in wooden ships that were crushed and frozen. They flew there in aircraft unable to withstand the constant winds of more than 180 miles per hour. But still they came, explorers and *adventurers, sealers and whalers, scientists and engineers. To learn the secrets of the Ice.*

Unmindful of humans, the Ice still answered only to the slow swing of the planet, the cycling rhythms of the sun.

As it had for more than ten million years, the Ice waited, stable, unchanging.

Until the final, inevitable day.

The day the soldiers came.

SHADOW FORGE

WEDNESDAY NOVEMBER 24

ONE

THE ICE

Three minutes from Gentle Two Five's point of no return, Antarctica disappeared.

With it also vanished any chance for Operation SHADOW FORGE to succeed. Only once before in his naval career had Mitch Webber faced certain failure at such an extreme level. And, as before, he refused to accept it.

The high-visibility-orange UH-1N Iroquois carrying Webber and four others thundered through the frigid air above the Ross Ice Shelf. The large 25 painted on the twin-engine helicopter's fuselage gave its call number. The call-sign prefix "Gentle" hadn't been heard in Antarctica for years, not since the U.S. Naval aviation unit, Development Squadron 6, had transferred its peacetime support mission to the New York Air National Guard 109th Air Wing. But this was no longer peacetime, and the Navy had returned to the Ice.

As of 1715 Global Positioning Satellite time, Gentle Two Five was 800 miles from the South Pole, 3,000 miles from Christchurch, New Zealand, and 500 feet above nothing. The wind-smeared, early-summer blizzard of loose snow and ice dust below shrouded all detail of what lay beneath. Three hundred feet above Gentle Two Five, the disorienting visual effect was repeated in clouds so violently churned by gale-force winds they had become little more than a featureless gray haze. Only the eastern horizon showed variation. There, an unnaturally thin and precise crease of almost pain-fully blue sky confirmed that at least a division between up and down still existed. But only the artificial horizon on the aircraft's instrument console could distinguish which of the two surfaces was above, and which below, as if when the seventh continent had van-ished, it had taken the rest of the world with it.

Mitch Webber had flown helicopters through worse—over the Iraqi desert, the Colombian rain forest; he'd even dodged through the office towers of San Francisco. But unlike those other active Forge alerts, this time no one fired up at him.

He was a fifteen-year veteran of the Navy, and if he had to sum up his recent career in one word, it would be *thief*—government-approved and sanctioned. Until he'd received the invitation from NAVSPECWARCOM—Naval Special Warfare Command—to join a new Development Unit, he had been a flight engineer and pilot by education and default. That invitation transformed him into a Spe-cial Operations SEAL by choice and determination. Now he was one of a handful of uniquely trained specialists on detached service to an intentionally low-key civilian agency—the otherwise nonde-script Department of Energy. Webber's new uniform consisted of a briefcase, a tie, and an office cubicle in Arlington, Virginia. Except during a Forge operation. Then Webber was Team Leader, Nuclear Emergency Search Team One, and his uniform was combat gear.

He stood in the center of the helicopter's cabin, one hand loosely twisted in a cargo net stowed overhead, easily keeping his footing as the deck bucked in the random buffeting of the winds. The helo's pair of 1,290-hp Pratt & Whitney twin turboshaft engines shook off the assault of the Antarctic storm as easily as Webber did. The craft was the offspring of the venerable UH-1H, the "Huey" of Vietnam, but it was generations more advanced than its war-fighting ances-tor. With the redundant safety factor of two engines, auxiliary fuel tanks, GPS navigation, and Doppler ranging, the Iroquois, Bell Heli-copter Model 212, ruled the Ice as easily as the first Hueys had ruled the Asian jungles.

On almost any other mission before joining the DOE, Webber might have been in the pilot's seat himself, taking control of his own life and safety, and those of his team. But his NEST function on a Forge alert, like that of Lieutenant "Ox" Bregoli behind him, near the starboard window, was defined by the clothing he wore. The pilot, the copilot, and NEST One's weapons specialist were dressed in bulky and colorful Extreme Cold Weather gear—the pilots in flight green, the engineer in red. Even their flight helmets were painted with Day-Glo orange panels. All three were dressed for survival on the Ice.

But Webber and Bregoli wore the white parka and leggings of PolarOps camouflage, their name badges, rank insignia, and the flags on their shoulders concealed by Velcro-secured white Goretex panels. In polar camouflage gear, even the massively built Bregoli would be unseen against ice and snow. Unlike the pilots and the engineer, Webber and Bregoli were dressed for combat—on a continent in which weapons were outlawed and there was nothing to fight over.

"Captain Webber. Coming up on final grid position." The pilot's voice crackled in Webber's helmet speaker, for a moment drowning out the hollow roar that filled the helicopter's cabin. Webber peered ahead, past the pilot and copilot, just able to look down through the lower nose windows at the gray haze streaming below at 120 miles an hour. He knew the Antarctic storm layer was no more than ten feet thick, yet it was opaque enough to completely obscure the startling flat expanse beneath them. It was, however, no barrier to the helo's radar. The pale amber glow of the radar display clearly revealed the Ross Ice Shelf, solid and eternal, beneath its stormy shroud.

Webber glanced back at his team's weapons specialist strapped into the unpadded, fold-down jump seat on the aft bulkhead. He was Hadrian Gowers, forty-something, overweight, uncomfortable, and one of the most important members of NEST One. Awkwardly balanced on the engineer's lap was a NEC Gladiator laptop computer, built to Department of Defense specifications for combat applications. The almost indestructible laptop was housed in a magnesium case, its hard drive encapsulated by a gelatin sleeve. Through the Iroquois's wiring harness, Gowers's deceptively compact computer was directly connected to the BO-105 gamma detector pod bolted onto the helo's starboard strut, and to the matching neutron detector on the port strut. Almost comical in his ECW gear, Gowers swayed back and forth in his seat as the headwinds struck the helo. He wasn't smiling. Unused to the rough ride, the weapons specialist had vomited twice in the past hour. But he was still the DOE's ranking expert on nuclear-trigger mechanisms, improvised or manufactured. If what the Defense Intelligence Agency feared was on the Ice *was* really there, Webber knew that Gowers was the man to have on the mission that found it, no matter how much the pudgy civilian hated fieldwork.

Webber pressed his fingers to his throat mike. "Gowers—status."

"No gamma detections," the engineer said. Webber knew that much. He waited for him to continue. "Not even random background fluctuations. It might be an equipment fault."

Lieutenant Bregoli shifted on his makeshift seat of bright yellow carryall bags—emergency shelter and food supplies, a necessity on any polar flight. "We're flying over shelf ice," he shouted back at Gowers. Bregoli kept his balance by bracing himself with the white-painted stock of his CAR-15. In his huge gloved hands, the already compact rifle looked childishly small.

Webber understood his lieutenant's assessment of the situation. On any military mission, knowing the terrain was essential. Directly below them was the Ross Ice Shelf, a single, solid sheet of ice, thirty percent of Antarctica's total shelf ice, roughly the same surface area as France—210,000 square miles. Directly under the Shelf was the Ross Sea. The thickness of the Shelf ranged from 600 feet at sea's edge to more than 2,000 feet hundreds of miles closer to land. Shelf ice meant there were no rocks or stony strata to provide the minor gamma sources that might naturally occur in ordinary terrain.

Gowers was clearly annoyed with Bregoli, impatient with Webber, much more tired than three hours in a helicopter should have made him. "I know," he said. "But even in a completely clean environment, we should be picking up random noise, spurious signals. Something. There's nothing."

Webber knew about spurious signals. The still-classified 1995 RAINBOW FORGE alert in San Francisco, in which the Federal Emergency Management Agency had come within three minutes of activating the Emergency Broadcast System and ordering an evacuation of the city, had bogged down precisely because of spurious signals. The coastal city contained hundreds of benign radiation sources, from hospital storerooms of medical isotopes, to university physics labs, engineering firms, mineralogical collections, and even fresh asphalt used for road repairs. NEST's desperate race to detect an IND—Improvised Nuclear Device—against that background clutter of legitimate point sources had been a nightmare of logistics.

In a jagged white lightning bolt down the left side of his chest, Webber still bore the scar from the last-minute, desperate shootout on the rooftop helicopter pad of the Bank of America building where the device had been recovered. One lucky round had struck him from behind, penetrating his left triceps, then angled inward to hit his ceramic body armor from the *inside*. Ricocheting down his ribs, the bullet had halted just above his belt, where it had burned an inch-deep hole in his flesh. He had remained unaware of his wound until three mercenaries lay dead beside a tied-down executive helicopter. Hadrian Gowers had been there to defuse the device—a lethally simple chemical bomb employing fifty pounds of homemade TNT and a wax-sealed Gatorade bottle filled with just over one pound of powdered plutonium that had been catalogued as "misdirected" more than two years earlier in Japan. The explosion would not have been nuclear, but the resultant spread of the toxic, radioactive metal would have given cancer to 400,000 civilians over the next ten years and rendered parts of San Francisco and Oakland uninhabitable for more than a century.

But at least during RAINBOW FORGE, NEST had known what the perpetrators had wanted, and that intelligence had enabled NEST operatives, working with the DOD's Joint Special Operations Forces, to anticipate the timing and the location of the threatened detonation.

NEST and Webber did not have the advantage of such knowledge now. Nor even any strong theories. The mission-background assessments Webber had been given when he and his team had arrived at McMurdo Station one week ago, only told him that as of November 15 the total population of Antarctica was less than three thousand, spread among sixty-six scientific and meteorological stations operated by fourteen different countries. There were no official national boundaries in Antarctica, no natural resources that could be exploited with currently available technology, and no clear reason why anyone would want to smuggle nuclear weapons to the continent.

But a twelve-month-long joint investigation by the Departments of Energy and Justice, the Defense Intelligence Agency, and the U.S. Special Operations Command had concluded, strongly, that someone *had* or *was* smuggling one or more of those weapons onto the Ice. It was Mitch Webber's mission to find those weapons, no matter how unlikely or illogical their presence.

The helo abruptly dropped ten feet in a downdraft. If there had been anything left in Gowers's stomach, the weapons specialist would have vomited again. Instead, he just moaned.

"What about neutron hits?" Webber asked.

Gowers's voice was uneven but determined. "Normal readings across the board."

Webber automatically consulted the operational flowchart he had constructed in his mind. With its inboard auxiliary tanks, the helo had just enough fuel to complete one more search grid on its way back to McMurdo, one hundred miles away, northwest. Was the possible malfunction of the helo's gamma detector reason enough to cancel that last grid?

Webber considered his options. It was unlikely the gamma detector had been tampered with. Who would do that without also sabotaging the matching neutron detector? Perhaps not in a city, but here on the Ice, where any radiation source should stand out like a flare at midnight, Webber reckoned the neutron pod would provide minimal, but acceptable, support for the mission.

Then again, minimal but acceptable took on a different meaning measured against the devastation of a nuclear explosion.

But devastation of what? Webber asked himself.

Then he saw the punctuated flash of a red running light, circling five miles ahead. *Typical*, Webber thought with a flash of irritation. "Patch me through," he told the pilot, and the helo banked toward the light.

"Gentle Three Zero," the pilot intoned, "this is Gentle Two Five. Over."

The pilot of the distant, second helicopter, already on station at the rendezvous coordinates, responded at once. She was followed by another, more familiar voice, rising and falling in the frequency distortion common to Antarctic radio communications. "Look who's last at the party again. What did you bring me? Over."

Webber noted Bregoli's start of surprise at hearing his commander addressed so informally. But Webber forced a smile. It was either that or admit he'd been outmaneuvered. Once again, Nick Young had reached the objective before him.

"NEST Two, this is NEST *One*," Webber replied. "What is your fuel status? Over."

"I'm at a big seven five zero pounds," Young radioed back. By now, Webber's helo had come within a quarter mile of Young's, and the two orange craft circled each other like belligerent dragonflies deciding whether they should engage in battle or go their separate ways. The columnar holes their downdrafts punched through the storm layer reached down to the ice, not directly beneath them, but almost 200 yards due west, attesting to the strength of the wind. "Plenty for one more grid on retrograde," Young continued. "Over."

Webber leaned forward between the pilot and copilot to check his own fuel status. Six hundred and seventy pounds. Even in the confusion of an Antarctic storm, Young had been able to find a tailwind to exploit. "Copy that," he said, suppressing any outward sign of emotional response to Young's challenge. A Forge alert was not the time to indulge in their usual sparring. "How are your detectors functioning? Over."

Young's response was not immediate. Apparently he had to confer with Glendon Morris, the DOE weapons specialist assigned to NEST Two.

"Glen says the neutron counter's nominal. But she's getting no background on the gamma. She thinks there might be a fault. Over."

Webber doubted both his and Young's gamma detectors could develop the same fault at the same time. If two gamma detectors on two different aircraft were reporting similar readings, or lack of readings, Webber was inclined to look for an exterior and natural cause. The Antarctic radio-spectrum environment was subject to a myriad violent electromagnetic events. A minor solar flare that might have no measurable effect on the rest of the planet could result in a Polar-Cap Absorption event, heavily ionizing the polar ionosphere and causing complete blackouts of HF and VHF communications. In addition to PCAs, disappearing solar filaments, coronal mass ejections, and coronal holes could all create geomagnetic storms with varying and unpredictable effects over the entire frequency spectrum.

"NEST Two," Webber transmitted, "are you good to go on neutron only? Over."

"That's a big affirmative." Young's instant reply was no surprise to Webber. He had no doubt Young would be willing to walk across the Ross Ice Shelf barefoot with only a Geiger counter to locate an IND. He was so obsessively committed to the overall NEST mission that in one tour at the Pentagon, he had almost single-handedly forced the creation of the DOD's Counterproliferation Support Program. Thanks to Young, the DOD was now developing effective responses to rogue bacteriological and chemical warfare threats, all patterned on the NEST scenarios intended for nuclear threats. Webber was about to reply to Young's anticipated positive mission assessment when he realized he hadn't heard the customary "over."

"I'm ready to fly search grid Baker Baker Two Two Four," Young continued. "If we split it, we'll be back at McMurdo within ninety minutes. What do you say? Over."

Webber studied the map clipped to the board in the center of the console. It was a "Grid North" navigational chart peculiar to Antarctica, with the South Pole at the top and north/south meridians running parallel to each other instead of converging on the pole. It was a confusing system for anyone trained in traditional navigation. But in a region where magnetic compasses were next to useless and even the Global Positioning Satellite constellation could only be accessed sporadically for certain hours of the day, Grid North was a useful, if arbitrary, system.

Webber's copilot understood what Webber was looking for and X'd in their current position on the chart. Young was suggesting they fly their final grid of the day to the chart's northwest, on a wide, outside curve back to McMurdo. Technically, with Young's helo and its extra fuel flying the outer area, they would cover more territory in the search. But that territory would be completely composed of more Shelf ice, more nothing.

Webber pointed to another grid, diagonally down from the first. "Negative, NEST Two. We will fly Baker Baker *Three* Two Four. Over." That, at least, would cover part of the Shelf's groundline. DOE analysts had come up with only one tentative theory to explain the presence of a nuclear device in Antarctica that made even the slightest bit of sense, and it required the presence of solid ground, not ice. It was the barest of straws, but after a week of no results, Webber was impatient enough to grasp at anything.

"NEST One," Young radioed back, and Webber could hear the condescension in his teammate's voice, "you might want to reconsider. We get close to those formations on the backside of Minna Bluff, we're going to be bouncing like a hooker's . . ." Young hesitated as if just remembering he had a female weapons specialist on his team. This was the modern Navy, after all. "It's going to be a rough ride, cowboy. Especially with low fuel. Over."

Webber couldn't resist the jab. "So leave the groundline to us, NEST Two. You take the Shelf. It'll be *easier*. Over."

This time Young's response was crisp and to the point, reminding Webber that only the best of the Navy's warriors were allowed into SEAL training, and only the best of the best completed that training. Already friends in the service, he and Young had gone in together and had emerged from the head-on competition with their friendship and their respect for each other even stronger. Webber knew there was a soldier every bit his equal inside Young. At least on those occasions when Young decided to take a mission seriously.

"No bullshit, Mitch," Young said. "And no offense to the pilots. But these are transport helos and transport crews. If you want to do any hairy flying, we'd better save it for the Special Ops pilots when they get here. Over."

Webber saw his pilot and copilot exchange a look. Then the pilot glanced back and carefully raised his hand, middle finger extended.

"Nick," Mitch radioed. "We're flying with *Navy* pilots. I have full confidence. Repeat: We will fly Baker Baker Three Two Four. Over."

The pilot gave Webber a thumbs-up, and then a sudden burst of radio distortion turned Young's response into an earsplitting banshee's wail. "You had full confidence in Baghdad, pal. I strongly suggest Baker Baker *Two* Two Four. Over."

Webber gripped the back of the copilot's chair as if he expected the helo to pitch. But the hover angle held steady.

It didn't help that Webber knew Young's suggestion had merit. This was a full Forge alert, but they weren't on a countdown. There had been no contact with rogue actors. No ultimatums delivered. But of all the arguments Young might have invoked, he had used the one that left Webber no choice. Baghdad.

"Screw you, too, pal," Webber said. He pressed again on his mike. "NEST Two, initiate search pattern for grid Baker Baker *Three* Two Four. Out." He touched the pilot on the shoulder. "Get us out of here." Then he moved back to the center of the cabin as the helo banked to come about and head straight into the unrelenting storm. Caught up in unwelcome memory, Webber did not acknowledge the inquiring look Bregoli gave him before he turned back to stare out the starboard window.

Twenty minutes more of flying elapsed, with no significant change in weather conditions before Young made contact again, this time to report that, according to the NEST Two weapons specialist, his helo's neutron detector was now malfunctioning. The search had to be called off for the day.

13

"NEST Two," Webber radioed, "we're halfway through our grid. Fly an intercept course and we'll head back together. Over."

Surprisingly, Young didn't put up a fight. "Copy that, NEST One. I'll be on your tail in ten. Out."

Webber pulled back his parka sleeve and checked one of his two watches—the cheap Timex digital set to McMurdo time. His second watch, a heavy, standard-issue Swiss Luminox, was always set to GPS mean time. For its most critical global operations, the U.S. military operated by only one clock, one time zone—Washington's.

It was 10:40 local time. Depending on the winds, they'd be landing at McMurdo by 11:30. Webber dug into a supply duffel held to the floor by two bungee cords. He broke out a dented, dull-green Thermos bottle, offered coffee to Bregoli and Gowers, who both declined, then poured some for himself in the bottle's cup lid. Unproductive, but it was his way of marking that today's mission was already over.

That was when Gowers shouted, "Neutron alarm, level three!"

Webber gulped down his coffee, moved swiftly to his engineer's side, and turned Gowers's laptop to read the spike in the display window. He checked the directional coordinates, bearing to the northeast, then shouted them to the pilot. The helo changed course as Webber replaced the lid on his Thermos. He shoved it back into the supply duffel on his way to the front of the craft to check the radar.

"There," the pilot said. His gloved finger tapped a smear of amber light on the display, twenty miles straight ahead.

"What is it?" Webber asked. The radar return was asymmetrical, as if he were looking at a cloud on weather radar.

The copilot checked the chart. "Hard to say," she answered. "No islands on the map. Probably an ice pressure ridge."

"ETA ten minutes," the pilot said.

According to the DOE's only theory, Webber knew that the presence of an ice pressure ridge made some sense. "Update NEST Two," he told the pilot. But before the pilot had even touched the frequency control, Young's voice came over the speakers. "From out of the dust, a galloping horse with the speed of light, and a hearty Hi-yo Silver!"

Webber followed the pilot's glance to port. A flashing red running light was closing.

The pilot snorted, unimpressed. "Fucking cavalry's here."

Webber's copilot tapped her screen to draw Webber's attention. NEST Two was no longer on the return leg to McMurdo. Young had apparently changed course to match Webber's.

Following protocol and using call signs, Young's pilot then came on to confirm that Gentle Three Zero was joining Gentle Two Five on the retrograde to base.

"What do you know that I don't?" Young radioed. "Over."

Webber answered. "Gowers picked up a neutron burst coming from the ridgelike radar target . . . twenty miles ahead. Over."

"Pick your bet," Young replied. "Rock outcropping or geo assay. Even odds. Over."

"You're the one who hangs in Vegas," Webber said. Young's helo was a quarter mile off now, still angling to match Webber's course. Webber could see Young's white combat helmet in the starboard main window. Young's bets and Las Vegas escapades were legend among the SEALs. He attacked the card tables and the showgirls as if Caesars were one of Saddam Hussein's palaces. "Over."

Young set the terms. "I'll take equipment malfunction against rock or geo team. Two to one odds—one Glenfiddich to two Absolut Peppar. Over."

The Absolut was Young's drink, Glenfiddich Webber's. Stateside, it was a nothing bet. But at McMurdo, where alcohol was not permitted in the mess hall, and liquor, wine, and beer rations were doled out and recorded on a week-by-week basis, the NEST Two leader might as well be wagering gold.

"Whatever," Webber said, not bothering to reply on the air, annoyed anew by Young's irrepressible desire to play games at all times.

But Young took silence for acceptance. "Wager accepted. Let's do it." Then his helo accelerated ahead, followed a few seconds later by a final, mocking "Out."

The NEST One pilot turned to Webber with an inquiring look. "Do we have the fuel to catch up and still make it to McMurdo?" Webber asked.

The pilot checked his instruments and the chart. "Depends on the winds on the way back."

"Worst-case scenario?"

"We sit on the ice for a few hours while they send snowmobiles with extra fuel."

"Take 'im down," Webber said.

Instantly, the deck of the helo angled down and the craft shot forward, rapidly hitting 140 miles an hour and gaining on Young.

A minute later, Webber's helo caught Young's and started to move ahead.

"Hey, cowboy," Young radioed. "You don't have the fuel for this. And I don't pick up hitchhikers. Over." Young's helo started closing the gap.

"What's your top speed?" Webber asked his pilot.

"With the pods and aux tanks, one fifty. Same as him."

"Then you'll just have to outfly him."

The pilot grinned. The helo pushed forward again.

Within another minute, the two craft were neck and neck, only one hundred yards apart. The winner would be decided by the vagaries of the wind.

The radar target they approached—by now, the secondary objective of the flight—was indeed a pressure ridge. Two thousand feet below, the ice river that flowed from the landmass of Antarctica across the surface of the Ross Sea had hit a slight upwelling in the seabed. The contact between ice and rock had slowed the movement of the ice and, over hundreds of years, had created a distortion at the ice surface, like the water of a fast-moving river deformed by a submerged rock.

To Webber, the pressure ridge looked like a small mountain rising a hundred feet above the blizzard. Veins of ice, compressed into exquisite, jewel-like bands of aquamarine and emerald green, were caught in the ridge folds. Glaciologists could calculate the age of the formation from its colors. But to Webber, the visual appearance of the target suggested it was solid ice, with no outcropping of rock buried within it that could account for the neutron burst. That meant either the neutron counter had malfunctioned as Young said, or that, somewhere near the pressure ridge, there was an accumulation of fissionable material.

They were two minutes from contact with the ridge, engines screaming in the race with Young, when Webber checked again with Gowers.

"Strong background count," the engineer confirmed. "Level two." An equipment malfunction was looking less likely the longer the readings continued. Webber knew what had to be done. No more games.

16

"NEST Two, this is NEST One. We have a *latent* Forge target. Repeat, *latent* Forge. Approach vector Romeo Zebra. Over."

Webber waited for Young to copy, then to hang back. The Romeo Zebra approach called for one NEST helo to stay airborne out of harm's way while the first landed to gather onsite intelligence. It was standard operating procedure.

But Young didn't copy.

"Nice try, cowboy. But you're not winning the race that way. Over."

Mitch cursed. "NEST Two acknowledge! Approach vector Romeo Zebra! We have a level-two neutron alarm!"

But Young's helo veered off to the east of the pressure ridge without answering.

Webber knew he had to make an alternate decision. He could deal with Young later. Right now, his pilot and his crew were looking to him for orders. It was his responsibility to give them.

"Circle to the west," he told the pilot. He looked back at Gowers. "Tune to narrow scan, full sensitivity."

NEST One's engineer rapidly typed on his keyboard, shifting his legs to hold the computer in place as the helo shuddered in a sudden crosswind. "Still at level two," he reported.

Webber's craft reached the far, southern side of the pressure ridge in less than a minute. Young's helo was already on station, hovering.

"Make that Absolut chilled," Young radioed.

"NEST Two Leader, you are in violation of procedures. This is an alert, not a drill. Over."

Looking out his own helo's canopy, Webber could see Young's white form between the pilot and the copilot of the second helo. Young waved. "Lighten up, Dark Knight. . . ." His voice warbled in the drifting radio frequency, despite the proximity of the helicopters, now less than fifty yards apart. "You're the one with the operational detector. We've been all around the ridge. Where's the source? Over." He said the last word with overprecise sarcasm.

Webber looked at Gowers. The weapons specialist shook his head. "Still level two." If they were anywhere close to a stockpile of fissionable material, the pod should have gone to a level-one alarm. "Gotta be a malfunction."

Webber exhaled. "Okay," he told the pilot. "Let's see how close to McMurdo we can . . ." He didn't finish. "What's this?" He pointed to an edge of the pressure-ridge boundary glowing on the radar display. There was a sharply symmetrical bar a few hundred yards from the upward sweep of the ridge, due south.

The pilot squinted through the canopy, past Young's helo, into the empty air between the two layers of wind-smeared clouds. "Something under the blizzard. Metal, maybe. Could be a fuel cache."

Webber reached for the binoculars in the pocket at the side of the copilot's seat.

The rotor blades of Young's helo were a blur at the edge of Webber's magnified field of vision as he scanned the storm. The clouds were so uniform he couldn't be certain if the binocs were in focus. Then there was a flash of white against the gray—a regular shape against the random visual noise of a natural landscape. Something was down there. Camouflaged.

Webber spoke into his mike. "NEST Two, I am declaring an *active* Forge alert. Approach vector Romeo Zebra. Over."

Young's response to Webber's call to action was immediate. His voice had lost its playful edge. "Standing by. Over."

Webber slipped the binoculars back into their pocket. He leaned toward the pilot. "I want you to fly over that, get it in the downdraft so I can see what it is. You up on your evasive maneuvers?"

Alert for the hunt, the pilot nodded and started forward, dropping altitude sharply. Webber was relieved that this time Young's helo held to the correct position. He turned to check on the other two members of his team. Gowers had placed his laptop on the deck, and was breaking out a small aluminum case containing a MACS Dual Modular radiation monitor. It was more sensitive than the exterior pods, but its limited range made it useful only for close-contact detection.

The pilot expertly brought Gentle Two Five over the camouflaged target, spun around 180 degrees, then slowly edged backward until the clear spot created by the main rotors' downdraft found the rest of the encampment—a drilling derrick, twenty-five-feet tall, with a diesel generator beside it, two pallets of fuel drums, and a large, eight-passenger Tucker Sno-Cat with treads and skis. All metal surfaces had been painted white. About twenty feet from the derrick, Webber could see a prefab cabin, twenty feet by fifteen. A supply pallet leaned close against it, almost blocking the only door, and there was another small generator behind it. Other supplies, perhaps four or five pallets' worth, were fifty feet away from the cabin, opposite the fuel drums, protected by a fluttering orange tarp, half-covered with snow.

The downdraft also revealed four frantically waving figures in red parkas and snow goggles, urgently signaling the helo to back off.

"Anyone know if they're from McMurdo?" Webber asked.

The pilot and copilot both said, "No," together. The pilot added, "I don't see any flag. Argentine maybe?"

Webber grimaced at the possibility. Argentina considered Antarctica an extension of the Patagonian archipelago, and had arbitrarily assigned a large wedge of the continent to Tierra del Fuego, Argentina's twenty-third province. In 1978, the government had airlifted a pregnant physician to the largest Argentine station in Antarctica and had promptly given the newborn baby Argentine citizenship, ostensibly establishing, though only to themselves, that Antarctica soil and Argentine soil were the same.

Argentina had also instigated the first and only military action within the Antarctic Convergence. Its helicopters and soldiers had attacked an outpost of British troops on South Georgia Island during the failed 1982 attempt to wrest control of the Falkland Islands from Great Britain.

The U.S. Department of Energy had reluctantly predicted that, if history were to be any guide, some of the more radical elements within the Argentine government might consider Argentina within its rights to use tactical nuclear explosives to begin extensive exploration of Antarctica's icebound mineral wealth. The Ross Sea, though, was nowhere near the region Argentina claimed as its own.

"Land," Webber said. He reached through a flap in his parka to remove the safety from his .45 automatic. If he were about to deal with Argentine nationals, at least he would be spared the sudden-death arena of a confrontation with terrorists. His rules of engagement stated that weapons would be used only to enforce Article V of the 1959 Antarctic Treaty, which prohibited nuclear explosives on the Ice. The International Court, rather than military action, could sort out the other details later.

Gentle Two Five scraped against the rough ice as it touched down in a veil of blowing snow and ice crystals. Bregoli instantly popped the starboard cargo door and slid it open, flooding the cabin with a sudden gust of freezing wind.

Webber jumped out, keeping one hand on the door frame until he was sure of his footing. Bregoli followed, stopping to help Gowers down. The pilot and copilot had flown for NEST before in this situation, the Iroquois was to be kept on instant-takeoff status until Webber ordered otherwise.

The helo had landed with its nose pointing directly at the derrick, and Webber sighted off the craft as he struck off through the stinging snow, Gowers at his side. In a few minutes, Webber knew he'd have to tug his fur-edged parka hood over his helmet and slip his gloved hands into the mittens hanging on his belt. But for this moment of contact, the bite of the cold was an acceptable trade-off. He needed to be able to see and hear without obstruction.

When the derrick appeared as a dark shadow within the snow squall, Webber turned to Gowers. The NEST One engineer, his apple-cheeked face almost as bright as the ECW gear he wore, shouted over the wind.

"Level one! Straight ahead!"

Webber glanced back at Bregoli, holding up his hand to signal the soldier to hang back. Bregoli already held his CAR-15 ready. Then Webber touched his fingers to his throat mike. "NEST Two, we have a confirmed target."

With that, three red figures appeared in the shifting curtains of snow, walking straight for them. None appeared to be carrying weapons. Webber knew that meant they could be part of a geological survey team. But still, there had been four people on the ground before the helicopter had landed. Before moving forward, Webber looked about for the fourth man but saw no sign of him. Now the snow squalls were so bad even Bregoli had disappeared from view. Webber spoke into his mike. "I am about to make contact with the on-site personnel. They do not appear to be armed. Over."

There was no response from NEST Two, but Webber had no time to question why. The first of the red figures was within ten feet, his face invisible behind snow goggles and the ice-frosted fur trim of his parka's hood. Webber sought out any markings on the parka—flags, corporate or mission patches. Nothing.

He raised his empty hand in greeting. "Hello!" he shouted. "Mitch Webber, United States Department of Energy."

The silent figure in red was joined by his two companions, also silent.

Webber trusted his instincts. These were not Argentine geologists. "Gowers—back off," Webber said in a low voice. He slipped his hand into his parka, about to grasp his weapon. Then the snow around him flashed yellow-orange a split second before the thump of an explosion pushed against his back.

Webber didn't have to look behind him to know that his pilot and copilot were dead. Gentle Two Five had just exploded, and with a greater release of energy than its remaining fuel could have provided. He dived forward, using the momentum of the explosive force to his advantage, .45 out and firing before he even hit the ground, shouting, "Abort! Abort!" into his mike.

One figure in red fell back, snow goggles shattered by two slugs from Webber's gun. The other two figures broke left and right, vanishing into a sudden eddy of blinding ice crystals—the unmistakable maneuver of trained soldiers.

Webber came out of his roll in a crouch, crusted with snow, his .45 held ready. He shot a glance over his shoulder, saw Gowers facedown on the ice, the radiation monitor beside him, its black case already white with drift. Webber's pulse quickened. Gowers had been taken out by a shooter hidden in the storm—the missing fourth man.

Even as he dropped the magazine from the .45 and slapped in a fresh one, Webber knew his situation was hopeless. The only cover was the drilling installation a hundred feet ahead of him. Undoubtedly, that was where the two hostiles had gone. Plus the fourth man who must have been behind him—the one, Webber knew, who had taken out Gowers and Gentle Two Five.

Webber scrambled across the ice for the body of the hostile he had dropped. Dark crystals of blood had already frozen around the demolished face, gore studded with shards from the snow goggles. Webber quickly searched the body's red parka, all the while attempting to raise NEST Two on his radio. Even though he knew his life might end at any moment, Webber's voice was even, controlled, and decisive. He had no thoughts except for the mission.

"Nick—we've been ambushed. Helo's been taken out. Four hostiles. No ID. I've taken out one. Gowers is down. No sign of Ox. Come back, over."

The body was clean. No personal effects—a terrorist signature.

No weapons—an anomaly. Webber scanned the immediate area. No sign of any movement. He hurried back to Gowers.

The weapons specialist was still breathing, but each intake of breath was a struggle. Webber kneeled down and carefully rolled Gowers onto his side. The spreading stain of blood on the engineer's chest was almost invisible against the orange of his parka, but it was large enough for Webber to know Gowers would never make it back to McMurdo on his own.

He pulled the chemical heating packs from the chest pockets on Gowers's parka, cracked them, kneaded them, then stuffed them up under the parka to provide more warmth. He leaned closer to the engineer, speaking loudly, trying to get him to focus. "Gowers! Did you see Ox?"

"Cold . . ." Gowers whispered.

Webber abandoned that strategy. The drilling installation might have a sheltered area. The Sno-Cat, at least, would have a heater, probably a radio more powerful than the one on his belt. The drilling installation became his target.

"I'll come back for you," Webber told the engineer. Though he knew if he didn't keep that promise in the next ten minutes, it would make no difference.

His hand still on Gowers's parka, Webber glanced back toward his helo. In the shifting billows of snow, he saw the orange glow of the fire consuming Gentle Two Five, but no other movement. He swiftly recalled the layout of the installation as he had seen it from the air, plotting his approach to bring the derrick between him and the Sno-Cat.

He turned back, released his grip on Gowers, and stood up.

He heard the crunch of ice behind him.

Webber knew that no one could have moved up behind him so quickly. At least, not in a red parka.

He whirled around to confront Nick Young. "You weren't supposed to land! There're hostiles all around!"

"No shit," Young said. He almost looked contrite. "Sorry, cowboy. End of the trail."

Then Nick Young raised his M-16 and fired point-blank into his best friend's chest.

TWO

THE PENTAGON

Though its masters would never admit it, the Pentagon and the more than 24,000 people who worked in it were expendable.

In peacetime, the existence of a centralized military command was a convenience. When a crisis arose which did not directly threaten the security of American soil, that centralized command was efficient, more or less. But in the event of a real war, the Pentagon was a bloated twenty-nine-acre target with an estimated lifetime that could be measured in minutes.

That was why U.S. Army General Charles Quincy Abbott could admit he looked forward to his duty hours in the National Military Command Center. For as long as the key component of the country's military command structure was located on the Pentagon's second floor, naked to all the world, America was not at risk.

Abbott would not say that crucial decisions were never made in this installation, or that American soldiers were never put in harm's way at the orders of the men and women who staffed it. But any military action that could be managed from the Pentagon was, to Abbott, a peripheral exercise at best.

Those few times, independent of training scenarios, when command actually had been transferred to the NMCC's mirror sites—in the Maryland hills, in Louisiana, or, in exceptional behind-the-scenes crises, to airborne EC-135 command centers which could stay aloft for weeks—were when real war or disaster had threatened the country, and the world. It was at those times, in the mirror sites in which he worked, that Abbott most enjoyed himself, though he would never admit that publicly. No soldier ever would, no matter how true such an admission might be.

But because of what its primacy signified about the state of the world and the security of the country, the Pentagon was Abbott's ultimate place of refuge, and he looked forward to his duty hours there, especially at this time of year. In the course of his thirty-two-year Army career, the general had spent only two Thanksgivings with his family. Thanks to his position on the Joint Staff and the needs of the Pentagon, this Thanksgiving would be no different. As he passed between the white-helmeted guards and through the smoothly opening double doors of the NMCC emergency action room, that knowledge soothed him. As always, in preparing for war, he found peace.

Following operational directives, the National Military Command Center was commanded by at least a two-star general, twenty-four hours a day, seven days a week. This holiday eve, Abbott had arrived to replace the previous shift's commander, Air Force General Norbert Morrow.

"Chuck, good to see you." Morrow was a large man, especially for an Air Force pilot, and his deskbound years in the Pentagon had allowed his girth to catch up with his impressive height. Abbott, who stood a head shorter than Morrow, yet weighed the same as when he had completed Basic Training almost three decades earlier, found Morrow's lack of physical control sloppy. He also disapproved of the general's approach to his work. Despite the fact that Abbott had not yet relieved him, Morrow was clearly set to leave, a United Shuttle ticket and a copy of *Sports Illustrated* on his closed briefcase. Abbott never brought recreational reading material into the EAR. The NMCC's briefing library, updated on a continual basis, would take decades to work through.

"Norbert," Abbott said, as he shook the larger man's hand. Though Morrow wore Air Force blue and Abbott Army green, as members of the Joint Staff they were both considered "purple suiters"—officers who had left their service rivalries behind. In Abbott's case, it was true, though he doubted if anyone else on the Joint Staff harbored his purity of feeling for the combined military forces. Army, Air Force, Navy, Marines, even Coast Guard—they were all his brothers- and sisters-in-arms, his family.

"I surely do appreciate you taking the extra shifts," Morrow said.

Abbott shrugged. Throughout the services, the Thanksgiving holiday was the most sought-after time period for leaves and furloughs, surpassing even Christmas. Traditionally, though never officially, it was the time at which the U.S. military was at its lowest state of operational readiness. Abbott didn't intend to contribute to that failing.

"Not that you're going to have a lot to do," Morrow added. He nodded at the big board—a high-definition, gas-plasma display screen fifteen feet wide, eight feet tall, that could present virtually any information possessed by the military. It had replaced the bulky, low-resolution television and computer monitors, and even the handwritten wall charts that had lined the north wall of the room in earlier years.

Abbott looked at the board. Morrow was right. At the moment, under the control of Air Force First Lieutenant Ann Yoshii, who sat at an elevated workstation at the opposite end of the conference table, the board displayed a world situation map. The map was the topmost layer of the Pentagon's ETEM system, and at Abbott's request virtually any spot on the globe could be brought up in enough photographic detail to show individual buildings. Where and when live satellite images were available, they could be incorporated into the existing map database in realtime.

The ETEM world map was, for now, overlaid with small video windows showing silent, East Coast feeds from the six networks, the American Forces Radio and Television Service, CNN International, MSNBC, and five additional international news channels. The window displaying CNN International was expanded and centered, showing coverage of the civil carnage in Islamabad.

"What's the situation with the riots?" Abbott asked.

"It's a non-starter. At thirteen hundred today, State got the word that India and Pakistan have reached a secret agreement. The Pakistani commandos will be found guilty by the Indian court, but will not be executed. In a month, they'll be deported home."

Abbott wasn't surprised. The Indo-Pakistani conflict had remained stable for longer than he had been in the Army. It affected no vital U.S. interests, other than the United States' determination to keep China from entering into any agreement that might upset the balance of power in the region.

"Chinese reaction?" Abbott asked.

Morrow eyed Abbott skeptically, knowing the reason for the question. "Remote, Chuck. As usual. Their country's existed for five thousand years. It gives those folks a unique perspective on patience."

Abbott didn't respond. The two generals were on opposite sides of what the Pentagon called the China Question. Morrow was confident that the growing move toward modernization and economic reform in China would transform the country, just as the Soviet Union had left its Communist past behind. But Abbott, and a growing number of senior officers, firmly believed that within the next ten to twenty years, China and the United States would engage in an inevitable military conflict. It was not a popular conclusion in a military force that as a matter of political reality and tradition would not consider first-strike scenarios.

As if to avoid the start of any debate between them, Morrow moved on with his impromptu briefing. "Berlin is under control. Colonel Frantello is running the CAT down the hall."

Abbott nodded without expression. The President's last-minute decision to visit Berlin to take part in an emergency World Bank conference on providing additional aid to North Korea's new leadership had necessitated the review of a score of contingency scenarios by J-7—the Joint Staff Operational Plans and Interoperability Directorate. According to the latest analysis from the Institute for National Strategic Studies, the growing separatist movement in the former West Germany considered U.S. trade involvement with the European Union a barrier to the re-creation of the two Germanys. The separatists wanted to preserve the western half's economic security by once again partitioning off the eastern half. Apparently, the assassination of the U.S. President while on German soil appealed to some of the more disaffected separatists as a way to ensure that America would want nothing more to do with Europe.

As a soldier loyal to the Constitution and the office of the Commander-in-Chief, Abbott refrained from thinking about the other benefits of an abrupt end to this particular President's tenure. To Morrow, he noted only that the Pentagon had cooperated with the Secret Service in providing impenetrable security for the President's visit. One of three Trumpet satellites passed over Berlin every twenty-eight minutes, monitoring all traffic around the Reichstag. Two Joint Special Forces anti-terrorist units had been deployed at NATO airbases, and a fighter-escort wing had and would provide cover for Air Force One throughout its flight. Frantello's Crisis Action Team was responsible for all military support to the President's trip.

But even if the worst should happen, with so many contingency plans already in place, Abbott knew it was unlikely that the NMCC would need to become involved.

With that, Abbott put the President out of his mind. It was an easy task. Any military commander who willingly provided aid and comfort to North Korea, an enemy who stood ready to use nuclear weapons on the American troops stationed in South Korea . . . well, Abbott believed the uniform code of military justice contained a word for that type of behavior, and any President guilty of that sin was not worth a moment of unnecessary thought.

"The Gulf?" Abbott asked.

"Same old, same old," Morrow answered. Despite their new alliance, Iraq and Iran still rattled their swords at each other and would for the next century, both too bankrupt and wary of Israel's stockpile of nuclear weapons to do anything more disruptive than occasionally interfere with the Straits of Hormuz.

Two flash points remained on the big board. Abbott asked for an update on the more important one—China.

"The PLAN maneuvers are continuing," Morrow said. Seven days ago, apparently in response to a radical Taiwanese newspaper's ongoing campaign for independence, the naval forces of the People's Liberation Army had begun a series of unannounced war games in the Taiwan Strait and the South China Sea. Though the PLA lacked the necessary military infrastructure to support an invasion of Taiwan, and was incapable of coordinating an effective sea and air blockade of the island, the merest threat of either would be enough to unsettle Taiwan and threaten the peace of the area.

As a warrior, Abbott would be sorry to miss the inevitable engagement between China and America, but the events of one or two decades in the future had little importance in the NMCC today. Like the Middle East and the Indo-Pakistan conflict, China was another flash point that could remain zeroed out for now.

"Don't you want to be briefed about Antarctica?" Morrow asked with a grin. This past week had been the first time the seventh continent had appeared on the NMCC watch list. Its inclusion was automatic, given that the Department of Energy had deployed two Nuclear Emergency Search Teams there. But the novelty of seeing the yellow warning icon flashing slowly at the bottom of the ETEM map caused most who saw it to respond as Morrow did—with amusement.

"Anything new?" Abbott asked. Amusement was not an appropriate response to any issue involving WMD—weapons of mass destruction.

"*Nada*," Morrow said. He checked his watch. "The NEST boys upload a daily report to the DOE at twenty-one hundred." He nodded to the first lieutenant at the workstation. "Lieutenant Yoshii can call up the action paper on the deployment. But it's still pretty much a joke."

"San Francisco wasn't a joke." Abbott had kept up to date on the threat of terrorist use of WMD, so he wasn't as quick as Morrow to discount the reasons for NEST's presence in Antarctica.

Morrow sighed, uncomfortable, the general could tell, with Abbott's strict adherence to proper military conduct. "C'mon, Chuck, San Francisco was an American city with a population of three-quarters of a million civilians. If someone's crazy enough to set off a nuke in Antarctica, we lose what? A couple of hundred penguins and polar bears?"

"There are no indigenous land mammals in Antarctica," Abbott said. He saw the momentary confusion in Morrow's eyes. "No polar bears. They're at the North Pole."

Morrow shrugged, dismissing Antarctica. "Whatever. If you want my professional operational assessment, they're on a wild-goose chase for some goddamn old chunk of Russian satellite crashed down there. End of story."

That was the end of the command-change briefing, too, as far as Abbott was concerned. He looked at the Shuttle ticket on Morrow's briefcase. "Going home?"

Morrow nodded as he gathered his belongings. "For four days of the three F's," he said with an even bigger grin. "Florida, football, and . . ." The complete lack of any sign of a smile on Abbott's face brought his recitation to an end. "Happy Thanksgiving, Chuck."

Morrow looked down the table to Lieutenant Yoshii. "Lieutenant—have a good one."

Yoshii glanced up from her workstation. "Thank you, sir. You, too."

Then Morrow nodded once at Abbott, and left the situation room.

Abbott at once felt more at ease. Small talk was not one of his strengths, and it had no place on duty, either.

He quickly thumbed the combination dials on his own briefcase, opened it, and laid out three folders of pending reports by the stacks of briefing papers and background books Morrow had left. He glanced back at the big board. The CNNI feed had switched to a story on the President. News footage showed him stepping off Air Force One in a swirl of snow, waving gamely as he negotiated the obviously slippery stairs.

Abbott let his attention wander to the flashing yellow disk at the bottom of the screen. He thought about it for a few moments. If a satellite with a plutonium reactor had come out of orbit over Antarctica, U.S. Space Command would have to have known about it in advance. NEST would be deployed, just as it had helped clean up the mess left when a Russian Cosmos satellite had crashed in the Canadian Arctic in 1978. But a nonmilitary cleanup and retrieval operation wouldn't warrant an NMCC alert.

Abbott tapped his finger against the side of his briefcase, then snapped it shut. "Lieutenant Yoshii, I'd like the background book on the operation in Antarctica."

Yoshii didn't look up. "It's the buff binder on the table, sir."

At least twenty binders were arranged in the center of the table, along with another dozen books and directories. Abbott reached over and took the binder labeled SHADOW FORGE. The binder had three-inch rings, but there were only twenty or so pages inside. Abbott frowned. A double-team deployment based on twenty pages of intel did seem like a wild-goose chase.

Abbott opened the book to the first text page. SHADOW FORGE had begun operation fourteen months earlier. The general ran his thumb along his jaw. How could an operation run for more than a year and only generate twenty pages? He started flipping through the pages, building a timeline of events.

"General Abbott, sir?"

Abbott looked up to see Lieutenant Yoshii holding a hand to her earphone.

"Sir, you have a personal call on outside line five."

Abbott stared at the flashing light on the phone set in front of him. "Who is it?" he asked, knowing the answer.

"Switchboard says it's your wife, sir."

"You know my rules, Lieutenant. No personal calls."

Yoshii nodded, acknowledging the rebuke in Abbott's tone. "Yes, sir."

Abbott returned his attention to the SHADOW FORGE book, ignoring the whispered conversation Yoshii had with whoever had been intemperate enough to transfer a personal call into the EAR. He came to the last page of the book: personnel lists of the two NEST teams deployed to Antarctica. Abbott recognized the team leaders from the San Francisco event. NEST One was commanded by Mitch Webber, Captain, USN. Thirty-eight. The compact build and quick eyes of a fighter pilot, one of the handful invited to endure SEAL training as part of USURP, a classified foreign technology retrieval program begun in 1989. The commander of NEST Two was Nick Young, same rank, two years younger. He was grinning in his ID photo, with the same sure confidence of all fighter pilots blazing from features that reflected both his Chinese and American heritage. Abbott approved of the DOE's selections. They had sent their best.

Abbott flipped back to the beginning of the book and started to read. Uncharacteristically, he became so caught up in the operational history of SHADOW FORGE that he didn't notice when CNNI ended their story on the President's trip to Berlin, and cut to a broadcast from a ship in the Ross Sea, approaching McMurdo Station.

Over the next few minutes, six other network feeds flickered over to carry the low-resolution video signal, until half the world had access to an unprecedented television transmission. The words LIVE FROM ANTARCTICA ran at the bottom of every screen on the big board.

But embraced by the security of the NMCC emergency action room, General Charles Quincy Abbott read on, undisturbed, in a world of his own.

THREE

THE ICE

Webber didn't feel the impact of the bullets. He didn't even see the rifle. All he saw was Young's face. All he thought was how could he have missed what Young had done, what he had become? Then he saw the streaming gray clouds and realized he was on his back on the snow. Then he realized he couldn't breathe.

There was static in his helmet speaker. He could hear voices calling for support from the police helos. The target had been found on the Bank of America building. Gowers was attempting to disarm it as the people of San Francisco carried on their business all around, unaware of the danger they faced.

No. Webber forced his thoughts into focus. *I'm not in San Francisco. That was years ago.*

He saw Young again. This time, his best friend was standing over him. Webber's breath came back in a ragged wheeze and a sudden explosion of excruciating pain.

Young jabbed at Webber's chest with the barrel of his rifle. Webber heard the scrape of metal as Young found the ceramic plates of his body armor.

"A vest." Young sounded amused and disappointed at the same time. "In Antarctica. I shouldn't be surprised. You were the only SEAL to drive a Volvo."

Webber opened his mouth to speak, but all that came out was another desperate gasp for air.

Young placed the open barrel of his rifle on Webber's forehead, looked apologetic. His chest heaving, Webber kept his eyes locked on Young's, refusing to look away.

This time, Webber did hear the gunshot. It was distant, a weak pop. But it hadn't come from Young's rifle, because Young jerked away from Webber without firing and was gone in an instant. Webber heard another shot, then the sound of approaching boots sinking heavily into the snow. Lieutenant Ox Bregoli leaned down and with one hand lifted him to his feet. Webber felt the lieutenant pat down his chest, searching for a wound. "Are you hit?"

Webber shook his head, amazed at the pain even that movement brought. He pulled off his helmet and let the cold air revive him. He was aware of every fire-laced rib, at least one of them cracked. Only his body armor had halted Young's bullets and dispersed their life-ending energy. Instead of being hit by supersonic projectiles focused on quarter-inch squares of flesh, his chest had been clubbed by one and a half square feet of ceramic plates traveling at about ten miles per hour. It was like being rammed by a slow-moving car, and every muscle in his body had recorded the strain of that impact. "It was Nick."

Bregoli grunted. His broad face was splotched with red. Ice crystals frosted his thick eyebrows. "I think I winged him, just before he could . . ." He pointed in the direction of the derrick. The structure faded in and out of sight, masked by the blowing ice crystals. "He took off that way."

"You okay?" Webber asked. He had just noticed Bregoli's left arm was hanging limply at his side, the white fabric of his PolarOps camouflage stained red.

"Yeah. What's the call?"

That simple question created a visual image in Webber's mind. It was how he always thought, in discrete blocks of color and texture, reducing every situation to a chess game played in three dimensions. Flying a MiG-29C Fulcrum from Baghdad, he had seen the area of pursuit and engagement like a cone of crystal, with the small points of light moving through it representing his position and those of the other MiGs scrambled by the enemy to bring him down. Webber wasn't particularly curious about whatever quirk of nature or nurture had wired his and other pilots' and strategists' brains in this way. He only cared that it gave him an indisputable advantage in tactical matters. The emotionless objectivity that accompanied it, however, had seldom been to his benefit in more personal situations. But here on the Ice, free of distractions, Webber saw all the game pieces on the board that confronted him move into position with perfect clarity.

Nick Young was the opposing king. Incredibly, whether it was because of gambling debts or a need for even more extreme challenges, somehow his longtime friend had been bought off, gone rogue. For Young to reveal himself in so blatant a manner, forever ruling out his return to active service, could only mean that the stakes were as high as they could be: There *was* an active Forge target at this drilling site. Young's motives, the strategic goals of whoever had brought a nuclear weapon to the Ice—none of that could stop Webber now. His mission remained what it had always been.

"There's a nuke in that drilling rig," Webber said. "We seize and disable."

"What about Nick?"

The necessary mind-set of combat was all that allowed Webber to say what he knew he must. "We see him, we take him down."

"Shit," Bregoli muttered. But he swung his injured arm up and grabbed his rifle with both hands.

Webber saw Bregoli's ruddy face pale. He took the heavy CAR-15 from the lieutenant and handed over his own .45, digging into his pockets for fresh clips.

Bregoli regarded the automatic pistol in his hand with a doubting expression. As a rule, SEALs didn't like pistols, and a .45 was not the latest word in modern weapons design. But it was dependable and proven in combat, qualities which, for Webber, always won out when compared with cutting-edge technology. A successful field commander never wanted to be the first to discover a design limitation.

"You go right," Webber told his lieutenant. "I'll circle from the left. Wait for me to stir things up, then support. I count three hostiles left in red. Nick's in white."

"What about the rest of NEST Two?"

Webber didn't know the answer. He assumed Young's pilot and copilot were dead—they had been selected as next up on the NEST duty roster, so it was unlikely they had been coopted with Young.

But Young's team—Lieutenant Rensberger and Glendon Morris, the weapons specialist—were another matter. They'd both been part of Nick's squad since San Francisco.

"If the pilots aren't with Young, they'll be with their helo. But Morris and Rensberger could be against us."

"So basically, we watch our backs."

"Welcome to the pointy end of the spear." Then Webber broke left.

Though each jarring impact of his boots sent sharp waves through his chest, it still didn't compare to BUD/S. The sheer torture of Hell Week during Basic Underwater Demolition/SEAL training had methodically and effectively demonstrated how much physical abuse a SEAL could endure and still function. A hard run with a cracked rib through an Antarctic blizzard came nowhere near the disorienting discomfort of a night swim in frigid waters off Coronado after four hours of sleep in four days, every fold of flesh raw from the abrading sand and salt water.

Still, to conserve his strength, Webber didn't dive to the ground when he saw the orange silhouette of Gentle Three Zero suddenly appear within a wall of wind-driven snow. Instead, he dropped to his knees, then stretched out on the ice.

All the while searching for any signs of the pilots' presence, he inched forward, crawling across the compacted snow. As soon as he was certain that there was no one in the cockpit, he rose to his feet and ran to the tail of the helo, keeping the craft between him and the drilling installation—for now, completely shrouded by the storm.

He had been right about Young's pilot and copilot. They were facedown in the snow, half-covered in drift. Unexpectedly, about ten feet away from the craft, a crumpled ball revealed itself to be Lieutenant Rensberger. Faint grooves in the snow showed he'd been dragged. There was no sign of Glendon Morris. Webber made the logical assessment. The NEST Two engineer was working with Young. That left the odds at five to two: He and Bregoli were up against Young, Morris, and at least three of the drilling rig's crew.

Aware of the heat inexorably seeping from his protective gear, Webber studied the area of engagement. The prefab cabin was in the center of a flat plain with only limited cover: the Sno-Cat, the two pallets of diesel fuel, the diesel generator, and whatever was hidden beneath the snow-covered tarp. The hostiles knew two SEALs were outside. Perhaps they knew Bregoli was wounded. But all the hostiles had to do was watch the four compass approaches and pick off their attackers when they made a mistake moving in. And he and Bregoli *would* have to move in at some point, simply because they could not maintain operational readiness at current temperatures for more than a few hours. Even evacuating in Young's helo was not a viable option. The polar-duty helos were slicks, carrying none of the armor or armament of their combat versions. As soon as the engine turned over, it would be a stationary target for at least two minutes. It would never make it off the ground.

Webber turned his attention to how he would defend the drilling rig, where he would place the killing zone. After a moment, he changed his strategy. How would *Young* defend the rig?

The answer was obvious.

Young was a ground fighter. He thought in two dimensions. Webber thought in three.

Webber backed off from the helo and ran through the blinding snow until he judged the derrick was between him and the cabin. He paused briefly before moving forward again, cautiously peering through the gusts for the first sign of the structure.

He saw it and hit the ground hard. He began crawling toward the white derrick, the chill of the ice beneath him overpowering the reawakened agony of his chest. He stopped moving when he was twenty-five feet from the tower, wary that he saw no sign of defensive positions. His opponent was either foolishly confident, or desperate. Webber trusted neither alternative.

He decided to up the stakes.

He rose up slightly, drew careful aim on the more distant pallet of diesel-fuel drums, fired, and then leapt to his feet. He was already at the base of the derrick when the first drum exploded with a dull concussion, sending a gout of dark smoke and twisting flame high in the air. A heartbeat later, a second thud signaled the eruption of another drum. The thunderous concussion that immediately followed—which he could actually see move through the wind-tossed snow and ice crystals—announced that the entire pallet had ignited.

Before the roiling red and black fireball had risen more than fifty feet, Webber was climbing the white-metal tower. Behind him, he could hear Bregoli join the action. The sound of the .45 was almost inaudible at this distance, especially upwind. He turned to see puffs of snow bounce off the tops of the fuel drums on the second pallet. They did not explode. Either the drums on the second pallet were empty, or had been used to bring in something other than fuel oil.

Heavy return fire sounded from a fully automatic machine gun, not the three-round bursts from Young's M-16. There was an answering pop from the .45, another roar, and then nothing. But by then, Webber was ten feet up the derrick, gloved hands numb on the metal crossbars, but still climbing.

He stopped at fifteen feet—the top height he knew he could jump from if necessary—hooked an arm around the corner brace, and held his rifle ready on the cabin's door in the center of one of its long walls. He didn't have to wait long.

The cabin door cracked open. Two men in red parkas eased out, crouched low behind the supply pallet that provided cover a few feet in front of them. Silent, they looked around, steadily, professionally, one pointing to the fire blazing where the fuel pallet used to be.

Webber didn't hesitate. At this distance, he didn't even have to compensate for the wind. His first shot slammed one hostile back into the cabin. His second shot dropped the other on the snow between the pallet and the doorway.

A third hostile in red appeared in the doorway, an AK-47 blazing in a horizontal sweep, covering thirty degrees left and right with constant fire. He remained a foot too far back for Webber to get a clear shot. Webber held his fire.

The hostile with the AK-47 slammed the door shut. The door and walls of the cabin were only thin metal with insulating foam plastic. In any other engagement, Webber would have fired right through the flimsy structure. But somewhere inside that cabin, he was sure, was a nuclear device.

His radio speaker crackled again. "Good shootin', cowboy."

Webber stayed silent. No need to let Young know the AK-47 bursts hadn't found a target.

"C'mon, good buddy," Young's static-filled voice continued. "We got Gowers. We just got Bregoli. And I torched your helo. You're on your lonesome out there."

Webber moved one hand off his rifle, squeezed and opened his fingers to keep blood moving through them. The wind seemed stronger up here at fifteen feet, gray sheets of snow obscuring the cabin for seconds at a time. His cheeks had lost all feeling.

"Oh, yeah," Young continued. "And while *you're* out there, guess who's in here? She's been dying to talk to you. Haven't you, Glen?"

Webber heard the sound of a slap, heard Glendon Morris cry out. Then her voice came over the speaker. "For God's sake, Webber! They've got a Bottle Rocket down here."

Webber's focus sharpened. The Bottle Rocket was a prototype U.S. weapon, a tactical nuclear explosive. Designed to be fired from the 120-millimeter main gun of a modified Abrams M1A1 tank, it was relatively clean with a yield of less than half a kiloton. Designed for theater operations against enemy troops in armored vehicles, it had a kill zone of one-eighth of a square mile. Technically useful in certain civilian mining applications—the use which this installation suggested—the device was small enough to have eluded Gentle Two Five's detectors, especially at their range of twenty miles. Unless the shell's casing was cracked.

Morris urgently continued as if she had read Webber's thoughts. "They haven't handled it properly. Webber—the casing's open. They're Argentine mining engineers. Don't have a clue what—" Morris's words ended in a strangled scream as Webber heard another impact.

"Look, cowboy," Young resumed. "I'm the first to admit it—this has turned a bit messy. All I signed up for was steering our guys away from the test site while my employers got their gold or titanium or whatever the hell they think is at the bottom of the Ross Sea."

It's too neat, Webber thought as he hung on the side of the derrick, listening to a man he'd clearly never known and whose behavior, therefore, he could no longer predict with confidence. Young was detailing a scenario that was almost identical to what the DIA had come up with. Webber's faith in the wisdom of his superiors did not allow for miracles.

"All I want now is out. So here's the deal. I let Glen go. You take her back to McMurdo on the helo, and I bug out on the Sno-Cat. You'll never hear from me again, and you can come back next week with NEST Three to clean this dump up. What do you say, pal? Everyone goes home? Nobody gets hurt? You won't get a better offer."

Webber shuffled the puzzle pieces. Why else would Young be

out here? Why else would he not have killed Morris? The scenario he described answered too many questions. And not enough of the key ones. Young's less than precise story had a convincing reality, but he and Young had been trained in the same special intelligence techniques. They both knew a carefully constructed lie was as deadly as any weapon.

Webber braced himself on the girder and put his thumb and forefinger to his throat mike. He hesitated a moment, but then decided his need for information was greater than his need for surprise. He was feeling cold now. Unlike BUD/S, if hypothermia set in out here, there was no trainer around to haul him out of the water before he died of exposure.

"Why'd you sell out, Nick?"

Webber could picture the cocky smirk on Young's face as he answered.

"Knew you were out there, pal."

"Tell me."

"The job was getting boring. You and I were running out of bad guys."

"Not good enough."

Webber saw the cabin door open slightly. Someone inside was peering out.

"Why does anyone sell out these days?" Young continued. "Politics? Not anymore. Money. It's the new ideology. Bet even you have a price."

Webber did recall that he had never heard Young talk politics, let alone "ideology." Besides Vegas and women, all Young had ever seemed to care about was pushing himself and others too far beyond reasonable limits. Webber had told him it would get him into trouble someday. Young had said that was the point.

Webber made the next move before Young could. "Send Glen out."

"You'll let me withdraw?"

Webber wasn't about to pilot the helo while Young and his shooter were within firing range. "I'll let you withdraw."

The door opened wider. Morris stumbled out, took a few steps around the dead man and the supply pallet at the threshold, then halted.

Webber spoke softly into his throat mike, though he doubted the wind would let his voice carry far enough to reveal his position. "Send her to the helo."

Someone from inside the cabin called out to the engineer. She turned to listen, nodded, looked around, started off.

From his perch, Webber intently studied the weapons specialist. Morris was a civilian. This was her first active alert. She didn't look nervous enough.

Webber again preempted whatever Young might have been planning next. "New condition: Carry the Bottle Rocket out where I can see it."

"No can do," Young answered. "The Argentines didn't handle it right. Counters going like a bad radio. No one's touching that thing."

"If that casing's cracked, you're breathing in a lot of rads. You'll cook before I freeze."

"Change of plans," Young said. "Glen's still in range. Get the fuck out of here, or I drop her. Five . . . four . . ."

Webber knew Young didn't bluff. It made the next decision easier.

He yelled at Morris to start running, and a split second later fired down in three-bullet bursts at the door, aiming some through the paneling over the door at whoever was back there, watching.

Sparks, then a barrage of shards of metal shook the derrick as Glendon Morris suddenly fired up at Webber's newly revealed position. Her voice reverberated in Webber's speaker. "He's on the derrick!" She fired up at him again.

Webber let go of the girder, trusting to the parachuting roll he'd mastered long ago. The bruising drop was broken only slightly by the give of the snow.

Crouched on the ground, between the base of the derrick and the prefab cabin, Webber returned fire to keep Morris suppressed. But after only two bullets, Bregoli's CAR-15 clicked empty.

A hostile in red—the last one—charged out from around the cabin. The AK-47 blew apart the snow beneath Webber's boots as he ran, dodging bullets to dive behind the cabin's other side.

The instant the hostile appeared around the corner, the stock of Webber's rifle cracked across his face. As much by instinct as by thought, Webber plunged his K-bar knife into the attacker's neck, sliced across the carotid, angled deep behind the trachea, and twisted the blade upward. The resulting wound was jagged, beyond holding closed.

He had the AK-47 and was running the opposite way around the cabin before the fountain of hot blood claimed the attacker's last breath.

Webber stopped at the next corner and took stock of his accelerated heartbeat, of his air-seared lungs straining to fill despite the protests of his battered ribs. But beyond noting the physical sensations and adjusting his next moves to compensate, he felt no urgency, no panic. His mission objective still lay before him like a readout on a heads-up display—seize and disable.

He shoved stiff fingers into his parka, drew out a small observation mirror on a telescoping handle, little different from what a dentist might use. He held it out just past the cabin's corner, angled it back and forth. No sign of Morris or Young. Only a Moga generator, five kilowatts at least, chugging away on a raised wooden platform, its cable running into the cabin's wall.

Webber took a moment for his breathing to steady and checked the settings on the AK-47. Then he popped the curved magazine from its well to do a visual confirm on the number of rounds remaining. Five. He checked the mirror again, then pocketed it and moved forward cautiously, listening for any movement in the cabin. Both the windows he passed—one on each side of the generator—were closed and blacked out by insulation panels.

Then he was at the last corner. Rounding it would bring him back to the side of the cabin with the door, with Young, and Morris. He used the mirror again.

Morris was waiting for him in the doorway, hunched down behind the pallet, holding a small Heckler & Koch MP5 submachine gun. Webber knew it had been Rensberger's weapon of choice—a "room broom," light and deadly effective in close-quarter engagements. The NEST Two weapons engineer moved her gaze from side to side, looking for him—she hadn't noticed the mirror—stopping only to talk over her shoulder to whoever was still in the cabin, presumably Young.

Webber visually rehearsed the moves he would have to make to reach the doorway, tap her, and then avoid Young's return fire. Every way he imagined it, the maneuver would cost him his five bullets, leaving him weaponless.

Suddenly, Morris took the decision from him. She bolted back inside the cabin as if responding to an emergency.

Webber ran for the doorway, swung in low, fired three rounds through the roof and yelled for everyone to drop their weapons. In a standard takedown, he would have swept the cabin's interior with his remaining rounds, but he had no intention of hitting an already cracked Bottle Rocket shell.

In the second Webber had to register the layout of the cabin, he perceived—at first—no surprises. He saw an open space with no dividers to provide cover. A string of utility lights along the walls put out dim but adequate light. He saw no heat source, but felt the mitigating effect of shelter from the wind outside.

Glendon Morris was not an operator. The first to respond to his shouted command, she dropped her H&K without conscious thought—a reaction born of fear, not training.

Nick Young—the only other person in the cabin—wasn't holding a weapon. His hands were on the controls of a large winch.

Several precious seconds elapsed before Webber comprehended the importance of what Young was about to do.

In the center of the ice floor of the cabin, there was a five-foot-wide hole. The winch hook was suspended over it. And dangling from the winch was a grease-covered chain. Attached to the chain was a four-foot-long, dark green metal cone marked with numbers and Cyrillic letters.

It was not an American tactical nuclear tank shell.

It was a 5.5-megaton-yield Russian Stiletto-class MIRV warhead. One component of six identical units from an SS-19 M3 ICBM. One component powerful enough to take out twenty square blocks of San Francisco.

Whatever the warhead was doing in the Antarctic, it wouldn't help Argentina look for mineral resources in the frozen Ross Sea. And if one MIRV warhead had been stolen, then Webber knew that, somewhere, there were five other warheads that NEST had to find.

Webber aimed the machine gun at Young. "Nick . . . step back. . . . I won't even count to five."

"So don't." Young punched a red button on the winch's control panel. A small motor whined, and with a deafening rattle of metal chain, the winch slipped out of gear.

The warhead began its descent into the ice. In the same distracting instant, Young shouted over the clatter. "It's set to go on contact! Twelve hundred feet down! Three minutes!"

"Stop it! Now!"

Young held up his hands, stepped back with a shrug. "Late again, cowboy."

As quickly as that, the warhead was gone.

FOUR

THE *FERNANDO PEREIRA*, McMURDO SOUND

Cory Rey looked away from the camera long enough to admire the expansive billows of red fabric growing behind her. The intensity of color was startling in the bright afternoon sun, especially after so many days of seeing only blue sky, green ocean, and white ice.

"Cory! They're getting ready to ram us!"

The cry from Johnny Rey, her brother, up on the signal deck of the *Fernando Pereira* brought Cory back to the moment. She faced the camera again, kept speaking, needing no notes, only a microphone and her passion.

"With this latest action, the United States is showing itself to be in flagrant disregard of the Antarctic Treaty, *and* in violation of international law." She glanced away from Hal Magnan, her camera operator, to see where the *Nathaniel B. Palmer* was now. The huge research vessel, more than 300 feet in length, was the flagship of USAP—the United States Antarctic Program. She was an icebreaker, and her reinforced hull was capable of smashing through three feet of ice, which made her more than a match for the hull of the *Fernando Pereira*. The smaller vessel, 120 feet long and flagship of Earthguard, was only an ice-class vessel, whose hull could push aside frazil, grease, and pancake ice, but could not slice through solid floe. And the *Palmer* was closing in on the *Pereira* at a good three knots, ice heaving up before her.

Cory waved to the cameraman. "Hal—show the *Palmer*."

Magnan angled to port to zoom in on the *Palmer*, her red hull as brilliant as the hot-air balloon taking shape on the *Pereira*'s helipad. The camera was an old Sony Betacam, purchased surplus from a television station in Seattle. But the sound and images it captured now were being relayed to the latest model of domed high-capacity uplink antennae above the bridge to be transmitted by satellite directly to Earthguard offices in Christchurch, Seattle, Halifax, and London, and from each of those sites into the Internet. This was the true power and promise of the pervasively networked age—an international civilian communications infrastructure which made possible live news reports that could not be censored. Even if no news channel in the world decided to broadcast Cory's message, it would still be available, in realtime and as a digital recording, to millions of witnesses on their own home computers.

Cory continued with her report, the lifelong conviction of her cause fueled by the rough pitch of the *Pereira*'s deck, the constant scrape and shudder of the ice the small ship pushed through, and the crisp bite of the Antarctic air blowing in from the continent. She was never more alive than when she was fighting back, and that truth shone in her flushed face and intense dark eyes. "Citizens of the world, the mission of Earthguard is vital to the preservation of the diversity of life in Earth's endangered environments—to support the rights of all species, not just humanity's right, to peaceful and uncontaminated existence. Today, we are here to investigate what may be a flagrant disregard of international law by the American government. Earthguard is here to defend your right to know the truth: Is the U.S. military-industrial complex preparing to return nuclear power stations to Antarctica? Have illegal nuclear weapons been lost on the Ice? Or—and this is a question that demands to be answered—are illegal nuclear weapons being *deployed* here? These are simple questions which require truthful answers—not acts of force, such as what you're seeing here today. Acts which could result in murder!"

The *Pereira*'s airhorn suddenly blasted out a collision warning signal. To Cory and the others on the forward deck, it was as if a cannon had gone off, thunderous, deafening.

Cory shouted up to her brother. "How's the balloon?"

Johnny waved back at her. "We're ready to go!"

Cory pushed her short black hair off her forehead and spoke

directly to the camera, directly to the world. "No country, no government, no *one* can stop the truth. We are coming to you live via the Internet and if you stay with us, you are going to see everything we see as Earthguard exposes the dangerous game being played here. C'mon, Hal! Let's get some answers!"

Then Cory ran toward the stern and the helipad, Magnan following, the jerky frames from his Betacam spraying into space at the speed of light, reaching an audience that also demanded answers—but not to the same questions Cory was asking.

NATIONAL MILITARY COMMAND CENTER/THE PENTAGON

"General Abbott, there's a transmission from McMurdo."

Abbott looked up from the SHADOW FORGE briefing binder, automatically checking his watch. General Morrow had said the NEST update was due from McMurdo at 2100 hours, so Lieutenant Yoshii must be mistaken. Then he saw the big board.

Yoshii had brought the video window for CNNI to the center of the ETEM map, expanding it to three feet. Whatever was going on, it wasn't an official transmission.

"What are we looking at, Lieutenant?" As far as Abbott could tell, the screen was filled with a red blob, labeled LIVE FROM ANTARCTICA. The image was repeated in five other video windows, some a few seconds out of synch with the others, others broken by static-filled freeze frames and diagonal slashes of interference.

Yoshii adjusted mixing controls at her workstation. "I believe it's a hot-air balloon, sir. I just noticed it on all those feeds. Bringing up audio for CNNI."

The voice of an unseen reporter, a man, came from the speakers above the board. ". . . an environmental activist group with a long record of exposing industrial polluters. In March of last year, Earthguard was responsible for the landmark two-hundred-million-dollar fine levied by British courts against—"

A female reporter broke in. "Mike, I've just been informed we've regained the audio from this unusual transmission. . . ."

Now another woman spoke, breathless, a familiar edge to her voice that Abbott associated with soldiers in combat. "We are now ascending from the *Fernando Pereira*—" Her voice was lost in a swelling uproar.

Abbott kept his eyes on the screen. "Give me a reference on the *Fernando Pereira*. What activist group are we looking at here? Greenpeace?"

The out-of-focus red blob suddenly swung off the screen and Abbott could see a spectacular aerial view of a blinding sea of ice fragments. For a few moments, the landscape jumped around the screen, the combination of handheld shakiness and a less-than-broadcast-standard rate of frames per second adding to the disconcerting documentary immediacy of the image. Then the camera moved on, flashing over an excited young woman with short dark hair, who was bundled in a parka that matched the red fabric flapping behind her. She was brandishing a small radio microphone and was obviously the commentator who had been speaking before the unidentified noise began.

The female CNNI reporter spoke over the noise, now muted. "Mike, I've been told that what we're hearing is the sound of the propane burner on the balloon."

Yoshii called to Abbott from her workstation. In addition to her headset, she was now cradling a phone to her other ear. "Sir, the activist group is Earthguard." She listened carefully for a few seconds. "About five years old. Two of the people who started it broke off from Greenpeace. Fernando Pereira was the photographer murdered when French commandos blew up Greenpeace's *Rainbow Warrior* in 1985. The breakaway group has a history of going after military bases for pollution offenses."

"McMurdo is *not* a military installation," Abbott said. Just then the handheld camera view swept around to zoom in on McMurdo Station itself—a collection of low, green- and white-roofed buildings and clusters of fuel-storage tanks sprawled against black volcanic rock, webbed by snow and ice at the shore of the frozen Ross Sea. Abbott estimated that the balloon must be at an altitude of two hundred feet, several miles out from the station.

The roaring stopped and the on-site woman's voice picked up again. "Okay, Hal . . . see there . . . right up on the shoreline . . . where that road sort of goes onto the ice . . . ?"

A man's voice answered. Hal, Abbott supposed, the woman's camera operator. "That triangle of black? To the right of the two buildings?"

"That's it. I've got it in my binoculars. Zoom in."

One of the CNNI reporters broke in. "Sandra, does anyone know what the activists are trying to show us?"

"Mike, Earthguard has called a press conference at their Seattle headquarters. We have a news team standing by waiting for that conference to begin. Perhaps then we can answer that question."

Abbott realized he knew the answer now. The black triangular area the camera was zooming in on was the station's helicopter landing pads, upper and lower. Abbott could see three helicopters parked there: a high-visibility-orange UH-1N, and two Aérospatiale 350B2s, more angular and in standard service green. But he also knew those weren't the aircraft the activists were interested in.

"I got 'em!" the camera operator on board the balloon called out as his lens found its target.

"Hold right there, Hal." Abbott could hear elation in the woman's voice. "McMurdo Station is the United States'—and Antarctica's—largest base. A base supposedly devoted to scientific research. So why—Earthguard asks the world—*why* are jet fighter planes, weapons of war, stationed here?"

"Oh, sweet Jesus," Abbott said. "She has no idea what she's talking about." There were warplanes on the helicopter landing pads. But they weren't what the activists thought.

Yoshii asked the question from her workstation. "Those are Harriers, aren't they, sir? But why the big canopies?"

"Modified AV-8Bs. They're two-seaters."

Yoshii frowned. "Trainers?" Abbott understood but did not condone her confusion. Harriers were among the most difficult fighters to fly, and McDonnell Douglas had responded by producing a two-seater version for pilot training. Yoshii should have known better. Trainers were generally painted white for easy identification. The Harriers at McMurdo were in European One shades—irregular splotches of light and dark gray. Urban camouflage. Those were active-duty craft. The general made a mental note to mark Yoshii's duty report with a strong recommendation she review the Project CLEAR DAY manuals regarding aircraft identification.

Abbott stood up. "They're part of the NEST deployment. The second seat is for a DOE weapons specialist." He took the briefing binder to Yoshii. "Lieutenant, I'm clearing you to read this. Go through the contacts list. I want to find out who's investigating how those civilians found out about SHADOW FORGE."

"Yes, sir."

Abbott returned to his chair at the table, his full attention now focused on the CNNI feed, calculating the security implications of what was being shown. In his experience, of all the dangers the United States faced in the new century, terrorist use of weapons of mass destruction was the most difficult to guard against. The constellations of surveillance satellites maintained by the military could easily detect the massing of hostile troops, unusual construction activity, even the launch of single missiles, so the possibility of a large-scale or high-technology-based surprise strike against America or her allies was remote. But unless intelligence assets instructed that surveillance system precisely where and when to look, a pickup truck with a homemade fission device, or a Piper Cub with a black-market Soviet warhead, could slip through the country's defenses unseen.

From his position on the Joint Staff, Abbott was acutely aware that despite the DOE's public assurances, of the almost two hundred NEST alerts initiated since the teams' creation by executive order in 1975, four had involved actual nuclear devices: an improvised radiation-dispersion bomb in San Francisco; a stolen American warhead in San Diego; and two sophisticated fission weapons, hand-built from old American plans available on the Internet, which had been intercepted while being smuggled into the country for use in Washington. When the Cold War ended, America's citizens had breathed their collective sigh of relief, but only because, in Abbott's view, they didn't—and couldn't—understand how the nature of the threat against them had changed. Where a hundred potential enemies had once been organized and constrained by the long-range strategic thinking of Moscow, now they were cut free. And they were still out there, Abbott knew, waiting for their chance to strike at a country that became more complacent, insular, and vulnerable each day.

In his judgment, what Earthguard was doing, live and in color, was broadcasting a training manual for those unseen enemies. Once alerted, Nuclear Emergency Search Teams had the technology and personnel to locate, seize, and disable almost any type of nuclear weapon. A broadcast of this kind, which might reveal the classified components of a NEST deployment, or identify personnel, only made it easier for the next hostile force to try its luck.

Abbott set aside Berlin and the Middle East, the riots in Islamabad. He even dismissed China from his thoughts. He was commander of the NMCC and a flash point had just gone hot.

"Lieutenant, have any of the networks identified the source of this transmission?"

"It's coming off the Internet, sir. The news feeds are getting it by logging on to an Earthguard site. It's fully accessible to the public."

Abbott steepled his long fingers as he studied the screens before him and considered his options. Through an elaborate system of computer viruses and override codes known as NIAGARA, the National Security Agency had developed and selectively demonstrated the ability to shut down the worldwide Internet in a matter of minutes via localized "data storms" which could block all attempts by individual users to connect. However, even the Pentagon recognized the constitutional issues involved in taking such an action, to say nothing of the international trade laws that would be broken. Thus, NIAGARA had been deemed a procedure to be employed only in the event of war, when all communications must be monitored. Abbott knew he would have no chance in requesting a NIAGARA implementation simply to stop a broadcast that *might* reveal a few technical secrets. Which clearly meant that he had to locate another way to shut down the Earthguard transmission from Antarctica *before* it reached the Internet.

"Lieutenant, show me our communications options with McMurdo—civilian and military."

In less than a minute, Yoshii had opened a data window on the big board, just beside the CNNI feed. In the new window was a list of all communications pathways linking McMurdo Station with the rest of the world. There were two indirect links: MARSGRAMS, a service of the Military Amateur Radio Service, which allowed station personnel to send up to two 50-line messages each week, which were then printed out and mailed in the U.S., and ham-radio contact, when electromagnetic conditions and the availability of licensed operators permitted. Of the direct links, there were precisely twelve: a fiber-optic underwater phone cable to New Zealand, and eleven satellite communications options, including INMARSAT—the International Marine Satellite communications network—and a classified link through the Defense Satellite Communications System. Since McMurdo wasn't a military installation, no matter what Earthguard implied, Abbott was somewhat surprised to see a DSCS link. But then, he knew, the Department of State also used the system, and presumably McMurdo would sometimes host members of government on fact-finding tours. Whatever the reason for the DSCS station, at least Earthguard would have no access to it.

Most of the other communications options were tagged to individual, conventional science missions—meteorology, seismology, upper atmospheric studies—involving specific windows for uploading data to satellites on whatever time blocks had been leased by participating universities or research institutes. Those links were extremely limited, involving clearly delineated access windows of only a few hours every few days. Since the links consisted of single satellite systems and not full constellations, anything uploaded would be stored by the satellite until it moved over a dedicated downlink site. That meant the scientific data uplinks were unsuitable for realtime transmissions. Earthguard would not be on this system, either.

That left only one communications option that was available to civilians *and* capable of handling a video signal—Motorola's Iridium system. It was a constellation of sixty-six LEO satellites, low-Earth-orbit, timed so that one was always above the horizon to provide satellite phone service around the world. With off-the-shelf modems, Iridium could readily handle the data stream necessary to transmit low-resolution digital video in realtime. And as a system wholly owned by an American company with extensive military contracts, Iridium was also a system that was completely transparent to Pentagon control.

Abbott saw the simplest strategy and implemented it at once. "Lieutenant, I'm setting up a Crisis Action Team. Find out who's at J-3 and get a response cell in here. Also from J-6. Then I need a direct link to civilian communications control at the NSA, and find me the chief engineer or whoever the hell's in charge of Iridium operations at Motorola."

"Permission to call in support staff, sir."

"Whatever it takes, Lieutenant."

Abbott fixed his gaze on the parka-clad young woman on the video feed. The camera was back on her and she was talking earnestly, leaning against the lip of a woven balloon carriage.

"Whoever the hell she is," Abbott said, "we're going to shut her down."

FIVE

THE ICE

Young was to Webber's left. Morris was to his right. Webber took the only action he could. He ran forward and jammed the AK-47 into the upper pulley of the winch.

The speeding chain sparked against the gun's barrel, wrenching it out of his hands as the chain jerked to a halt with a shriek of metal. Somewhere in the hole carved through the cabin's ice floor, Webber knew, the Soviet warhead was swinging back and forth, momentarily halted, but still primed to detonate when it hit bottom.

Young shouted at Morris. *"The gun!"*

For an instant, Webber's eyes met Young's. Then, as Morris scrambled for her H&K submachine gun and kicked it, spinning it across the ice toward Young, Webber dove for it.

So did Young.

Webber's hand hit the weapon just as Young landed on both.

They stretched on the ice, side by side, eye to eye, inches apart, Webber's arm buried under Young's chest; twenty years of friendship vanished in the standoff of betrayal and defiance.

Webber closed his finger on the H&K's trigger.

Young's body went into spasms with the force of the bullets that ripped the weapon from Webber's buried hand.

Then Young was on his back, hands across his gut. Webber didn't know if any of his bullets had connected, but the scorching gases

51

from the barrel must have gone off against Young's chest like a small grenade.

Webber dropped the H&K and struggled to his feet, aware once more of the rib he'd cracked when Young had shot him. Then, through the ringing in his ears from the submachine gun's burst, he heard another rhythmic sound.

The motor on the winch had a safety transmission and it was slipping in and out of gear, alternately winding and rewinding the drive chain, rocking the AK-47 in and out, working the rifle free from the pulley.

Young was now sitting up on the ice, though doubled over. Webber made his decision swiftly and kicked his heavy PolarOps boot into the side of Young's head with the intent of crushing his temple. The bulky combat gear robbed Webber's blow of full force and made his aim less precise, but Young fell over on his side with a grunt.

Then an explosion of black stars burst before Webber as a four-foot ice auger swung into his neck from behind. Morris.

Webber dropped to his knees, reflexively covering his head and rolling as a second blow from the auger bit drove down into the ice. He swept out his leg, knocking Morris off her feet, flinging her backward and slamming her head into the stone-hard surface of the ice as she fell.

Now the only thing that moved in the cabin was the winding and unwinding chain on the winch. Another thirty seconds would dislodge the AK-47, allowing the warhead to resume its controlled descent. Three minutes past that and the warhead would detonate.

Morris was unconscious. Young lay in a fetal position, groaning, as he cradled his head in his hands. Webber staggered to the winch panel. He had trouble focusing on the controls. He put his hand to the back of his head. His glove came back with blood. He leaned closer to the panel.

Then the AK-47 fell clear, into the hole in the ice, clattering down toward a warhead set to explode on contact. Webber's chest felt as if the falling AK-47 had taken with it all the breathable air and he were adrift in the vacuum of space. A dull metallic crash echoed from the hole.

Nothing else.

The winch motor hummed and the chain began to unwind again.

Three minutes.

Webber reached out to the control panel, found the power switch, hit it. The motor shut down and the chain stopped. Webber resumed breathing.

The click of the H&K submachine gun echoed in the small cabin.

"Story of your life, pal. Always outmaneuvered."

The front of Young's white parka was black with powder burns, yet obviously no bullets had hit him. Instead, blood dripped down the side of his head. Webber's boot had missed Young's temple but gashed his scalp. Vapor steamed from the wound in the unheated air of the cabin.

"C'mon. Ask me why again," Young said.

"Doesn't matter anymore."

Something flickered across Young's face, maybe pain, maybe regret. Webber couldn't be certain. "Yeah, but it used to, right?"

Then Morris stirred, pushed herself up from the ice, dry-heaved. Young's eyes and weapon remained steady on Webber.

Webber saw Morris jerk as she saw the chain swaying gently in the hole. "Jesus, Nick. We have to—"

Her head blew apart in a spray of blood, flesh, and bone. Young's gun was back on Webber before the engineer's twitching body had settled back onto the cabin's ice floor.

But Webber had heard the faint click of the trigger being released long enough after the last round had fired to know the H&K was no longer in the equation. The clip was empty. And Webber knew Young well enough to see that his friend, his enemy, knew it, too.

Young hit the power switch, reactivating the winch. Again, the chain began unwinding.

At the same instant, Webber drew his knife from the scabbard on his leg.

Reflexively, Young pulled the trigger on the H&K, just in case, but the clip was spent as both had known. He threw it to the side and pulled out his own knife.

The two soldiers faced each other, each in a half crouch, each waiting for the other to make the first move, the first mistake. Once contact had been made, any knife fight between two SEALs would be over in less than a minute. The most optimistic outcome would be one dead, one badly wounded. But this time, there was another outcome possible as the two former teammates circled each other and the chain kept unwinding. In less than two minutes, the warhead would hit bottom.

Webber kept his attention on Young's eyes, not his knife. To survive, he had to respond to intent. To respond to action meant he was already dead. "Whatever's going on here, Nick, are you willing to die for it?"

For a fraction of a second, Young hesitated. Suddenly Webber knew Young did not expect to die in a matter of minutes. He was still fighting to get away. "So it's not set to go off on impact," Webber said.

"Are *you* willing to die to find out?"

Webber chose his primary and secondary target: a feint to Young's neck, followed by a thrust to the stomach, angling upward to the heart. The front of Young's parka was so badly damaged it wouldn't offer any resistance.

But before Webber could attack, Young spun around, and leapt into the air to kick out one of the three metal support legs of the winch. The center pulley crashed down into the ice hole, wedging into a precarious hold with the other two splayed legs. The chain slipped off the pulley and began to rattle out independent of the motor.

Young ran for the door.

Webber threw his knife, but the weapon struck Young's back in midspin and bounced off the intact back of Young's parka. Then the NEST Two leader was out the door and away.

The chain played out, moving faster now, less than a minute left by Webber's estimate. He was certain the warhead wouldn't detonate on impact, but there was no guarantee the casing wouldn't crack. If he could stop the warhead in place, an ordinary work gang could haul the warhead out with another winch. If not, NEST faced a potentially major nuclear incident just in the cleanup.

Webber spotted the manual brake lever, lunged at it, and felt it buck back up against him. The last links of the chain rattled into the hole. Only seconds were left.

Sweat ran down his face as he changed his grip, applying greater and greater pressure until he saw and heard the spool begin to slow, mere inches of chain left to play out.

He increased the pressure, putting more and more effort into it until his full body weight leaned against the lever.

Then all movement ended. The spool stopped unwinding.

Webber flipped the lock bar over the lever, jammed it shut, tried loosening it to be sure it was secure, then slowly let up on the lever. The bar held. The chain was locked.

For a brief moment, as a shrieking howl from outside suddenly vibrated the cabin, Webber thought another warhead had detonated. Then he ran to the door, almost slipping in Morris's slick frozen blood.

Outside, snow eddies swirled thickly as if the blizzard had suddenly worsened. Webber grabbed an AK-47 from the hostile he had shot outside the door, then ran around to the back of the cabin, half expecting to see the Sno-Cat coming at him hauling a sledge of burning fuel drums.

But a screaming blast of flame from *above* threw him down into the snow-encrusted ice—snow that splashed as he hit it, snow already liquid from sudden heat.

He cupped his hands over his ears as he heard the cabin explode in flames behind him, then the scream trailed off, lost in the wind. The rich scent of jet fuel burned in his nostrils.

Drenched, Webber looked back to see the cabin collapse inward on itself, burning embers shooting skyward within the dancing flurries of snow.

He got awkwardly to his feet, remembering the supplies fifty feet away, covered by the orange tarp. Ignoring his stiffening clothing and the stinging of the storm's windborne ice crystals on his exposed face and hands, he made his way to the supply cache, found the bright orange tarp blowing free.

The cache was empty, only a flame-blackened surface of wood planks.

But Webber recognized the centralized burn pattern and the size of the wooden surface, and instantly knew what had been hidden under the tarp.

He looked up into the storm and the darkening cover of gusting snow, reassessing all the intelligence he thought he had already gathered. It was one thing for a terrorist group to steal or buy six Soviet warheads. But what kind of group had the means to bring a jump jet onto the Ice? The logistics alone meant such a group had immensely powerful backers. Each Clear Day NEST Harrier back at McMurdo needed a flight crew of four to maintain operational readiness, and the full support of the New York Air National Guard for service between flights.

Webber shivered as the wind completed the icy conversion of the water soaking his gear, but it wasn't just the temperature that affected him. Whoever had bought Nick Young, their resources were the equal of NEST's, which meant their resources were the equal of America's.

That was an enemy NEST was not ready to face, alone.

Mitch Webber needed the Pentagon.

SIX

Fifteen minutes after giving the order, General Abbott had a Crisis Action Team of fifteen Joint Staff personnel assembled to deal with the breach of security on SHADOW FORGE. Nine worked outside the emergency action room on the adjacent NMCC watch floor. Six had positions in the EAR itself: Lieutenant Yoshii as systems coordinator; two NCO communications specialists who had been taken from their workstations in the China section of the National Military Command Center to provide Yoshii with systems support; Air Force Captain Alan Woolman, from the Office of the Secretary of Defense; Army Major Prospero Chennault, senior on-duty Defense Intelligence Agency liaison to the National Security Agency; and Abbott himself.

Everyone involved had been through enough drills and training exercises that the Crisis Action Team had been self-organizing. Only its objectives were unique. Indeed, Abbott thought, they were unprecedented.

Lieutenant Yoshii's clear voice called out over the hum of conversation in the room. "General, I have Clifton Ferris of Motorola on SVTS."

Abbott checked his watch. When he had given the order to form the CAT, he had started the stopwatch function in the digital display set in the timepiece's analog face. It had taken Yoshii seventeen minutes to locate the engineer responsible for the Iridium system this holiday weekend. That wasn't good enough, though Abbott didn't consider that a sign of Yoshii's shortcomings. Anyone in the active chain of command was no more than two minutes removed from communication with the NMCC. But as more and more of the military's functions were piecemealed out to civilian companies, the lag time for locating nonmilitary specialists was rising dramatically. More than once, Abbott had issued reports stating that one day that lack of organization would result in unacceptable delay and disaster. So far, the Joint Chiefs of Staff had declined to act on his recommendations. This apparently minor crisis might be the proof his argument required.

On the big board, a new video window opened, making three that were front and center. They were overlaid on an expanded ETEM map showing the Ross Sea—precisely speaking, more of a bay, like a bite taken out of the generally circular shape of Antarctica, directly at the bottom of the Pacific Basin. McMurdo Station was marked as a blue square on the western edge of the sea, just at the seasonal minimum extent of the Ross Ice Shelf. It was the southernmost point of land in the Antarctic that could be reached by ship. The yellow warning icon still flashed beside the station's square.

The center video window continued to carry the CNNI feed. The Earthguard activists continued to upload their signal, making their outrageous and uninformed claims. Abbott had seen enough to know that there were three people in the balloon. The dark-haired woman, whom CNNI had identified as Dr. Corazon Rey, an oceanographer and director of Earthguard; the camera operator, known only as Hal; and an unidentified younger male, whose appearance, to Abbott, suggested some familial relationship to Rey.

The balloon was now directly over the Station, still at about 200 feet. Someone on the ground had taken the proper initiative and covered the NEST Harriers with tarps, to hide the specialized science packages each carried. The mere shape of the radiation detectors slung under the jets' wings could provide potential enemies with useful clues about the equipment's range and sensitivity.

The second video window was a low-resolution feed from the National Security Agency, relayed through the government's Secure Video Teleconference System. Elrey Boyd, an African-American who to Abbott appeared to be no older than twenty, was standing by to take part in the videoconference with the representative from Motorola. That representative was the person who appeared in the third window, also in an SVTS feed, from the Iridium master control facility in northern Virginia.

As the static faded from the Motorola connection, Yoshii gave Abbott the go status he waited for. "Everyone's in synch, General."

Ferris, a balding, middle-aged man in a loosened tie, who had the look of someone who had accomplished nothing of significance in his life, seemed surprised to hear Abbott's rank. Abbott had no idea what the civilian had been told about this conference call, and didn't care. "General . . . I'm Clifton Ferris. How are things at . . . the Pentagon?"

Abbott ignored the question. Serving civilians was one thing. Having to deal with them was another. Who could think of responding to an emergency communications from the Pentagon with idle small talk? "Mr. Ferris, a video signal compromising the security of a classified government operation is being transmitted through your Iridium system."

Ferris's eyes widened. "It is?"

"Trust me. Under FCC regulations, I have the authority to request that you stop that signal from propagating through your system. At once."

Ferris seemed genuinely flustered, but Abbott felt some relief that the engineer didn't immediately say he would have to consult with his company's lawyers or make some other delaying excuse.

"General . . . I have sixty-six satellites up there. Each handles three thousand, eight hundred and forty channels. That's more than a quarter-million possible links. I'll . . . I'll have to find out what grid the signal's coming from, isolate the transponder—"

The kid from the NSA broke in. "Mr. Ferris, Elrey Boyd, NSA. The signal's originating at 77 degrees, 55 minutes south, 166 degrees, 40 minutes east. That puts it in your proprietary grid number 12-12-12, currently served by satellite 48, transponder 6, with a handoff to satellite 18 coming up in . . . 6 minutes."

Ferris's mouth opened, just a little, as he seemed to realize the capabilities of the people he was dealing with. "That . . . uh, that does make it much simpler. Um, I don't suppose you happen to have the phone numbers? Of the sending unit and the receiving circuit?"

Abbott waited as Boyd read out the twelve-digit Iridium phone number used by Earthguard on their ship, and the landline numbers of the Earthguard offices who were patched into the call around the world.

Ferris stood up with a notepad, then bent down to look back into the teleconferencing camera on his computer monitor. "Uh, if you'll give me a moment." Then he moved out of camera sight.

Abbott spoke to the big board. There were several small video cameras mounted above it, and Yoshii had instructed one to follow the general, or, more accurately, to follow the smart badge the general had pinned to his lapel upon coming on duty. The small, plastic-covered tag, not much larger than a watch battery, continually broadcast an extremely short-range FM radio ID code, so that the Pentagon's internal communications system would know at all times exactly where he was in the building. The camera responded to the same signal to keep its lens constantly focused on the badge, and by default, the general. "Mr. Boyd, how long should this take him?"

The young man gazed up for a moment. "If he doesn't have to walk too far to a terminal, say thirty seconds to type in the ID numbers, a minute for the system to process the command, upload it from the TTACs in, let's say Hawaii . . . under two minutes."

"At three minutes, I would like the NSA to interrupt the signal."

Boyd looked noncommittal. "This is peacetime. That'll be an illegal act."

"My authorization. That broadcast could threaten the future safety of NEST operatives."

Abbott could see that Boyd was still not comfortable with the command. "General, with such short notice, we will have to disrupt the entire Iridium system."

"But you can do it."

Boyd blinked as if Abbott had asked a question for which the answer was self-evident. "Of course."

Abbott knew the question was self-evident. Thanks to the foresight of the National Security Policy Commission established by a previous Administration, which in turn had led to the creation of both the Army's Digitized Office and the Information Warfare Centers of the Navy and the Air Force, the United States' ability to wage electronic warfare was absolute, unparalleled, and largely unsuspected by the civilian population. Abbott was proud to have

60

been one of the soldiers who had helped show the way to this new era of warfare.

Almost fifteen years ago, as a major in the Gulf War, Abbott had been inserted behind Iraqi defensive lines by a five-member SEAL team. Operation Desert Shield had yet to become Desert Storm, and at that point, almost all direct contact between Allied and Iraqi forces had been accidental or covert.

The SEALs had brought Abbott to a buried junction box 200 yards from an Iraqi Intercept Operation Center, part of a linked air-defense network which coordinated more than 500 radar posts and 8,000 anti-aircraft guns throughout the country. Two hours of painfully slow and quiet digging in the sand had unearthed a military communications link. Using only an inductance interface, which did not require a physical connection to any of the wires and thus did not risk a detectable change in current, Abbott had used a specially manufactured portable computer to override the command and control system in the IOC. Though he then had the capability to shut down the center, Abbott's plan had been more far-reaching. He had simply inserted into the center's master control program two extra lines of computer code. Then he had removed the interface and with the SEALs spent an additional hour reburying the junction so that no one would ever suspect it had been uncovered.

By the time Abbott had been debriefed that morning, following a successful and uneventful extraction, those two lines of code had begun to spread through the entire Iraqi air defense computer network. Operation BLINDSPOT became the first use of a computer virus in wartime.

One week later, on the night of January 16, as twenty F-117A Stealth fighters flew into Iraqi airspace to deliver the first round of Desert Storm's aerial bombardment, those two lines of code, triggered by a standard time signal, systematically interrupted and blanked out the transmission of all radar contacts throughout forty-two percent of the Iraqi defensive network. Since the Gulf War, further studies had indicated that if the virus had been allowed to spread over three weeks, more than ninety percent of the Iraqi system would have been infected. And if the same operation were to be carried out today, refinements in the Army's ongoing development of computer viruses would permit the infected system to display the radar returns of its own aircraft, while selectively ignoring American planes, including non-stealthy ones. In some cases, Abbott knew, even the physical insertion of viruses would no longer be a necessary step of the operation. They had already been hard-wired into computer chips that the State Department believed would be sold illegally to countries under technology-transfer restrictions.

At two minutes thirty seconds, Clifton Ferris reappeared in the SVTS window. "Uh, General . . . the system should cut off the signal within the next half minute."

Abbott checked his watch, then fixed his attention on the CNNI feed. Dr. Rey was self-righteously holding forth for the world. "Volume up," Abbott said.

"—to summarize: Article One of the Antarctic Treaty states Antarctica shall be used for peaceful purposes only. All military measures—*all* military measures—including weapons and testing are prohibited. And Article Ten states that contracting parties, of which the United States is one, shall insure that no activity contrary to the Treaty is—"

Dr. Corazon Rey dissolved into a field of random static, where she belonged.

Abbott watched approvingly as she also disappeared from the other news feeds on the board. "Thank you, Mr. Ferris. You've done your country a great service. You will be receiving formal notification and authorization paperwork within twenty-four hours. However, at this time I must inform you that the law restrains you from discussing this action, verbally or in writing, with anyone. Failure to abide by this requirement will subject you to a fine of not more than five thousand dollars and a sentence of not more than one year in a military prison. Do you understand these conditions?"

"I'm . . . going to have to tell the system supervisor."

Abbott allowed a hint of threat to color his authoritative tone. "No, Mr. Ferris. The law specifically restrains you from discussing this with *anyone*. Your supervisor and all appropriate company officials will be notified in accordance with the law. Do you understand?"

Ferris blinked several times as if some internal circuit in his brain were resetting itself. "Yes, sir . . . General . . . I understand."

"Thank you. I will expect that no further transmissions will be accepted from the Earthguard satellite phone in that grid sector."

"I'll keep it locked out, sir."

Abbott smiled his approval, trying to put the man at ease, knowing Ferris had never served a day in the military. The draft had been more than a way to maintain the country's armed forces; it had been a tool to teach the necessary lessons of discipline and respect—two qualities that Ferris would forever lack, to the detriment of his country and his life. "That is all, Mr. Ferris. Carry on."

Abbott signaled to Yoshii, and the hapless Mr. Ferris disappeared from the screen.

CNNI had switched back to a news anchor in Atlanta commenting on the unprecedented transmission from Antarctica while the network attempted to reestablish the signal. In the other video window, Boyd stretched back in his chair and cracked his knuckles. "Anything else I can do for you, General?"

"Stand by for the moment." Abbott motioned to Captain Woolman and Major Chennault to join him in a corner of the room. Woolman had the slim, compact build and air of precision that made him instantly identifiable as a pilot. Abbott had never worked with him, but knew the type. The captain had understood enough about the way the military worked to lobby for a position with the Office of the Secretary of Defense and the career opportunities that would open up in the years ahead. But he had the caged-tiger look that told Abbott he lived for the day he could return to active flying.

Chennault, on the other hand, was a known quantity. He had made Washington his home and had worked with Abbott on several projects in which the electronic-interception capabilities of the NSA had been required. Chennault had seen active duty as part of the Army's counterterrorism Delta Force, then moved to a desk assignment in the Pentagon, first with the Defense Intelligence Agency, then with the J-2 Directorate, which served as liaison between the DIA and the Joint Staff. He was at least fifty, though he hid his age by affecting a completely shaven scalp, leaving only a mustache to reveal streaks of gray. Had his career path been different, Abbott had no doubt Chennault would also be a general by now. But those soldiers who specialized in special warfare and covert operations often lagged behind their peers in promotions, because so many of their accomplishments could never appear in their service records. Abbott believed that when the system worked properly, it was because of men like Woolman and Chennault. He was pleased to have both officers on his team.

"Gentlemen, we've now contained the security leak and the next step is to isolate the perpetrators. Apparently, McMurdo has a DSCS satellite link. Is that a backup, or are there military personnel on duty there, other than Air National Guard support?"

Woolman and Chennault exchanged a glance which told Abbott that he had unexpectedly requested classified information. Though he maintained a Top Secret security clearance, it did not mean he could legitimately have access to all programs at that same level of secrecy. It was possible that of all the personnel in this room with Top Secret clearances, none of them shared knowledge of a single program.

Captain Woolman, as the least senior officer, excused himself from the decision that had to be made. "General, this is outside my classification."

Major Chennault thought for a few moments, clearly choosing the best way to frame his response to Abbott's request, without revealing more than was necessary. "The Defense Satellite Communications System in McMurdo is primarily a backup. The Air National Guard has authorization to use it in the event of an emergency."

"Would ANG personnel on station consider the Earthguard transmission an emergency?"

"Doubtful. They would think in terms of medical emergencies, a major air crash—" Chennault smiled. "—eruption of Mount Erebus. But the NEST personnel at McMurdo would understand the significance of Earthguard's presence."

Abbott had suspected that. It raised a troubling question. "Do you have any explanation for why we haven't heard from them?"

"To be blunt, they haven't been having much luck down there. Both teams have been going out to run a search grid every day and my interpretation is that no one in authority is present at the station at this time."

"Someone pulled the tarps over those Harriers."

"That's SOP. We have good flight crews."

Then Abbott realized the distinction Chennault had made in response to his first question.

"You said the DSCS is 'primarily' a backup. Is it there for a reason other than emergencies?"

"Sir, I have to inform you that you are straying into compartmentalized information."

Abbott waited. An NMCC Crisis Action Team was ample precedent for establishing need to know.

Chennault looked at Captain Woolman. "Captain, if you'd excuse us."

Woolman instantly walked away. Abbott approved his lack of hesitation. Information was the lifeblood of the Pentagon, and too often proper procedures were overlooked in the quest to expand one's knowledge and thus influence. But Woolman showed the behavior expected of officers on the Joint Staff.

Chennault shifted his position so that he faced only Abbott, and dropped his voice. "There is a black program currently under way at the Amundsen-Scott Station at the geographic South Pole."

"I take it it's not in compliance with the Treaty."

Chennault shrugged. "A matter of interpretation. It's an R-and-D project."

Abbott was intrigued. Black programs, those projects most protected by the Pentagon's multilayered webs of secrecy, fell into four general categories: operational, involving spycraft and covert actions; space, the fourth dimension of warfare; HUMINT, human intelligence, chiefly from unfriendly regions; and R&D, involving hardware. Abbott found himself pressed to imagine what sort of weapons system might be best developed in one of the most extreme and inaccessible environments on the planet.

Chennault seemed to sense Abbott's unspoken question and tried to provide an answer. "It's not nuclear and . . . it's not what would be traditionally thought of as a weapons installation. But, the station has been closed since 1990 in order to . . . avoid facing the legal technicalities that might arise if the project suddenly turned white."

"Could the NEST operation be connected to the South Pole project?"

"Extremely doubtful. Fewer than one hundred people in the country know what's going on there."

"What about another country?"

From Chennault's reaction to the question, Abbott could see that that was a question the Defense Intelligence Agency had already considered. "The DIA has no indication that the current suspected introduction of nuclear devices into Antarctica is targeted at operations at Amundsen-Scott."

Abbott decided he had remained in the dark long enough. "Major, the SHADOW FORGE briefing book provided us by the DOE contains twenty-two pages. It's obvious that the operational details have been sanitized. If this CAT is to achieve its objective to contain the security leak, I am going to have to have the complete background to the current NEST deployment. Do you have a problem with that?"

Chennault squared his shoulders. "No, sir, I do not." He glanced around the room. "However, I do suggest we continue this conversation in a more secure environment."

Abbott considered that a reasonable request. "The Tempest room. Five minutes. Do you need to contact anyone at the DIA?"

"No, sir. I believe conditions warrant a full briefing."

"Thank you, Major." Abbott dismissed Chennault with a quick nod, then went over to Yoshii to be certain the Earthguard feed had not resumed. It had not.

For a few moments, then, Abbott observed the hive of activity his orders had brought into being. The Pentagon, the pinnacle of the military structure of the Earth's greatest nation, was responding smoothly and expertly to the unexpected. He felt a sense of completeness. And he knew that in a few minutes, that feeling would be substantiated as he learned all the details behind NEST's deployment at McMurdo.

Information, Abbott thought, it was more than the lifeblood of the Pentagon. In this new era, when the electromagnetic spectrum itself had become the *fifth* dimension of warfare, information was the most powerful weapon of all. And in any confrontation, the combatant with the most powerful weapon was more often than not the winner.

Whatever else General Abbott was, he was that winner. And it was his duty, and his dream, to do all that history demanded of him to ensure his country was one as well.

SEVEN

McMURDO STATION

"Hold it, Cory! Stop!"

But that was the last thing Cory Rey wanted to do. Even without her binoculars, aloft in the red Earthguard balloon, 200 feet over McMurdo Station, she could see that the diminutive Earthguard ship, the *Fernando Pereira*, was being boarded by crew from the *Nathaniel B. Palmer*. In international waters no less. The world had to see. The world had to *know*.

But Hal Magnan, her videocam operator, reached out to lower her small mike before she could share her indignation with those viewers witnessing what she knew was a government cover-up that she was determined to expose. He showed her his handheld SABER two-way radio. "We've lost our ship uplink."

Cory's indignation turned to outrage. "That's a criminal act."

"Cory, it wasn't deliberate. We all knew the satellite coverage was going to be spotty." But the lack of conviction in Johnny Rey's statement betrayed that he knew Cory would not listen to him.

She tugged at the Velcroed sleeve of her red parka to check her watch. "We've got coverage for at least the next hour. I timed this perfectly! We can still transmit."

Shrugging at Hal, Johnny gave up, as he usually did in any argument with his older sister. They shared the same slight build and angular features, the same dark hair and impenetrably black eyes, but Cory knew she had ten times the passion and social indignation of her brother for their present endeavor. It was that same passion their parents had shown as they marched with Cesar Chavez to better their lives in their new country. It was that same refusal to accept defeat that had earned her an unprecedented engineering scholarship to MIT at sixteen. And it was that same uncompromising drive that had led her to take her degree in fluid-mechanics engineering. A short two years later, she'd graduated and begun all over again, earning a doctorate in oceanography at the University of California, San Diego. It'd been no surprise to anyone who knew her that she'd chosen to focus her studies on natural systems and environmental preservation. Her causes were well known to her few close friends and her family.

Not many people could keep up with her. Johnny, six years her junior, was, like Hal and most of her colleagues in Earthguard, content merely to be swept along in her wake. "Okay, so maybe it's temporary. When do you want me to land us?"

The large basket abruptly shifted as the balloon was caught in the sudden surge of a katabatic wind—a wave of cold, dense air driven by gravity, not temperature, rolling down from the continental plateau to the sea. The movement was eerie, because there was no sound from the moving air that had captured them. Since Cory and her team traveled at the same speed as the air current, they offered no resistance to the wind. Thus, when the burner was off, the balloon soared in a world without sound. Cory didn't like being cut off from the world. But she did enjoy the heart-stopping view. It gave her hope when she saw how impossibly small McMurdo Station was against the ice. Surely the destructive effects of the works of humans could be similarly reduced in their power over the works of nature.

She braced herself against the lip of the basket. "Johnny, if we land, they confiscate our camera. Anything we record will be erased. We have to keep transmitting from up here. That's the only way to save the material."

Johnny checked the altimeter bolted to one of the burner support pipes. Cory could feel the gradual drop in altitude, like descending in a slow elevator. The wind was cooling the reservoir of hot air in the fabric shell above them, and they were losing lift. Johnny double-checked the propane gauge. "We can stay up another half hour, sis. Less if the winds keep us dicking around to hold position."

Hal looked up from his camera. He was taking advantage of the time-out to replace a small digital Betacam cassette with a fresh one from his equipment bag. "The cold's really draining the batteries. They're lasting about half as long as they should."

"Guys, don't tell me your problems. Tell me what you're going to *do*."

Cory discounted the look of silent exasperation that Hal and her brother shared, because to her the solution was simple. At heart, most things were, she'd found.

Hal hefted the camera onto his shoulder and checked to be sure the small antenna on it was unencumbered, still able to transmit directly to the *Fernando Pereira*'s satellite uplink. "I'm going to keep recording until the batteries are dead."

Johnny dialed the squelch on his radio until Cory could hear the hash of static. "I'll keep us up here as long as the propane lasts, and keep trying to reconnect the call."

Cory smiled encouragingly for her team. "Simple, right?"

Johnny and Hal nodded, both knowing their place in this outing.

Cory wiped at her running nose with the back of her mitten and faced the camera. Her face felt stiff and she could feel the intense cold beginning to penetrate through to the thermal underwear she wore next to her skin. But she still had a lot she wanted to say. She always did. "Ready to roll."

Johnny grabbed the burner control. "I'll get us some more height."

Cory nodded. The burner roared, making conversation almost impossible. She basked in the blast of heat as she felt the balloon rise, filled with warm air. Far below, McMurdo became smaller and even more insignificant.

The noise resonated deep within her chest, connecting her to the world through visceral experience. She craved that sense of connection. She'd always sought it out wherever, whenever she could. She focused on that connection now, knowing it would help prepare her for the fight to come when she landed.

And knowing she was going to win that fight, Cory Rey couldn't wait to engage the enemy.

GENTLE THREE ZERO

"Mayday, mayday, mayday . . ."

Mitch Webber took care to speak slowly and clearly. The damaged helo fought every command he gave it, but he was its master, the outcome of their struggle never in doubt. If a machine had the capability to take to the air, Mitch Webber could fly it. It was in his job description.

He ceased speaking and the VOX radio built into the orange flight helmet he wore switched automatically from transmit to listen. All he heard in his helmet speakers was soft static. But he knew his broadcast, which was strictly line of sight, would most likely be received by a civilian science team camped on the Ice, so he allowed extra time for a response to come back. He couldn't expect the same instant reaction speed he would get from a military listening post.

The helo tried again to veer to port, the annoying response of damaged hydraulics. To maintain a straight flight path, Webber forced his foot to maintain constant pressure on the right antitorque pedal. At the same time, the helo's collective had been slow to respond since liftoff, so Webber never allowed his left hand to relax on the pitch lever, and he flew high to insure an extra margin of safety in case of an unexpected drop in altitude. Fortunately, he had long ago flown beyond the low-altitude blizzard that had scoured the Ross Shelf. The sky was now cloudless and deep blue above him, the land below impossibly white, raked by long indigo shadows from the slowly setting sun.

Webber moved off channel 7, the Science Net, to channel 10, Movement Control Center. He had no expectations that McMurdo would hear his VHF transmission, but there were a number of automated repeater stations on the peaks of the Royal Society Range of mountains he flew past. There was always a chance that some other air traffic might intercept a relayed message. A life depended on that chance: Behind him, Hadrian Gowers, his severely wounded weapons engineer, was strapped securely to the deck of the cargo hold. "Mayday, mayday, mayday . . ."

At least part of the damage to the helo was an aid, not a hindrance. The starboard door wouldn't slide shut because its frame had been warped by the heat of the exhaust from Nick Young's jump jet. The constant harsh whistle of the stream of freezing air it admitted kept Webber awake and alert. If Young's jet had lingered another few seconds over Gentle Three Zero, the NEST Two helo would have been inoperable. Given its fuel reserves, it might have exploded into flames together with the drilling-rig cabin and Gentle Two Five.

But wherever Young had been headed, he had been in a hurry. The NEST Two helo's upper fuselage had only been blackened, not destroyed, by Young's jet exhaust, and some panels bore only blistered paint as evidence of Young's treachery. The starboard observation window was cracked and the radio antenna leads had been damaged, except for the VHF. But the craft was still flightworthy, which meant that the helicopter race which had begun as Webber and Young had closed in on the drilling installation was still under way. To win, Webber had to reach McMurdo before Young arrived at whatever his destination would be. There still were five other warheads to track down, and the full resources of NEST would be needed to discover where else they had been deployed. And why.

Beyond that, as he flew onward, one part of Webber's mind had already diverted to his next challenge: calculating the strategies necessary to contain and investigate the drilling site and its deadly secret. Webber had recorded the GPS coordinates of the landing site, so finding the ruins of the installation on the expanse of ice would not be a problem. Then, since SEALs never left behind their weapons or their fellow warriors, the NEST containment team would retrieve the bodies of Bregoli and Rensberger, along with those of the four pilots and whatever was left of NEST Two's turncoat engineer, Glendon Morris.

Webber returned to channel seven to try again for a science team. "Mayday, mayday, mayday . . ." This time, the response was almost immediate.

"Mayday, this is Sierra Zero One Four. Copy you loud and clear. Please identify. Over." From the easy Southern drawl of those words, Webber guessed he had made contact with a U.S. team that was operating at a put-in site. Its McMurdo designation was Event S-014.

"Sierra Zero One Four, this is Gentle Three Zero. My HF is damaged. I need to relay an urgent message to MacOps. Repeat urgent. Over."

The scientist came back at once, standing by to relay Webber's next message.

"Advise MacOps my ETA is twenty-seven minutes. I have wounded. Gunshot injury requiring immediate medical attention. Relay and come back for additional message, over."

Webber flew on as the scientist said he would switch to his PRC-1099 radio to contact McMurdo. Behind Webber, no sound emerged from Hadrian Gowers as a gust of wind savagely shook the damaged helo. Amazingly, the DOE weapons specialist had been alive, though not conscious, when Webber had returned to find him, half-buried in the snow outside the drilling-rig cabin, the chemical-heating packs exhausted. From the briefings Webber had received on polar combat, he concluded that the extreme cold had helped lower Gowers's heart rate, decreasing the output of blood. But now the hypothermic shock was also responsible for bringing the engineer perilously close to death.

Webber scanned the snow-swept rocky terrain of the territory ahead, trying to find some indication of the science team he had contacted. At the speed he was traveling, he would not be able to maintain a line-of-sight comm link much longer. His mind continued its run-through of the preparations he still had to set in motion.

After arranging for Gowers's medical treatment and informing NEST that five other warheads were loose, tracking Young would become Webber's next priority. If Young's jump jet was a Harrier, then in the time it would take Webber to reach McMurdo, Young could have covered more than 350 miles. Though there were not enough data to predict his ultimate destination, from the maps on the helo Webber estimated that there were thirteen bases within the Harrier's 1,300-mile range. Five were American, including the Amundsen-Scott base at the South Pole, though Webber was inclined to dismiss those as possible landing sites. There were Air National Guard personnel at all the U.S. bases and news of a Harrier's landing would spread quickly.

But three of the bases within range were Russian. Given the source of the warhead Young had been deploying, those couldn't be discounted. Though given that country's fragile and fractured economy, it was unlikely that the Russian government itself was involved in nuclear activities in Antarctica, there was still the possibility that a third party had taken over one of those stations on a cash basis.

Young's other potential landing bases were French, German, or Australian, also all unlikely. But since, Webber knew, a Harrier could set down like a helicopter on anything from an aircraft carrier to the deck of a small ship, that was the more probable, and more dangerous, possibility he would have to consider. Once a Harrier was camouflaged by a cover of false cargo containers, it would be undetectable. That meant the only chance NEST had of finding Young's jet was to detect it in flight. Against the ice of Antarctica, the heat from a jet's engines would be an easy target for almost any reconnaissance satellite passing over Antarctica—even civilian Landsats with IR, infrared, capability. As long as Young remained aloft for at least one more hour, Webber was confident the Air Force Space Command and the National Reconnaissance Office would readily locate him.

Channel 7 came back to life. "Gentle Three Zero, this is Sierra Zero One Four. MacOps acknowledges your communications. A medical team will be standing by. MacOps also asks for your name. Over."

With his next communication, Webber understood he would be compromising some of NEST's latest operational codes, but he also knew the system was robust and the next set of codes in the sequence would be in place within ten hours. He told his ground contact that what he said next must be relayed immediately and word for word through MacOps to the Department of Energy's Emergency Operations Center, as coming from Mitch Webber.

"SHADOW FORGE went active eighteen hundred hours, Golf Papa Sierra. NEST Two leader rogue. Forge on site. Loose crimson. Status blue niner. Request immediate realtime heat lock on Harrier-class aircraft in transit, one-thousand-mile radius from McMurdo."

Straining to hear the last few words as static began to encroach on the signal, Webber had the scientist repeat the message back to him. Wherever the scientist was based below, Webber was flying out of range.

A minute later, a final confirmation came back, most words garbled. At the end of the transmission, the scientist added an odd warning. "Gentle Three . . . advises caution on . . . civilian traffic . . . helipad . . . peat . . . void heli . . ." Uninterrupted static followed.

Webber's helo streaked over three orange tents grouped together near the snowless top of a low mountain, another scientific survey team. But he was so close to McMurdo now that he wasted no time in trying to establish a new contact. Gowers was going to get his chance. In two or three minutes he'd be within line of sight of the station itself. Within ten minutes he'd be landing.

He switched to channel 11, Helo Operations Net. "MacOps, this is Gentle Three Zero, over."

Garbled static filled the cockpit. Webber flew another minute before trying again. This time, the reply was heavy with interference, but intelligible.

"Gentle Three Zero, this is MacOps. Your mayday is a go. Medical team is standing by at the Transition Ramp."

Webber frowned. The Transition Ramp was the roadway that extended from the shoreline to the sea ice. It was close to the helipads, but not a landing site.

Webber radioed back. "Say again, MacOps. Should I land at the helipad or the Transition Ramp? Over."

The helo shuddered noisily as it encountered a wind flurry. Smooth filaments of thick cloud smeared across the land ahead. McMurdo Station was just a few miles beyond, for now still obscured from sight.

"Negative, Gentle Three Zero. Land at the Transition Ramp. *Not* the helipad. We have civilian traffic there. Over."

Considering that civilian aircraft were forbidden to land at McMurdo, Webber thought it best not to question flight control. It was probably a long story. And now that he was so close to his goal, the reserves of strength he had drawn on were running low, as if his body were anticipating an end to the tension he had been operating under.

"Copy that, MacOps. Were you able to relay my message to the DOE? Over."

"Gentle Three Zero. Not yet. We're experiencing communications difficulties. Should have them resolved in the next half hour. Over."

Webber swore to himself. His week in Antarctica had taught him how completely he had come to accept the instantaneous communications options of the developed world as routine. Even though, this far south, instant communications could not be counted upon, he would hold MacOps to their thirty-minute promise. That half hour could give Young another 350 miles of travel.

Webber checked his fuel. He was good for at least another twenty miles before having to land and McMurdo couldn't be farther than five. He risked looking back to check Gowers, but couldn't see if the engineer was still breathing or not. He called back. "Five more minutes, Gowers. You're almost there." There was no response.

With his radar out, Webber couldn't be certain what his exact approach to McMurdo was going to be, so he pulled back on the cyclic to drop his airspeed, at the same time easing up on the collective to increase his altitude in order to rise above the katabatic cloud stretched before him.

As he rose above the cloud, he saw Mount Erebus first, the largest of the four major volcanoes that formed Ross Island. When Sir James Ross had discovered it, in 1841, it had been actively spewing smoke and flame up to 2,000 feet above its crater. Since then, though, the largest volcanic events had been a series of explosive gas ventings in the austral summer of '84-'85 and a minor eruption in '93 that caused damage only to monitoring equipment at the summit.

Finally, Webber glimpsed McMurdo. Or, rather, he saw what was on McMurdo's helipad—an enormous red sphere. The sight was so unexpected that Webber's first startled reaction was that he was witnessing an explosive fireball. When the sphere didn't expand, though, he recognized it for what it was. He radioed MacOps again.

"MacOps, I have you in sight. Is that balloon your civilian traffic? Over."

"That's affirmative. It's uncontrolled, so approach from the sea ice. Over."

Webber swung the helo offshore to approach from the southwest. Several miles out, he could see two ships at the edge of the ice, unusually close to each other. He recognized one as the *Palmer*, but the other didn't appear to be part of the USAP. Later in the summer season, in late December, the sea ice would be thin enough here for the large supply ships to break through and come right to shore for off-loading. For now, though, all ship traffic remained well at sea. As Webber fought the controls to bring the balky helo in smoothly over the ice, en route for the Transition Ramp and the ANG ambulances parked there, he put the two unexpected elements together and decided that the balloon must have come from the smaller ship. *Some tourist party gone astray,* he thought. It was precisely because of the time lost to rescuing tourist expeditions in the past that most U.S. bases in the Antarctic severely restricted civilian access. Webber appreciated the problem. His own experience had taught him that civilian and military strategies seldom were compatible, even though their goals were ultimately the same—survival.

The helo bucked but he set it down neatly, fifty feet from the two ambulances, following the waved instructions from the ground control crew to land beside the Transition Road, not on it. If the two ships couldn't break through the shoreline edge of the sea ice, Webber felt certain it was thick enough to support the aircraft.

When the helo's rotor had slowed below takeoff requirements and the sparkling cloud of snow he had kicked up cleared, Webber gave the ground crew a thumbs-up and instantly the medevac team ran forward with a stretcher. Webber unfastened his seat belt, yanked off his helmet, and moved to the partially open starboard door. The medevac team saw him attempting to shift it on its twisted frame, joined in, and had it open in seconds. Then Webber knew enough to get out of the way as the station's force medical officer and medics scrambled in and went to work on Gowers.

Webber jumped out onto the ice and was surprised to find the exterior temperature felt warm. He was aware enough of his situation to understand that meant he could be entering a hypothermic state himself. The front of his bullet-shredded white parka was still crusted with ice.

Elizabeth Germer, station operations manager, was beside him at once, pale cheeks flushed red in the cold wind, a fringe of short gray hair fluttering from the edge of her tightly tied hood. She had an extra green parka ready for Webber. She grimaced at the state of his own parka. "Take that off." The ops manager of McMurdo was a civilian, employed by the National Science Foundation, but she had the voice of a good commanding officer. Webber fumbled with the Velcro flap on his parka, surprised he couldn't get his fingers to grip it. He began to shiver violently.

Six-two to his five-eleven, and at least twenty years older, Germer grabbed him by the shoulders and deftly aimed him for the closer ambulance. "In there, soldier."

The ambulance interior was blasted with warm air from a retrofitted overhead gas heater that operated independently of the engine. Shivering completely overtook Webber as Germer peeled him out of his combat parka and had him strip off his sweater, body-armor vest, shirt, and T-shirt. Every piece of clothing was soaked.

"Cripes. Did you hit water?"

Webber shook his head as best he could, suddenly unable even to speak.

Germer instructed the driver to take them to the medical building at once. As the ambulance clunked into gear, and moved slowly off over the icy, black rock road, Germer poured Webber warm chicken soup from a Thermos, to bring up his body core temperature and restore his electrolyte balance. "Where's the other chopper?"

"Didn't make it." Webber's hands shook too much to allow him to hold the soup cup.

Germer took the cup from him, and wedged it onto a supply shelf. She reached over and pulled out a thin, blue blanket from a side cubbyhole and tucked it snugly around him, then draped the green parka over his shoulders. "Pilots, too?"

"Me and Gowers. That's it." Webber left it at that. Germer had been given Secret clearance in order to facilitate NEST's deployment at McMurdo, but Young's defection and the possibility of five Soviet warheads under hostile control was information to be saved only for command.

"Did you find something out there?"

Webber couldn't be sure if she could tell the difference between his shaking and the nodding of his head. "Did MacOps pass on my message?"

"We've lost our satellite link ahead of schedule. I've got a team chopping out to the dish site on Black Island. Probably just a loose connection. You get hundred-and-seventy-mile-per-hour wind out there, metal contraction from the cold. Breakdowns happen all the time."

Webber knew the geosynchronous satellites the Station depended upon for most of its communications were so low on the horizon at this latitude that direct contact with them was blocked by Mt. Erebus, twenty miles away. Black Island was an automated relay site, twenty miles across the sea ice, powered in part by low-maintenance wind turbines, and far enough away from McMurdo to avoid the volcano and maintain a clear line of sight—when weather, solar events, and satellite wobble permitted. Still, Webber remained suspicious of Germer's ready explanation. In his work, coincidences were always cause for suspicion. The one that troubled him most was that Young had had a jump jet prepped on the ice. That type of aircraft was not easily come by. Which suggested another possibility. "Both Harriers still on the pad?"

The ops manager nodded. "Your flight teams covered them up with tarps so the Earthguard people couldn't film them."

"Earthguard? The environmental group?"

"Our friends in the red balloon." Germer looked apologetic. "We had to let them land. We're, uh, pretending to keep them in custody." There were no containment facilities in McMurdo. When necessary, troublemakers could be locked in an infirmary room, their own quarters, or—in austral winter, when the Station was virtually deserted—in a separate barracks building. But even for the military personnel, there was no official brig.

Earthguard was an organization Webber knew quite well, and even as he asked the next question, he suspected he already knew the answer. "Why are they here?"

Germer held out the steaming cup of soup for Webber again. "You're not going to like this. They have some sort of idea that . . . the U.S. government has either installed or lost nuclear material down here."

"Shit. They know about the deployment."

"For what it's worth, they didn't mention NEST in their broadcast."

Webber stared at the ops manager. She knew what he wanted.

"They were broadcasting a video report. From the balloon. Satellite uplink into the Internet."

Webber let out his breath noisily and for a moment his shivering stopped. A good sign. He was just cold, not hypothermic. But since he still had so much to do, the potential breach of security suggested by Earthguard's presence here had to be the least of his priorities.

"Sounds like them."

Germer looked interested. "You know those guys?"

Webber shrugged, bringing on another round of uncontrollable shaking. This was not the time to tell the story of his life. "It is extremely important that I contact the DOE, or Space Command, or any military communications system, right away."

Germer looked serious. "Captain, are the people at this base in any danger?"

"No. But . . . one of the bad guys is getting away."

The ambulance lurched to a stop. The ops manager stood up, automatically ducking down to avoid the vehicle's roof, while bracing herself against the supply cupboards. "I want you to get checked out here. I'll noodge the techs on Black Island, and I'll get the DSCS transmitter prepped. Just in case."

Webber was surprised to hear Germer mention the Defense Satellite Communications System. The standard equipment carried by NEST included portable DSCS satellite phones, but both units had proved useless at McMurdo because of Mt. Erebus. "You have DSCS capability?"

"More of a backup, really."

"How do you get yours to work?"

"The dish is on Black Island, too."

The back doors swung open with a metallic clang and blast of freezing air. The driver waited to escort Webber into the infirmary. The sun was setting and outdoor floodlights had come on, catching swirls of blowing snow against the darkening sky. At night, under the brilliant stars of the southern skies, McMurdo might as well be a colony on a distant planet. Its isolation from the rest of the world was that profound.

"Look," Webber said, "if you have any other communications options available, explore them, okay? The people we're up against are using sophisticated techniques, and whatever happened at Black Island—"

"Might be sabotage. I'm aware of that, Captain. I'll see what else I can arrange."

Webber eased out the back of the ambulance and, with the driver's assistance, mounted the wooden stairs to the medical building. Like every other structure in McMurdo, it was raised on stilts to keep above the winter snows. He glanced over his shoulder to see the second ambulance approaching, a red light flashing on top. Another good sign, he thought. Gowers might make it.

Then he was indoors, being guided along a narrow corridor beneath flickering fluorescent lights. The driver pushed open a wide door and helped Webber through it. The area beyond was like a small emergency room, with four hospital beds, medical monitors, and overhead examination lights on telescoping arms. Two hulking mechanics from the 109th's power-plant division—a master sergeant and a senior airman—were off to the side. The target of their menacing attention was a group of three civilians seated on the farthest bed, each cocooned in a blue warming blanket like Webber's. The oldest of them, a male with a gray ponytail, was clearly nonmilitary. Webber assumed he was one of the Earthguard activists who had—

"Oh my God."

The clear voice stopped all thought for Webber.

"Mitchell?"

Webber's voice cracked in disbelief. "Cory."

One of the civilians had gotten to her feet and was walking toward him, her thermal blanket trailing on the floor like the train of a gown as she pushed imperiously past the puzzled airman, who didn't know if he should try to restrain her. It was just the sort of dramatic entrance Mitch Webber associated with Corazon Rey. And it felt all the more bizarre to be witnessing it in a small, stripped-down medical ward on a remote base in Antarctica.

The heart-shaped face that had given her her name was pale with anger as she confronted him. "You're part of this, aren't you? You and your SEAL assassins are bringing nuclear weapons to the last peaceful continent on the planet!"

Webber's stomach tightened. From bittersweet experience, he knew he could never hope to convince Cory of anything she didn't want to hear, no matter what approach he used. But she was always so wrong. Always. And once again, he couldn't help telling her so.

"Cory, I'm here to *stop* the nuclear weapons."

The woman who had been closer to him than anyone in his life drew herself up like a Caesar acknowledging a tribute. "Good," she said. "So am I."

EIGHT

NATIONAL MILITARY COMMAND CENTER/THE PENTAGON

The Tempest facility off the National Military Command Center watch floor was a small conference room designed to ensure that certain conversations and briefings could remain secure. There was no window on the green door, the floor and inner walls "floated" on rubber pads, and a mechanical oscillation system transmitted random noise through the exterior walls and floor and ceiling supports at the same frequencies as most human speech. As it was, under current antisurveillance standards, those precautions were considered minimal. If the small room had been located in a civilian office building, even more elaborate precautions would have been required to make it as safe against eavesdropping as it was in the NMCC. But the technology required to defeat first-level Tempest safeguards had little chance of making it through the Pentagon's metal detectors and thermal imagers.

Major Chennault was already waiting when General Abbott entered. Abbott carried a cafeteria tray with an insulated coffeepot and two mugs adorned with the NMCC mission crest. It was in the military's nature to label everything, and coffee mugs were too tempting a target to leave unadorned. Abbott took special pleasure in one particular mug in his collection, that he kept locked in a cabinet in his office in D ring. It carried the crest of the National

81

Security Agency, and he had obtained it two years before the government had even admitted the agency existed.

Abbott poured coffee for Chennault, his way of telling the major that this room was a "no-hats" zone, a sanctuary from the usual military structure. They could speak freely here. "Black?"

Chennault took the mug without adding creamer or sugar. "It goes with the territory."

The two soldiers sat down, facing each other across the highly polished wood table. Neither had chosen to sit at the head of it. At the highest levels, Abbott knew, the best warriors were all equals. That was how he chose to work with Chennault.

As Abbott had expected he would, the major got directly to the point. "I'm going to give you the short form. Interrupt anytime you'd like additional information."

Abbott found that efficient and acceptable. He nodded but did not speak, intent on what he was about to hear.

"SHADOW FORGE became operational thirteen months ago when a radiation monitor in a cargo warehouse at Los Angeles International Airport was tripped. The warehouse handled medical isotopes. The monitor was a standard part of the safety system. But there were no isotopes being processed at the time.

"It took a while, but the alarm was traced to a Mercedes S-class flown in from Honolulu. It belonged to . . . a businessman."

Chennault didn't name the man. "Is it important to know who he is?" Abbott asked.

"Was. And no, it isn't." Chennault directed a glance toward the door. The active status board above it showed that no electronic surveillance measures were being detected. "The Mercedes was specially equipped, armored, bullet-proof glass . . . he took it with him on business trips."

"Government business?"

"No. Strictly investments, joint projects, a lot of work in Hong Kong. All legitimate. At least, as legitimate as international finance can be. There was some government involvement in that he had to work with regulators, but he was not employed by governments. Any government." Chennault sipped his coffee. Abbott waited. With the Earthguard transmission from Antarctica terminated, time was no longer a critical issue. "The car was routinely searched for drugs every time it entered the country. Most of the time it was inspected for contraband. But the man had no record, no known criminal associations."

"But the car was carrying something radioactive?"

"Yes. And no. Customs found that the car was definitely hot, though not dangerously so, and informed the DOE. The Customs officials wanted a team to check it out, then tell them it was okay to tear the car apart in a search."

Abbott knew how the Department of Energy worked in these cases and immediately saw the scenario that had been played out. "Except, the DOE said, Don't search the car. Follow it."

Chennault nodded. "The detectors made it clear the car wasn't carrying anything. At least, not in terms of plutonium or uranium or an explosive device. But it *had* carried something. So Energy made it a NEST operation and initiated SHADOW FORGE to follow the car and see if there was any kind of smuggling network involved. Energy didn't assign any artillery. Just two weapons specialists and a DIA agent trained in surveillance. Two weeks later, the businessman died from lethal exposure. Somewhere on the order of eight hundred rad."

Abbott understood the implications of that kind of exposure. Two hundred rad caused debilitating radiation sickness. Just over twice that amount was a thirty-day death sentence for half the people exposed. Eight hundred was fatal. He was surprised the businessman had lasted two weeks.

"Do you know when he was exposed? Do you know what he was exposed to?"

"I do. But that's where the mystery starts. The car's door panels were filled with bundles of cash. Five million dollars in circulated hundred-dollar bills. The plastic the bills were wrapped in had once been used to wrap an unshielded plutonium core and was still dirty with it. Minute particles of Pu-239. Weapons grade. The poor bastard must have wrapped the money himself. His hands were swollen from contact exposure. All his skin had sloughed off by the time we found him. Had to go with dental records for the ID. He even had burns in his lungs from inhaling the shit."

Abbott knew exactly what had happened. "He sold someone a nuke."

"That was the first guess. But DIA found out he was just a middleman. Probably only transported the material. In the car."

From a strictly professional standpoint, Abbott wanted to know more about the initial operation. Who was the nameless man? With whom had he done business in Hong Kong and in the United States? But before Abbott concentrated on details, he needed to know the answer to the question that had puzzled him since the moment he had read the SHADOW FORGE background material—what there was of it. "So far, Major, everything you've said makes it sound like a textbook smuggling scenario. Which doesn't explain why the DOE briefing book was sanitized."

Chennault leaned forward, dropping his voice as he had in the emergency action room, as if even the Tempest facility would not be able to contain what he must say. "This guy usually had his Mercedes shipped by air, Hong Kong to LAX. On this trip, he took a liner from Hong Kong to Honolulu, *then* flew. The NRO went back through satellite coverage of the Pacific. The liner made contact with a sub."

Abbott's eyes narrowed. "Whose?"

Chennault turned his palms up. "That's only one problem among many. The NRO hadn't specifically targeted the rendezvous point at the time contact took place, so they didn't have an unbroken surveillance track. The sub was definitely diesel. It was definitely in contact with the liner. It seemed to be heading south afterward. Then . . . nothing. And the liner's crew . . . we're still trying to track them down."

"The NRO can't find a diesel sub?" Abbott found that state of affairs hard to believe. The National Reconnaissance Office managed the nation's surveillance satellites. Their assets could identify individual nuclear-powered subs sitting motionless a mile deep on the ocean floor. From 400 miles up, they could identify the type of rifles carried by enemy soldiers during night maneuvers, under cloud cover.

"General, they can find any diesel anywhere, anytime—*if* they're looking for it. But they can't ID which one made the rendezvous. PLAN . . . Korean . . . Japanese . . . there're even two old British subs being operated by the Colombian cartels. It could have been any of them."

"That part of the operation is missing from the briefing book." Chennault said nothing and Abbott read the reason for the silence. "Are you saying it could have been an American sub, Major?"

The major looked pained, but he responded. "That I don't know, sir. But I think the NSA knows. I saw the preliminary reports attempting to correlate the NRO's observational data with the NSA's communications intercepts. I never saw the end results. My impression—and I have nothing to base it on other than my gut—is that somebody ID'ed the sub, and it would cause a shitload of trouble if that ID got out. The only other option would be that somehow the sub turned invisible. They wouldn't want that to get out either."

Abbott's fingers stoked the handle of his coffee cup. The major's response was all too familiar to him. Perhaps the best-loved military acronym at the Pentagon was CYA—cover your assets. He chose another line of attack.

"Why Antarctica?"

Chennault's rueful expression was to Abbott an admission of defeat. "That, I guarantee you, *no* one understands. About two years ago, there was another NEST operation, WINDOW FORGE, that intercepted a loose nuke on a Russian science vessel hired out to a travel company, taking tourists to Antarctica. The components were sealed in an inflatable lifeboat container. No one knows how they got there, or why. Only that they *were* headed for Antarctica. Thirteen months ago, our mystery sub was also heading south. And three weeks ago, one of the science teams at McMurdo tested out some mining survey equipment, got readings that suggested there was uranium under *sea ice*. Absolutely impossible. The NSA intercepted the report the scientists uploaded back to their university, told the DIA, who told Energy, who sent two NEST teams down to run a search. They're on-site now. And *that* is all I know."

Despite Chennault's candor, Abbott was uncomfortable with such a significant gap in the story. The NSA and NRO seldom drew blanks. "Other than the project at the South Pole, are there *any* U.S. military assets in Antarctica?"

"Mostly ANG support services. A defense mapping project at Palmer. I looked into that myself. Just why anyone would want to take nukes to the Ice has been driving everyone at the DIA apeshit."

And then the solution became apparent, and obvious, to Abbott.

" 'March by an indirect route and divert the enemy by enticing him with a bait.' " The general looked at the younger man for his reaction and was not disappointed.

Chennault, like any good officer, recognized the quote. "Sun Tzu." Whether or not a Chinese warlord by that name had ever existed, the book attributed to him, *The Art of War*, was at least 2,400 years old, had guided Eastern military thought for centuries, and had informed American military theory for decades. Sun Tzu's pronouncements on strategy and tactics were a distillation of the forces shaping any conflict, independent of politics and technology, as true today as when they had been written.

Knowing the hold Sun Tzu had on China's military leaders, Abbott had long ago committed the work to memory. To understand Sun Tzu was, the general believed, to understand the enemy he knew America would inevitably face.

"So you think this is a feint?" Chennault asked.

To Abbott, it was the only answer that made sense. "If Antarctica has no assets or resources, the only advantage to be gained by placing nukes there is to lure our forces away from where they're needed. Two NEST teams ten thousand miles from home cuts Energy's assets by almost half."

"And you think other nukes are slipping through the cracks left unguarded."

"A shell game. Exactly."

Chennault leaned back in his chair. The overhead lights gleamed from his shaven scalp. "One problem. Who has that many nukes? I mean, most terrorist groups would piss their pants to get a pound of plutonium. You're talking about somebody who can afford to trade off at least two nukes just as a diversion to bring others into the country."

"And I'm talking about someone who can also afford a submarine. As for where the other nukes are going, that's still unknown."

Abbott could see that Chennault was processing this new possibility. "You're saying we're dealing with a major power."

Abbott shrugged. He had his theories but knew better than to voice them under the current leadership. "I'm suggesting that Energy's facing someone with more assets than NEST's equipped to handle." And with those words, Abbott suddenly saw the wheels turning within the wheels. "The DIA knows it, too."

At least the look of puzzlement on Chennault was genuine. If Abbott was being kept in the dark, then so was the Joint Staff's DIA liaison.

"That's why the briefing book was sanitized," Abbott explained, thinking aloud. "At some level, someone in command knows whatever's happening in Antarctica is a blind. But they're not going to admit it, so they're making it look as if we're going along with the diversion."

"The NEST deployment is a smoke screen?"

"You described the strategy yourself. Customs finds a radioactive car and the Department of Energy says, Don't intercept. Let's play the smugglers along. See where it takes us. Same thing's in operation here. Someone wants us to *think* there're nukes in Antarctica, all right, let's play them along, too. Meanwhile, we compartmentalize what we know and stand by to intercept the smugglers' real operation."

Chennault sounded as if he were trying to talk himself into sharing Abbott's conviction. "Everything fits . . . to a point. But who the hell decides to keep the Joint Staff out of the loop?"

Abbott's thoughts were already elsewhere as he sorted out what he had learned and, more importantly, what he still had to uncover. "It happens. The Joint Chiefs probably know. But cutting out the rest of us was a good call."

Chennault looked astounded. No one on the Joint Staff ever wanted to be cut out of any operation.

"Look at those Earthguard activists," Abbott said. "How'd they find out about the NEST deployment? There's a leak somewhere."

Chennault appeared to give up. "So what I was told about the operation . . ."

"Was part of the cover story, too."

Chennault rubbed his hands over his face. "Six years with DIA and I never saw it. So much for your Crisis Action Team."

But that wasn't what Abbott had in mind. "Oh, no. I'll keep that going. That's part of the smoke screen, too. To make sure the Pentagon's response is exactly what it would be if we thought the threat in Antarctica was real."

Chennault had run out of arguments. Abbott stood. "Major, I can't order you to do this, but it might be helpful if you reported this conversation to your superior at the DIA. If we've managed to penetrate the cover story, someone else could do it, too. So it might be useful if we were all brought onside."

Chennault swallowed the last of his coffee, grimaced. "I'll give it a try. But if you hear I've been reassigned to Nome, you'll know how it went."

The two soldiers walked to the door. Chennault reached for the first of the three locks securing it, then stopped. "You know, General, there's another possibility here."

Abbott knew a commander was only as good as his troops. When time and circumstances permitted, he was always ready to encourage thoughtful discussion of the mission at hand. "I am open to all suggestions."

Chennault spoke slowly, choosing his words with care. "This shadow operation you think we've uncovered, it's based on an extremely optimistic assessment of our intelligence capabilities. We're assuming the people above us have information unavailable to us."

"Go on."

"What if they don't? What if SHADOW FORGE is just what the briefing book says it is: a screwed-up operation because no one knows what the fuck's going on? Sir."

Abbott considered Chennault's suggestion for two seconds. He patted the younger man's shoulder. "Have faith in the system, Major. I do." Then Abbott opened the three locks and pushed the door open, just in time to see Lieutenant Yoshii running across the watch floor, urgently calling his name.

NINE

McMURDO STATION

Before Webber could say anything more to Cory Rey, the main door to the emergency ward burst open and a gurney crashed in, Gowers on it, red ECW gear sliced off, one medic holding a respirator mask to the engineer's white face, the force medical officer shouting at everyone else to clear out.

Cory seemed mesmerized by Gowers's blood-soaked chest as the master sergeant, one of the two mechanics guarding her, gripped her by her shoulders, as if getting ready to drag her from the room. Webber wasn't surprised to see Cory fiercely elbow her guard.

"Get your hands off me!"

The sergeant outweighed her by at least 150 pounds and towered over her by more than a foot, but Webber recognized the caution the man displayed as he promptly backed off. Cory was best approached as an unexploded bomb. "I'm following the doctor's orders, ma'am."

"Well you can do it without groping me!"

The mechanic's face turned red. "Ma'am, I was . . . I didn't . . ."

Webber stepped in. "I'll take care of this, Sergeant."

"Like hell you will, Mitchell Webber!"

In the preceding eight hours, Webber had been shot at, kicked, beaten, almost burned alive by jet exhaust, and yet had maintained objectivity during each assault, the perfect soldier's response to the fog of battle. But five serene years free of the torment of life with Corazon Rey dissipated in the less than ten seconds that it now took for Webber to completely lose his temper. "Will you just shut up! Gowers almost died trying to stop the goddamn nukes you're so concerned about. Now, do what you're told and get the hell into the hallway!"

Cory's dark eyes flashed dangerously. But sometime in the past five years even she must have learned some semblance of self-control. All she said was "We've got a lot to talk about, Mitchell."

"No, we don't." Webber gestured toward the door.

Cory flicked the trailing end of her thermal blanket over her shoulder and walked out slowly, regally.

The sergeant looked at Webber. "Whoa."

Webber nodded. He glanced back at Gowers. A transfusion had been started. The force medical officer was working on a wound near the engineer's shoulder. One of the medics was attaching EKG leads. Webber had no idea what the patient's status was and didn't want to disturb the medical team in their frenzied activity. The second medic saw Webber staring at Gowers and immediately drew the faded green curtain around the bed. Webber turned back to the sergeant.

"If I keep my eye on the tree-hugger out there, when one of those medics comes up for air, you want to ask how that guy's doing?"

The mechanic was clearly relieved to be free of Cory. "Sure thing, Captain."

Webber walked into the hallway. Cory and the ponytail were sitting in battered wooden chairs at a corridor intersection twenty feet away. The burly airman stood beside them, arms folded purposefully. But Johnny Rey was at the emergency room door, waiting for Webber.

"Hey, Mitch. Long time, huh?"

Webber had no argument with Cory's brother. The last time they had seen each other had been a tense lunch with Cory at the Coronado Hotel in San Diego. Johnny was nineteen, saving up for a car. He had been eager to see what his sister's Navy pilot boyfriend drove. Webber smiled as he remembered Johnny's openmouthed look of disappointment when he had seen Webber's calculated choice for secure ground travel—a Volvo. And even worse, it was a station wagon. Webber didn't believe in taking any risks that weren't necessary.

"Good to see you, kid."

Johnny smiled, so much like his sister, but without the tinge of restless discontent that always seemed to haunt her. "If you say so." He glanced back at Cory down the corridor. She wasn't looking at them. "So . . . I guess we're a bit of a surprise."

Webber knew the kid meant well. Under oath, he'd probably have to admit that even Cory did, too. But this was no reunion. "We lost seven people today, Johnny. My guy in there might make it eight. You're in the middle of something serious."

Johnny's smile faded. Unlike his sister, he understood reality.

"So what I need to know is, what're you doing here?"

There was a nervousness to Johnny now. Another trait unlike his sister. "Well, you can't have nuclear weapons in Antarctica. That's the law, right?"

Webber shook his head. "It's not the law. It's a treaty agreement. Two different things. Important question: Why does your sister's group think nuclear weapons are involved?"

"Because the government sent the Nuclear Emergency Search Team here. Cory told me that's a special group of scientists, engineers, and—"

"I'm team commander, NEST One."

Johnny blinked at him in surprise. "Oh."

"Answer the question."

"I, uh . . . some friends of Cory's, some Earthguard people, they found out about it. A conspiracy newsgroup on the Web."

Webber studied Johnny Rey, unhappy with the evasion he sensed, but aware that Cory's young brother was his best chance to trace a potentially dangerous security leak. He knew Cory wouldn't tell him the time of day if she thought there was an important principle at stake. And her companion with the ponytail wasn't likely to be more cooperative. "Are you part of Earthguard?"

"Not really. I need to work a year. I already got my BSc, but I want to go for my masters. So I have to save up, you know. Cory's the one got me this job."

That rang true to Webber. Cory was exceptionally good at taking control of everyone's life but her own. "So you just tag along, do what you're told, and don't ask questions."

Johnny smiled. "You know Cory, man."

Webber refused to smile back. "What's your major?" When Johnny looked at him blankly, Webber added, "For your degree."

"Oh, yeah, biochem."

"Good choice. Just don't become Cory's biological-warfare expert." Webber shrugged off Germer's spare parka, too small for his shoulders to fit into easily, and wrapped his blanket more securely around his ribs, wishing he had thought to ask for a new shirt or sweater. "Hold this. I'm going to talk to your sister."

Johnny nodded, taking the green parka that Webber held out, his next words studiously offhand. "You want to know if she's seeing anyone?"

"No," Webber said, and meant it. He just didn't bother to add that it had taken him all of the last five years to achieve that level of conviction.

Even with the ponytail and the airman-mechanic both watching Webber walk down the hall toward them, Cory didn't bother to look up at him until he was right in front of her chair. She always managed to create at least the illusion of being the one in control, Webber remembered. "*Now* we have to talk," he said to her. "Alone."

Cory leaned back in her chair, not going anywhere. "Are we under arrest?"

"Would you like to be?"

Cory's brief, triumphant smile let him know that she knew she'd provoked him. "Arrest away. There's no such thing as bad publicity, Commander."

"Captain."

"A promotion. How impressive."

Webber pointed to an alcove down the hall. He didn't know what the airman's security clearance was, and he knew he didn't want another civilian listening to the questions he had to ask. "This is important. I need to ask you some questions. Down there."

The man with the ponytail stood up, belligerent. "Stay where you are, Cory. You are not splitting us up, man. I know how you bastards work."

Webber studied him for a few seconds, chose his strategy. "Then you know that I can kill you where you stand in twelve different ways before you can open your mouth to annoy me again."

"Oh, fuck y—"

Webber jabbed his fingers up into the man's trachea, just below his Adam's apple, cutting off the next word and his breath at the same time.

Cory leapt to her feet to strike at Webber, but he fended her off easily.

Ponytail clawed at his throat, his eyes bulged, then he stumbled backward into the airman's arms, wheezing.

"You could have killed him!" Cory's voice shook.

"I could have." Webber hooked his arm through hers and half-lifted, half-dragged her down the corridor before she had fully re-covered from the shock, as he had intended. Then he turned her around and pushed her into the alcove, keeping his body close to hers, to prevent her escape. "This is not the time to make things difficult. This is life and death. The real world."

"That's why I'm here, you monster."

"No. You're here because someone told you and your sorry-ass friends some made-up story about loose nukes on the Ice."

Cory made a face. Her voice was bitter. "Loose nukes. Very smart. Trivialize the most lethal weapons in human history. Make them sound kind of cute. Who'd worry about a couple of little loose nukes?"

Webber fought unsuccessfully to check his emotions. If Cory had been a BUD/S instructor, nobody would have lasted a day. "Don't you fucking understand the stakes?"

"Mitchell, don't *you* understand that's why I'm here? Because I *do* fucking understand the fucking stakes!"

Webber took a breath and stepped back. She'd done it again. How could he argue with someone who in some perversion of twisted logic ended up agreeing with him? He spoke very slowly. "I need to know how you found out about the NEST deployment."

She answered with the same slow precision. "No fucking way." She folded her arms. The next move was his. But before Webber could say anything to break the impasse, the master sergeant he had left in the emergency room appeared in the hallway.

"Captain Webber—" the sergeant began. Webber turned to him. The sergeant shook his head.

Webber's hands tightened into fists. Bregoli and Rensberger, the pilots, they were soldiers. As their commander, Webber took re-sponsibility for their deaths. But because they were professionals killed in the line of duty, somehow, he could accept their loss more easily than that of Gowers. Not that the soldiers' lives were worth less, but when they had sworn to defend their country, they had knowingly accepted the price they might someday have to pay. The weapons specialist had never been given the choice. "Gowers was a civilian, Cory. He volunteered because he understood the stakes. If you and I are really here for the same reason, then help me. Don't fight me."

For a moment, something like comprehension, or compassion, appeared in Cory's eyes. Something in her face softened. Then the sound of running boots hammering down the hallway caught Webber's attention and he turned to see a first lieutenant jogging toward him with a SABER two-way radio. "Captain! Germer wants you ASAP!"

"Where?"

The lieutenant shoved the radio into Webber's hand. "She's on this!"

Webber hit the transmit button. "Webber here, over."

Germer's voice came back at him, urgent, tense. "Captain, I'm in MacOps. The team at Black Island reported in. It *was* sabotage. All the lines are burned out. They were wrapped around flares set off by a timer. Over."

It was as if Cory had disappeared for Webber. He had no doubt that whoever had sabotaged the communications lines had also done same to the radiation detectors on the helos. Nick Young was working with an expert group. Webber knew he needed immediate support and he told Germer what he had to do. "I have to take a satellite phone far enough out to avoid the mountain. Arrange a snowmobile crew. I'll be there in five minutes. Over."

But McMurdo's station operations manager came back with a faster option. "The team out there now can uplink through the DSCS dish. It's undamaged and they can run the transmitter off batteries while we do a voice patch on UHF from MacOps. Over."

Webber allowed himself the small luxury of feeling relief. At last, he had been given a tactical advantage. "Great work. Have your people initiate an emergency broadcast. I want immediate contact with Air Force Space Command. Over." He eyed the first lieutenant as Germer stated her acknowledgment. "Lieutenant, I need your parka and your shirt," Webber said. The young officer hesitated. Webber dropped his blanket to show he was shirtless. "Now, Lieutenant."

As the lieutenant quickly complied, stripping off his green parka and handing it to Webber before beginning to unbutton his shirt, Webber caught Cory staring at his chest. "Mitchell, what happened?" She reached out to touch the white lightning bolt that blazed down his taut, muscled chest—the trace of the bullet his armor had stopped from the inside, back in San Francisco. Her smooth fingers brushed his skin and a thousand memories were reborn in him.

Webber took her hand, moved it away.

"You're cold," she said, and for the first time there was no challenge or bluster in her tone. She was Cory as Webber had first known her.

He let go of her hand. She held it in place for a moment, then lowered it to her side.

"Mitchell," she said. But she was stopped from saying more by the sudden rumble of a deafening thunderclap and the instantaneous loss of all lights.

Even as Mitch Webber flew through the darkness to smash against the buckling wooden wall, he knew the unthinkable had happened.

Somewhere on the Ice, a nuclear warhead had exploded.

EVENT MINUS 4 HOURS
10 MINUTES

The Ice trembled.

For thirty thousand years it had slipped gently into the southern ocean at 300 feet per year, fed by the glaciers of the Ross Embayment, diminished by the waves and the warmer temperature of the seas it invaded. Each year, enough ice calved off the Ross Ice Shelf to raise sea level around the world by a single millimeter. But each year, as well, sea level dropped by the same amount as water evaporated from the ocean surrounding Earth's seventh continent to fall as snow on the western Antarctic glaciers. Thus the balance was maintained.

Until now.

One drilling site had been discovered on the Shelf. There were five more that had not. Traced on a map, those six sites were arranged along the same curve as the long-hidden shore of the sea that lay buried beneath miles and millennia of the ice of the Shelf.

Though each site was more than a hundred miles distant from the next, each was located above one of six key rocky underwater ridges and uprisings that anchored the Shelf to the land.

At 2050 GPS, precisely, thanks to the use of the Global Positioning Satellites, six warheads detonated at once, freeing the Shelf from its six anchors.

Little of the energy released by those explosions reached the surface of the ice, thousands of feet above. Instead, the fireballs they generated created half-mile-wide pockets of superheated gas and water vapor within the Shelf.

The gas-filled pockets now began to rise, carrying upward hundreds of millions of tons of shelf ice.

But the Shelf, though no longer bound to the land that ringed its shores, was still bound by hundreds of feet of sheet ice overlapping the shore of Antarctica and the frozen Ross Sea. That ice was unsupported, and as the Shelf rose up and fell back, straining for its freedom, far beneath the Shelf the still-liquid Ross Sea shuddered with the impact. A ripple of pressure waves now formed in the long-buried waters, waves that continued to rebound and amplify the force of the first six explosions.

The movement flexed the unsupported ice sheet far above. The flexing of the sheet created heat and the heat further weakened the unsupported sheet. With the next surge of the buried sea, the sheet above it flexed even more.

Where and when the flexing movement and the heat it caused reached a critical level, cracks formed in the sheet and the cracks became fissures.

As if the sheet were a pane of glass collapsing under its own weight, the fissures spread out along the weakened ice layer linking the sea to the land.

The Ice growled as the fissures ripped through it at up to forty miles an hour, like ghostly trains throwing giant spouts of ice powder hundreds of feet into the air.

The line the fissures formed were curves, jagged here and there as they broke around accumulations of harder ice, but all moving toward the same six locations that ringed the Shelf where it bit into the land—the crumpled, steaming depressions that marked where six devices brought by soldiers had given birth to fire.

For now the Ice trembled.

But soon it would move.

TEN

NATIONAL MILITARY COMMAND CENTER/THE PENTAGON

Despite the urgency she obviously felt, Lieutenant Yoshii stopped inches from General Abbott to quietly whisper the message she had for him. "Sir, Falcon has received an emergency communications request from McMurdo, on DSCS."

"From whom?"

"They don't know, sir. They're waiting for a voice patch."

Chennault caught Abbott's attention. "Should I stay?"

Abbott decided he should. "It's probably the daily NEST update, but let's be sure."

Accompanied by Chennault and his lieutenant, Abbott left the Tempest room and crossed the watch floor, weaving through the maze of high-walled cubicles where rapt analysts stared into the hypnotic glow of their computer screens, monitoring the state of the world. He felt a familiar surge of adrenaline shoot through him, his body's response to the power of this place whose tendrils of influence reached out across the globe, all at his command. Training was essential, periods of quiet reflection necessary, but no soldier could exist without action, and all around him Abbott could feel the potential for action building. It was why a career in the military had drawn him, it was why he embraced each moment he spent in the NMCC. General Abbott came alive here as he did at no other time. This was where history was made.

When he reentered the emergency action room, once again three video windows were open over the ETEM map of the Ross Sea region of Antarctica. One window was still identified as the CNNI feed, though now it displayed a car commercial for the latest hybrid-engine runabout from Ford. That told Abbott that the network had decided that whatever was going on at McMurdo wasn't important enough for them to switch to breaking-news-style coverage. And that told the world that McMurdo wasn't important. The first problem of his shift had been contained.

In the second video window, Elrey Boyd of the NSA could be seen doing paperwork at his desk, still standing by as Abbott had requested. But the third window was new. In it, the general could see a somber Air Force major waiting, her intent eyes darting back and forth at something beyond the camera that watched her. The major was African-American, with a dusting of silver in the black hair she wore tightly pulled back. From the blue duty sweater she wore, and the constellation of multicolored, out-of-focus lights sparkling in the background behind her, Abbott recognized her location. The major was based at Cheyenne Mountain, and that surprised him. The Defense Satellite Communications System was run from the Falcon Air Force Base in Colorado, not from Space Command.

Lieutenant Yoshii addressed the big board. "Major Bailey, General Abbott is now present."

In her SVTS window, the major took her eyes from whatever she was watching and faced her teleconference camera. "General, I'm Major Bailey."

"Major. I take it you're with SPACECOM."

The major's serious expression broke for a moment as she flashed a smile that lit her face. "On this Thanksgiving Eve, sir, I *am* SPACECOM. Until two o'clock tomorrow morning."

Abbott nodded his understanding. Major Bailey had pulled extra holiday duty as well, either as a volunteer or simply because she was the officer with the least seniority. "Lieutenant Yoshii reported Falcon had picked up an emergency DSCS communications request from McMurdo Station."

"That's correct, sir."

"Which makes me wonder why I'm talking to you in the mountain and not someone with the Third Satellite Control Squadron."

Major Bailey had a quick answer for him. "Whoever made the

communications request asked to be put through to Earth Surveillance, so Falcon handed off to us."

Abbott didn't like what Bailey's answer implied. "You said, 'whoever made the request.' You don't know?"

"They've gone offline, sir. We had a strong signal. One of my techs had an exchange with the sender. The sender evidently was also a tech. They were waiting for someone else to be added to the circuit on a voice patch. And then, nothing."

"Can you reestablish contact?"

Bailey's eyes flashed and Abbott realized this was not an officer who appreciated being asked the obvious. "Sir, I've got about ten billion dollars' worth of the taxpayers' equipment here trying to do exactly that. I'm contacting you about this because McMurdo is on the NMCC hot list this week and what I need to know is, first, do you know who the sender might have been, and second, if so, does the sender have any other communications options through which we could attempt to reestablish contact?"

Abbott sensed a kindred spirit in her and decided she had volunteered for holiday duty. "Point taken, Major. We receive an update from personnel on station at twenty-one hundred hours, each day. I believe this might have been that report."

In the video window, Major Bailey held up a printout and glanced at it. "Sir, I have the McMurdo communications log here. NEST One and NEST Two are currently deployed there. Their report is usually made by an encrypted phone call on the dedicated military phone system, cable through New Zealand to New York Air National Guard support in Christchurch, then satellite transfer to Florida, and then to D.C. But the NEST contact we just logged was originated through the DSCS, and it was ten minutes early for their regular report." When she did not receive an immediate response, Bailey added, "Let me put it another way. Is this a matter you would like SPACECOM to pursue?"

Abbott appreciated what Bailey was offering: If the NMCC was operating a classified operation that should remain classified, she was ready to bow out. But Abbott believed in pursuing all options.

"Major, I understand there are twelve different communications channels available at McMurdo."

"Correct, sir. Eleven are satellite-based, of which . . ." She glanced away from the camera, looked up, and Abbott concluded she was checking a satellite positioning display. ". . . only three are currently available. DSCS. The Iridium system, recently accessed by five mobile units in McMurdo. And a Celestri uplink to a civilian geosynchronous satellite. Though that's right on the edge of the horizon now and would not provide a robust link."

Abbott knew the Celestri system incorporated both geosynchronous and low-Earth-orbit satellites to provide variable bandwidth capabilities for civilian users who needed to transfer large amounts of data, including broadcast video. He supposed he should be grateful that a private operation like Earthguard didn't seem to have had the resources to send their signal through that system. He had no doubt the NSA could disable a geosynchronous satellite as easily as the Iridium system, but such an action might have disrupted communications for a larger and more vocal group than just the five Iridium phone users in McMurdo. "I take it you've tried the Iridium and Celestri systems to make contact."

"Those are both civilian systems, sir. I don't have access to them." That almost mischievous, transfiguring smile suddenly animated Bailey's face, again for just a moment. "Except through my desk phone."

"Major, I'm going to ask you to stand by. But if you could keep trying to reestablish DSCS contact, I'd appreciate it."

Bailey nodded once, as if she had no feelings either way about being cut out of the loop or not. Abbott noted her professionalism. "Very good, sir."

He raised his voice to address Lieutenant Yoshii who had returned to her elevated workstation at the end of the conference table. "Lieutenant, cut the sound and video feed to SPACECOM, but keep the link active. Bring up Mr. Boyd at NSA."

The words STANDING BY appeared over Major Bailey's image as she spoke to someone out of camera range. Abbott could see her but she couldn't see him. At the same time, Elrey Boyd looked up from his desk. "Yes, General?"

"There are other Iridium phones at McMurdo, and at least one Celestri station."

Boyd misunderstood what the general meant. He took it as a criticism. "Well, that's right. But none of them are listed as belonging to Earthguard and . . ." He checked something off camera. ". . . none of them are in use."

"Do you have the phone numbers available?"

"General, we're the NSA."

"Then start calling them. I'll speak to whoever answers."

"You got it." Boyd picked up a handset from his desk, and Abbott could see him type a string of numbers into his computer keyboard.

Chennault took advantage of the lull to ask Abbott if he should remain in the EAR, or report to DIA.

Abbott still saw no reason for urgency, and under those conditions, he preferred to have as much intelligence in place as possible. Only in the heat of battle were actions based on best guesses and instinct permissible. "I want you here until we get the NEST update. Or decide we're not getting it."

Chennault withdrew to the conference table where the two NCO communications specialists spoke on two secured phones. With great military gravity, they were ordering pizzas from Domino's.

On the big board, Boyd waved for Abbott's attention. "General, I'm ringing through to McMurdo on all satellite lines. There is one Celestri station at the base that appears to be dedicated to a computer network, and there are four Iridium phones registered to various civilians in addition to the Earthguard unit. Unfortunately, the Celestri antenna is totally passive, so I can't tell if it's operational. And the Iridium phones don't appear to be switched on."

Abbott sighed. He hated the next suggestion he was going to make, but he had to be certain all possibilities were accounted for. "Can you try the Earthguard phone?"

The young man seemed amused. "It's currently deactivated. I'll have to contact our friend at Motorola."

"Do that," Abbott said. He had no desire to contact the rabid environmentalists. He was merely interested in confirming that McMurdo hadn't gone up in a radioactive fireball, though he wasn't about to state that aloud. Not that he thought it likely.

Chennault returned to Abbott's side. "General, may I make another suggestion?" Abbott nodded for the major to continue. "The . . . operation we discussed at the South Pole has been known to have a . . . detrimental effect on communications. What we're seeing here might be the result of a . . . systems test."

Abbott was intrigued. "Is there a way you can find out?"

"The fastest way would be through SPACECOM."

Abbott gestured to the board, telling Chennault to proceed. "The more information, the better informed." Then he called back to Yoshii. "Lieutenant, bring Major Bailey back in synch."

The STANDING BY legend flashed off, and Bailey looked into her teleconference camera. "Yes, sir?"

Abbott didn't bother to ask if she had had any luck reestablishing contact, because, if he were in her position, he'd resent the question as well. If she had reestablished contact, she would have told him and he left it at that. "Major Bailey, this is Major Chennault, Defense Intelligence Agency. He has some questions for you."

"This is the place for answers. Go ahead, Major."

"Are you able to establish communications with the Amundsen-Scott base at the South Pole?"

Abbott was curious to see Bailey hesitate before she checked the satellite board again. "That base is below the horizon for all geosynchronous satellites right now, and . . . about four hours away from anything that will provide a realtime link. Other than that, we'd have to patch through McMurdo, which is a no-go, or try through one of the other USAP bases."

"Major, I believe you should be able to make contact through the FLTSATCOM system."

With that mention of the Fleet Satellite Communications System, Abbott definitely perceived an undercurrent of tension in the exchange between the two majors.

Bailey's expression was unreadable. "FLTSATCOM is a geosynchronous constellation, Major. The base is below their horizon."

Chennault responded with an equal absence of emotion. "I'm not suggesting you use the satellite component."

Bailey tightened her lips, then spoke to Abbott. "General, there seem to be a lot of people with you in that room, and the major is suggesting something that might not be covered by appropriate security clearances."

Abbott was pleased to see that his suspicions had been correct. It seemed that Bailey also knew about the black op under way at the pole and was as reluctant as Chennault to discuss it. "Understood, Major." In less than a minute, he had the emergency action room cleared of everyone except himself and Chennault. "We are now secure."

Bailey looked stern as she addressed the general again. "Sir, Major Chennault has suggested that I use a communications system that I am under strict orders not to access except during specific drills or in the event of dire emergency. Is this a dire emergency, sir?"

JUDITH & GARFIELD REEVES-STEVENS

Abbott left the question to Chennault. "What is your assessment, Major?"

Chennault had it worked out. "It depends, sir. If there has been . . ." He didn't seem happy about saying his next words. ". . . an unscheduled discharge, that could account for the observed communications difficulties and it could also imply that something has gone wrong at the base. Given the circumstances, I believe it would be permissible for Major Bailey, acting under your orders, to send a simple query to the base, asking if there has been a discharge, scheduled or not."

"What is this communications system you're trying to preserve?" Abbott asked Bailey.

Bailey replied with the same type of obscure detail Chennault had used in alluding to the technically illegal operation at the pole. "It's a classified variation of the extreme-low-frequency system used to communicate with submerged subs. It's very slow, but it's not dependent on satellite or affected by the electromagnetic effects of the pole. We can get through to Amundsen-Scott at any time, under any conditions."

Abbott was familiar with ELF communications. The operational frequency was so low, it could take up to fifteen seconds to transmit a single letter or digit, so most transmissions consisted of short codes which the recipient used to look up standard, already formulated messages contained in a large book. On submarines, ELF transmissions were generally used to instruct submerged vessels to come to periscope depth and use their other communications systems to contact command. But unless a sub had the time and opportunity to unspool an ELF antenna that could be miles long, it was not a two-way system. "If Amundsen-Scott can receive ELF transmissions, how does it respond?"

Bailey looked more serious than she had at any time since she first appeared on the big board. "For that, sir, you will need a Presidential order."

Abbott acquiesced. "I will declare this a dire emergency, unless the Amundsen-Scott base can tell us they're in good shape. Is that acceptable, Major?"

Bailey was determined to go by the book. "Is that an order, sir?"

"Yes, Major, that is an order."

"Then that is acceptable. This could take up to twenty minutes."

"We're standing by."

Bailey began manipulating controls on the desktop out of range of the teleconference camera. Abbott watched the distance her hands traveled back and forth and decided her entire desk was a control board of some kind. It appeared she was capable of sending the classified ELF message from her own station. Space Command had become more centralized and efficient in the past few years. This tight integration of command and control of the military's communications and surveillance systems was the worthwhile result.

As Bailey worked, Abbott took Chennault aside, turning away from the cameras above the big board and their directional microphones. Though Abbott and Chennault were still alone in the EAR, without Lieutenant Yoshii, Abbott had no way of controlling the sound feed to Bailey. "All this secrecy over the black op at the South Pole convinces me even more that the upper levels know exactly what's going on there."

Chennault kept his back to the board as well. "I agree. It is a possibility."

"But you're still not convinced."

For a moment, Chennault reminded Abbott of his own son, the way Sam had looked when he'd finally blurted out that he didn't want to continue at West Point. Chennault had the same air of nervous regret that suggested he felt he was being forced to say something he knew Abbott didn't want to hear. "Sir, there're a great many complex systems involved in this, and all of them are prone to breaking down, almost at random. But the human brain . . . we're wired to look for patterns, so when we see a DSCS contact switch off because of what might only be a blown fuse, and an Earthguard protest start up because of some rumor someone's read on the Internet, and a NEST deployment go astray because of . . . I don't know, bad weather, someone caught a cold, something mundane like that . . . our tendency is to connect them all as if they're related parts of a single problem and not just . . . the random collection of unremarkable and inevitable glitches they really are."

Abbott wondered where Sam was at this moment. Inbound to Washington, most likely. The flight was due in tonight.

"Sir?" Chennault prompted.

Like closing a door, Abbott shut off the unwelcome, distracting thoughts of family. Compartmentalization. A most effective technique. "I'm not looking for trouble where none exists," he told the major, effortlessly picking up their conversation. "But before I make the judgment that conditions are normal, I want to be able to rule out all possible *ab*normalities."

Chennault looked relieved. "Very prudent, sir."

Abbott smiled at the word. It had a unique association at the Pentagon. "Now, there was a President." He saw Chennault's nervousness fade as he realized he could speak his mind to the general, even disagree, without provoking a knee-jerk response. But he still wasn't completely at ease. "Something else, Major?" Abbott asked.

"Sir, if NEST has run into something down there, what happens if . . . the worst case happens?"

Abbott studied the ETEM map. He doubted there were more than thirty dots on the wide white band of Antarctica that formed its bottom frame—each dot representing an isolated research base, a handful of researchers, workers, ANG personnel. The entire continent was a giant slab of ice and rock in the middle of nowhere, worth nothing to no one. And that gave Abbott his answer.

"Nothing, Major. Absolutely nothing."

The general was sure the answer lay elsewhere. It had to.

ELEVEN

McMURDO STATION

In the dim light of the battery-powered emergency lights, Cory pushed herself to her feet and looked around for Webber. He was already down the hallway, searching for an explanation of the explosion. A blast of cold air hit her, telling her that an exterior wall had fallen away from the medical building. Judging from the extreme slant to the floor, it had fallen off its stilts as well.

"The radio," she heard Webber say to a soldier slumped sideways on the floor. "What happened to the radio?"

The soldier had obviously been half out of his parka when the lights had gone out. He looked confused, blood trickling down from his forehead. He straightened up, found the radio beneath his hip, handed it up to Webber.

By the time Cory was at Webber's side, he was already trying to raise Germer on the radio, but wasn't getting any response. His face was flushed.

Cory never liked it when Webber got agitated. He was one of the most emotional involvements she had ever had, and she had always wondered how he had managed to survive in a profession that demanded he remain clearheaded under fire. "Calm down, Mitchell," she told him. "It's only an earthquake."

Webber glared at her. "That was a blast concussion."

She slipped out of her thermal blanket and thrust it at him. Web-

107

ber was still bare-chested and Cory knew he must be freezing. "Okay, so maybe it was a six. Or a six two. I've been through worse in L.A."

Webber stared at her, taking the blanket only when she waved it. He obviously didn't know what she was talking about.

"Earthquake, Mitchell?" Cory looked past him to see her brother and Hal coming down the corridor, moving gingerly as they tried to negotiate the slanted floor. Both of them looked unhurt. She turned her attention back to Webber. "I'm the scientist, remember? A blast concussion is a single wave. Bang and it's over. Sound familiar? But this time, the ground shook. It lasted a good five seconds."

Webber looked at her sourly. Then shot out his hand to brace himself as the building again shook violently, its framework creaking audibly.

"Aftershock," Cory said with satisfaction. She looked up at the loose ceiling tiles dangling above her. "And before there's another, we should haul out of here."

Leaving the medical building was awkward. At the main entrance, the second floor had crashed down to the first. Cory, Webber, Johnny, and Hal had to double back and exit through a side door, jumping down five feet to the icy ground. Ten other base personnel they'd met up with on the way were right behind them.

Pale orange light glimmered through the windows of the nearby buildings—more battery lights. Cory was surprised that the floodlights used to illuminate the roads and walkways were all out. It appeared there were no battery backups for the exterior lights.

While Webber, now wearing a medic's parka he had found on the floor, tried his radio again, Cory felt another lesser tremor, this time a four. From somewhere closer to the center of the base, she heard the muffled crunching of a building collapsing and distant shouts of caution.

Then the darkness, eased only by the glowing windows and a few flashlight beams swinging back and forth, turned day bright. Like the others with her, Cory instinctively turned to the source of the light, only to feel Webber's arm snake around her and pull her close to his chest, keeping her from seeing anything as he shouted to the others, *"Close your eyes!"*

She felt an incredible blast of heat as another rumbling explosive sound enveloped them.

It wasn't until that moment that she realized what Webber had anticipated.

Not just a bomb blast.

A nuclear explosion.

She stared up at him as he squinted into the distance, face lit by a flickering orange light shining from above. She pushed him away.

"You *did* bring the bomb down here!"

"No. Someone else did. And that wasn't it." He pointed toward the hills. One of the fuel storage tanks, up in the surrounding hills about half a mile away, had exploded. The fireball that rose from it faded into a black cloud, outlined by the flames blazing below it. The ground thumped again. Another four. *Definitely an earthquake.* Now Cory could hear muffled screams in the cold air, shouting voices. When would people learn? When would the lies stop?

"Then what *are* you doing here?" she demanded. "Was someone here stupid enough to run an underground test in a geologically active region?"

But Webber met her eyes directly, and no matter how much Cory had come to despise him for the choice he had made, she knew him well enough to know that whatever he said next would be the truth. In his own twisted way, Mitchell Webber was an honorable person. Misguided, but honorable.

"This is absolutely off the record, and I'm only telling you so you don't go back to your ship spreading lies. Understand?"

Cory nodded, accepting the condition. If Webber told her something really important, she'd know how to get it from someone else, freeing her to report it to the world.

"I found a nuclear warhead on the Ice Shelf. Maybe sixty, seventy miles from here. It wasn't in rock. It was about a thousand feet down in the ice."

Cory watched Webber's dark green eyes carefully for any sign of prevarication. "What was its yield?"

"What do you want to know yield for? You're an oceanographer."

"Don't tell me what I am. What kind of warhead? How big?"

Webber cocked his head back. She knew the look. He thought he was calling her bluff. "According to specs, it contained twenty-seven point five kilograms of Pu-two-thirty-nine."

Cory smiled pleasantly at him. "At twenty kilotons per kilogram, that's five hundred and fifty kilotons, smart guy. Right?"

Webber wouldn't say so, but she could tell he was surprised, and that she was correct in her estimate.

"Whatever the yield," he said, "that's one mother of a hole in the ice."

"If it goes off. It didn't."

Webber shook his head as if she were an ignorant child in need of his guidance. "Cory, that wasn't an earthquake."

"Listen, soldier boy! One bomb going off in a thousand feet of ice sixty miles from here does not flatten buildings. The concussion is absorbed by the steam and liquid water the fireball creates from the ice. Whatever major blast effect reaches the surface—and a thousand feet of ice is a damn good insulator—is vented straight up. And whatever minor overpressure effect propagates along the surface is deflected by the mountains all around us. Your warhead didn't blow. Bet you're sorry you told me now."

Webber's upper lip trembled the way it always did when his temper was about to go critical, but he turned away as a siren approached.

A humvee skidded to a stop near the ruined medical building. Station Manager Elizabeth Germer was in it, wearing a large bandage across her right cheek. Webber abruptly abandoned Cory and sprinted over to Germer.

"See you on CNN," Cory yelled after him. Then Johnny and Hal were at her side. "You guys okay?"

Hal was pale and shaken, but Cory saw that her brother was wired. He had no clue about the precarious position they were in and was excited by what had happened.

"Wipe the smile off your face," she told her brother. "If their power plant is down, we're going to be building igloos and camping around fires."

Johnny kept grinning. "Who says? We're civilians. We can head back to the ship."

But Cory knew that wasn't going to happen. Not for a long time, at least. "Take a look at this place, Johnny. There're going to be people trapped in the buildings, injuries, supplies that need salvaging. We're here for a while. And there's going to be a lot of work to do."

Cory could see that her brother didn't like that assessment of their situation. "Sis, this isn't our responsibility. It's the military's."

If Johnny had said that when he had been ten, she would have explained the situation to him in about ten seconds by twisting his ear until he begged for mercy. He had been much easier to deal with at that age. Unfortunately, these days she had to invest time in logic and persuasion to get her way. "Johnny, *everything* is our responsibility. That's what Earthguard is about. That's why we're here. To take responsibility for our country, and our planet. We're staying here to help these people, military goons or not. End of story."

Hal pulled up his parka hood, jammed his trembling hands in his pockets, started looking around.

"Where're you going?" Cory asked him.

"I'm going to find out where they locked up my camera. This is news. When we get our uplink back, we can sell the footage for enough to pay for chartering the ship."

"That's thinking," Cory said approvingly. She stopped then, mentally running through a rough calculation, wondering if the *Fernando Pereira* might have been affected by the quake.

"What?" Johnny asked. He knew her moods as well as she knew Webber's.

"If that was an inland quake, the energy couldn't travel through the water to the ship, so they're okay. But if that was an offshore quake, there might have been some water displacement." She looked at Hal. "First thing you do when you find our gear is call the ship. Make sure everyone's okay." She glanced back at the humvee. Webber was in a heated exchange with Germer and five other people with Air Force insignia on their parkas. For some unfathomable reason, all the Air Force personnel at McMurdo were sporting mottled green-and-brown camouflage parkas. But since Cory's past experience with Webber had thoroughly convinced her that she would never understand the military mind, she wasted no time wondering what made some far-removed military planner decide Antarctica had jungles. "Johnny and I'll stay here. We'll try to borrow a radio from these guys."

Johnny gave her a puzzled look.

"Mitchell's one of them, but he'll know how this place is organized, so he's going to be on top of whatever disaster plan they have. If we stick with him, they won't be able to hide anything from us."

"Like what?" Johnny asked.

For now, Cory decided she'd keep her promise to Webber. She

wouldn't say anything about the warhead he had found. "Like what NEST is doing here," she said, and left it at that.

Johnny gave her his most obnoxious little-brother smirk. "You still like him, huh?"

She couldn't help herself. She reached out and grabbed his ear, but he laughed and backed away before she could twist. "This is going great," he said.

Another sudden flash of light followed by another blast of heat-seared air prepared Cory for the sharp ground tremor announcing the detonation of a second fuel-storage tank high in the hills.

"No, it isn't," she said. Then she hurried off to join Mitch Webber, telling herself that she was only seeking him out because he was useful.

But before she could reach him, a huge pillar of fire from the northeast streaked high into the sky, and the concussion was so long in coming that when it finally hit, there was no question in anyone's mind what had happened.

For the first time in more than a century, Mount Erebus fully erupted. And the now-glowing volcanic cone was only twenty miles from McMurdo.

TWELVE

NATIONAL MILITARY COMMAND CENTER/THE PENTAGON

"General Abbott?"

Abbott turned back to the big board and saw Major Bailey looking out at him from her SVTS window. "I have a response from Amundsen-Scott. I sent them a standard coded query asking if Project SHAARP had been operational in the past six hours. Their response is an unambiguous negative. But then they transmitted a second coded reply. 'Anomalous seismic readings detected, 2050 GPS.' "

Chennault rubbed his hand over his scalp. "Christ. That's it. Something detonated."

But Abbott held up his hand, unwilling to jump to any conclusions, and fascinated that Bailey had revealed the name of the black op based at the South Pole. He had never heard of Project SHAARP. "Major Bailey, bear with me. I'm unfamiliar with your standard code book. Did Amundsen-Scott have a prearranged code option to report an earthquake?"

Bailey typed something, read a display screen. "Yes, sir. They have a series of in-place, three-letter codes to report earthquake, local region; earthquake, Antarctica; seismic disturbances in various sectors of the southern ocean; and then codes for force measurements, timing, and estimated location."

"So, since they specifically broadcast 'anomalous seismic readings,' we can conclude that they do not *know* the cause or location, or even if it was an earthquake, correct?"

"Correct, sir."

Then Abbott asked the question that he knew Chennault was sure already had been answered. "Major Bailey, does Amundsen-Scott have standard codes to report detection of a nuclear detonation?"

Abbott saw Bailey take in a quick, short breath. She hadn't known what he was building toward.

She typed again, read the screen, looked surprised. "Yes, sir. They do. Several options . . . oh, I see. Sir, their seismic station is part of IMS. That's the international monitoring system for the Comprehensive Test Ban Treaty."

"So, again, since they did not specifically report a nuclear detonation, is it because they did not detect one?"

Abbott saw Chennault paying careful attention to Bailey's reply.

"General, my expertise is in surveillance systems and . . . there is no seismic station anywhere that can instantly and unambiguously identify a nuclear detonation. The IMS works by transmitting data from around the world to several different processing and analysis centers, including the U.S. Geological Survey. It can take days to work that data to develop a location, force reading, and probable cause for an anomalous event."

"Then why does the station have the codes in place to describe a nuclear explosion?"

"That's not my area, sir. But I would think that they're intended to be used when the station has prior knowledge of an event. Maybe to monitor a French or Chinese test blast. Something like that."

Abbott didn't want suppositions. He wanted an expert opinion, something to base further action upon. "In your estimation then, does the message suggest that a nuclear detonation might have occurred in Antarctica?"

"Sir, without additional observational data, it would be reckless to venture an opinion on something with such far-reaching consequences."

Abbott wanted to tell Bailey that she was being stubborn. He could order her to offer her opinion, but if she responded to pressure the way he did, she still wouldn't give in. There was only one way to go. "Major Bailey, I want you to get me that additional observational data."

"Sir?"

"You're Space Command. I want images of Antarctica. Specifically, the region around McMurdo Station."

Bailey leaned back from the camera as if Abbott had just told her a ridiculous joke. "Sir, with respect, you're talking about the South Pole."

Abbott was losing patience. "I am talking about receiving operational intelligence from a division of the U.S. military that exists specifically to cover every goddamn inch of this planet in realtime. What is your problem, Major?"

Bailey leaned back toward the camera, lips tight, eyes hard. "Space surveillance assets are designed to provide intelligence on our potential enemies and to inform us of theater conditions. The geographic regions selected for observation are based on historical precedent. The South Pole has not been and is not now our enemy. It is not a likely theater of operation. Thus, it is below the horizon of our Keyhole birds in geosynchronous orbits. The poles are not consistently covered by our Big Birds, our Trumpets, or even by our Landsats *or* NASA's. I *can* provide you with daylight weather imagery from the Defense Meteorological Satellite Program—as of four hours ago—but we will not be receiving another realtime pass for two hours and I guarantee the resolution will not even show the largest McMurdo buildings, even if there are no clouds in the way."

Abbott's hands tightened into fists at his side, though his face remained impassive. The one thing he required of all his officers was that they never tell him that what he asked for was impossible. If Bailey didn't finish her tirade with some suggestions for obtaining the information he required, her next posting for the Air Force would involve sentry duty in Guam.

Fortunately for Bailey and her career, she came through. "General, if you want to know what the traffic conditions are in Beijing, or Baghdad, I can show you pictures in under five minutes that'll let you read how much time is left on a parking meter. But if you need to see Antarctica in realtime, you have three options: One, launch a TACSAT. Two, scramble a Blackbird. Three, go there yourself."

Abbott could sense Chennault shrinking back out of sight, in case Abbott was about to tear into Bailey. But the general did not intend to criticize one officer's attitude in front of another. He pressed on. "How long until I could have a tactical satellite over McMurdo?"

Bailey operated controls on her desktop, read a screen, seemed to do some calculations in her head. "Vandenburg has a three-hour-to-launch program. They mate a Pegasus to a B-52, launch into a polar orbit . . . it'll take two orbits to pass over the Ross Sea . . . so . . . you could get about three minutes of realtime observation in six hours, sir."

"Not good enough, Major."

Bailey consulted her screen again. "There are NRO Blackbirds on standby in Okinawa. They're flying daily sorties near Taiwan, keeping tabs on the PLAN maneuvers. If you can free one of them, arrange for refueling, you could have multispectrum realtime imagery in a little under three hours from launch."

If Bailey was suggesting the Blackbirds as a solution to his request, Abbott wondered why she hadn't provided him with the fourth, even better option. "Major, what is the operational status of Nevada Rain?"

Bailey frowned as if Abbott were out of line to even state aloud the randomly assigned name of the HST spyplane. "Sir, if you had full-color photos and signed affidavits attesting to the presence of a nuclear weapon under the President's bed, you *might* have a chance of getting the NRO to scramble the Nevada Rain to go look for it. But they're not even flying it over Taiwan."

Abbott liked a challenge, especially against the military bureaucracy. "Strictly out of curiosity, Major Bailey, how long would Nevada Rain take to overfly McMurdo?"

Bailey smiled at him. *Her civilian smile* was what he had come to think of it as. It seemed to spring from her whenever circumstances took her military persona by surprise, revealing the person beneath the uniform. "From Hawaii to McMurdo, with refueling, maybe an hour."

Chennault whistled softly and Abbott understood why. Bailey was suggesting the top-secret craft could attain a speed close to Mach 10—almost 7,600 mph.

"Is it available?" Abbott asked. He could go directly to the Joint Staff with his request to use the plane, and he felt certain they would approve it. The hypersonic aircraft could prove its value by performing a mission that would not bring it anywhere near a combat zone.

"It is on active status," Bailey said. "But to arrange the refueling assets you'd need to support a direct flight from Oahu to McMurdo, that could take two or three days, sir. The Blackbirds are already operational in the South Pacific with their own refueling tankers. I'd say they're your best bet."

"I don't gamble, Major."

"Then go with the Blackbirds, sir. They're a sure thing."

Abbott knew that sometimes it was more important for a commander to make a decision—any decision—rather than to keep his troops in suspense as he worked out the right one. He had kept his crisis action team out of the EAR long enough. There was a communications glitch at a remote location where a government agency was searching for a rogue nuclear weapon. Scrambling a Blackbird was a reasonable response. He could put his request in motion and in the hour it would take for the Blackbird to be retasked and launched, communications might be restored and the mission could be scrubbed without harm. If communications were not restored in that time, then on-site imagery would be more important than ever. And no matter how any of this turned out, Abbott had added two important facts to his store of informational wealth, the currency of the Pentagon—the speed of the Nevada Rain, and the existence of something called SHAARP.

"Major Bailey, you will initiate a Blackbird sortie to McMurdo, looking for evidence of explosive damage within . . . a hundred-mile radius of the base. The mission is to proceed at once and will have the capability to relay realtime imagery through SPACECOM to the NMCC. Is that understood?"

"Yes, sir."

Abbott walked to the room's side door. The camera above the big board whined as it tracked his smart badge. "I'll expect that bird to be up in an hour. Keep me informed."

He heard Bailey acknowledge the order, then opened the door. His crisis action team was huddled around a stack of red, white, and blue pizza boxes. Lieutenant Yoshii was gathering money from everyone to repay the MP who had had to accept the delivery at the Mall entrance.

As the team members realized the general had reappeared, Abbott motioned over his shoulder with his thumb. "Everyone in for a briefing, people. We've got a situation under way." But when he saw the NCOs start to double-time away from a desk, leaving their Coke and their pizza behind, Abbott added, "Bring your food with you."

The mood of the team changed as quickly as he said the words, and Abbott knew he was making the necessary connection with his staff. He went over to Yoshii and gave her a twenty-dollar bill to add to the pot. "The next order's on me," he told her. "We might be here for a while."

Yoshii and Captain Woolman carried the last of the pizza boxes into the EAR. Abbott sniffed the air, realized he also was hungry. Then he saw Chennault, eager to be on his way.

"I'm going to brief my boss on what we've got going here," the major said.

But Abbott didn't dismiss him at once. "I want clearance to be informed about this Project SHAARP."

Chennault seemed surprised. "Bailey said the base reported that they haven't been active."

"I'm commander of this CAT, Major. I say I have a clear need to know about any program that could impinge on the success of the surveillance sortie I've ordered, and any other action I might have to take as a follow-up. I don't want to be caught ordering a support mission only to have you whispering in my ear that it could interfere with something else I don't know about. Am I making myself clear?"

Chennault drew himself up and saluted Abbott. "Perfectly, sir."

Abbott returned the salute and smiled to himself as Chennault marched quickly away. Then the general looked over the watch floor, saw the glow of the screens, heard the hum of all the hard drives at work, the excited conversations in the emergency action room behind him. Something was happening here, something that he had brought into being, something that was his to control.

He strode into the room, secretly hoping that NEST *had* found something terrible in the Antarctic—something that would require his quick thought and careful action to contain. After all, what was the sense in commanding the greatest military force in the history of the world, if he never had a chance to use it?

THIRTEEN

McMURDO STATION

The tactical picture Mitch Webber built in his mind was not promising. McMurdo was being squeezed by a growing vise of fire, and the only escape was across a plain of sea ice already showing stress fractures from the constant onslaught of aftershocks.

In the foothills that surrounded the station to the north and east, the fuel-storage tanks and bunkers raged with angry flames, and billows of black smoke reached hundreds of feet into the night sky. The stars were obscured and the air was filled with the diesel-like stench of JP-8 fumes. Beyond them, twenty miles to the northeast, the fiery lava fountains of Mount Erebus brought a false dawn to midnight.

A snowfall of eerily enormous flakes of ash had begun to fall on McMurdo only minutes after the first explosive eruption. In the frigid Antarctic air, the powdery debris from the volcano cooled quickly and did not remain aloft for long. But the residual warmth of the ash turned snow and ice to slush, making the few roadways dangerous, some impassable. The scientific base had become a cauldron of confusion.

Evacuation of McMurdo was clearly required, but the logistics of such a move were considerable. According to Elizabeth Germer's count, there were 820 station personnel, 3 Earthguard activists, and 22 residents from New Zealand's Scott Base two miles along the shore, all of whom would have to be airlifted to Christchurch. Webber knew that only two airstrip facilities had been built on the Ross Ice Shelf.

Williams Field was the permanent facility, six miles away, with a 6,000-foot ski-way, a control tower, and quarters for pilots and maintenance personnel. But only aircraft equipped with landing skiis could use it. A second, seasonal facility, the Pegasus Blue Ice Runway, operated from early October to mid-December, and was several miles farther out.

To Webber, the prospects of a timely evacuation were dismal. Currently, there were eleven LC-130 Hercules transports at Williams Field—ten belonging to the New York Air National Guard's 109th Air Wing, and one which belonged to the Royal New Zealand Air Force. At Pegasus, there were four C-141 Starlifters, which included the two Naval aircraft that had brought both NEST teams and their Harriers and helicopters to McMurdo, and one C-130 Hercules with wheeled landing gear. If only passengers were carried on the cargo planes, no equipment or luggage allowed, just under half of the 845 people needing evacuation might be able to fly out after sunrise. And even that, Germer had said, was based on the flight crews being able to check out, prep, and fuel all sixteen aircraft in one operational day. Considering that at least three of the Hercs were undergoing heavy maintenance and probably couldn't be certified for another twenty-four hours, and that the weather forecast called for morning high winds and blowing snow that would restrict flight operations, McMurdo's ops manager told Webber that it might be a week before all personnel could safely leave.

As he had spoken with Germer by her humvee near the collapsed medical building, Webber could only wish her luck. His first and most important task was to make contact with any communications system that could patch him through to the Department of Energy or U.S. Space Command. He didn't for a moment accept Cory's explanation that the first earth tremor that had damaged the medical building and the subsequent shock waves, unrelated to fuel-tank explosions, were a result of natural tectonic activity. Webber was certain that the warhead Nick Young had deployed had detonated, and he had hated Cory's smug smile as she pointed to the first blazing gout of lava soaring a thousand feet above Erebus. The volcano itself could not be seen from the lower elevations of the station, where the medical building was located, but everyone had instantly realized what had happened.

"See?" Cory had said. "Ross Island is geologically active. We're experiencing *earthquakes* and there's your proof."

Webber had told Cory and Johnny to leave then, return to their ship. But Cory, in her ongoing mission to save the world, had insisted on staying to help organize the evacuation effort.

"These people are professionals," Webber had reminded her.

"Then why don't they have an evacuation plan?" Cory had retorted. Then Webber had watched in frustration as Cory interrupted Germer and began offering advice.

Webber tried to pull Cory away. Germer had too much to contend with as it was. But, inevitably, as he remembered her doing so many times before, Cory said something that at first seemed to be reasonable. She was good at getting people's attention that way. That's how she'd drawn him into her naive idealism in the past.

"We can take at least twenty extra people on the *Fernando Pereira*," Cory told Germer.

Germer could see that Webber was trying to cut Cory off, but the ops manager stopped him. "This is helpful, Captain. Let her continue."

Cory flashed that maddening smile at Webber again, then spoke to the station operations manager. "It'll be crowded, but you can bring them in fast with your helicopters, drop them off on our helipad, and get us on our way in under an hour. And you could probably get another fifty or so on the *Nathaniel Palmer*."

"No helipad on the *Palmer*," Germer said, "but that's a good idea." She turned to the ANG pilot who had accompanied her in the humvee. "Colonel, get your pilots ready to chop some passengers to Dr. Rey's ship. If the ice is in good condition, see about using the Twin Otters, too, to land beside it."

Webber couldn't help himself. "You can't send a helo out at night to land on something she *says* is a helipad. It's a private vessel owned by a shoestring operation. What kind of safety certification does it have?"

Cory pushed Webber aside. The clouds of vapor she exhaled as she spoke seemed to be an indication of her mood. "Earthguard has an excellent safety record, Ms. Germer. We hired a helicopter service to operate off the *Pereira* all summer to document illegal

Norwegian whaling up north, and we had no problems, not even in storms."

Webber tried to call her bluff again. "What were you flying all summer?" She glared at him. "What kind of *helicopter*, Cory?"

"It was like that orange one we landed by. A Baby Huey or something, right?"

Germer interrupted. Her voice betrayed the strain she was under, physical and mental. "Captain, this isn't your concern. We have no electricity, there's not an intact building on the island, and we don't have enough heaters to support the whole population. I have to get my people out of here any way I can." She pressed a hand to the bandage she wore over her right cheek. Frost was collecting on it and any blood it had absorbed would be frozen, drawing heat from the wound it covered.

Then a new tactical picture came together in Webber's mind. "Look, I have to get a satellite phone out to where I can make contact with the DSCS. I'll snowmobile these people to their ship—"

"The sea ice is off-limits," Germer said. "And even if it weren't, you're not driving on it at night."

But Webber countered her objection. "And those pilots aren't landing on an unknown vessel's pad at night, either. I'll contact the ship, get their GPS. They can send up flares to mark their location when we get close enough, and there's enough light from the volcano to see the condition of the ice. I'll check the pad. If it's okay, I'll radio back and you can start an airlift while I contact my command."

Cory gave Webber a measuring look. "You almost sound reasonable. What's the catch?"

Webber didn't consider what he had left unsaid a catch, but added a distraction to keep her from questioning him further. "If the pad checks out, you'll be transporting one of my Harriers."

Cory's puzzled expression told him he'd been successful. "Harriers?"

"The jets by the orange helicopters. Vertical takeoff and landing. If your ship can carry a helo, it can carry a Harrier." *If the pad's strong enough*, Webber added for himself. The weight difference between a fully loaded UH-1N and an empty Harrier was about 3,000 pounds. He planned on checking the pad supports with diligence.

"Earthguard does not transport weapons."

"Those are not fighters. They carry scientific instrumentation only."

"Then why were they covered up when I started broadcasting their pictures?"

"You did what?"

Germer regarded Webber and Cory with a troubled look. "Do you two know each other?"

"We used to," Webber said.

"Not anymore," Cory added.

Germer looked sternly at them both, like a mother breaking up a fight between siblings. "Let me put a stop to this. Frankly, Captain, I'd rather their ship carried one of my choppers instead of your plane."

Webber countered again. "Look, you can buy one of your helicopters off the shelf for under six million dollars. A NEST Harrier costs the taxpayers a hundred and twenty million. Think what the network anchors can do with that."

Another tremor rolled beneath them. The medical building creaked, long and slow as it shifted. Germer made her decision. "Whatever you do," she said, "make it fast." Then she climbed onto the hood of the humvee, stood up, and began shouting instructions for everyone to start a convoy to Williams Field—no personal effects, only food, tents, and Preway heaters.

Webber took Cory's arm. "This way."

But she stood her ground and shook him off. "Forget it. I'm not transporting a weapon of war."

Webber struggled to keep his voice level. He was cold, tired, hungry, and filled with the frustrating knowledge that each second's delay made Nick Young harder to find. "Trust me, you don't have a choice."

"Trust me, I do."

They glared at each other, motionless, as the chaos of the shattered station swirled around them like the blowing snow and ash. Webber had a sudden flash of another time they had faced each other like this, in San Diego, a Sunday morning, in her small ocean-view apartment, sheer curtains billowing with a seductive California spring breeze. Each detail of that moment still vivid in him, the moment when he had known it was over between them, the moment he had known he would do anything to stay with her except the one thing she wanted him to do. Five years and 9,000 miles from San Diego, they were still locked in that same impasse. Except now their joint stubbornness would not just change their lives, it might end them both.

This time the balance was broken by Johnny as he stepped in to separate them. "What're you two doing?" he said. He looked at Webber. "I thought you had a satellite call to make." He turned to his sister. "And what are you doing? You've got a chance to save the government a hundred and twenty *million* bucks! I mean, we're talking you and Earthguard on the cover of *People* at least, right?"

Shockingly, Cory started laughing, and Webber remembered that sound and knew he had missed it. She patted her brother's cheek with her bear-paw mitten. "You're hopeless, Johnny." Then her smile and laughter faded as she faced Webber. "Okay. I'm your taxi driver. But you're damn well going to help with the publicity when we get to Christchurch."

Without trusting himself to reply, Webber simply turned and started jogging along the roadway crowded with wandering personnel, heading away from the medical building and toward the helicopter hangar where the NEST equipment was stowed. As soon as he heard Cory and Johnny behind him, their rubber boots splashing in the slush, he picked up the pace.

Now, within half an hour of Cory's acceptance of his plan, Webber had placed fresh batteries in the portable DSCS satellite phone and packed it in its aluminum container, which looked little different from a metal-walled suitcase. He had also commandeered two Alpine 2 Skidoo snowmobiles, the heaviest available at the station and, with their wide tread and single forward ski, the ones best suited for travel off the area's snowmobile trails.

Webber tied his phone case securely to the tail cargo deck of his Alpine. He would ride alone. Johnny and Cory would follow him on the second snowmobile, Johnny driving. Johnny claimed the controls weren't that much different from the Jet Skis he skimmed the waves with back home, and he enthusiastically demonstrated to Webber that he could control the clutch, brake, and throttle. Along with the mandatory survival packs, they took a pair of SABER radios. Cory had raised the captain of the *Fernando Pereira*, had him relay his GPS coordinates, then told him to fire off a white flare in thirty minutes. She would contact him again then.

With all preparations complete, Webber pulled down on his snow goggles, carefully placed his double-mittened hands on the Alpine's handlebars, then slowly moved out from the Mechanized Equipment Center, bearing left toward the Transition Road and the Ice Shelf. Cory and Johnny followed close behind.

Though the ice field beyond the shore was only a dim orange expanse in the glow from distant Mount Erebus, the ice road to Williams Field was clearly inscribed across it by the stream of red taillights of the truck and humvee convoy that carried the first evacuees.

Webber waved Johnny to a stop at the edge of the Transition Ramp, and they stayed there, engines racing, until a large orange Ford transport truck slowed and the driver gave Webber a thumbs-up.

Webber twisted the throttle of the Alpine and shot onto the ramp, accelerating down its 300-foot length until he hit the ice and caught up with traffic. He fishtailed as he swerved around the next truck in the convoy, then bounced over the raised edge of the road and onto the raw ice beside it. He slowed then, checking over his shoulder to see Johnny soar over the road edge in a burst of snow as Cory whooped in surprise. Then Johnny sped toward him and, as he had been strictly ordered, swung in directly behind Webber, keeping him centered in the cone of his headlight beam.

Webber was gratified to see the kid had more sense than his sister and knew how to do exactly what he was told. He looked down at the directional display on the Magellan GPS unit held to the Alpine's control panel by two strips of duct tape. He had entered the *Fernando Pereira*'s position into the navigation unit and it would now continue to point the way, no matter how much he had to twist and turn as his two-vehicle convoy made its way across the wind-carved ice field.

He hunched his shoulders, trying to keep his nose buried in the fur trim of his parka, trying not to breathe the air too deeply, because each inhalation felt like a knife slicing into his lungs. The snowmobile mechanic had told him that though the thermometer read –10° Fahrenheit, the Antarctic summer winds were now gusting at 25 mph on the ice, which made the windchill temperature –59°. Flash-freezing of exposed skin was a definite risk. According to the GPS unit, the *Fernando Pereira* was only four and a half miles away to the west and Webber was counting on the trip taking less than half an hour. If any of the three of them did develop frostbite in that time, at least it wouldn't be debilitating. Or so he hoped.

For fifteen minutes, the ride was uneventful. Webber's own headlight flashed and probed across the ice, and only twice did he stop to scout ahead and be sure a dark line of shadow was just a ridge of ice and not a crevasse. Johnny obediently kept his place behind Webber, and sometimes Webber's own shadow, cast by Johnny's headlight, shot out across the ice like a blade of night, only to be lost in other darkness.

But two miles from the *Pereira's* position, everything changed. Webber felt something go wrong with his Alpine. The sound of the motor altered, as if it were misfiring or out of balance. Webber slowed so he could listen to the engine more clearly. He held up his hand to signal Johnny to do the same, then tugged back on his hood, feeling crusted ice and snow splinter beneath his mitt.

Johnny's Alpine pulled up beside him. The thrumming of the second engine partially masked Webber's. Webber waved him off. "There's something wrong with my engine. Listen."

Johnny and Cory pulled at the side of their own hoods. "Maybe that's not your engine," Johnny shouted.

As Webber felt the vibration grow in the machine, he realized the kid could be right. He throttled down to a low idle. The machine shook, but not because of anything it was doing to itself.

"Feels like another earthquake," Johnny yelled. "Aftershock."

Webber saw the expression of alarm on Cory's face as she called out, "Not on ice it isn't."

Then it was as if an oncoming train were shrieking toward them from a direction no one could see. Webber grabbed for the Alpine's handlebars to keep from being thrown. The vibrations in the ice shook Cory off the back of the second snowmobile, and she tumbled onto the ice field as Johnny, fighting to keep in position, squeezed the throttle by mistake and spun the Alpine around. The spray of snow that shot out from his tread covered Webber's goggles.

Webber shook his head in vain to clear his goggles, then risked using a mitt, hoping his Alpine wouldn't buck him free if he held on with only one hand. His vision restored, he looked up to see Johnny's headlight angle straight up and spiral like a searchlight as the Alpine tipped backward into a black and yawning crevasse.

Then the ice rushed up beneath Webber, propelling him from his machine like a diving board suddenly released. Deafened by the roar of the cracking ice, he hit the snow rolling, to see his Alpine lying on its side, ten feet away, the crucial satellite phone still strapped to its cargo deck.

As he ran toward the crevasse in the dim orange glow from

Mount Erebus, he called out for Cory and Johnny, then saw some-one in orange ECW gear stretched out on the ice.

It was Cory who answered him, pleading for help. Only her hand on the hood of Johnny's parka was supporting her brother as he dangled in midair over darkness.

And Cory's body was slowly slipping forward.

Ripping off his goggles, Webber threw himself down on the ice. Ignoring the piercing pain of his cracked rib, he stretched himself out behind Cory to increase the friction of his body in an attempt to stop her movement. Slamming one hand across the back of her boot, he forced it into the snow, trying to dig a trench so she could wedge the toes of her boots into position.

"Keep as still as you can!" he told her. "I'll brace you!" But his soft mittens made no headway in the hard frozen surface. He tugged them off with his teeth, began futilely digging with one bare hand—a hand that was numb within seconds.

Cory kept slipping, toward the abyss.

"There's a rope on the snowmobile!" she cried out. Webber could hear the panic building in her, the effort she was making to keep it in control.

"It's too far away." Webber half-rolled on his side, still keeping pressure on the back of Cory's boot, reaching up beneath his parka for the 9mm Beretta he carried. It had been Rensberger's, still stowed with the NEST equipment in the hangar, and Webber's training had made it impossible for him to continue on a mission without at least one weapon.

He pulled the handgun free and for the briefest of instants, he felt how warm the metal was. Then the chilling wind froze it and his hand was numb again.

Webber clubbed at the snowy ice, using the pistol's grip as an ice hammer. But with each blow, he felt Cory slip another inch, and this time Webber was slipping with her on the sloping ice.

"This isn't working! Johnny's got to climb! Tell him to climb while we can still brace him!"

"If he moves we'll all fall!"

"Cory, I can't keep us braced!" Webber shouted as loudly as he could, "Johnny! CLIMB!"

Cory joined in. Her voice was high and desperate. "Johnny, you have to! Swing up! Grab my hand!"

Webber gripped both of Cory's boots, pressed them down as hard as he could, feeling her body suddenly shift from side to side, knowing it meant Johnny was swinging up to get a grip on her.

Webber and Cory jerked another foot forward, stopping only when Webber jammed his face in the ice, pushing down with every ounce of strength he possessed.

"He's got my hand," Cory gasped despairingly. "But I can't pull him up."

"You have to tell him to climb."

"He can't, Mitchell. He can't."

They slid forward again. Another foot. Then another.

Cory's head and shoulders were now over the edge, about to lose purchase. The scenario to come played out in Webber's mind.

Cory would fall. And he would fall with her. Washington would never know about Young and the warhead. About the other five warheads. About what had happened on the Ice.

"JOHNNY!" Webber turned his face to the side and bellowed. "CLIMB GODDAMN YOU! I WON'T FALL WITH YOU! DO YOU UNDERSTAND! I CAN'T!"

Cory screamed back at him. "STOP IT!"

Webber felt tears of rage freeze on his cheeks. "I HAVE TO CONTACT WASHINGTON! I'LL LET YOU GO, JOHNNY! I SWEAR I'LL LET YOU GO! *CLIMB!*"

Cory sobbed, Cory pleaded.

Then the wind grew stronger. Webber felt its push on them increasing.

But there were five nuclear warheads to find.

The mission *couldn't* fail.

No matter the cost.

He whispered to the snow and the ice, his words stolen by the wind. "Kid, I'm sorry . . ."

The pressure disappeared.

The pull on them gone as if it had never existed.

Cory's wail of horror pierced the night. Webber pulled her back from the edge.

"You bastard!" Cory shrieked as her fists pounded against him. *"You made him let go!"*

Then the ice field reached out for them as it splintered again, the coldness of its grip beyond human capacity to feel.

FOURTEEN

THE ICE

When Cory Rey had been twelve years old, she had wanted to fly. Not for-real flying. She knew the difference between cartoons and real life. But between the house and the garage, *that* distance she could jump. She'd be so high in the air over the breezeway, *that* would count as flying.

She had been methodical about it. She'd rehearsed her plan by putting her back against the house and jumping with all her might across the gap on ground level. Then she had climbed the roof and thrown her Barbies across, carefully plotting how high they had to arc to make it from one roof to the next.

Even at the age of twelve, she had been very scientific. She even drew diagrams.

She would have done it, too. If not for Johnny.

He had watched her and her ever-loyal followers climb the twisted old walnut tree that made it so easy to get to the roof of the house. Johnny was only six. He couldn't climb no matter how badly he wanted to follow his big sister.

So he had run back and forth in the front yard, watching her on the roof, watching her get ready to jump for her admirers. And he had screamed and cried and told her not to, told her he would tell their parents, their aunt and uncles, everyone, if she jumped. But if she came down, he promised not to tell.

129

The fear in his eyes, a fear born of pure love, had stopped Cory that day. A few months later, trying the running broad jump on her school's field day, she realized she would have missed the garage roof by a good four feet.

Johnny had saved her that day. Johnny had clung to her when she had climbed down the walnut tree. He had told her through his tears that she always, always, *always* had to listen to him, because he would keep her safe. And then he had done what she really hadn't expected him to do. He had kept his promise not to tell.

But when it had been her turn to keep him safe, when he had needed her most, Cory had felt her brother release her hand and fall into oblivion, eyes wide, without reproach, because of Mitchell Webber.

Cory hated Webber as she struck him. She hated him as the ice field cracked again, hurling them both against the rock-hard hummocks of compacted snow. She hated him as he staggered to his feet and half-dragged her to his snowmobile. She hadn't helped him as he strained to rock the machine upright again. But she hadn't resisted as he had pulled her onto the snowmobile with him and sped away from Johnny's hungry grave.

In time, the tears frozen on her face stopped stinging and a part of her understood that frostbite was setting in on her cheeks and her nose. Listlessly, she shifted to look past Webber's broad back, to see how close they were to the ship.

Instead, she saw a gateway to hell—Erebus, still erupting. Webber was heading back to McMurdo.

"Where are you going?!" she cried out above the snowmobile's roar. When he didn't answer, she punched his back. "Answer me, you bastard!"

He twisted around to look at her, and even through the snow that caked his goggles and hood, she could see the conflicting emotions that ravaged him. "The shelf is breaking up!" he shouted at her. And then he saw something behind them that drove the conflict from his face.

Cory twisted to look back even as Webber hunched forward and gunned the engine, no longer swerving and banking around the rises of snow, but shooting up them as if they were ramps, flying forward, jarring her teeth and her back with each impact.

And Cory knew why.

Behind them, more cracks were forming, black lines weaving

across the hellishly lit ice like black lightning. Where the cracks converged, snow and ice exploded, and slabs the size of cars flew up and crashed together.

The fissures were multiplying, and they were gaining on Webber's snowmobile. Reaching out for her like Johnny's hands, to pull her down with him into the void.

No, she thought as she wrapped her arms tighter around Webber, feeling the snowmobile drop beneath her with each jump he took, never knowing if she would remain on it when they landed. *Johnny wouldn't do that. Johnny would take care of me. That's why*— But she couldn't finish the thought. It was all Webber's fault. Johnny had died for Webber's "mission." But no mission was worth Johnny's life. Somehow she had to survive to make Mitchell Webber pay.

Then the snowmobile skidded sideways as Webber sat back up, raising his head to stare to the side. Cory followed his gaze.

She saw the roadway to Williams Field, picked out by a chain of taillights and headlights.

About to be intersected by a speeding black ridge of shadow.

Webber accelerated again. McMurdo—solid land—was only half a mile away. But Cory couldn't take her eyes off the roadway.

The fissure reached the convoy.

The lights of four trucks were gone so quickly Cory couldn't tell if they had been thrown into the air or pulled down through the sea ice.

Then another group of trucks seemed to pivot, headlights blazing up into the sky, catching the blowing snow to make it look as if stars danced overhead.

The trucks reared skyward, and then they fell, sliding down to hit other trucks behind them.

A gas tank blossomed like a brilliant red night flower.

Another explosion engulfed two more trucks. Part of the roadway twisted to the side. The trucks that slipped there hit nothing, swallowed by that same long fall that had claimed her brother.

It hit her then. It wasn't just Johnny. Everyone was going to die.

The ice moved beneath the snowmobile. It seemed to Cory that the mind-numbing roar of the disfigured surface that surrounded them was growing even louder, if possible.

She looked back over her shoulder.

Into the maw of a pursuing crevasse.

"MITCHELL!"

The snowmobile shot to the left just as the ice split beneath them. Cory saw the snow from their tread cascade into empty space, and then the snowmobile rolled as it dug into the ice and Cory kept going.

Her mouth was filled with snow and blood and she felt Webber nearly dislocate her shoulder as he hauled her to her feet.

"Run," he yelled. Then he pulled her along with him, the Transition Ramp just two hundred feet away.

Cory didn't know if her feet were touching the ice. Her face burned with icy cold. Her exposed hands felt nothing. She felt as if she were in a slow-motion nightmare, being dragged through something thick and unyielding, with each impossible breath an explosion of agony.

But Webber's grip was like steel around her wrist and she knew if she stumbled he would just keep pulling.

The Transition Ramp from the ice-covered sea to the ice-covered land was a hundred feet away now, clogged with trucks and humvees, and people fleeing back to the land.

With a shriek so loud it was like a physical blow, a section of ice beside Cory and Webber suddenly thrust into the air where it exploded, eight-foot-thick sections of it slamming back down to hit the exposed Ross Sea, spraying them with a sheet of salt water colder than freezing.

The shock of it took what was left of Cory's breath away. She fell to her knees, forcing Webber to a stop.

Dazed, she looked up, saw him speaking her name, but couldn't hear him because another noise—

Some other part of her mind took over as she realized a crevasse was opening right behind her and she was lifted up bodily, propelled forward by Webber, who pushed her up the side of the ramp, toward the grasping hands of the McMurdo personnel above.

A final spray of icy salt water washed over her. Then she was on the ramp, safe from the ice, doubled over, hands on her knees, struggling to breathe. She lifted her head to look out across the ice and saw that the road to Williams Field was gone. A few lone sets of vehicle lights were scattered out to the horizon. Some trucks still burned.

She could see Webber talking to the others on the ramp. Then he came back to her side. "The airfields are gone."

"All those people," Cory said. *All those people gone with Johnny.*

"Time to go," Webber grabbed her arm and started guiding her farther up the ramp.

"Why?" she said.

"We can't stay here."

She looked at the station in ruins before her. At least five buildings were on fire now. She saw and heard detonations emanating from what seemed to be a large pit in the foothills to the north. A river of liquid fire coursed into it, fed by the blazing storage tanks. If Erebus had been an entrance to hell, McMurdo was the underworld itself.

She nodded her head, unable to argue. She didn't want to be here anymore.

They moved up the ramp together.

By the time they reached the station's helipad, Cory had almost caught her breath again. But she was shivering badly. The thermal underwear, microfleece leggings, and sweater she wore under her parka were sodden with sweat and seawater and her body was running out of the energy necessary to generate heat.

She saw uniformed figures working around the helicopters—the large orange one and one of the green ones. There had been another green helicopter here when she had landed. She guessed it was the one that had gone to Black Island.

The helipad area glowed with bright blue light from portable floodlights powered by small generators. Snow blew everywhere, and volcanic ash had made the ground soft gray. Automatically, she started to move toward the basket of the balloon that had carried her here, wondering only now where Hal and his camera had ended up. But Webber tugged her back.

"We're taking that." He pointed to one of the planes the station personnel had hidden under a tarp. "The Harrier."

"To the *Pereira?*"

"I'll land it on a damn iceberg if I have to." Webber started pulling on the tarp, peeling it back from the plane. The ash that had collected on it sloughed off in clouds. Cory was surprised by how large the aircraft was. The top of its oddly bulging canopy was at least twice as tall as Webber.

Webber left the tarp to Cory as he sprinted off to talk with the people working on the helicopters. After a moment, Cory began to wrestle with the heavy canvas cover and succeeded in dragging it off and away from the Harrier before Webber came back with two uniformed men. One had a small ladder, which they took to the side of the plane. Cory saw the clear canopy lift up. It was hinged at the back, like the mouth of a child's toy alligator. Webber waved her over to his side.

"Sorry," he said, "but we'll get warm once were airborne." Then he tugged open her parka. "There's no room for this."

Cory gasped as she lost the wind protection of the Goretex and the sweat in her layered clothing instantly froze. The onset of shivering was immediate. She tried to speak but only unintelligible stuttering came out.

"Five more minutes," Webber promised her. Then he pushed her back to sit on one of the steps of the ladder so he could pull off her boots and waterproof pants.

Cory hugged herself, trying not to fall off the ladder as Webber struggled with her boots. She had to duck as one of the helicopter men took a half-moon-shaped cover out of the engine intake beside her. The intake was large enough that she could fit into it. She wondered what it was doing right beside the cockpit and not on the wing where most planes put their engines. And then she was standing in the middle of Antarctica, at night, in frozen thermal underwear.

"Okay," Webber said. "Climb."

Cory turned to the ladder. Her hands wouldn't close over the rungs. She felt Webber's hands on her waist, balancing her, forcing her up as he climbed behind her.

"Backseat," he said.

She looked in. "There's no room."

"You'll fit. Hurry."

Once, Cory had spent half a day paddling a kayak off Baja, looking for humpbacks. The kayak had more room than the space Webber was forcing her into.

Awkwardly, she stood on the seat, then stepped down, still shivering, until there was no more room and nothing more she could do except bend her knees and plop on her backside like a kid in a stroller.

The seat was hard, cold, though with a bit more space around it than she had thought. But her part of the cockpit remained crowded as Webber leaned in and pushed her from side to side as he fastened her flight harness, connecting four straps over her chest. Then he pulled off her balaclava, and jammed a heavy flight helmet down over her head until she couldn't see.

"Okay," Webber said as he plugged a wire from the helmet into something at the side of the seat, then positioned a breathing mask over her mouth and nose. "Keep your hands on the safety straps at all times. Don't touch anything. I mean it. Nothing."

Cory nodded. Her fingers no longer worked. She couldn't touch anything if she wanted to. The mask smelled of old sweat and rubber.

"Once we're up, we'll be able to talk through our helmets. You okay?"

She nodded again, though she doubted anything got through the shivering.

"Five more minutes," Webber told her.

"Y-you said that t-ten minutes ago."

Webber disappeared. Cory sat and trembled and watched snow and ash build up on all the complicated-looking dials and screens in front of her. Numb with cold and shock at losing Johnny, she felt her mind and attention wander as she waited for Webber to tell her what to do next. She drifted in the present, safe for the moment from reliving the past.

Then Webber was back, also in his thermal underwear, already wearing his helmet and gloves. He stepped over the high side of the cockpit and smoothly slipped into position.

Cory heard his voice crackle over her helmet speakers. "I'm closing the canopy. Keep your hands on the straps."

"K-kay," Cory managed. She heard a loud clunk behind her and the canopy began to scissor shut above.

As soon as the large plastic bubble had closed, the wind stopped and she felt warmer. She heard more thunkings in the plane all around her. She risked moving one unresponsive hand up and clumsily adjusted the angle of her helmet so she could look around. To either side, the edge of the cockpit was about level with her nose and all she could see was the floodlights. But her seat was almost two feet higher than Webber's, so she had an almost uninterrupted view straight ahead. Someone was standing about forty feet in front of the plane, just like at an airport, a flashlight in each hand, pointing straight up.

Suddenly, with a whine, all the lights on the control panels came to life in a spectrum of colors. Two blank screens dead center flickered and displayed status readings for equipment and systems identified only by mysterious acronyms.

Cory jerked against her seat restraints as a deafening scream hit her from both sides. The engine was starting. Seconds later, a blast of warm air hit her feet. The instant shock of sensation in her reawakened flesh brought sharp tears to her eyes.

The Harrier seemed to rock in time to various whines and clunks, but since she couldn't see any part of the aircraft, she had no idea if the wing flaps were moving or panels were opening or closing or what was going on.

Then a muffled thumping came from her left and she looked over the edge of the cockpit in time to see the orange helicopter taking off.

Webber spoke to her through the helmet radio. "We're just going to let the helos get out of here, then we're next."

"Where're they going?"

Webber's reply was grim. "Out to the airfield. Look for survivors. How're your hands and feet?"

"Can't feel my fingers. Feet are warming up."

"We'll be okay."

Cory didn't respond. Nothing would be okay again.

The green helicopter took off, and then the Harrier rocked forward a few feet.

"Here we go," Webber said. "Nice and easy."

The whine of the engine pulsated through Cory and she clutched her safety straps hard, expecting to be jammed into her seat like an astronaut in a rocket. For a moment she was relieved to realize that her cold-stiffened hands could move on the straps, and then she noticed that the floodlights were gone. The Harrier was rising straight up, so slowly she didn't even feel the motion.

"Changing vector," Webber said.

This movement Cory could feel. A gentle rise and forward motion. She could see the orange glow of Mount Erebus against the clouds above, but that was all. There was nothing else to see through the canopy except a complex display of colored lines and numbers that flashed on a sheet of something transparent in front of Webber's face.

"How're you doing?" Webber asked her.

"Still here," she said.

"We're going to gain some altitude."

To Cory, that seemed a reasonable thing for a plane to do, and she wiggled her fingers against the safety straps. Suddenly she was shoved to the side of the cockpit as the Harrier banked and she was looking straight down at—

"Oh God."

It was McMurdo, but already less than half the size it had appeared from her balloon, roughly outlined by small clusters of portable floodlights. She could see the blazing fuel-storage tanks, each one inconsequential from this height. She could see the blinking lights of the helicopters that had taken off before the Harrier, hundreds of feet below and over the ice.

In the volcano's light, she could also see the web of cracks and fissures that had torn the ice to pieces. Cory frowned, suddenly struck by the thought that there might possibly be something more to the seismic disturbances she had felt than just an earthquake.

And then the sun came up.

Cory stared in surprise. It still felt as if it should be the middle of the night. But there the sun was, high in the east . . .

"DON'T LOOK!" Webber shouted.

Cory reflexively closed her eyes. Saw red as an intense burst of light—so strong she felt its heat—played across her.

Then it was gone as the Harrier leveled out, pointing west. She opened her eyes, looked down past Webber to see light flickering over the Ice Shelf below. "What was—"

There was an explosion on the ice.

"Oh, no . . ." Webber growled over the radio.

Cory leaned against her straps to stare down and to the side as the Harrier banked again and the false sunlight faded.

"What is—"

She saw the orange dot that was the Huey helicopter as it plunged abruptly to the ice. A second explosion flared. Overwhelming fear woke her deadened senses. Somehow, she knew that the light had caused the helicopters to crash. "What happened to the helicopters? What happened to them?"

When Webber replied, Cory had never heard such anger in him, never such rage.

"Electromagnetic pulse," he said. "That flash of light. It was an airburst. A thermonuclear detonation in the upper atmosphere."

For a brief, sickening moment, Cory wondered if the Harrier would drop from the sky like the helicopters. Then Johnny, the ice and the cold, and her hatred all fell away as she remembered what she and Webber had said to each other when they'd met again in the last place on Earth.

Cory, I'm here to stop *the nuclear weapons.*

Good. So am I.

But they both had failed.

The time was 0100 GPS.

Event minus zero.

It had begun.

PACIFIC SHIELD

THURSDAY NOVEMBER 25
THANKSGIVING

EVENT MINUS 3 MINUTES

The final components were launched from a camouflaged position 350 miles southeast of McMurdo Station, midway between ice-locked Roosevelt Island and the Crary Ice Rise. In case of failure, all markings and serial numbers had been removed. Subsystems originally designed to enable the missiles to fly more than 1,100 miles had been eliminated or altered. The distinctive control chips and gyroscopes had been replaced with equivalent units from four different countries. In case of failure, no one would know who had attempted the unthinkable.

But the missiles reached their optimum burst heights and the devices they carried did not fail.

One hundred and fifty-six miles above the Ice, the first device detonated. One hundred times greater than the weapon that had obliterated Hiroshima, its yield was twenty megatons. The explosion was far too high to cause any physical damage, but not all damage caused by nuclear explosions is physical.

The device had been "salted," wrapped with layers of cobalt 59 and iridium. The iridium was there simply to confuse. In the months ahead, when scientific missions returned to the blast site to sample the air, the presence of iridium would point to a natural event, a meteoroid burning up in the atmosphere over Antarctica. It would not be a definitive answer, but it would cause endless debates and scientific arguments.

141

But the cobalt isotope had a more important role to play than misdirection. Its presence dramatically increased the production of gamma rays in the first 10 nanoseconds of the fusion reaction. The gamma rays struck the electrons of the molecules of air in the thick layer of atmosphere beneath the explosion, and initiated the Compton effect—a cascade reaction, releasing 30,000 high-energy electrons for each gamma impact.

The energy of those electrons peaked at 100 gigawatts—the combined power output of almost 100 nuclear generating plants all at once—to produce a region of intense ionization. Over more than half of Antarctica, destructive electric currents induced by that ionization disabled every unprotected phone wire, computer chip, radio antenna, engine ignition, power cable, and electrical wire.

The region of ionization did not just extend to the icy landmass below the explosion, but spread through space as well, amplified by the Earth's own electromagnetic field. The power surge affected every satellite south of the 50th parallel toward the Pacific, and south of the 60th toward Africa.

As its creators had intended, there could be no warning now for what would happen next.

A single mile above the Ice, the fission trigger of the second device formed a new sun: a fusion reaction with the destructive force of 80 megatons of conventional chemical explosives, more than 400 times greater than the Hiroshima bomb. The second device became the most powerful nuclear bomb ever detonated in the atmosphere, though by no means the most powerful one ever built. And, unlike the first bomb, this one was low enough to cause physical damage.

In 0.83 seconds, the shock wave of released energy impacted the surface of the Ross Ice Shelf. Any observers standing directly below the fireball, at the hypocenter, when the shock wave arrived, would have been instantly reduced to a smear of protein and pulverized bone, though they would not have known it, for the initial burst of radiation had traveled at the speed of light—intense enough at that range to boil away flesh and to convert the upper twenty-three inches of snow and ice into superheated steam.

The atmospheric shock wave hit that steam. The steam, in turn, transferred that mechanical energy to the Ice. Some of that energy went into the Ice at once. Some of it was reflected back to form a second shock wave that combined with the first. As the two met, they created an even more powerful shock wave than that which the bomb had created. In the language of physicists, this was called the Mach effect.

Had the Ross Ice Shelf still been connected to the land, still been in one piece, it would have shattered like the unyielding tree that resists the wind. Hundreds of thousands of ice slabs would have formed, dissipating the energy of the blast, changing the Ross Sea into a churning mass of pack ice. Over the next six months, sea levels around the world might have risen by as much as two and a half feet in a gradual series of progressively higher tides.

But the Shelf was no longer a rigid, unyielding sheet connected to the land.

The fractures caused by the six warhead explosions deep within the ice had changed the Shelf into a single, isolated object. A single object that contained enough ice to build a mile-thick wall around the Earth's equator, two miles high. A single object with the mass of seven billion tons of ice. And the spreading circle of the amplified shock wave that raced across the massive Shelf now gave the ice an extra push of 300 miles per hour.

After 30,000 years of being anchored to Antarctica, the Ross Ice Shelf flexed like a reed bending before the fury of a storm. Then it moved.

The Ross Sea trapped beneath it had nowhere to go.

What happened next would not take six months.

It would take hours.

ONE

USSPACECOM/EARTH SURVEILLANCE CENTER/CHEYENNE MOUNTAIN

One thousand, seven hundred and fifty feet beneath the surface of Colorado, Major Wilhemina Bailey looked across a dark and cavernous room, over the heads of twenty-four Air Force intelligence officers, technicians, and air staff, to gaze down upon the world as if from heaven. Though she didn't know where each sparrow fell, the efforts of the Space Surveillance Center, 500 yards away, reached out through a maze of unmarked steel corridors to provide her with absolute realtime access to every *object* in orbit of the Earth, from the classified optical-surveillance satellites whose design had been adapted to create the Hubble Space Telescope, to the errant tools and cameras dropped by two generations of careless spacewalkers.

It was in Bailey's Earth Surveillance Center that the onslaught of data produced by the American observational components of Earth's orbital array was combined, sifted, and displayed on the immense map display on the wall fifty feet across from her elevated duty station, a display even more detailed and elaborate than General Abbott's ETEM map in the National Military Command Center in Washington, D.C. If she touched a control on her situation panel, as large and complex as a music mixing board in a recording studio, she could call up the position of every civilian satellite currently on orbit. Another control showed her U.S. military communications satellites. Another, surveillance satellites, or foreign satellites, or the abandoned hulk of the *Mir* station, the still-under-construction International Space Station, or even AOO-221, the mysterious object long rumored to hold the body of a Soviet cosmonaut lost almost forty years ago, and destined not to reenter the atmosphere for another three hundred years.

Major Bailey loved the Air Force, loved her job, and most of all loved the thrill of knowledge her new position as ESC shift supervisor gave her in this cave-like facility where the hum of the VAX processors was soft and soothing. Like most Americans born in the sixties, Bailey had grown up in a world in which even those loyal to their government could not completely trust it because of all the questions unanswered. What about the assassinations and Watergate? What about orbital nuclear weapons and Star Wars space defense, Irangate, even UFOs and Roswell? There were so many secrets hidden in those innocuous folders marked Classified, Secret, Top Secret, and Above, so many nagging puzzles that could be so simply solved, just by reading a few typewritten pages.

As a career military officer, Bailey knew there was good reason for the government to keep *some* secrets. It was a dangerous world and America and her allies faced deadly enemies, even with the Cold War a swiftly receding memory.

But still, at just a basic human level, she had always wanted to *know* what those secrets were. Some of them, at least—the ones that would not endanger her country by her knowing them. Now, as a senior intelligence officer for Space Command, she knew things she would never have been able to even imagine ten years ago.

The world was safer than it had been in many decades. It had survived threats the American people barely recognized. And the most fascinating parts of America's history over the past fifty years would only come to light decades after the generations who had lived through them had passed to dust.

But Bailey knew that history now.

It was an extremely satisfying feeling. It was also ephemeral, she had found. For after only two months as ESC shift supervisor, this evening as she had walked through the three-foot-thick blast doors that secured Cheyenne Mountain and its command centers from the rest of the world, her sense of self-satisfaction was being challenged by a new obsession: How was she going to lose those last six pounds before Thanksgiving dinner tomorrow night?

Every year, it seemed to be the same. Thanksgiving, Christmas, and Kwaanza brought those extra inches that never managed to go away by summer. Not that she minded being a few pounds—all right, twenty pounds—over Air Force guidelines for her height. And not that the few significant men in her life over the years had minded either.

But Major Bailey was determined to retire from the Air Force a general, and she knew she had a good shot at it. The only problem was that the Air Force was an environment shaped by those damned fighter pilots who treated an ounce of superfluous fat like the enemy. Consequently, however unfair, the Air Force remained a world in which the pressure to conform to the minimum health guidelines for weight was stronger than in any other service.

Bailey didn't make those rules, but she had long ago made up her mind to play by them, because that was the easiest way to win. Then, when she was *General* Bailey, she'd have a crack at changing the rules, and at getting a few more women—and sisters—into the cockpit of a few more fighters. Then the Air Force would come around and look more like the nation it served.

Her Thanksgiving weight-loss goal became suddenly inconsequential when Falcon AFB handed off the DSCS communications attempt from McMurdo Station. For this shift, for a change, Bailey's job was no longer to observe, but to take action. Which was exactly what she was doing now—provided the satellites cooperated. That was another secret the public wasn't aware of: The more complex the technology, the more frequently it behaved in ways its designers never anticipated.

Commander Dominic Huber, Bailey's crew chief and senior orbital analyst, and ten years her junior, carefully negotiated the four steps leading to her duty station while cradling a tea mug. There was a special, high-lipped plastic shelf built into Bailey's situation panel, with deep indentations specifically meant to hold hot drinks and pop cans without spilling. The Air Force had borrowed from the car industry for that one.

Huber put the tea down, looked at his watch. "Four more minutes," he told her. Bailey's precise concern about her tea had become known to her staff within the first three hours of her new assignment. Every officer was allowed one foible. Herbal tea was hers.

But herbal tea didn't get in the way of her mission. "Are we set to transmit the NOAA pictures directly to General Abbott?" One of the Department of Commerce's National Oceanic and Atmospheric Administration weather satellites was over McMurdo now. The first shots would be ready to be transmitted through a TDRSS interlink any moment.

Huber was in no rush. "Standard procedure is to scan them here first, see if they need to be reprocessed before forwarding."

But Bailey knew that nothing about Abbott's request was standard. "You heard the general. This is time-critical. We'll upload the raw data directly to the NMCC as we get it. If it needs reprocessing, we'll just keep updating him on the fly."

Huber nodded, no argument. For all the systems that Bailey could access from her own workstation, Huber was the shift's key "knob turner," the person who handled the myriad subsystems that made her control possible. Impossibly thin—which she tried not to hold against him—Huber had a mind almost as fast as the computers he wrangled and always seemed to know a different way to make them work together. She had felt somewhat discomfited when he had begun bringing her her tea. There were other, more junior air staff who could act as aides. But Huber had persisted, saying he had to talk with Bailey so often during duty hours, bringing tea made the process more efficient. She'd begun to wonder if the commander had a crush on her.

"Seriously," Bailey added, "is there any chance a weather shot's going to show anything useful at McMurdo?"

Huber ran a hand back and forth over his short, spiky red hair. Bailey was learning that this gesture was Huber's way of saying that to give a full answer to the question just put to him would require an hour-long lecture describing innumerable technical considerations, pro and con. Thus, she knew, he was going to deliver a short answer that didn't please him. "It's night there, so you're not going to see anything in ordinary light. But the infrared should show a blob or two where the buildings are grouped, depending on how well insulated the roofs are. And if the general was serious about a . . . nuclear explosion, you'll have no trouble picking up a crater. No trouble."

A green indicator light flashed above one of the six flat-screen computer displays angled up from Bailey's situation panel. They each had an image area the size of a fourteen-inch, old-fashioned television tube, but they were only three inches thick. Within the next five years, there wouldn't be a single television vacuum-picture-tube in service anywhere in the American military. "There you go," Huber said.

A NOAA access code printed out across the bottom of the screen and a black-and-white image of the bottom of the world began to spray across the top. According to the coordinates shown, the terminator marking the division between night and day was running along the Antarctic Peninsula—the long finger of land extending from the continent's near-circular shape toward the tip of South America. That put the Ross Sea region in the middle of night.

"They're putting out a lot of light," Huber said.

Bailey didn't know what he meant. "Who?"

"McMurdo." Huber reached past Bailey to tap his finger on the display. Deep in the shadow area, she saw a small blob of white. "That's them."

"You sure that's light from the station?"

Huber shot a quick glance at her, knowing what she meant. "Major, the odds of this satellite taking a picture of the region at the *exact second* a bomb went off is . . . improbable." He straightened up and folded his arms across his narrow chest. "Wait for the update . . ."

Just then, the next image, taken one minute after the first, showed the same blob of light in the same position. It had not been a nuclear fireball.

Bailey activated her SVTS link to the NMCC and waited for General Abbott's aide, the detail-obsessed Lieutenant Yoshii, to bring her into synch. A moment later, the general appeared on the far-left screen. Wherever the teleconference cameras had been mounted in Abbott's emergency action room, Bailey thought their placement certainly didn't flatter the general. The extreme downward camera angles made it look as if she were peering down at someone whose extraordinarily large head was perched on an absurdly small body.

"General Abbott, we've just started receiving the NOAA images. The first in the series should be coming on your ETEM now." Bailey watched Abbott watching his map board. "That point of light at four o'clock is from the building lights at McMurdo."

On the screen, Abbott scratched at his jaw. "What is the curved line starting just east of the light?"

Bailey studied her screen. She couldn't see any line, curved or otherwise, near the lights of McMurdo. "Just a moment, sir. These are raw data. We'll clean them up." Bailey looked at Huber, silently asking him what was going on.

Huber adjusted some of her controls, changing the contrast on the image. There *was* a curve there, starting right beside the station, extending to the southeast. "We have it, sir. Should have an ID in a moment."

Bailey mouthed the word *Clouds?* at Huber.

Huber brought up the second image on another screen, adjusted its contrast, too. The curve was there again, and it had changed, becoming slightly thicker.

Bailey knew she couldn't keep the general waiting. She guessed that, to him, any information was better than none. "Sir, here comes the second visible-spectrum image. Our preliminary analysis suggests the curve is a high-altitude cloud formation, maybe picking up backscatter from the moon. We're working on it."

Another NOAA screen came up, on a fourth display screen, displacing the weather-radar image Bailey had called up for San Diego. She'd promised her parents she'd keep them informed about the chance of rain on Thanksgiving.

"Here comes the infrared," Huber said. Then he added, "Holy shit."

Bailey switched off her station mike. "Commander, you'd better give me something better to say to the general than 'Holy shit,' because I am not saying that to him."

Huber's fingers flew across the controls. Bailey saw the infrared image from the satellite suddenly expand on the wall map. The satellite's IR capability was used to study cloud patterns, and the false colors assigned to all the different levels of temperature readings made the top half of the image, the sunlit side of Antarctica, a garish combination of blue, yellow, and red. The bottom half of the image, the night side, was mostly blue, except for a green curve and several blobs of yellow and red at the location where the visible-light image had shown only one.

"That's a volcano," Huber said. "That big red blob to the north of the others. Very distinctive heat signature. A full eruption."

Bailey toggled her mike back on, hoping for the best. "General, we're looking at an infrared image now, and my analyst believes a volcano has erupted near the station." She chewed her lip. "Sir, *is* there a known volcano near the station?"

"That's affirmative, Major. Mount Erebus. Last minor eruption was ninety-three. Does your analyst know if the curved clouds are related to the eruption?"

Huber looked at Bailey. "I don't know the geology down there, but if the ejecta went high enough, we could be looking at volcanic gases being transported through the upper atmosphere. Why they're curved like that, like they're in a jet stream or something, I don't know."

Bailey passed the analysis on to the general. He didn't seem troubled by it. "I suppose that could have had something to do with interrupting a transmission, correct, Major?"

Bailey wasn't sure what Abbott was after, but she allowed as how the sudden active status of a volcano next door might make her think of relocating to a safer location before attempting to establish radio contact.

"Major," General Abbott said, "is your analyst at hand?"

Bailey looked at Huber. He wasn't going anywhere. "Yes, sir."

"Is there any sign of explosive damage near the station?"

Huber fiddled with more controls as Bailey commanded the small, teleconference camera to turn toward the commander.

Huber glanced rapidly back and forth from the camera to the wall display. "Hard to say, sir; I'm looking at the lights where the station is located and I'm seeing a lot of variation. That could be atmospheric churning, or it could be fires. These pictures should really go to NPIC."

Inwardly, Bailey winced. The National Photographic Interpretation Center was part of the CIA. No one in the military liked working with them.

"That won't be necessary," Abbott said. "The Blackbird mission is a go and we should have more definitive images within the next three hours. In the meantime, I thank you, Major. You've provided considerable information. I'll inform the ANG Air Wing at Christchurch that they should gear up for a relief mission to McMurdo, in case that eruption is serious."

Bailey was surprised that her involvement in the situation at McMurdo was ending so soon. "Do you need additional follow-up, General?"

"I'll be relying on SPACECOM to relay the Blackbird's data when it arrives McMurdo. Until then, unless you can come up with some way to observe the station, you're on standby."

"Understood, General. SPACECOM ESC standing by for acquisition of Blackbird transmission."

Bailey watched the general give a signal to someone offscreen, probably Yoshii, then the screen went dark, displaying only the words NMCC STANDING BY.

Bailey glanced up at Huber, sharing with him the letdown of the anticlimactic end to what had promised to be an intriguing round of work. "And that is that." She reached for her tea mug and grimaced as she lifted out the tea bag, knowing the drink was already oversteeped. Then she realized that Huber was fixated on the control floor's wall map display, fifty feet away.

The second NOAA infrared image was frozen on the screen, only half the picture painted. Bailey watched for several seconds. The image did not continue to grow. "What's the holdup?"

"We lost the signal," Huber said.

Bailey raised her eyebrows. "My cable company loses the signal. This is Space Command."

Huber typed instructions into the small section of Bailey's situation panel that was a keyboard. He pointed to the data that printed out on yet another of the six screens. "There. LOS. Loss of signal."

"We didn't lose the satellite."

"I'm not saying you did. What I am saying is that the satellite stopped transmitting." Huber tapped the screen. "Says so right there."

Bailey stared at the control room's huge wall display. The section of the display that showed the NOAA image was clear, no sign of trouble. But the satellite weather photo remained incomplete.

"Can we talk to it?" Bailey asked.

Huber touched a readout window on her situation panel. "The ATAMS's been trying for the past six minutes."

Bailey knew the Automated Tracking and Monitoring System was the heart of the Space Surveillance Center. There were too many objects in orbit for the human mind to keep track of. The possibilities for attacking North America, from space, from submarines, from bombers disguised as passenger jets, were too complex. Thus, the first layer of observation and detection had been given to machines. And the machines had responded to the NOAA glitch before Bailey had even known a problem had existed.

"It's not responding," Huber said.

Bailey was aware no satellite was perfect. That's why hundreds of millions of dollars were spent to launch "spares"—fully functional, duplicate, sleeper satellites that stayed silently in orbit, until another satellite broke down and there was no time to build and launch another. Even the sixty-six satellites of the civilian Iridium system had six spares in orbit, in anticipation of a failure rate approaching ten percent.

"Winston's Corollary," Huber said with a grin. Winston being some long-forgotten satellite engineer, second cousin to Murphy, author of the infamous Law. Winston's Corollary stated that the likelihood of a satellite's malfunctioning increased in direct proportion to the importance of the information it was about to provide.

But Bailey wasn't feeling lighthearted. She and the ESC staff were so used to dealing in the world of military satellites that they sometimes forgot about the limitations of civilian birds. "Commander Huber, what is it that might make a satellite malfunction?"

"Loss of orientation. Loss of power. Impact with a foreign body."

Bailey puzzled over the frozen image on the wall display. "A loss of orientation would have given us signal fade. The last few lines of data would have been weakened, then garbled. Loss of power, same thing—we should have been seeing a gradual decay of signal strength."

"Impact?"

"That is why we're here, Commander. If anything was going to hit that satellite, the computers would have made a collision prediction months ago."

"A meteor then?"

Bailey could see Huber was thinking like a soldier. "Add this to the equation: It was a civilian satellite. Not hardened for war."

Huber's eyes brightened. "The NEST team."

"Exactly," Bailey said. "Electromagnetic pulse from a nuclear explosion."

"Are you going to contact the general?"

Bailey knew better than to inflict her wild guesses on Command. Earlier in her shift she had refused to speculate on the possibility of a nuclear explosion. She wasn't about to now. Not without evidence. "Not yet. First, set up a task unit with Space Surveillance. I want to know if that bird is still up there. Second, I'm going to get on the gold phone to Falcon and ask for a complete status check of every operational satellite within McMurdo's horizon at the time the NOAA shutdown. Let's see if anything else was affected."

"And then?"

Bailey sipped her bitter, lukewarm tea, no longer aware of the taste or the temperature. "Then, we might be able to tell General Abbott that not only did we find that nuke he was looking for, as improbable as it might seem, we took a picture of it just as it was going off."

She shrugged at Huber, letting him know she understood the irony of her statement. It was a good way to hide the fear she felt.

Any nuclear explosion near an American facility was an act of war, one which unquestionably demanded a full and decisive response. But to Bailey, the key mission of the U.S. military was deterrence. And whenever events required that the greatest military force in the history of the world had to be used, that meant that the country which controlled that force had already failed in its mission of peace.

At the center of the most powerful and complex web of electronic surveillance in the world, Major Wilhemina Bailey went looking for a bomb, hoping she would not find it.

TWO

CLEAR DAY ONE/ROSS SEA

Shouting to Cory not to look at the flash in the night sky, Mitch Webber squeezed his own eyes tightly shut and threw the Harrier into a 4g turn, tightening the trajectory to a seemingly impossible acute angle by vectoring the craft's turbofans to 30 degrees.

Then he opened one eye to check the light reflected from the flash on the ice far below. For a moment it was as if full daylight had taken the place of night. He opened both eyes as soon as he saw the shadows pointing away from the Harrier. The fireball's light was now behind them and he and Cory could no longer be blinded. A painful dark spot floating at the edge of his vision was the only evidence of what might have been. Webber knew that even in the first microseconds of its life, a nuclear fireball could be *trillions* of times brighter than the surface of the sun. If he was lucky, the detonation had been far enough away and the afterimage would not be permanent.

Cory's voice reached him over the cockpit radio. "What was—"

Her question was cut short as a small silent flare blossomed ahead of them—the AS/350B2 helicopter had plummeted nose-first into the ice.

Next, as the radiance of the distant fireball faded, an orange helicopter spiraled downward, exploding on impact. The last UH-1N was gone.

Webber heard the fear thinning Cory's voice as she asked him why the helos had crashed.

"Electromagnetic pulse," he said, as he fought the rage he felt at the destruction Nick Young had set in motion. "It was an airburst. A thermonuclear detonation in the upper atmosphere. The helos weren't shielded for EMP."

Then he answered the question she did not ask. "We're okay. We won't crash. The Harrier's shielded." What Webber did not share with Cory was his knowledge that absolute protection from electromagnetic pulse was not a sure thing. The best shielding designs could be rendered useless by moisture, ordinary dirt, or a connection incompletely sealed. But since any EMP damage would have occurred in the first instants of the detonation, and they were still airborne, he also knew that Clear Day One's shielding had worked.

In the last of the light from the fireball, Webber saw the condition of the Ross Ice Shelf. The once-solid ice block now resembled shattered white china, thousands of fragments afloat in dark water. Webber had difficulty conceiving the force required to break up something so massive so completely.

"What . . . what's the plan?" Cory asked. His passenger's voice was almost inaudible against the all-surrounding roar of the Harrier's Rolls-Royce Pegasus 11-61 engine. Frankly, Webber was surprised she was still functioning at any level. For all her scientific knowledge and personal bravery, Cory was still an untrained civilian in a combat arena. He couldn't expect her to behave like a soldier and set aside her grief and anger at her brother's death until the mission was over. She had no part in the mission. He had to accept that she would blame him for Johnny until the time came he could bring her into the picture—if that time came. But those personal concerns were for the future. His next goal was clear.

"I have to contact Washington. Let them know what happened."

"How?"

"This plane has an emergency channel for contacting AFSAT-COM." Then Webber corrected himself, allowing for Cory's outsider status. "Air Force Satellite Communications System. It's part of a combined Air Force/Navy network. Not a lot of planes have it, but there're five satellites up there listening for us."

"Can we fly on to New Zealand?"

"Not in this plane. It's a fighter, not a transport. We'd only make it halfway. But we can land at McMurdo right after I make my report. Washington'll be sending relief teams out from Christchurch and they could use our help." To Webber, escape from McMurdo was no longer required. The worst had already happened. The relief teams would welcome anyone with knowledge of nuclear-blast and radiation effects.

Webber started to climb. The Harrier's operational service ceiling was 50,000 feet, and in the cold dense air of Antarctica he could reach that altitude in about three minutes. That would give him the widest possible horizon in which to contact a FLTSATCOM satellite. And the higher altitude would help minimize the jet's encounter with the bomb's shock wave when it arrived. He had no way of knowing how far away the detonation had occurred, but from its effect on the helicopters' engine systems, he guessed it was within ten to twenty miles.

"What about radiation?" Cory asked.

Either Cory's mind was still operating like a scientist's, Webber decided, again impressed by her resilience, or it was her way of blanking out all other thoughts. Whatever the reason, it was probably best to keep her talking and distracted.

"Minimal for now. The foothills should have protected the people on the ground from the initial burst." He tried not to think about Germer's evacuation convoy on the ice road, heading for the Williams Field airstrip. From his view of the field, there'd been nothing to stand on, and survival time in polar water could be little more than seconds. "Depends on the altitude it went off at, if it kicked up any radioactive snow or ice. And that depends on the wind, whether or not it was blowing toward . . ."

Webber stopped as he saw the error in his logic. The warhead Nick Young had been trying to deploy in the ice had been a Soviet Stiletto-class MIRV warhead, one of six carried on an SS-19 M3 ICBM. It had been removed from its reentry shroud. There was no way it could have been recovered from the ice, mated to a missile, and launched for an airburst detonation, not in such a short time. And the Stiletto only had a yield of 5.5 megatons. At twenty miles, the EMP from a low-altitude blast of that size would have been negligible. The two helicopters might have lost communications because their radio antennas would tend to attract the pulse, but their engine systems would have had enough shielding behind the helos' airframes to have survived.

"Hey, up there?" Cory prompted. "What *about* the wind?"

"Forget the wind." Webber spoke his sudden insight aloud. "Cory, there were *two* nuclear detonations. That first one, the one you thought was an earthquake. And then the airburst."

"So?"

"So, if you set off a nuclear airburst high enough, it doesn't destroy anything. All it's intended to do is spread radiation."

"Radiation bursts *kill* people, Mitchell. That's destruction to me."

"But you have to be close. And . . . there just aren't enough people in Antarctica . . . I mean, if it had gone off directly *over* McMurdo, that might make some sense."

"Maybe to you and those military sickos you work for. But not to the rest of us."

Webber didn't rise to the bait. "I didn't detonate the bombs, Cory. I'm only trying to understand the motives of the people who did."

"To make helicopters crash?" Her voice was thick with disbelief.

There were easier ways to take out helicopters, but, to Webber, Cory was on to something. *The electromagnetic pulse.* "Not to crash the helicopters," Webber said slowly. "To crash communications." The puzzle was finally resolving itself in his mind. "The second blast, the airburst, was designed to prevent anyone from knowing about the *first* one—the one in the ice. The airburst—that's the important one."

"Important for what?"

But that part of the image remained obscure. "I don't know," Webber said. "It's got to have something to do with the ice, too. But what?"

Even Cory didn't have an answer for that.

They flew the last 10,000 feet in silence, beneath a panorama of stars as dazzling and remote as the ice they illuminated. The Harrier's instruments still showed no sign of disruption from the EMP. The well-shielded aircraft had originally been designed and built by Hawker Siddeley in the 1960s, and remained the only true vertical-takeoff fighter in production. But the version Webber now flew, a two-seat modification of the McDonnell Douglas/British Aerospace AV-8B Harrier II joint project, was almost a completely different model. The British version had been designed to allow full fighter capability on the smaller aircraft carriers used by the Royal Navy, which did not support the longer runways required by traditional fighters. The second-generation Harrier II had been modified to serve the U.S. Marines. To the U.S. military leaders, carrier operations were not as important as the ability to place fighters close to the front lines. Harriers could provide quick-reaction close support by their ability to take off vertically from fields and roads.

When the Department of Energy saw that helicopters were not always fast enough to respond to the Nuclear Emergency Search Teams' requests, the AV-8B jet became the favored backup aircraft. It could cover territory at close to 700 mph, yet slow down to a hover when the radiation pods detected a likely target. While the basic model was designed to be flown by one pilot, the two-seater training version provided an already integrated passenger seat for a DOE weapons specialist dedicated to full-time surveillance. With the elimination of the Harrier's weapons packages and bomb load, the custom-built NEST Harriers had a faster speed and greater range than their combat forerunners, even with the additional weight of the second seat and passenger life-support, and the negligible mass of the radiation detectors.

The DOE had purchased four of the jets, code-named CLEAR DAY 1 through 4. Webber had never flown an active Forge mission in one, but his training in handling the challengingly responsive aircraft was paying off now.

Before he reached 50,000 feet and leveled off, he had worked through the rest of the logic of the airburst. Not only would the electromagnetic pulse generated by the atmospheric nuclear explosion have overloaded all unshielded electronic components at ground level, its effects would also reach into space. Webber doubted there was a single functioning satellite over the southern Pacific within a thousand miles of ground zero. While the military birds would be shielded, because, like the Harrier, they were specifically designed to resist and recover from EMP scintillation, it could take several hours for them to come back online and reestablish themselves within the military network.

If Webber had been designing the device used in the airburst, he knew he'd have made sure it was modified to produce the strongest possible pulse. He had read the DOE studies indicating that a single nuclear detonation at an altitude of 300 miles could shut down 90 percent of North America's telecommunications and computer-based activity in under two seconds. That particular scenario had remained the responsibility of military planners, though, because NEST hadn't identified any potential terrorist group or rogue actor with the capabilities to manufacture or steal such a powerful weapon, and then gain access to the technology required for a space launch. So far.

A great many things would change because of what had happened here, Webber knew. But *why* those things had happened still eluded him.

At 50,000 feet, Webber leveled off and began a slow circle that would keep Clear Day One close to McMurdo. His FLIR—Forward-Looking Infrared system—detected no other air traffic. As he expected, his radar was useless. It would likely take hours for the electric charge built up in the atmosphere by the EMP to bleed off enough for radar waves to function. Even though he also knew what the result would be, he activated the emergency AFSAT-COM beacon.

Nothing.

Every frequency he tried produced nothing but static.

Webber knew his best choice now was to fly out of the range of the EMP shadow and try to pick up any open channel. But he also knew that might require flying beyond the operational radius of the Harrier—700 miles out was the point of no return.

And the Harrier could not land at sea.

His other option was less optimal, but still viable. And he would not have to make a life-or-death decision for Cory.

He brought the Harrier around on a return vector to McMurdo. "We're heading back," he informed his long-silent passenger.

"What? Back where?" Cory sounded startled, confused, almost as if she had been drifting off to sleep, though Webber knew it was more likely she'd been about to pass out from exhaustion. "The airburst has screwed up all the satellites. I'm going to refuel, then try to reach a clear area."

"A clear area where?"

"I'll figure it out. How's the heat back there?"

"I'm soaked."

"Me, too," Webber said.

"Yeah, but you can take it, right? SEALs do stuff like this just for fun."

"Not for fun," he said. "Practice." The Harrier leveled out, back on course to the station. Webber began his descent. He couldn't pick up a GPS signal, so he was flying on inertial guidance only.

"How *did* you survive SEAL boot camp?" Cory asked. "Something so bad nothing could be worse, right?"

Webber regretted having said anything. But somehow he found himself still talking to her, still trying to explain, no, justify himself to her. "You tell yourself, as bad as it gets, the instructors aren't really trying to kill you. Knowing that takes most of the pressure off right away. Then, it's mostly about pain. But since it's pain that won't kill you . . . and you know what the limit is, and there's an end to it, you take it. You just keep telling yourself, it'll get better. And it does. Eventually."

They were descending through clouds and the Harrier shook slightly. But Cory didn't seem to notice the buffeting. By now, Webber hoped, she probably was beyond caring.

"Actually, after the fourth day," he went on, "nobody's even conscious. You're just running on instinct. I don't even remember the last days. I don't think I've ever met any SEAL who did."

"Why would anyone put themselves through all that on purpose?"

Finally, Webber thought, a question with a simple answer. "I wanted to fly."

"You already could. When we met, you were flying for the Navy. And what do the SEALs have to do with flying, anyway? Aren't they like, underwater commandos or something? Swimming up from submarines, blowing up shit?"

Overstressed or not, Cory's mind was up to its usual zigzagging attack. "Well, now you've just uncovered a deep dark government secret. You see, sometimes it takes SEALs to sneak into places to blow shit up. And sometimes they sneak into places to bring shit out. I was one of the guys who brought shit out."

"What kind of shit?"

There was a standard SEAL response to that kind of question— *I could tell you, but then I'd have to kill you.* Webber decided against using it. "I can't tell you, but you could probably guess."

Cory only had to think for a moment. "Airplanes. You steal airplanes for the government."

She was still sharp. That's what made it so hard for us to stay together, Webber thought. *She hates secrets.* "The word is *liberate.* Or, sometimes, *borrow and return,* or . . . this is all hypothetical, you understand."

"Mitchell, why are we having this conversation? I know your job is classified. You told me that often enough."

Webber didn't know. Was he starting to think of her as a fellow soldier? Because of what they'd gone through together on the Ice?

"I don't know," he admitted, honestly puzzled.

Clear Day One slipped through the clouds. Webber scanned the black landscape below the jet for the fiery spout of Mount Erebus. That would be his best visual landmark. He saw a red spot of light on the horizon, adjusted his course by a few degrees.

Cory asked him something else then, but Webber was concentrating on his heads-up display. Something wasn't right. The center image in the floating window of softly glowing coordinate lines, numbers, and systems readouts held the FLIR display. Toward the bottom, it was a patchwork of random mottling—the temperature pattern of the shattered ice at about 14°F against the slightly warmer sea at about 30°. The salt in the sea kept it from freezing at 32° as freshwater did.

About halfway up, he could see the even warmer signature of the land, with a few hot spots representing the burning fuel tanks at McMurdo. But at the top of the display was a solid, pale green bar, so straight it couldn't be natural—only an equipment failure could produce that reading.

"You still awake up there?"

"Just a second. I'm . . . changing over navigation. Radar might be back up now." Webber switched from FLIR to radar. Nothing. Radar still wasn't operational. Forgetting that Cory could hear him, he swore as he toggled back to FLIR, then kept shifting views between the Forward-Looking system and the Downward-Looking one.

"What's wrong?"

"I'm getting a strange reading on the infrared." The shape was vaguely familiar, but the strength of the signal return was not. In one sense, it almost looked like a weather front moving in. Sometimes radar signals could bounce off a thermal inversion layer, but infrared was generated by targets, not reflected from them.

Webber blinked as he saw the speed readout in the laser rangefinder window. What kind of inversion layer moved at 300 miles an hour?

The shock wave. That's what his instruments were reading—the wall of air created by the airburst. He checked the time display in the HUD, did the math, knew he had to be wrong. At 300 miles per hour, if the atmospheric shock wave were approaching Mc-

Murdo just now, it would mean the airburst had occurred more than a hundred miles away. Which meant the shock wave should have dissipated.

"This isn't right," Webber said.

"What isn't?" Cory demanded. Seconds passed. "Talk to me, Mitchell!"

Webber started to climb again, attempting to hit the shock wave head-on. If he tried to turn and race it, he could stall out if it caught him from behind. "Hold on," he told Cory. "We're about to hit a pocket of turbulence."

"From the airburst?"

"I don't know." The laser collision-alert chime sounded, telling Webber that impact with something solid was one minute away.

Solid?

He forced the Harrier into a steeper climb for a few seconds but no longer, not wanting to present too broad a surface for the shock wave when it hit.

"What's that sound, Mitchell? There's a little red light back here that says 'collision alert.' Is that a collision-alert sound?"

"C'mon, Cory, we're at two thousand feet." He spoke sharply to cut her off, but, to be fair, nothing was making sense, not even to him. Then the top edge of the bar appeared in the display window. Whatever was coming at them had a top—sharp and clearly defined. The collision alert stopped chiming. Webber checked the display again. The green bar was still moving.

"The little light went out. Guess you knew that."

"Thank you," Webber said. He frowned, deep in thought.

The Harrier was coming toward McMurdo from the northwest, about five miles out. At his current airspeed they'd be over the station in less than a minute. Webber magnified the FLIR display. He could just make out the shapes of the fuel tanks, the buildings, and even the small vertical smears that represented the base personnel milling about near the shore.

Showing a temperature of 212°, the green bar approached McMurdo from the southeast. Even the temperature reading made no sense. No nuclear bomb could create a firestorm out of ice. And a firestorm would show temperatures above a thousand degrees, not a reading just at the boiling point of—

"*Water*," Webber exclaimed. "Cory, can a wall of water be a thousand feet high?"

"No—it's impossible under normal weather conditions. Maximum height's a hundred and ninety-eight feet. Water can't support its own weight above that height. It—"

On Webber's display, the green bar swept over McMurdo and the station was gone in an eyeblink. No fires, no buildings, no people. Only smooth land, radiating at 50°.

A swift-moving wall of air hit the Harrier and it shot straight up, as if ejected from a cannon. Webber heard Cory's body slam hard against her seat as he fought the unresponsive controls, the jet shaking like a child's rattle. Every alarm in the cockpit chimed, every emergency light flashed.

Then the Harrier stalled, forward speed completely lost, the plane's aerodynamic capabilities now like that of a dropped brick.

The plane was drawn, tail-first, into a death spiral, pushing Webber up from his seat and against his restraints. He could feel himself growing dizzy. He couldn't focus on the instruments or the HUD. He grabbed the stick with his left hand, pushing it forward to bring the nose down, while at the same time adjusting the turbofan vector to match the angle of the fall.

At one thousand feet, the Harrier slowed, hung for a moment, then pitched sharply forward. Webber was jammed backward into his seat now, but an uncontrolled nosedive was a simpler trajectory to recover from than a tail-drop. By 800 feet, the Harrier was his again.

Cory threw up behind him.

"Sorry about that," he said.

She gasped something back at him. The beginning was unintelligible. But it ended with a question. " . . . the hell was that?"

"What *we* hit was turbulence. But something else hit McMurdo." Webber brought the Harrier back on course for another flyover of the station, now from the southeast. This time, the FLIR gave him a glimpse of the landscape beyond the wave—or whatever it was— that had passed. But all was flat, no sign of ice, only featureless seawater. Water with a surface temperature close to 80°.

"That wasn't a wave," Cory said as she coughed, half-choked. The air in the cockpit was suddenly acrid.

"There're two display screens in front of you, right in the middle. See them?"

"Yeah."

"By the upper right corner of the right-hand screen, there's a switch marked FLIR."

"Found it."

"Push it on."

"What does it do?"

Webber slowed the Harrier. "Just push it, will you? Then you'll see what I can see."

"Okay. I see it. Green and blurry, right? Like infrared?"

"It is infrared. See what's on the screen now?"

"Yeah."

"That's McMurdo. One minute ago, I could see the fuel tanks, buildings, even people. Now there's nothing."

"There's something wrong with the system. Look for the *Fernando Pereira* or the *Palmer*. They have to be down there somewhere."

But Webber could hear the hesitation in Cory's voice. He pulled back on the magnification as they approached, so Cory could see the shoreline. "Recognize the terrain? See Hut Point?"

McMurdo slipped off the screen before Cory spoke again. "It wasn't a wave."

"Well, it was something," Webber said. "I'm switching to a forward view. Check the display. It should still be—there!"

The bar was there again, this time moving away from the Harrier.

"Give me the stats, Mitchell."

Webber translated the readings from the instruments. "Solid, four hundred feet high, absolute speed in excess of three hundred miles per hour . . . from horizon to horizon."

"It *can't* be a wave . . . unless . . . oh, Mitchell . . . oh, God . . . I know what's happened. The Ice Shelf . . . it's collapsed. The ships are gone."

Webber didn't understand the ultimate ramifications of Cory's pronouncement. But he did understand that if the Shelf had collapsed, that collapse wasn't natural.

"How far can that wave go?"

"It *can't* be a wave! At least, not like—"

"Don't keep telling me what it can't be! I can see it. It's right there in front of us! How far?"

"Uh . . . storms down here . . . Antarctic storms, they've sent waves up to Hawaii. Forty-foot breakers. But if the whole Shelf's dropped, something that big, with the water displacement—the energy alone—it could get to Alaska. And every place in between."

Almost a thousand people dead already. The Harrier's engine screamed as Webber applied full power. If Cory was right, the entire Pacific Rim was at risk.

"What are you doing?" Cory asked.

"That wave's moving at three hundred miles per hour. We can do seven hundred. We've got to pass it, get out of the EMP shadow, and warn . . . warn the world."

He was gaining on the wave. The dark sea behind it was unnaturally smooth.

Against the growing whine of the engine, Cory's voice sounded unnaturally calm. "And then what? You said we couldn't reach New Zealand. After we warn everyone, where do we land?"

"We don't," he said. There was silence behind him.

Once again, there was only the mission and, in ninety-two minutes, certain death in the sea.

EVENT MINUS ZERO

The physics were simple: The Ross Ice Shelf moved down, all at once, into the Ross Sea beneath it. With nowhere for the sea to escape, the kinetic energy of 7,000,000,000 tons of ice moving at 300 mph was transformed into heat.

The seawater changed to steam in less than a second. The steam escaped at supersonic velocities through the fissures that had separated the Shelf from the land. Shooting miles into the glacial air, the steam became geysers of ice crystals and formed a billowing, cloudlike curtain that followed the curve of the sea, just at the limits of resolution of the NOAA satellite that passed overhead.

But where there were no fissure outlets, the superheated seawater endured such pressure that even as its temperature rose past the boiling point, the force of the descending Ice Shelf caused the water to remain liquid, and the scalding liquid became a reservoir of energy seeking release.

And because that reservoir was contained to the east, south, and west by the land, only one release was possible.

To the north. Open ocean.

Like the expanding gases in a gun barrel, the superheated seawater beneath the collapsing Shelf shot forward, and the energy stored as heat was once again released as motion.

A liquid wall bulged from the mouth of the sea—a displacement wave of 3,250,000,000 tons of water, 500 miles long, 350 feet thick, rising 1,400 feet in just over eight seconds.

The displacement wave was not as perfect as theory or computer models might predict. It was lower in places where the sea was shallower, or where the descending Shelf had shattered instead of remaining whole, and thus reduced the concentration of the energy released. But over its 500-mile length, the variations were minor. The displacement wave was sufficient in size to initiate the next stages of the process, and that was all that mattered.

The sudden release of pressure that had created the displacement wave transformed almost 20 percent of the collapsing Shelf's energy into sound. Vaporizing the top two inches of water for the first eight miles of its path, the sound blasted through the ocean at 3,400 mph, killing every living fish, bird, and mammal in the first 100 miles.

The sound of that gunshot would reach Hawaii in two hours, its cause at first a mystery. It would echo around the world for days.

But before that sound had even traveled its first mile, the 1,400-foot-high displacement wave of water began to collapse.

The wall took nine seconds to fall. The titanic impact deformed the sea bottom where it struck, setting off seismic waves that over the next six hours would confound observers at the more than 10,000 seismic stations around the world.

Then the kinetic energy of the collapsing displacement wave met the final burst of steam from the superheated seawater escaping the Shelf. Now the two pulses of monumental energy—heat and motion—their movements timed by gravity and the precision of the Shelf's collapse, met and merged at the mouth of the Ross Sea, and became a whole greater than the sum of the parts.

It took two minutes for the two energy systems to fall into perfect step.

Time enough for an 800-foot wave to wipe McMurdo Station from existence.

Time enough for the moving mass of water to seek the equilibrium mandated by gravity and the sea's own density, as it diminished to the maximum height that ordinary physics could support.

Five hundred and ten seconds after the initial displacement wave had appeared, a solitary wave radiated northward from the mouth of the sea to the open ocean. Like a single ripple in a pond.

A wave 190 feet tall. Its speed, 200 miles per hour.

And unlike waves formed by wind and storm, this one was self-sustaining. It would move endlessly forward to fill the trough that formed before it.

Though it moved through the water, and the water rose with it in response, it was not a wave of water. It was a wave of energy, and it had many names. In the language of sailors, it was a freak wave, a rogue. In the language of oceanographers, it was a gravity wave. In the language of physics, a soliton. But all of its names described the same phenomenon.

What now spread across the ocean was a wave that would not lose momentum or power. It would not crest, or break, or in any way slow down.

Until it hit something other than water.

The wave would reach New Zealand in ten hours. Hawaii, in thirty-five. Japan, thirty-eight. California, forty.

The dead would number in the millions.

The economic devastation would take decades to reverse.

Because no one knew what was coming except those who set it in motion.

Or so they had planned.

THREE

USSPACECOM/EARTH SURVEILLANCE CENTER/CHEYENNE MOUNTAIN

The first entry in the catalog of Earth-orbiting objects maintained by the Space Surveillance Center of USSPACECOM was the Soviet Union's *Sputnik I*, launched in 1957. Over the next 43 years, more than 22,000 additional entries had been made. Of those, and the ones added in the first years of the new century, on this Thanksgiving morning 7,437 objects remained in orbit.

The vast majority were classified as debris—spent boosters, launch hardware, dead satellites. Ten were individual metal screws, each one-eighth of an inch in diameter, ejected from the space shuttle in 1984. One was a glove that floated out an open hatch on *Gemini 4* almost twenty years earlier. And at any one time, a handful were labeled Anomalous Orbital Objects. Three or four of those had been tentatively linked to failed Soviet missions, including the notorious Object 221. But most AO2s corresponded to no known launches, were small and dark enough to be difficult to observe in detail from the ground, and inexplicably disappeared from their orbital tracks on those few times when a space shuttle attempted to move within viewing range. They were objects that were not officially discussed outside the multi-ton blast doors of Colorado's Cheyenne Mountain.

But Major Bailey's concern this early morning was the 116 government-operated, unclassified satellites that were the basis of America's, and a good part of the world's, communications, weather-monitoring, mapping, and environmental-assessment infrastructure. Slowly, and without anyone noticing it, the United States had become a space-based society.

Though the orbits of all 7,437 objects were known to the SSC's computers, the objects themselves were not subject to constant tracking. Instead, Earth orbital space was constantly "sampled" by the sensor stations of the U.S. Space Surveillance Network around the world. The phased array radar at Elgin AFB alone could provide up to 10,000 observations each day, though only of those objects within its observational horizon.

When objects were detected, contact information was forwarded to the SSC in Cheyenne Mountain, and to its backup facility, the Alternate Space Surveillance Center, in Dahlgren, Virginia. There, computer systems independently matched the objects to established orbits and updated path predictions, assessing the chances for reentry or collision.

Now, seventy minutes after the failure of NOAA-20 in mid-transmission of its image of the Ross Sea region, Bailey waited in her underground control center for confirmation from Hawaii's MOTIF—Maui Optical Tracking and Identification Facility—that the satellite still existed. MOTIF's dual telescopes, with the capability of tracking objects in both near- and deep-space orbits, would be able to locate NOAA-20 by passive infrared radiation. Other, more precise methods of tracking satellites were also available to Bailey, among them the SSN's CROSS and PAVE PAWS tracking stations. But it would be hours before NOAA-20 came within range of any of those facilities. And tonight, she knew, speed was of the essence.

Commander Dominic Huber waited at her side. Both officers stared across the darkened Earth Surveillance Center operations room as they waited for MOTIF's results to go up on the wall display. For now, a small red dot followed the orbital track predicted for NOAA-20. The color red indicated that it was not under active contact.

The dot reached the yellow circle that defined MOTIF's optimum observational range. Because it was a passive surveillance station, MOTIF was limited by clouds, winds, humidity, and the brightness of the moon. The station's actual observational range varied from night to night, sometimes hour to hour.

The red dot moved farther into the circle.

On one of the six small screens angled up from Bailey's situation panel, a realtime television feed from MOTIF was being processed by SSC computers. Stars were automatically dropped from the image, which resembled a constantly shifting field of dark patches sliding over each other—the random visual noise of a highly magnified empty section of sky.

The other screens carried automatic update reports from the systems and diagnostic tests Bailey had requested be run on the military communications nets, including NATO III, FLTSATCOM, DSCS, and the Milstar components. So far, no obvious problems had been detected, though few of those assets were involved with communications from the extreme polar regions. Except for meteorological purposes, the icy expanses of the North and South Poles were simply dead zones that satellites passed over on their way to fulfill their real functions above Europe, Asia, and North and South America.

When Bailey had sent her Action Message to request a full system test, General Jaime Gutierrez, commander, AFSPACECOM at Falcon AFB, had explained that he was not about to interrupt all satellite communications based on *suspicions*. Unless she could come back to him with something concrete, that is, direct evidence that a nuclear event had taken place in Antarctica, he would pass her request through channels, incorporating the diagnostics into regular operations. Bailey could expect a full systems-integrity report to be available to her within thirty hours.

Then a thin white streak appeared at the bottom of the MOTIF screen. Bailey snapped her fingers. "That's it."

On the wall display, the red dot changed to blue—positive contact had been made.

"We've got a dead bird," Bailey said.

Huber had the Operations Manual in his hand, a finger marking the section where EMP Recovery Procedures were listed. He opened the thick binder and placed it on the fold-out desk surface beside Bailey's panel.

Bailey scanned the contents list—all four pages. She looked up at Huber. "There's nothing listed for polar incidents."

Huber frowned. "There has to be something for the Arctic. That's where Soviet missiles would have come from in the Cold War. EMP over the Arctic was a precursor to missile launch."

Bailey spun the manual around. "You check it."

As Huber paged through the index, Bailey activated the standby SVTS link to the NMCC. She was certain when she told General Abbott she had a dead bird showing every indication it had been burned out by EMP, he would light a fire under the AFSPACECOM commander and get her the system check she needed *now*. Most military satellites would recover from scintillation effects, and if she could get a listing of which satellites had been affected and how long their recovery had taken, she'd be able to confirm the site of the blast.

"Here's the problem," Huber said. He pointed to the cover sheet. "Last update was July. Russia isn't a bad guy anymore. The polar launch scenarios have been obsoleted."

Bailey could think of a few more things she'd change in the Air Force when she became a general. One of them was the vocabulary. "That's not a real word."

"Works for me. They're not in the manual."

"Where would they be?"

"I'll call them up in the archives."

Huber was already halfway down the stairs as Lieutenant Yoshii appeared on the SVTS feed.

"Lieutenant," Bailey said, "I need to speak with General Abbott at once."

"The general is not in the room. I'll track him down."

Bailey decided to let it all hit the fan. "When you find him, Lieutenant, let him know that I believe we're looking at a SNAP BLUE scenario."

Yoshii's surprise flickered across her face for a moment, but she quickly and professionally recovered. "He'll want confirmation."

"That's why I'm calling. I'll stand by."

Bailey shut off her station mike, then picked up her secure phone to contact Falcon one more time. There were four SNAP scenarios in the Department of Energy's current training procedures to stop nuclear terrorism—RED, GREEN, BLACK, and WHITE. Then there was the fifth SNAP scenario that was used when the first four had failed.

SNAP BLUE meant the terrorist weapon had already detonated.

If that didn't get the attention of the AFSATCOM commander, she'd have to start wondering whose side he was on.

NATIONAL MILITARY COMMAND CENTER/THE PENTAGON

General Abbott could feel himself gearing down from the evening's earlier excitement. It was apparent what had happened in Antarctica, and after the late-night pizza had been demolished by his adrenaline-drained staff in the EAR, he had cut his Crisis Action Team in half. Those personnel who remained were now on the watch floor, working directly with the New York Air National Guard 109th Air Wing in Christchurch, New Zealand, to coordinate the relief mission that would be necessary.

For his part, Abbott had forwarded a brief report to the Office of the Secretary of Defense, which would in turn condense it to a single sentence for the President's next daily brief in Berlin.

Abbott's report stated that operations of the United States Antarctic Program at McMurdo Station, including the activities of NEST 1 and NEST 2, had been interrupted by the eruption of Mount Erebus, an active volcano. Terrorist involvement related to the NEST mission was judged extremely unlikely. A Blackbird SR-71 would overfly the station by 0400 GPS and provide realtime assessment of the damage. An LC-130 Hercules transport loaded with pallets of emergency supplies had already been scrambled from Christchurch with a KC-135 refueling tanker and would arrive McMurdo in seven hours. If landing facilities were not operational at either of the station's two airstrips, the supplies could be air-dropped and the Hercules would continue to the Amundsen-Scott base at the South Pole. In the meantime, four additional transports and their refueling tankers were standing by at Christchurch for the Blackbird intelligence. Once the station's immediate needs had been determined, the transports would be loaded and airborne within two hours, arriving McMurdo eight hours later. Thus, full relief was expected to be provided within fourteen hours of the time the eruption had first been noticed.

That precisely outlined schedule brought an intense feeling of satisfaction to Abbott. American personnel had been put in harm's way almost 10,000 miles from Washington, D.C., and in less than a day all their needs would be met. It was what the U.S. military did so well—anticipate, train, and respond. Its incredible bureaucracy ensured that no emergency would ever be faced by personnel wondering what to do. All possible actions and reactions had already been defined and rehearsed, so that all that was left to do in any crisis was take action.

But with McMurdo dealt with, taking action of a different sort was what Abbott was concerned with now. He was downstairs in the NMCC, in the facility's small mess room, sharing another cup of coffee with Major Prospero Chennault. The major had briefed his section leader at the DIA on Abbott's concerns that the NEST mission in Antarctica was merely a diversionary operation.

"What was his response?" Abbott asked.

"He wouldn't confirm or deny."

The two officers sat in a corner of the mess room, the only staff present. Here, the tables were plastic laminate, with fake wood-grain designs. The chairs were bright orange and silver metal. Food service this evening was provided by a wall of dispensing machines offering plastic-wrapped turkey sandwiches, candy bars, powdered coffee and hot chocolate, and individual servings of soup that could be placed in the small microwave oven next to the self-serve napkins and utensils. In keeping with a long-standing Pentagon tradition, the food service in the building remained uninspiring.

"That's confirmation," Abbott said. "If I was wrong, he would have said so."

"General, I can't speculate. I have to go with what he said."

"And that was all?"

Chennault glanced around the mess room, making sure they were still alone. "I am cleared to tell you about SHAARP. The section leader said it might have a bearing on Antarctic operations."

Abbott kept his expression neutral. "In terms of communications or the NEST mission?"

"Communications."

Abbott concealed his disappointment as well as he had his interest. He had been developing a scenario that postulated a terrorist attack on a secret military installation at the South Pole. Supplying troops there would have been an intriguing logistical problem, and he had reviewed the assets of the 109th Air Wing with that in mind.

"So what have we got down there?" Abbott asked. "A tunnel to the center of the Earth?"

Chennault sipped his coffee. "Have you heard of Project HAARP?"

Abbott nodded, surprised the explanation was that obvious. "High-frequency Active Auroral Research Program?"

Chennault nodded.

"And SHAARP would be the *Southern* High-frequency, etcetera?"

"That's it," Chennault said. "Top Secret. Need-to-know only. You'll get a formal briefing and background papers next week."

Abbott had been hoping for something more exotic. He had already read a briefing paper on the HAARP project, an immensely powerful microwave transmitter operating outside of Gakona, Alaska. Certain test broadcasts from the transmitter could interrupt normal radio communications and interfere with aircraft navigation systems, so operational tests were carefully scheduled, and all military commands with activities in Alaska and the surrounding regions were alerted beforehand.

But there was some controversy surrounding the project. Despite the innocuous and unclassified name, the members of the public who perversely delighted in finding conspiracies behind all military activities claimed that HAARP was everything from a weapon to be used against attacking flying saucers, to a device to manipulate weather, or even a transmitter to control people's thoughts. But according to the briefing paper, it was an over-the-horizon radar installation which had still to be perfected, even though the day it became operational it would be in violation of the START II treaty.

As Abbott understood the project, microwaves could be selectively tuned to reflect from ionized regions in the upper atmosphere to reach over the horizon. But still to be solved were the technological requirements of detecting the returning microwaves and using them to build an image of whatever reflected them back to the ionized region.

"So, tell me, why do we need over-the-horizon radar at the South Pole?" Abbott prepared himself for a boring dissertation.

But Chennault glanced away, lowering his voice. "That's just the cover story."

Abbott leaned forward, berating himself. He knew how to identify a cover story. They contained too much information, usually consisting of extensive detail. The HAARP briefing paper had been properly vague. It hadn't even been classified. And Abbott had fallen for it.

"*Are* we shooting down flying saucers?" he asked.

Almost nervous, Chennault pressed on without the hint of a return smile. "In a nutshell, it's theoretically possible to short-circuit parts of the Earth's magnetic field. That's why we need two HAARP installations. One near the north magnetic pole. One near the south. When the two installations come on at the same time, and atmospheric conditions are right, they establish a current in the magnetosphere. Not strong, but if a number of factors are adjusted for, the current creates phase interference, producing a band, north to south, in which the magnetic field is, in effect, switched off."

Abbott was out of his depth. He understood that perturbations in the magnetic field could play havoc with radio, but there were simpler and more precise ways to interfere with an enemy's lines of communications. "And what, exactly, is the point of this process?" He had a sudden, exciting flash of inspiration. "*Is* it weather control?"

But Chennault shook his head. "The Earth's magnetic field is what protects us from cosmic and solar radiation. And you know what happens when an energetic solar flare is powerful enough to punch through the magnetic field and hit the Earth."

In the NMCC mirror sites, Abbott had fought war-game scenarios in which solar flares suddenly disrupted vital communications links, cutting off all units from command. He was well aware of their effects. "Power grids overload. Satellites fade. Radio frequencies are smeared by interference. It's like a small electromagnetic pulse."

Chennault nodded. "That's the point. What if we could selectively turn off a region of the magnetic field that stretched, for example, north to south over Iraq? Or Korea? Every power grid shut down. Every computer disabled. Every form of electromagnetic communication useless. It *is* the equivalent of EMP. But without a weapon being fired. Without a single soldier's life at risk. Without any American presence within thousands of miles of hostile territory. And . . . as long as the technology remains classified, the event is indistinguishable from a random natural occurrence."

Abbott was staggered. He whistled softly. "Does anyone else have it?"

"For the moment, no. The Soviets never believed in it. China appears to have a single test facility capable of generating microwaves of the appropriate power, but they could actually be experimenting with over-the-horizon radar. Maybe in twenty years they'll figure it out. But for right now, we're the only ones who can afford it, so we've got a lock."

Twenty years, Abbott thought. Just about when he predicted China would feel ready to take on the U.S. That made the next question the most important. "Is it operational?"

"The tests show that the field *can* be switched off. The trick is to control the size of the affected region. Right now, if we tried to hit North Korea, we'd certainly hit South Korea as well. Maybe even Japan. Same for Iraq. We could nail Baghdad, but we'd probably hit Israel, and we'd definitely hit Saudi Arabia and Turkey. In a 'High Noon' scenario, if we were going up against the old Soviet Union, say, all or nothing for the world, then that kind of collateral damage wouldn't be important. We could take out every missile and bomber over hundreds of thousands of square miles. But for regional conflicts, we need to be able to focus the effect much more precisely."

Chennault shook his head as if scarcely believing the system he described. "Theoretically, they think it'll be possible to refine the focus to the point where they'll be able to target individual aircraft in transit. Can you imagine?"

Abbott wanted to. Desperately. America would have a weapon that could reach around the world and take out its enemies without having to fire a shot. It was breathtaking. An entirely new concept of war. And it also made it perfectly clear to Abbott why there was so much concern at the DIA over unanticipated problems in Antarctica. A nuclear explosion there was of no importance to anyone. But the possibility that Project SHAARP might "go white"—be exposed—would mean that America could lose the biggest tactical advantage of the century.

"That's . . . incredible." Abbott had no other words to describe it.

"And I think it explains why the SHADOW FORGE briefing book was sanitized. A lot of people read NEST deployment reports, and SHAARP would have been prominently listed as a critical asset in the target area. Same thing for that sub contact with the ocean liner. Thousands of personnel would have become involved. Secrecy would be compromised."

Chennault drained the last of his coffee and crumpled the paper cup. "Sometimes I think we have too many secrets. Too many compartments. We'll end up not being able to talk to each other at all." He stood up. "Anyway, General, if you don't mind, this marks the end of my day."

Abbott stood also. Chennault's abruptness disturbed him. The only extenuating circumstance he could think of was that the major had someplace else he'd rather be this Thanksgiving. "Are you spending the holiday with family?"

Chennault frowned as if to dismiss any further questions. "Not this year. What about you?"

"No. I'll be spending it here."

"Ever vigilant."

Abbott noted the tone Chennault was using. It seemed almost veiled criticism. But before he could comment on it, the wall phone across the room rang. It was for internal messaging only. Abbott nodded at Chennault, indicating that the major should answer it.

But Chennault shook his head, making no effort to move. "You're the one with the smart badge, sir. It'll be for you."

The major's behavior wasn't quite insubordination, so Abbott let it go. He answered the phone himself. It was Yoshii.

"Sir, I have Major Bailey on the board. She's calling a SNAP BLUE."

Abbott reacted as unemotionally as if this were a tactical exercise. "I take it she means at McMurdo?"

"Yes, sir."

"And she has some evidence?"

"She'd better," Yoshii said. "She's about to give a Flash Alert to General Gutierrez at AFSATCOM. She says she has evidence of EMP."

"No." Abbott gave the command at once. "You tell Major Bailey I am ordering her to sit on this until I've spoken with her and reviewed her evidence myself. I'm on my way."

As Yoshii confirmed the order, Abbott beckoned to Chennault. "How much would someone in Major Bailey's position know about SHAARP?" Abbott asked, as he hung up the wall phone.

"The cover story. A classified radar installation that can occasionally disrupt communications. She has to know that for her job."

"Then you're with me," Abbott said, leading the way to the door. "The major's about to call too much attention to McMurdo. You and I are going to change her mind."

FOUR

CLEAR DAY ONE/OPEN OCEAN/900 MILES NORTH OF McMURDO

"Mayday, mayday, mayday . . . this is Clear Day One out of McMurdo . . . any station . . ."

The entire radio spectrum was still a sea of static and the Harrier II had less than twelve minutes of fuel remaining, good for perhaps another 140 miles. Mitch Webber told himself the EMP shadow would end before then. It had to. If not, he and Cory would die for nothing.

Webber reset the radio controls to begin on the emergency-beacon frequencies again, watching the small, glowing green window of the signal-strength indicator for any sign of clearing. The stars hung brilliantly around and above him. Far below there was only pale moonlight on dense clouds. The dark sea was hidden, though its presence was certain and inescapable.

"It's beautiful up here," Cory said. Her voice sounded almost serene in Webber's helmet speakers. She hadn't said much since he had explained what he had to do, what that meant about their survival. He didn't know if her silence was a sign of acceptance, or defeat.

But as he looked out through the cockpit, at the vista of stars that filled the horizon, he knew what she meant. "On a night without a moon, the stars go on forever. You see colors in them. Solid, intense . . ."

"This is why you want to fly, isn't it?"

"Part of it." Webber kept his eyes fixed on the indicator. He *had* to get out at least one message. The world had to know what was behind them, racing forward at 200 miles an hour. He tried again. "Mayday, mayday, mayday . . . this is Clear Day One out of McMurdo . . . any station . . ."

"You ask most people about what flying means and I bet all they think of is being squashed into coach, eating bad food, and staring through a scratched-up bit of Plexiglas. Not very romantic. Or inspiring."

"That's not flying," Webber said. "That's transportation." *Nothing.* He set the radio back to the beginning again, started cycling. At the same time he toggled on the radar, searching for other air traffic. But even here, almost a thousand miles from McMurdo, he was still flying through the ionized region created by the airburst. *A second airburst,* he thought. *Extremely high altitude. Salted with something to increase the gamma count.* The technical answers for what had happened could be solved easily enough. But the most important question for Webber still wasn't one physics or engineering could answer; it was why Nick Young had done this.

"What will it be like?" Cory asked suddenly. "When we hit?"

From 50,000 feet, in an unpowered controlled dive, Webber knew they'd impact the ocean at at least 300 miles per hour. At that speed there was no difference between water and the side of a mountain. But it was better than trying to ditch and spending their last few moments of consciousness drowning in freezing water. Of the two options—dying quickly and dying slowly—Webber preferred the first.

"We'll be going too fast. We'll never know."

"Well, you may be jackass-stubborn, insensitive, and selfish, but at least you're honest. You always were."

"Glad you saw something in me."

"You having *any* luck up there?"

"Nope. This isn't like anything I've ever read about coming from a low-altitude burst. I'm thinking there must have been a second airburst. Something specifically designed to create an intense EMP." He delivered his mayday again.

"We only saw one flash."

"That was the one that was close to the ground. If it was intense enough, we might even have seen an atmospheric reflection from a detonation point past the horizon."

"Reflected from what?"

"Ice crystals suspended in the air. They can act like a prism in Antarctica. That's what makes sun dogs and mirages down here."

"Was it worth it?"

Webber watched the signal-strength indicator for a few seconds before he realized that Cory had changed the subject. "What?"

"Bringing nuclear weapons to Antarctica."

Webber felt a rush of instant anger well up in him so quickly he almost didn't contain it in time. In ten minutes, their fuel would be gone. In thirteen minutes, they'd be a slick of fragmented debris spread out over a quarter square mile of ocean, erased from the world and history. He didn't intend to go out arguing. "For the last time, I didn't take them there, Cory. The U.S. had nothing to do with it at all. Someone else brought them and I was supposed to find them and . . . bring them out."

"Oh, right. The almighty mission. How could I forget that?"

He didn't understand it. When they sparred like this, each word she spoke hit him like a slap in the face. Still. "We had this argument five years ago. Considering the circumstances, let's drop it."

But Cory seemed intent on raising the stakes. "Well, I'm not you, Captain Zen Warrior. I am *not* going out peacefully. I *want* to feel it when we hit. I want *you* to feel it. Just like my brother. Just like all those people on the sea ice." She added quite matter-of-factly, "You know you killed them, too."

Fighting to keep his mind clear, Webber repeated his mayday message like a mantra. He'd switch on the Harrier's landing lights in the final dive. He wanted to see the ocean approaching. He wanted to experience everything up to the last possible microsecond, focused and in control. It was how he had lived his life, how he did his job, and how he would die.

But Cory couldn't go out without continuing her struggle to understand and judge everything and everyone. "So maybe you didn't set off the bomb yourself," she went on. "Or the bombs, however many there were. But one way or another, the people who think like you brought them there."

A pattern appeared in the static, right on the edge of the third emergency channel. Webber immediately slid the volume control to full, straining to catch whatever was hidden in the rush of white noise.

"And people like you built them, Mitchell. You're all responsible for a world in which they could even exist. Five years ago you didn't know what I was talking about when I told you to quit the Navy. But now you do. Because now *you're* going to—"

"*Cory, shut up!*"

"No, I won't be—"

"*I hear something!*"

Cory was instantly silent.

A voice rose up from the interference like a beacon in the night. ". . . say again, Clear . . . Ranger Ten respond . . . your may . . . over."

Webber shouted his mayday again, addressing it to Ranger Ten. He checked his radar. Still useless. He toggled to infrared.

A bright spot moved toward him from 40,000 feet, twenty miles and closing. And the bright spot spoke to him with a distinct British accent. "Clear Day One, this Ranger Ten out of the *Illustrious*. I have you on infrared and am reading you five by five. Where did you say you were from? Over."

"Ranger Ten, this is Clear Day One. I am a civilian jet from McMurdo Station. I am low on fuel and have an urgent message for any U.S. military command. Can you patch me through? Over." Now Webber could see Ranger Ten's acquisition lights, flashing ahead to the northwest.

"First things first, mate. How low on fuel and what are you flying?"

Webber told him. The British pilot seemed skeptical of the idea of a *civilian* Harrier, but quickly gave Webber the coordinates of his homebase, the aircraft carrier HMS *Illustrious*, ninety-seven miles northwest of their current position. If the winds held, Webber calculated, he would have just enough fuel to reach the ship and land on it. "Though we might have to get out and push it the last mile," he told the British pilot.

The British jet took up position on Clear Day One's left wing, no doubt to check out the claim of civilian status, Webber knew. Ranger Ten was a British Sea Harrier, her markings visible only in the strobelike flashes of her running lights.

"First time I've seen a civilian jet with camouflage," the British pilot radioed. "Are you a trainer?"

"First things first," Webber reminded him. "What is the status of your fleet communications?"

"All bollixed up, I'm afraid. The tech boys are laying it on either the biggest solar flare in recorded history, or scintillation from a nuclear detonation."

"It was nuclear," Webber confirmed.

"At McMurdo!?"

But Webber didn't have time for a conversation. "Look, the situation's critical. All or part of the Ross Ice Shelf has collapsed." Webber kept talking over the pilot's interjections. "The collapse has generated a wave. Like a tsunami. And it's spreading. We need to contact someone outside the EMP shadow and warn . . . just about everyone in the Pacific Rim."

"That's going to be difficult, friend. Our scintillation shielding wasn't up to par. No way to test it in the field, really. So we have no communications with the fleet. Or with anyone. Out of nine Harriers, two are functioning. The captain dispatched us to see if we could find a clear spot to relay our own distress call." The planes flew on as Webber waited for the question he knew must come. "Just how large would this wave be?"

Webber would never forget the laser range and velocity readings displayed in his HUD as he had overflown the wave. "Two hundred feet. Moving at two hundred miles an hour."

Ranger Ten did not respond for almost half a minute, and then, in a quiet voice, said only, "We've eleven hundred souls on the *Illustrious.*"

Then, together, Clear Day One and Ranger Ten dropped through the clouds and made their approach to the doomed ship.

THE *ILLUSTRIOUS*

Cory's first sight of the British aircraft carrier was a quick glimpse of a handful of tiny lights, undulating in a sea of absolute darkness. Then Webber banked the Harrier to bring it in on final approach and she could see nothing over his head. She hoped he at least had his sights on something other than what seemed to be the complicated video game glowing on his heads-up display. Fifteen minutes earlier, for the second time in three hours, she had prepared herself to face death, but with the arrival of Ranger Ten, now she had a mission of her own. Something to live for.

Webber had said he wanted to warn the world about the Ice Shelf's collapse. Cory was going to tell the world who had *caused* that collapse. Maybe then the ordinary people of the world would take responsibility for their planet and force the age of the military-industrial complex to its too-long-delayed end.

Webber spoke to her over her helmet speakers. She could feel the Harrier slowing and descending at the same time. "Brace yourself. There's no way I can try a normal landing the way the flight deck's dancing around, so we're going in vertically."

"Isn't that easier?" Cory asked. The vertical takeoff at McMurdo had seemed simple enough.

"It takes a lot more fuel, and we're already on empty. We could drop the last few feet real fast, so . . ."

Cory gripped her safety straps and pulled them in tight, jamming her arms to her side and her helmet to the back of her seat. "I'm—*ahhh!*"

Like a theme-park thrill ride—which Cory hated fervently and Johnny had loved—the Harrier dropped out from beneath her, then came to a sudden, jarring, and noisy stop.

The helmet snapped down over Cory's eyes, making it impossible to see anything. She could feel the plane bounce, then sway, and it took her almost a minute to realize that the swaying was actually the slow pitch of the ship they had landed on.

Then her ears popped as the canopy whined open and a cold blast of sea air and diesel fumes hit her, reminding her that her sole garment, her thermal long underwear, was still uncomfortably damp.

Something banged the side of the plane and she hunched down in her seat, in case the Harrier started to bounce again. She heard Webber shouting to someone, but she couldn't tell what he was saying, because a terrible roar was starting up. She let go of her safety straps and pushed up on her helmet just in time to see Webber slip out of the cockpit.

"Mitchell!" she called out. But by then the roar was so loud even she couldn't hear herself.

She waited for a moment as the roar died down. The smell of burning diesel fuel grew stronger, and she guessed that the other jet must be landing, too. She looked down at the metal disk on her chest where all her straps connected. She looked for a button to push. Or a lever to pull. Or something to unhook. Nothing. She grabbed likely parts of it and twisted. Still nothing.

"Hello!" she shouted in frustration. She heard other shouts, machinery, banging, but no answer. "Hey, someone! Anyone!" She waved her hand over the edge of the cockpit. All she could see was a glow in the moisture-laden air. There was a bright light somewhere behind her, but the only direction that was open to her was directly ahead over the pilot's seat. And there was still nothing to see there.

Then she heard another bang right beside her and looked up to see—

"Johnny?"

Cory felt her heart flutter and her stomach contract. And then the young man spoke and it wasn't Johnny at all, just a British sailor, no more than nineteen. With that, Johnny's death became doubly real to Cory and misery engulfed her again.

The young sailor grinned down at her. "Got yourself in a bit of a bind, eh, mate?"

Cory took her hands off the locking disk. The sailor reached down with both hands, grabbing the disk with one and bracing himself against her breast with—

The sailor straightened up as if struck by lightning. "Oh, God, ma'am, miss, God, I'm sorry, I . . ."

Cory watched him turn red as he sputtered, his errant hand held to the side as if he expected it to burst into flames.

"You'll get over it," Cory told him, her amusement helping her regain control of her emotions. "Now, just get me the hell out of here."

The hapless sailor blinked at her, then sped into action. "Yes, sir—miss. Right away."

This time, he braced himself on her shoulder and worked some magic on the locking disk so that the straps slipped away in two pairs. He straightened up again, holding out his hand to help Cory to her feet.

Her backside was numb, her legs didn't want to straighten out, and one of her wet sock feet slipped in what she knew had to be the remains of the last meal she had eaten. The young sailor was wearing a badly rumpled, oil-stained yellow parka but he was out of it in an instant, offering it to her. Gratefully shrugging into its warmth, Cory then tugged off her helmet. The expression on the shocked young sailor's face told her she was having a very, very bad hair day. And she was unsteady enough to accept his help without protest as he guided her down the ladder on the outside of the jet.

She and Webber had flown a thousand miles north and it wasn't as cold here as it had been at McMurdo, but by the time she stepped onto the deck of the carrier, she had started shivering again. Beneath her wet socks, the deck felt like a road surface, some kind of icy-slick asphalt. With his hand firmly under her elbow, the young sailor indicated she should follow him. "I think you should get inside, miss. Get some dry things, see the doc, have a cuppa."

But Cory pointed back at the Harrier II. Technicians were already working on it, like a pit crew at a car race. "The pilot. Where'd he go?"

"I believe he's up with the captain, miss."

"Then that's where I'm going."

Cory kept her eyes fixed fiercely on the sailor's. If she looked like a gorgon, then she'd damn well act like one.

It worked. The sailor gave in in less than five seconds. "I'll . . . I'll show you the way."

Feeling slightly stronger from the combination of fresh sea air and movement, Cory followed him across the flight deck, which she thought was unusually small for a carrier, no more than fifty feet across. They were heading for a large, metal-walled control tower rising up by the side of the flight deck, wrapped by walkways and studded by portholes. Ahead, on the bow of the ship, the deck curved up like a ski jump. Aft, she could see a line of other Harriers, and at least ten helicopters, most about the size of a Huey, and three almost half again as large.

For all that the structures on the ship were impressive, Cory couldn't help but feel there was something unfinished about it. She could see floodlights on the walkways that weren't lit. Sailors near the parked Harriers and helicopters ran back and forth with flash-lights. It reminded her of McMurdo. Battle damage.

The young sailor held open a heavy metal door for her. It was deeply crusted in paint. He pointed out the lip of thick metal at the curved threshold. "Watch your step, miss." Then he guided her along a cramped corridor to a metal stairway. "Six flights," he said, almost apologetically.

By the time they reached the bridge, Cory's legs were trembling. An hour and a half of being crammed into the Harrier's cockpit had left her ready to crawl, if not collapse. But she wasn't letting Webber out of her sight.

The sailor opened the final door for Cory and she felt she stepped into another world. It was warm again, the lighting was soft, some indirect, much coming from the colorful displays on the control consoles. Intent men in crisp white shirts talked softly by computer monitors. A few technicians in mechanics' overalls were stretched out on the carpeted floor probing the complex interiors of other consoles which were dark.

Then Cory saw Webber, standing with a tall man in uniform, by a large table. Webber also wore a stained yellow parka over his thermal long underwear. As Cory and the young sailor approached, she could see navigation charts spread across it. She recognized the south island of New Zealand on one of them.

The young sailor suddenly went rigid and snapped a salute so forcefully that Cory thought he was going to knock himself unconscious. "Captain, the lady wanted to join her pilot, sir."

The captain returned the salute, far less forcefully, then took in Cory's condition like a livestock appraiser. "Dr. Rey?"

Cory was pleased that Webber had seen fit to mention her existence. She nodded. "Captain . . ." She looked at the name badge clipped above his pocket. "Sofronski."

Captain Sofronski waved his hand at the young sailor. "Take the doctor to sickbay, get her some dry things, and—"

"There's no time for that," Cory said. "I know this ocean, Captain."

The captain looked at her as if no one had ever interrupted him before. "I assure you, *Doctor*, that after twenty-two years in Her Majesty's navy, so do I. And as for the story told by your colleague here . . ." The captain hesitated, apparently having a hard time finding the precise words he wanted. "Well, frankly, I find it most improbable."

"Well, it isn't, Captain, because something very much like it has happened before." *That got your attention*, Cory thought. And Webber's, too. When he'd probably thought she was dozing or struck dumb with fear, she'd been reviewing whatever she knew that might prove relevant. And she had remembered something that confirmed that both she *and* Mitchell had been right. It *wasn't* a simple displacement wave of water, and it *had* been as high as Webber's display had indicated when it hit McMurdo.

"Approximately two million years ago," she began, "an asteroid slammed into the Bellingshausen Sea, right off the shore of Antarctica, just off Palmer Land at the base of the Antarctic Peninsula. It wasn't all that big, somewhere between a little over half a mile to maybe two and a half miles across. But it was traveling so fast it hit like a hundred *billion* tons of TNT. Do you know how high the asteroid's initial displacement wave was, Captain?"

Sofronski cleared his throat, as if to speak, but Cory didn't wait for his response.

"Try three miles," she said. *"Three miles,* a three-mile-high column of water rising straight up, in *less than a minute.* That explains why they're finding sea-bottom microfossils on Antarctic mountains where the fossils don't match the strata. A three-mile-high wave splashing down on the landscape causes a little bit of planetary rearrangement."

Out of the corner of her eye, Cory saw Webber make a circling motion with one hand, urging her to get to the point. She ignored him and continued outlining her argument. "As for the rest of the world, waves one hundred and thirty feet high moved up the coast of South America at more than one hundred miles an hour. Two million years later, we can still see the damage those waves left behind. So if the entire Ross Ice Shelf *has* collapsed, as Captain Webber and I believe, well, it's going to make the Bellingshausen asteroid look like a summer squall."

The captain made another attempt to regain control of the discussion. "Doctor, even if the Shelf did collapse, you're surely not saying it could travel anywhere near the thousands of miles per hour an asteroid would?"

Cory looked over at Webber who shrugged. His message was clear: It was her argument, so she should be able to defend it. "Fair enough, let's do some back-of-the-envelope work here." She closed her eyes, creating a mental grid like a spreadsheet, ready to plug in the numbers she needed. She knew how Webber thought his way through problems. She wondered if he'd ever realized that that was something else they had had in common. Then she focused her gaze firmly on the captain just as she had on the sailor.

"Let's say the Bellingshausen asteroid *was* its largest estimated size: two and a half miles across. Four pi *r* to the third over three gives us . . . let's round it to eight cubic miles. We'll make it an iron asteroid, too, the heaviest kind. Iron's almost five hundred pounds a cubic foot. We've got eight cubic miles . . ." She closed her eyes again, briefly, watching the numbers fall into the grid, and read off the answer. ". . . So we're at almost three hundred *billion* tons of mass punching a hole into five square miles of water. I'll give you a head-on collision, too. The asteroid traveling in one direction, the Earth traveling the opposite. That's a speed of . . . one hundred thirty-five thousand miles an hour. Still with me?"

"Impressive, but still not conclusive."

Cory played her ace. "I spoke at an international ecology conference last year. The threat of global warming. I developed environmental models of what might happen if the ice caps began to melt. There's a considerable mass of ice in the Ross Shelf, Captain Sofronski. *Seven* hundred billion tons, to be precise. And that's more than *twice* the Bellingshausen asteroid's mass."

Corey glanced at Webber, but he was now leaning back against the door frame, silent, as if relieved someone other than he was the focus of her attention.

"Regardless, Doctor," Sofronski said, "I find it most difficult to accept that all that ice would be traveling at one hundred thirty-five thousand miles per hour when it collapsed."

Cory had him. "Ah, but it doesn't have to." All she needed now was one last example to present to him, something that would concretely connect a scientific principle to the life of a military officer. *Think,* she told herself, *what have you learned from dealing with Webber?* She had it. "Think of the asteroid as a bullet. Three hundred billion tons, one hundred thirty-five thousand miles an hour, all focused on five square miles of ocean. Pow! The bullet goes right through you, right? But what if you're wearing a bullet-proof vest?" Cory caught the flash of understanding that appeared in Webber's face. *Right, he's probably already been shot in a bullet-proof vest,* she thought. *Everyday occurrence for a military masochist.* She turned her attention back to the captain. "If you're in a vest and that same bullet hits you, the armor plates spread the bullet's kinetic energy over a greater area. Your body still absorbs the same momentum from the bullet, the same energy, so you react the same way and go flying back, but the bullet doesn't go through you because the impact isn't focused on a single square inch of your skin.

"So," she concluded, "three hundred billion tons at one hundred thirty-five thousand miles per hour applied against five square miles is the equivalent force to the same mass hitting *ten* square miles at *sixty-seven* thousand, five hundred miles an hour. Or *twenty* square miles at thirty-three thousand, seven hundred and fifty miles per hour . . . see how it works? The greater the area, the less energy is applied per square mile."

Clearly unable to refute her data, the captain became testy, behaving as if she had launched a personal attack on him.

"See here, Dr. Rey, I do not need to be lectured like a schoolboy."

"Maybe you do," Cory said, raising her voice enough to know that everyone else on the bridge would be looking at her. "The Ice Shelf averages two hundred and ten thousand square miles. And remember, the Shelf is more than twice the Bellingshausen asteroid's mass, and it was moving at . . ." Cory looked at Webber. "How fast does a nuclear shock wave travel?"

Webber answered without having to think, telling Cory that he had had no difficulty following her calculations. "After the first second, say three hundred miles an hour."

"Do the math, Captain. That Ice Shelf hit the water with more than *a thousand* times the energy of the Bellingshausen asteroid. And if you don't start paying attention to Captain Webber, you and your ship are, as we say in America, fucked." Cory couldn't resist. "Royally."

Captain Sofronski's lips tightened, but Cory intuitively understood that no matter how much he wanted to, he would not permit himself to raise his voice to a female, even a rude American female, in front of his officers.

Webber straightened up and moved away from the door frame. "Captain Sofronski, your ship has experienced electromagnetic pulse, so you know a nuclear detonation was involved. And if Dr. Rey's calculations are right—"

"What do you mean, *'if'?*" Cory demanded.

But Webber silenced her by holding up his hand and continuing. "*If* they're right, then you have less than two hours before the wave reaches this position. That's two hours to help us get some warning to the rest of the world. Help us for those two hours. And if there is no wave, then throw us in the brig and . . . think of the stories you can tell about the crazy Yanks you picked up out of nowhere." Cory saw that Webber had won. "Two hours, Captain. That's all we're asking for."

The captain stared down at the charts on the table. "I'll see you both on the flight deck." He glanced up at Cory. "Those . . . outfits . . . can't be comfortable." He looked at Webber. "It will take a few minutes to get the flight crew assembled. I suggest you use that time to change, get something to eat." Then the captain nodded dismissal of them both and turned to a wall phone.

Webber gestured to Cory to follow him to the door. "Why are we going back to the flight deck?" Cory asked, as Webber opened the door and she stepped through after him.

Webber started walking down the corridor to the stairway. Cory stayed at his side. The young sailor followed them. "We're fifteen hundred miles from Christchurch, and the Harrier only has a range of about thirteen hundred miles. Captain Sofronksi's flight crew is going to strip off our radiation-detector pods and see if they can adapt their Sea Harrier drop tanks—extra fuel tanks—to get us the extra two hundred miles we need."

Cory didn't approve of the way Webber concentrated on the technical aspects, ignoring the human side of what they faced. "That works for us. But what about them?"

Webber stopped at the top of the first flight of stairs. "If the captain's right, nothing will happen to his ship. If you're right, there's nothing we can do for them."

Cory caught the look of fear on the young sailor's face. "There's a chance," she said.

Webber shook his head, obviously not aware of the effect their conversation was having on the sailor. "A two-hundred-foot wave at two hundred miles an hour? The *Illustrious* can't survive that."

"We don't know that. Not for sure. And there are things they could do to increase their chances."

"Such as?"

Cory knew she was now working on instinct more than science. But if Webber was willing to write off this ship and her crew, she wasn't. "You look after the plane." She turned to the sailor. "What's your name?"

"Liam Andrews, miss." The young man coughed nervously, then added. "Cadet First Class."

"Okay, Cadet Andrews. I need to talk to someone about the size and shape of the ship. Her draft, weight distribution, blueprints would help. Who would that be?"

"Uh, the chief engineer, miss."

"Take me to him."

"But . . . what about your clothes, Doctor?"

"Would everyone please stop worrying about the way I look and get busy around here?"

"Whatever happens, we're taking off in sixty minutes," Webber said. He started down the stairs without looking back for Cory's confirmation.

As the clanging of his footsteps faded away, Andrews turned to Cory. "Miss, what you were saying in there to the captain . . . are we all going to die?"

Cory looked at the cadet and saw only Johnny, felt only Johnny's hand first clutching hers, then letting go. Deliberately. Because of what Webber had said.

She put her hand on the young man's arm, squeezed tightly, the way she should have held on to her brother.

"Not if I can help it."

But even as she said the words, Cory Rey feared she would fail again.

FIVE

"Don't make me repeat myself, Major. You do not have enough information to warrant your conclusions."

Major Bailey stared at General Abbott on the SVTS display, barely able to keep her mouth closed. "With respect, sir, what other explanation is possible?"

"Space is an unforgiving environment. Satellites fail for no reason all the time."

But to Bailey, those were fighting words. "No, sir, they do not. If a satellite fails, it is *always* for a reason. Maybe it's a loose wire. Maybe it's a meteor strike. Or maybe it's little green men from Mars stealing hubcaps. But if I see an *effect*, I guarantee you there's a *cause*."

"Let me make it simple, Major. I am ordering you not to transmit a Flash Alert to General Gutierrez."

And that was the end of the fight. To Major Bailey, the chain of command was inviolable. Without it, the military could not function, the country could not survive. As the general had said, it was simple.

"Yes, sir," Bailey acknowledged. "I will not transmit a Flash Alert to the general."

Abbott smiled on the screen. By now Bailey had determined that

193

the smile was a calculated expression, probably rehearsed in front of a mirror.

"However," Bailey continued, "do I have your permission to continue to investigate the loss of NOAA-20 and the DSCS transmission from McMurdo?"

"By all means. I'd concentrate on the weather satellite, though." Abbott looked at something offscreen. "We'll be getting realtime images from McMurdo within the hour. I believe that will explain why we lost satellite communications."

"Thank you, sir." Bailey was set to switch the NMCC feed to STANDING BY, her new plan already taking shape. But the general pulled a flanking maneuver.

"One last thing, Major. Also an order. You are to report the results of your investigation directly to me, and only to me. Understood?"

Bailey sighed. So much for going laterally through the chain of command to inform NORAD, and letting *them* issue a Flash Alert. "Understood, sir."

Abbott seemed to sense her disagreement. "Major, I assure you I am not acting capriciously. There are other factors involved of which you are unaware. I am determined not to put other operations at risk."

Bailey was surprised that a general would actually stop to explain himself to her. Maybe he was a human being after all, and not just a set of walking, talking brass stars.

"Thank you, sir. I'll keep you informed."

Then Abbott put the feed on STANDING BY at his end, once again outmaneuvering her.

"What was that all about?" Huber asked. He had come up the stairs toward the end of Bailey's conversation with the general, discreetly staying beyond the range of the teleconference camera.

"Abbott says we don't have enough data to prove a claim of EMP."

Huber's naturally pale, freckled face looked puzzled. "Of course not. But we have enough to *suggest* EMP. That's cause for further investigation."

Bailey stood up to stretch her legs. It had been a long shift and there were five more hours to go before it ended. Even with her family's infamously rich and calorie-laden Thanksgiving dinner looming before her, she was hungry, and this might be the perfect time to slip off to the commissary. Then she saw the printout sheets Huber had. "What's that?"

"I searched the online archives for scenarios that had been dropped from the procedures manual since they figured out that EMP was a strategic threat."

"And?"

Huber carefully folded back two sheets to show Bailey where he had marked five lines of text. "Five scenarios were developed and tested involving EMP over polar regions." He read them out. "1983: Operation TRIPWIRE. 1986: Operation LIGHTS OUT. 1986 again: Project BOUNCEBACK. 1988: Operation RED SNOW. And this last one. Icefire."

Bailey took the sheets and scanned the archive control numbers printed out beneath each entry. The Icefire scenario was missing most of its numbers. "No date?"

"And no designation. It's not a project. It's not an operation."

Bailey was intrigued. A project designation usually meant that something was being designed or built. An operation involved taking action, such as war games or troop deployments. She presumed that whatever technology had been developed as part of Project BOUNCEBACK in 1986 had been tested during Operation LIGHTS OUT of that same year. But Icefire, standing out on its own, was a definite anomaly.

Bailey handed the sheets back to Huber. "Print 'em out, I guess."

"I'm doing that now. Except for Icefire. It's not in the online archives."

Bailey didn't believe that. She looked sternly at Huber. She had hoped he was going to be more than just a pretty face. "Those are permanent computer library files, Commander. The sum total of more than fifty years of defending North America from attack."

"I found *all* the other scenarios, Major. We'll have hardcopies in the next half hour. But for Icefire: file not found."

Bailey sat back down again. Satellites didn't fail for no reason. Military planning documents didn't vanish from classified archives on their own. "So how do we find it?"

Huber grinned at her. *Now, that's a* real *smile,* Bailey thought, amused. He was letting her know he had already anticipated what she'd want. "I sent out a system request. To the Pentagon, CIA, NSA, everywhere. We probably won't be able to get a printout through channels till Monday, but at least we'll know where it's being kept, and that'll tell us who to go to and ask for a favor."

"Good work."

"Thanks. I . . ."

Bailey waited, wondering what else her junior officer wanted her to know. But Huber left it at that. "Thank you, Major. I'll get those printouts. Oh, and . . . can I get you something from the commissary?"

Bailey appreciated the offer, but she'd decided if she left her food choice up to Huber, he'd probably come back with a plate of lettuce and a side of cottage cheese. Come to think of it, she couldn't remember ever having seen him eat. No wonder he was so scrawny. "No, you go to the print shop and I'll hit the commissary. Can I get *you* something?"

Huber dug into his pocket for some cash. "Sure. The sloppy joe, fries, chocolate milk, and . . . if they have any more of those double-fudge cupcakes, two of those."

Bailey limited her reaction to a single blink. *Maybe he only eats once a month,* she thought. She took the bills he gave her, then told him to get the printouts. As Huber took the stairs two at a time, Bailey logged off her situation panel, handing control to her second, Captain Freedman, at the workstation just below hers.

When Freedman acknowledged that he had her displays, Bailey made sure her smart badge was secure on the front of her sweater, then walked down the staircase from her elevated platform to the control-room floor, heading for the polished steel corridor that would take her to the commissary.

Along the way, she thought about all the different combinations of events that could lead to a satellite being accidentally disabled. She even spared a stray thought or two for Commander Huber's smile—definitely spontaneous. But she didn't think about Icefire or why its file was missing from the archives of Cheyenne Mountain.

The scenario's omission from her thoughts, was, in fact, the reason for its omission in the archives.

No one was supposed to think of Icefire at all.

NATIONAL MILITARY COMMAND CENTER/THE PENTAGON

Abbott watched the big board as Lieutenant Yoshii adjusted the ETEM map so McMurdo Station filled the left-hand side. He could see every building and the roadways between them. There were even helicopters on the helipads. The photo image was from the U.S. Geographical Survey, taken two years earlier, and now seamlessly incorporated into the ETEM database of satellite maps and, where available, aerial photography.

An insert window floated over the upper right-hand side of the station. In it was a yellow outline of Ross Island and the western shore of the Ross Sea. To the northwest of the insert map, a small red dot flashed—the projected location of Archangel Four, the advanced SR-71 spyplane that had begun its descent to image the extent of the damage caused to McMurdo by the eruption of Mount Erebus.

More than other commanders outside the Joint Staff, Abbott had always admired the Blackbirds, perhaps because he knew more about the aircraft's true capabilities. The Lockheed SR-71, first flown in 1964, had been based on the A-11 supersonic reconnaissance aircraft developed to outrun the Soviet SAM missiles that were successfully shooting down U-2 spyplanes. For the next twenty-five years, the Lockheed SR-71 had been the country's preeminent intelligence-gathering tool. In the sixties, it could photograph any part of the Earth's surface within six hours, and became the first aircraft to fly faster than Mach 3—more than 2,000 mph—for sustained periods. By the time of that first model's "retirement" in 1990, through constant improvements to its engines and startling breakthroughs in its fuels, flight time to target acquisition had been cut to just under four hours. Though of course, Abbott knew, the Air Force, somewhat comically, continued to report only the plane's 1964 performance statistics to the outside world.

In the nineties, the Blackbirds had been caught up in a Kafkaesque game of military secrecy. So many improvements had been made to them over the years that the planes had long deserved a new model number. But the Pentagon didn't want to publicly acknowledge those improvements, and so the designation never changed. Pentagon planners even went out of their way to ask Congress not to fund SR-71 operations any longer. Eventually, the

Blackbirds were called dinosaurs of the Cold War. Three were kept by NASA for mundane science experiments. The same paltry number were kept by the Air Force on a standby basis only. It appeared that the age of satellites had made the Blackbirds outmoded.

However, the most sophisticated surveillance satellite could acquire detailed images of a given point on Earth within four hours only if the satellite happened, by chance, to be passing over that point in that time. Satellites had not supplanted the SR-71s—at least, not yet. The jets were still needed.

Behind the scenes, even as the Pentagon stated that it did *not* want to keep operating Blackbirds, Pentagon officials made sure that congressional committees added SR-71 funding back to the military budget every year. The money was minimal by military standards, only enough to keep the six official planes at the lowest standard of readiness. A thirty-day call-up period would be required to bring them to full operation. But the few millions that Congress added each year, apparently unasked for and in defiance of all logic, provided the cover story the Pentagon needed in case one of the twelve *unofficial* Blackbirds, flown by the National Reconnaissance Office, the National Security Agency, and the Central Intelligence Agency, happened to crash in the Middle East, or in China, or South America. After all, it would be difficult to explain why a retired spyplane should fall out of the sky if it was supposed to be in a museum. By playing a shell game with its budget requests, the Pentagon ensured that it would always be able to identify a crashed SR-71—which was really an SR-75 or an SR-80—as one of the six antiques kept in service by a sentimental Congress. In the meantime, the Pentagon sent a message to the rest of the world implying that because America no longer needed the Blackbirds, she clearly must have something better.

Someday soon, Abbott knew, America would have that something better. The Mach 10 Nevada Rain. The day the Nevada Rain was fully operational was the day all the Blackbirds would stop flying for real. But until then, they would continue to mysteriously evade the line-item veto and congressional oversight committees, an elaborate charade for an invaluable tool.

Major Bailey at the Earth Surveillance Center appeared in an SVTS window to the right of the maps. "General Abbott, we're receiving communications from Archangel Four. He's seven minutes from target."

Abbott made certain his next question had no hidden meanings in it, and he hoped Major Bailey would take it the right way. Abbott liked Bailey. She was a bit overeager, perhaps, but that was a quality to be guided in the military, not suppressed, and overall she showed great promise for even further advancement up the ranks. *If only,* he thought, *someone could alert her, discreetly, of course, in these politically correct times, to do something about her weight.*

"Major, what is the quality of the communications?"

Bailey responded crisply. "Excellent, sir." But it was clear she knew why he had asked. "No indication of adverse effects from EMP."

Abbott nodded, not wishing to belabor the fact that he was right and she had been wrong. Bailey was an intelligent officer. She would learn her lesson. "Very good, Major."

"Of course, General, we're routing the communications link through a Milstar bird that was not within range of McMurdo at the time we lost the other signal."

Beside Abbott, Major Chennault raised his hand to hide his lower face and whispered, "She never gives up, does she?"

Abbott did have to give Bailey points for trying. In the past hour, she had made three attempts to suggest ways she could ask for a full systems check of all U.S. military satellites in order to ascertain if any, within range of McMurdo when NOAA-20 transmission had been lost, showed signs of EMP. Abbott had overruled each request. There was no sense in sending out an alarm that might accomplish nothing except to jeopardize Project SHAARP.

"Thank you, Major. Put me through to Major Bardeen."

On the board, Bailey operated her arcane controls. "Lieutenant Yoshii, Archangel Four is live on feed two."

Yoshii adjusted something at her own workstation and a buzz of static came over the room's speakers. Abbott marveled anew at the system. Through an intricate web of fiber-optics and encrypted microwave transmissions, he was now directly connected to an aircraft 10,000 miles away. He dreamed of the day SHAARP promised, when an enemy aircraft at that distance could be plucked from the air just as easily.

"Archangel Four, this is General Abbott at the National Military Command Center. How do you read me?"

The voice that responded had the comfortable drawl of an experienced Air Force pilot, completely at ease with the machine he controlled. "General Abbott, I'm reading you loud and clear, sir. I'm following the coast of Victoria Land, five minutes from McMurdo."

"What do you see, son?"

Major Bardeen chuckled. "Well, sir, I can't exactly see anything out there. Visually, it's night still and I'm flying over clouds. There're an awful lot of them. Nothing like the weather maps I got at launch. But my RSO is activating infrared scanning. Should have something for you momentarily."

Abbott looked over at Yoshii. "Lieutenant, who is Bardeen's Reconnaissance Systems Officer?"

Yoshii checked a note on her workstation. "Captain Rosinski, sir."

Abbott returned his attention to the screen. It was always important to know the names of his troops. They could never be numbers, never faceless windup soldiers.

Bardeen's voice came back over the speakers. "I'm advised we are uploading IR data now."

Abbott watched Bailey as she worked her panel. A moment later, another window opened on the big board: night vision from the Blackbird.

"I am slowing to two hundred nautical miles," Bardeen reported. "On internal guidance. No GPS fix is available."

Abbott glanced at Chennault. "That's normal for Antarctica, Major." Failure of the Global Positioning Satellite system in that region was not a sign of EMP, Abbott knew, simply an indication of the continent's remoteness.

But Chennault seemed puzzled by something else.

"What?" Abbott asked.

"That's a remarkably clean coastline return, General. Shouldn't we be seeing ice?"

Abbott studied the moving IR display. It appeared in false colors, adjusted to match the expected terrain. Thus, the surface of the sea was black, the scattered chunks of ice on it were white, land was brown, and snow had a pinkish cast. "Those bits of white on the water. That's ice."

"That's pack ice. All broken up." Chennault pointed to the left side of the board. "Look at the ETEM. There should be solid ice all down the shore this time of year."

Abbott decided to check in with the expert. "Captain Rosinski, General Abbott here. Are you seeing anything unusual?"

A female voice responded. Abbott noticed Major Bailey flash a smile as she also heard the captain. "I wouldn't say unusual, General. But it does seem warmer than I was told to expect. The ocean temp is close to forty degrees. Snow cover on the land is light."

Abbott considered the possibilities, turned to Chennault. "What do you think? Volcanic gases trapped beneath low-lying clouds?"

Chennault shook his head. "I'm not a meteorologist."

"Lieutenant Yoshii," Abbott said, "get me someone from the watch floor with meteorological background. Whoever's available."

Yoshii had her phone up and was dialing before Abbott had even finished speaking.

"Coming up on McMurdo," Bardeen announced. "Speed holding at two hundred nautical miles, should give us a real good look."

"Whoa!" Rosinski added, and Abbott could instantly see why. A bright yellow smear had suddenly flashed in the upper right-hand side of the IR image. "We found your volcano, General."

An adolescent-looking naval lieutenant commander came running into the EAR from the watch floor. Yoshii pointed at Abbott and the young officer saluted, breathlessly. "Lieutenant Commander Tishler, sir. You had a meteorological question?"

"Here comes the station," Bardeen announced.

Abbott pointed to the IR window. "That's Antarctica. McMurdo Station. Why is it so warm?"

Clearly baffled, the lieutenant commander stared at the IR image.

The IR window changed to show an east-west shoreline; then the framing locked and the image changed only as the angle of the Blackbird's position moved over it.

But there was obviously something wrong.

Rosinski was the only one talking. "Uh, Major Bardeen, I'm on the right coordinates . . ."

"What's the problem?" Abbott asked, concerned that he might already know the answer.

The IR window showed a familiar shoreline, one that matched the ETEM map exactly. But instead of solid sea ice, Abbott saw only the shattered pieces of a puzzle. And instead of buildings and roadways and fuel tanks and transmitting towers, he saw only black rock, devoid of snow, and radiating heat at 30 degrees.

"General Abbott," Rosinski said. "There's nothing down there. McMurdo Station, sir . . . it's gone."

SIX

THE *ILLUSTRIOUS*

The work on Webber's Harrier was taking longer than anyone expected. For some obscure reason, the British Hawker Siddeley–built Sea Harriers used fuel-coupling connectors that were a different size from the ones used on the American McDonnell Douglas Harrier II. As planned, the Royal Navy flight crew from the British carrier, the *Illustrious*, had expertly disconnected the outboard radiation-detector pods under the Harrier II's wings, dropping at least 300 pounds from the aircraft. And they were ready to bolt the inboard drop tanks into position. But there seemed to be no way to connect the drop tanks to the main fuel lines.

Mitch Webber checked his combat watch. The soft glow of the tritium gas indicators showed that Cory's mega-tsunami was no more than thirty minutes away. His second watch, the Timex, told him that in Washington everyone would be asleep. By the time anyone got around to checking why the NEST teams had missed their scheduled report from McMurdo, the shoreline of half the Pacific Rim would be inundated.

And he still didn't know why.

Three mechanics under the Harrier's wing suddenly shouted and jumped back as fuel spilled out of the wing's underside. They yelled at another mechanic on top of the wing to shut off the flow. Webber grimaced. About fifty gallons of fuel had just been lost A couple of cadets were doggedly using a hand pump to drain fuel drums to fill Webber's jet—a time-consuming and physically arduous process. None of the EMP-disabled electric pumps were working.

Webber had had enough. "Okay," he shouted, waving his arms at the mechanics and cadets to stop what they were doing. He sprinted toward his Harrier. At least he was warm. The Brits had provided a change of clothes, a flight suit, and a parka. But it was time to get airborne. "Forget the drop tanks. Just top up the wings and seal her up."

The white-haired flight-crew chief was Commander Shastri, a deeply tanned man who in his person suggested the sweep of the British Empire by looking Pakistani and sounding Australian. He didn't agree with Webber's call. "My blokes can do this. We're cutting new couplers onto the fuel leads. Ten minutes is all."

Webber calculated the odds. The drop tanks would make the difference between setting down on farmland on New Zealand's south island, or making it all the way to Christchurch and the 109th Air Wing. He looked out at the southern horizon as if he might see something in the darkness.

"We're right for it, aren't we, mate?" Shastri asked.

Webber nodded, unable and unwilling to lie to this man.

"Then give us the chance to do our jobs."

Webber looked into the eyes of someone who knew he was dead, but who had no intention of giving up. "Ten minutes. But start topping the wings now."

Shastri gave him a quick salute. "That's the lad."

Webber headed for the control tower, fast. Some sailors were standing around, off duty, hunched against the cold wind, cradling cigarettes, looking angry. They saw Webber approaching.

"Can one of you find Dr. Rey for me? She was the woman on my plane. She should be with your chief engineer." Webber didn't care if he disrupted Cory's meeting. She was mistaken when she said she thought there was a chance the carrier could survive the wave. She might be able to reel off the numbers but she still had no concept of the physical reality of the forces she'd described to Captain Sofronski. And she was about to have a head-on collision with the real world.

The sailors stared at Webber.

"They say you Yanks set off a bomb down there. Made the wave in the first place," one said.

Webber heard the challenge in the man's voice and instinctively shifted into fighting stance, keeping his hands loose and ready at his sides. "No. That's not true."

"That's not what I hear," another sailor added. "And I hear the only ones to get off this ship is two Harrier pilots and as many boys as can fit in the three Sea Kings what still fly. I put that at twenty-four. And then there's you two. You and your passenger."

Webber faced the sailors without backing down. He might be able to take them on and walk away, but he knew he'd be in no condition to fly. His cracked rib still flashed with pain at every breath.

"Talk to your captain," Webber said quietly.

One of the sailors threw down a cigarette, and it blew into the night before it hit the deck. The wind was picking up.

"Captain's not here, is he?" a sailor said, the one who thought the wave was Webber's fault.

Then the control-tower door clanged open and Cadet Andrews stepped out, followed by Captain Sofronski and Cory. Cory was also in a new flight suit, only two sizes too large.

The sailors snapped to attention and saluted the captain. Looking sharply at Webber and the sailors' respective positions, the captain seemed to grasp exactly what he had interrupted. To the sailors he said, "I'd get below, lads. Make certain all the hatches are dogged."

The sailors moved off, not wanting to, but compelled by their training to do what the captain said.

When they were gone, Sofronski shook hands with Cory. "Not that it will do them a bloody bit of good." He nodded to Webber. "Someday you might want to acquaint the good doctor with the fundamentals of marine engineering."

Webber looked at Cory. She shook her head, chagrined. "Inertia," she said. "I thought, since the water isn't really moving forward, it's the energy moving through the water, that the ship could float up the side of wave, if it was sealed tightly enough. Like a cork. But at two hundred miles an hour . . ."

The captain patted Cadet Andrew's shoulder.

Webber understood what Cory had left unsaid. The carrier couldn't move fast enough to keep up with the growth of the wave.

"How's your plane coming?" the captain asked Webber.

"It'll be ready in five minutes."

The captain reached into his parka and pulled out a large leather envelope. The ship's name was embossed on it. "Make room for this, would you. Ship's log, on disk. A few letters."

"Shouldn't one of your pilots carry it?"

The captain looked away for a moment, then back at Webber. "The helicopters won't actually be going anywhere. They'll go straight up, hope to ride out the turbulence. Then the best they can do is a controlled ditch a few hundred klicks north. The boys might be able to last three days in inflatables, but their radio beacons are all pulsed out, so . . ." The captain straightened his shoulders abruptly. "Our Harriers don't have the range yours has, even with drop tanks. So the pilots drew straws and two of them are going to try to make it to Young Island, a few hundred klicks south. With what they can carry, maybe they can last a week. Tell your Navy friends about them, would you?"

Webber took the envelope, held it under his arm, saluted the captain. "What changed your mind?" he asked.

"The bugger's on the radar screen. Radar's working finally. Just in time." The captain pulled his parka closer, tightening it around his neck. "I blame the bloody Argentine nationalists. They stirred up that mess in the Falklands, so every year we're down here, showing the flag, letting them know we're watching. And this is what happens. Goddamn *bloody* Argentines."

A huge gust of wind struck so suddenly that Cory was blown forward a few feet. The captain reached out to steady her. The ship groaned as it rolled heavily.

"Time you were away," Sofronski said. "I'll walk you. Make sure there's no trouble."

They started forward. Webber saw Cadet Andrews move closer to Cory, to whisper to her. He handed her something. She looked at it, nodded, slipped it into her pocket. Then she put her arms around him. The cadet turned away. Webber could see tears streak in the wind across his crimson cheeks.

Then they were by the Harrier. Commander Shastri's crew were closing the wing panels, rolling away their platforms. Two cadets were still frantically pumping fuel from a drum.

"Drop tanks are on, sealed, and full," Shastri reported proudly. "Another minute to top the tanks and—"

The ship shuddered and lurched to one side.

The cadets pumping the fuel lost their footing, stumbled against the almost empty drum, knocking it over. The last of the fuel spilled.

Webber grabbed for Cory's baggy flight suit. "What was that?"

Cory shook her head, no idea.

The wind gusted again, its whine turning to a scream.

"Air displacement?" Webber asked.

Cory looked up at him, worried. "There'll be some, but this is too early."

The deck pitched steeply beneath their feet as the carrier heeled heavily. From the port side, he heard a sailor's hoarse cry, "HERE SHE COMES, BOYS!"

Another deep shudder shook the carrier as it began to lose its battle against the growing current and wind. Cory pressed her face into Webber's back as he leaned into the gale that threatened to separate them.

"God be with you!" Shastri shouted.

Captain Sofronski was already waving at the Sea King helicopters, to tell them to take off as, beyond them, two Sea Harriers kicked off the deck, wavered in the air, then angled forward and shot off into the night.

As the ship lunged upward, a mechanic's wheeled platform fell heavily to the deck, sending up sparks as the metal hit the asphalt.

The sparks found the spilled fuel.

Webber and Cory could only watch as a river of flickering blue flame flashed from the fuel drum to the Harrier, leaping onto the fuel line, shooting up to the wing opening and—

But just before Clear Day One could explode, the wave hit the carrier.

Webber had just enough time to think, *That's lucky*, and then he was lifted from the deck and hurled into darkness.

Cory's vision blurred as her head smashed against the control-tower bulkhead. She struggled to push herself up but her hand kept slipping in the salt water. Then she felt the deck shift beneath her and the water rushed away. She tried to remember why she was using only one hand to help herself. *Oh, right, Mitchell.*

Her other hand was still locked on to the sleeve of Webber's parka. He was lying beside her, faceup, choking up water.

She jumped to her feet and pulled him up, too. Mitchell couldn't die on her now.

Webber took in a deep, ragged breath as the deck rocked again, so slowly and ponderously that Cory felt sickened. Then he stared at her in shock, in surprise, and finally with a stupid hopeful grin. "That was it?"

But Cory knew better, finally understanding. "Harmonic wave," she yelled at him, over the wind. "The three sisters." Webber was still staring at her blankly. "The big one's still out there. And it's close. Two minutes max."

At that, Webber nodded and coughed out more water, gesturing for her to follow him back to the Harrier.

Cory ran after him, the wind blowing at her back, making her feel as if she'd take off on her own at any step. There were no more floodlights on the lower levels of the control tower. The only light came from fixtures higher up, out of the spray of the last wave. Cory estimated it at forty feet, guessed it would have formed about six miles in front of the main wave.

Webber skidded to a stop by the Harrier. There was no sign of the mechanics or the cadets. He turned to look aft.

Turning with him, Cory saw what he saw. The helicopters were gone. Someone was crawling along the flight deck, but that was all. She realized then that anyone who hadn't been swept up against the control tower would have been swept off into the sea. She thought of Cadet Andrews. Reached into her pocket, felt the letter he had given her still there.

"Shit! Shit! SHIT!" Webber said. Cory saw him looking around the deck. "No ladder."

Cory looked up at the Harrier's cockpit as if it were Everest.

"Let's go!" Webber was now crouched down by the plane, hands cupped together.

She placed one hand on his shoulder, one foot in his hands, jumped up as he pushed, and landed with her stomach on the sharp edge of the cockpit.

"Move it!" Webber called up to her.

Cory kicked her way headfirst onto the observer's seat, then flipped around and scrambled to her feet. Webber had thrown off his bulky parka and pulled himself up into the jet intake, swinging up onto the wing. She saw him shut a small panel on the wing's surface, then crawl forward to pull himself past her and into the front of the cockpit.

She became aware of a sound, somewhere distant, unlike any she had ever heard, including the terrible shriek of the splintering ice field. The sound was getting louder. Together with the wind. Then it was more than hearing—she *felt* the sound.

"Down!" Webber shouted. "Helmet on! Strap in!"

Cory was still standing, reaching behind her for the helmet on her seat. She grabbed it, looked out, saw a line of sailors about twenty feet away.

They were standing together, arms linked, canted against the wind, watching her.

One of them broke rank to blow her a kiss. She couldn't tell if it was Andrews. She thought she heard them singing. But the sound was louder now, in her chest, in her bones.

Something clunked behind her and she quickly dropped down to the seat as the canopy closed over her. Webber started the engine before the canopy had sealed and for a few seconds its reassuring rumble drowned out the sound of what was coming.

She fought with her safety straps first, but then realized Webber was talking to her and she couldn't hear him. She tugged on the helmet, remembered that she had to plug in a wire to connect the microphone and speakers, but had no idea where.

The plane began to dip forward. She peered out the side of the canopy, rising up just enough to see the deck. The whole ship was dipping forward.

The engine roared behind her. The plane lurched forward, then pivoted, throwing her to the side. She twisted desperately to keep from hitting any of the controls, having no idea what any of them might do.

Cory grabbed again at her safety straps, tugged them over her shoulders, held them together with her shaking hands. She still didn't know how to work the locking disk.

Then a vibration built up in the plane, but it wasn't a vibration she had experienced the last time they had taken off. She felt herself pressed back into her seat, judging that they must be at a 30-degree angle at least. She pictured the *Illustrious* balanced on the brink of the trough that would form. She thought of the sailors, arms linked together, no longer able to stand upright on the tilted deck.

She saw them tumbling, falling, sucked down into darkness, into—

Something struck the Harrier and made it shake, made her gasp.

Then the jet-engine scream rose higher and the vibration stopped and she knew they were airborne.

Cory's eyes were squeezed shut, but she could still see what was coming for them, reaching out to pluck them back with the wind that would be drawn into its curve. *How fast could the Harrier go in that wind? How fast could it climb?*

She heard Webber calling out to her, but his words could not reach her.

The Harrier trembled, bucked, gained speed, gained height. But whether fast enough or high enough, Cory still didn't know.

In the moment in which she existed, all her knowledge and all her bravery left her, until she had nothing.

Except fear of the wave.

EVENT PLUS 3 HOURS

Awakened by the Ice, the ocean rose from itself like Leviathan, and the Illustrious, 20,000 tons of steel and electronics and human life, could not stand in its way.

The first wave to strike had been a mere 20-foot swell, though it traveled at 200 miles an hour. It was an accident of physics, an oscillation in the backflow of water that rushed in to feed the monster that followed.

The first wave damaged the carrier, but did no serious harm, except to those who stood on the deck unprotected, swept away, not by the water, but by the force of its impact.

Then, locked in step six miles behind, the real wave came. The freak, the rogue, the gravity wave. The soliton.

As the Harrier on the flight deck started its engine, the ocean's surface was already beginning to dip as water rushed to fill the volume of the deformation that approached.

As the Harrier strained to roll forward on the deck, the trough preceding the wave became an open pit—a monstrous Niagara of cascading water.

And just as the Harrier lifted off from the raised ramp at the bow, the Illustrious paused, left behind by the advancing trough, so that for one eternal instant, all of its 686-foot length hung over nothingness.

Then, like a match, the ship snapped in two.

The pressure change—from the interior of the sealed carrier to the near-vacuum gale of the wind in the trough—was sufficient to pull the sailors from the now-open lower decks as if they were astronauts in a spaceship ruptured in orbit.

For a single heartbeat, long enough to be aware and know they were still conscious, those sailors saw their ship fly and tumble with them, a fragile plaything tossed by a giant's hand. They saw a water mountain grow so large, so fast, their senses could not comprehend it. And then it struck them so quickly that they were crushed even before they penetrated its surface.

Their ship, though, was stronger than flesh and withstood the first impact as its bulkheads crumpled and every hatch and porthole blew out. Then, suddenly, the two halves of the carrier were swept into the wave's embrace. And just as suddenly, both halves imploded like a submarine beyond its depth.

Eleven hundred souls. Three seconds. The length of time it took the wave to move from stern to bow.

Then the rogue was gone, the sea curiously flat behind it, but for a second swell of forty feet, another oscillation, that followed three miles behind.

All that remained of the Illustrious was a fine mist of bubbles hissing on the water's surface. In a few hours, some debris might surface—a life jacket, some few shards of wood and plastic.

The wave had come, the wave had gone.

New Zealand in seven hours now. Hawaii, thirty-two. Japan, thirty-five. California, thirty-seven.

Like Leviathan, the wave moved on.

SEVEN

NATIONAL MILITARY COMMAND CENTER/THE PENTAGON

General Abbott stared at the IR image coming in to the ETEM wall board from Archangel Four, now above McMurdo. Around him, the emergency action room was silent. Also on screen in her SVTS window, Major Bailey of SPACECOM, in Colorado's Cheyenne Mountain, was so motionless she appeared to be caught in a freeze-frame. And all Abbott could think was that this was a situation that had never been described in any training scenario.

He had been prepared to see a station in ruins, in flames, even undergoing evacuation as lava crept nearer, or any combination of the above.

But what kind of force wiped away *everything* as if it had never existed?

There was only one possible explanation.

"Equipment failure," Abbott said. "Major Bardeen, I want you to make another pass, below the cloud cover, and give me a visual confirm."

But the reply that came in over the speakers was as unexpected as the image. "Uh, sir, if we suck volcanic ash into these engines, we've got one dead aircraft."

Major Chennault supported the pilot's caution. "An Air New Zealand DC-ten crashed on Mount Erebus in seventy-nine. Volcanic ash in the intakes."

Then Bardeen's RSO, Captain Rosinski, reported another complication. "We are also experiencing problems with our radar, General Abbott. I have no confidence we can avoid the terrain below the cloud ceiling."

As much as Abbott burned to know what had happened to the station, this wasn't the time to risk the costly Blackbird. Not to study an event that had already taken place.

"Major Bardeen, Captain Rosinski, I understand your concerns. At your discretion, please attempt another flyby. Anything you can do to increase the resolution of the image without endangering the aircraft will be useful."

Abbott could hear the relief in Bardeen's response. He was a pilot who had been prepared to take his plane lower if he had been so ordered. "Thank you, General. I'm starting my turnaround."

Then Bailey spoke from the board. "General Abbott, may I check some technical readings with Archangel Four?"

"Go ahead."

Abbott turned away from the board to half-lean, half-stand against the EAR conference table as he rubbed the bridge of his nose. To help himself concentrate, he closed his eyes, trying to develop a theory to explain what Bardeen's Blackbird had revealed. He heard, but paid little attention to, Bailey's follow-up with Rosinski.

"Captain Rosinski, Major Bailey, SPACECOM. Can you describe your radar glitch?"

The replies from the Blackbird were slightly delayed, attesting to the complex, secured route the signals were taking through the Milstar system, up and down to geosynchronous satellites, then through Falcon and Cheyenne, before being relayed on to the Pentagon, repeatedly encrypted and decrypted at each listening point along the way. "Muddy returns, Major. Not getting clean signals coming back."

"Have you considered atmospheric ionization?"

Instantly, Abbott opened his eyes, knowing what Bailey was after. Chennault had been right about her. She was tenacious.

"That's my guess," the Blackbird's RSO replied. "I was briefed on the auroral effects we'd find down here."

As Abbott knew she would, Bailey went for the touchdown. He made no attempt to stop her, allowing Bailey to bury herself. "Captain, would you characterize the radar glitch as similar to that caused by ionization due to electromagnetic pulse?"

"That's an affirmative," Rosinski said. "If we weren't a thousand miles from the south magnetic pole, that would have been my first guess."

That was a new piece of information to Abbott. He looked up at Lieutenant Yoshii, who stood ready to change the display on the board at his request. "Lieutenant, show me the location of the south magnetic pole."

The ETEM map of McMurdo shrank by fifty percent to show the bulk of the Antarctic continent curving up to the west of the Ross Sea. A green dot eighty miles off the Adelie Coast, a thousand miles northwest of McMurdo, began to flash. "There it is, sir," Yoshii said. Abbott hoped Rosinski was correct about auroral effects near the pole. That would be a much easier explanation.

But Bailey kept pursuing her own agenda and now spoke to him directly. "General Abbott, that's three strong pieces of circumstantial evidence pointing to a nuclear detonation in the McMurdo region. Loss of signal on the DSCS transmission. Loss of signal on NOAA-20. *And* atmospheric ionization interfering with radar."

With that, the major had pushed too far and too hard. Abbott decided it was time to dispense with her involvement. "Then what happened to McMurdo Station, Major?" He stood up, approaching the big board as if he were speaking to Bailey in the flesh. "I don't see a superheated crater from an on-site detonation. I don't see ruins or any signs of blast damage from a nearby detonation. All I see is a blank slate. Do you know what kind of nuclear detonation makes buildings disappear without damaging the landscape? I sure as hell don't." He was ten seconds from telling Bailey she was relieved.

"Sir, if the weapon detonated in the water, a wave could have washed the station away."

Chennault was staring at the screen. "Good God." His shaven scalp glistened with perspiration.

Abbott began to speak, to dismiss Bailey, but then stopped. The major had just presented him with the solution he had been searching for, though she would have no idea how she had just liberated him. He no longer had to think of unique solutions to an unprecedented situation. He now had ready-made scenarios to draw upon: terrorist attacks on U.S. installations. Tens of thousands of pages of move and countermove had already been laid out for him, developed by the best minds in the Pentagon.

He only had one last condition to check. "An intriguing scenario, Major. Before we run with it, though, I'd like you to confirm with Amundsen-Scott base that they are unharmed and operational."

"At once, sir. Lieutenant Yoshii, I'm turning over Archangel Four to my second, Captain Freedman. He will run the patch to the NMCC."

Yoshii confirmed the handoff and Bailey put her SVTS window on standby.

Chennault lifted a hand to wipe away the sweat beading his forehead. "You think that's it, General?"

"I think that's it," Abbott said. "I just want to confirm that it was a terrorist attack on McMurdo and not on Amundsen-Scott and SHAARP."

"Who would target McMurdo?"

Abbott hadn't proved that part of the equation yet. But he did have a direction to pursue. "Before all this started, there was that broadcast from the environmental nuts."

Chennault frowned. "Earthguard? They're more anti-nuke than Greenpeace."

Abbott had already considered that, and it only confirmed his growing suspicions. "Exactly. So what better way to get the world's attention than to give us all a taste of what they've been warning us about?"

Chennault shook his head. "General, the environmentalists are wackos, no question. And maybe there are some of them extreme enough to cause a real disaster to teach the world a lesson. But you can't honestly believe a bunch of loser longhairs were able to obtain at least three nukes, smuggle one of them onto a rogue submarine, give up two as a diversionary tactic, and then . . . *detonate* one on purpose?"

"Maybe the detonation was accidental," Abbott said. "But here's something else to consider, it was on the news report when all this started: Earthguard just won some huge lawsuit in England. Two hundred million dollars. You can make quite a statement with that kind of money."

Chennault's expression showed he was still unconvinced. Abbott put his hand on the major's shoulder. "Think it through, Major. Who *else* could it be? If any of the terrorist groups on the hot list had a nuke, you think they'd waste it in Antarctica? No. They'd hit the U.N., D.C., London . . . someplace where they'd get a higher kill rate and more publicity. Provided Bailey can tell us that Amundsen-Scott is unharmed, that SHAARP wasn't the real target, then we're likely dealing with a radical green group."

"You're probably right," Chennault said, coming around as Abbott had trusted he would. "I just hope we're not missing something obvious."

Abbott gave Chennault's shoulder a paternal squeeze, then returned to the big board to give Lieutenant Yoshii a string of orders.

"Lieutenant, we are preparing for a SNAP BLUE response. I am going to need in this room representatives from the DOE, the DIA, Justice, the Interior, and the OSD—we're going to need to brief the President. And get me a public-affairs officer." He checked his watch. "As soon as Major Bailey makes her report, I'll want a press conference within the hour." Abbott smiled as he pictured the reaction in America as U.S. citizens woke up this Thanksgiving morning to find their military hard at work tracking down those responsible for a horrendous terrorist act. *That* was the type of lesson Americans really needed, so they would appreciate the men and women who served them, who had been so often and so wrongly ignored.

The room buzzed with purposeful reaction as new IR images appeared on the board from Archangel Four's second flyby, showing the complete absence of McMurdo. Now that he had a target, now that he had an adversary, now that he had a *mission*, General Abbott felt the same exhilarating current energize him as well. He felt alive. He felt needed.

It was going to be a good Thanksgiving after all.

USSPACECOM/EARTH SURVEILLANCE CENTER/CHEYENNE MOUNTAIN

Major Wilhemina Bailey had noticed General Abbott's fixation on Amundsen-Scott base. She thought back to his saying something earlier about not wanting to risk other operations. Presumably, that meant that either Project SHAARP, or some other classified program at the South Pole station, was the reason for his concern. But if someone wanted to compromise Amundsen-Scott, why not attack *it?* Why go after McMurdo?

Unless, she suddenly thought, *we're looking at collateral damage. What if even McMurdo wasn't the target? Just something caught in the cross fire?*

Bailey tapped her fingers on the edge of her situation panel as she waited for the inexorably slow, ELF return from Amundsen-Scott. She couldn't help but feel that everything she was doing would be considerably easier if the general would simply tell her everything he knew.

Huber mounted the stairs to her workstation much more slowly than usual. He was juggling a thick stack of printed documents and was looking for a place to drop them.

Bailey got up and cleared the remains of their combined total of three commissary trays from the chart table behind her chair. She slipped the stacked trays under the table, ready for an airman with some time on his hands.

Huber dropped the documents with a thump, then spread them out on the chart table. He patted the one titled Project BOUNCE-BACK. "This one's hilarious."

Bailey kept one eye on her panel, waiting for Amundsen-Scott's reply. "Just give me the short form, Commander."

Huber picked up the BOUNCEBACK document, all 400 classified pages, and flipped through it as he talked. "Overall—it was a project to develop electronic equipment that could withstand EMP. Specifically—it was to be used to detect incoming Soviet missiles after a high-altitude burst had blanked out NORAD's long-range detectors." Huber rolled his eyes. "So they started building computers out of *vacuum tubes.* Like from the nineteen-forties. Only this was the nineteen-eighties." He stopped his page-flipping at a dark photograph showing someone in a white lab coat standing beside a metal cabinet the size of three refrigerators strapped together. "Can you believe that's a 128K computer?" Huber asked as Bailey studied the photograph. "IBM provided the circuit diagrams, based on their own desktop models, and that thing ended up about eight thousand times bigger than a printed-circuit board. And get this, the screen display was mechanical—made of little pieces of plastic that flipped around to show a black side or a white side. Incredible."

"Did it work?" Bailey asked.

"Yeah, but not as fast as someone with a pencil and a mechanical adding machine. Big surprise."

Bailey resumed watching her panel. There was a single letter on the ELF screen. Amundsen-Scott had received her query and was replying. Another five minutes and she should have the code sequence that would give her their prepackaged message.

"Anything interesting in any of the other reports?" Bailey asked.

"I just scanned the contents pages. LIGHTS OUT was the only one to deal seriously with EMP interacting with the polar aurora, but that was in the Arctic. Unless there's something buried in an index or a footnote, it looks like no one's ever run a full-scale nuclear-war-game scenario based on Antarctic conditions. Except maybe for Icefire."

"You found something?"

"Not exactly, but the contents listing for Operation RED SNOW has an appendix that includes Icefire in its title." Huber again flipped open the thick report.

On the ELF screen, Bailey saw that another letter had been received.

"Here," Huber said as he pointed to the RED SNOW contents page. " 'Icefire Potential of Greenland.' "

"Icefire *potential*?" Bailey repeated. "What's the appendix say?"

Huber closed the report. "The appendix is classified, under separate cover. Not in the archives."

"Potential . . . Sounds like an assessment for development. Something you get from Greenland *and* Antarctica."

Huber lifted an eyebrow. "Uh . . . could that be ice?"

There was a playful streak in Dominic Huber that Bailey found engaging, but this was serious. "Colorado has ice, Commander. Way too much of it. Alaska has ice. Canada, Russia, Scandinavia . . . there's got to be something else important, valuable, that Greenland and Antarctica have in common."

Huber shrugged. "Leave it to me." He started to turn to go.

"And follow up with those queries you made to the other agencies," Bailey said.

Huber paused at the top of the stairs and gave her a sharp salute. "All automated, Major. I dispatched a knowbot into the system. It'll keep checking for Icefire references until it finds one and brings it back."

"A 'knowbot'?" Bailey repeated.

Huber grinned like a kid contemplating a new puppy. "It's a computer program. For automatic searches. It makes its own decisions, chooses which archives to check. Saves a lot of time."

" 'Knowbot.' Thank you, Young Skywalker. You're dismissed."

Huber left on the run. Bailey wondered how old he actually was. *I'm probably old enough to be his* . . . She decided not to pursue that particular thought. Next thing, she'd be fixing him up with the girls in data input.

The major sat back down at her workstation. There were five letters in the ELF window. One more to go. Fifteen seconds later, it came up.

Bailey typed in her access code and somewhere in the mountain a VAX computer looked up the six-letter code in a classified list, then printed out the text on her screen.

STATUS NOMINAL. SEVERE ANOMALOUS SEISMIC READINGS ONGOING. ORIGIN OTHER.

"Other?" Bailey hated coded messages created by engineers and not by real people. She called up the list of possible seismic signal-origination messages available to Amundsen-Scott. "Other" was at the bottom of the list, the category used when the signal fit no previously described profile. That meant Amundsen-Scott was telling her they were picking up seismic readings unlike any ever detected before. Which definitely ruled out any kind of bomb blast. "Damn." She was back to the beginning, and worse: Abbott was right.

As Bailey reset her controls and went to get her feed to the NMCC back in synch, she slowly became aware of a buzz of conversation in the dark confines of the workstations on the floor between her and the wall display. She glanced over toward the display, to the world map with key satellite orbits traced on it, three insert screens showing numerical readouts, and a single insert with a satellite image, and briefly wondered what was going on. Then she looked again at the satellite image. She didn't recognize its format. There were no code listings down the side, no coordinates she could read. And because of a jarring imaging error—a computer-graphing glitch had created a perfect, circular curve through the lower left corner of the image—she couldn't even tell what part of the world she was looking at. Then she noticed a line of clouds below the curve that were aligned to match it. Her throat tightened. The curve was not a computer artifact.

"Captain Freedman," she called out.

In front of her control panel, her second glanced back at her. "Yes, Major?"

"What are we looking at?"

Freedman was worried. "South Pacific, ma'am." He glanced over his shoulder at the satellite image. "Right at the top, that's New Zealand."

Bailey checked the satellite orbits on the tracking map. "We don't have anything down there."

"No, ma'am," Freedman said. "It's from a Japanese satellite. The ADEOS-III." It was the latest in the series of Japan's Advanced Earth Observation Satellites, and the first to offer true realtime imagery.

"What the hell is a Japanese data stream doing in the United States Space Command?"

Freedman bit his lip. "Major, it's not a Japanese feed. It's CNN."

Bailey felt as if she had been sucker-punched. How many billions, no, *trillions* of dollars' worth of American equipment had she been trying to juggle around the world, only to have the data she needed dropped in her lap by a lousy Japanese civilian bird? And why hadn't she noticed what was going on on her own floor before this? *Because I was sitting around daydreaming of being a general, or trying to outsmart one.* She was so disgusted with herself she could barely bring herself to speak. "Why is CNN showing a Japanese satellite image?"

The image blurred, then updated. From the barely perceptible change in position of the terminator, Bailey guessed it was a one-minute jump. But the imaging artifact that wasn't an artifact was still there—that precise curve.

"That . . . that line, ma'am? The announcer says it's a wave. And in two hours, it's going to hit New Zealand."

Bailey at once filled in what the CNN announcers and her second hadn't said. Any wave large enough to show up on a satellite weather image wasn't going to stop at New Zealand.

It might not stop for anything.

EIGHT

CLEAR DAY ONE/APPROACHING NEW ZEALAND

Cory awoke to warmth and brilliant sunshine. Her first thought was to stretch, but she had forgotten where she was—in the cockpit of Webber's Harrier. With that, her neck cramped and went into a spasm and then everything hit her at once, stiff legs, sore back, a pounding head.

She braced her helmet with both hands as she took a sharp intake of breath, tried to straighten up, to see the wave.

But to her right, the sea was glorious, deep blue stretching toward a golden sunrise, so perfect it seemed nothing could disturb it. To her left, she could see rich green forests wreathed in morning mist. Eden. And straight ahead, she saw Webber's right hand waving over the back of his seat, holding a black wire with an input jack on the end. He was jabbing it down on the right-hand side. It was clear what he was telling her to do.

Cory shifted in her seat, every movement agony, until she could see hidden away to the side a small panel with inputs. The panel had been invisible in the darkness last night. She stiffened, recalling the sailors again, arms linked on the deck, one of them blowing a kiss to her as the sound she'd felt more than heard had engulfed them.

She shoved the wire from her helmet into an input labeled INT, guessing the letters meant intercom, or something internal. She

221

winced as her helmet speakers crackled with static. What seemed to be a volume control was located next to the input. She adjusted the control and the speaker hiss faded. "Is this working?" she asked.

"Welcome back," Webber said. Ahead of her, he raised his hand in a thumbs-up.

"Where are we?" All she could remember was the absence of stars above her, the roar of the engine, her hands squeezing the safety straps because she couldn't fasten them. It seemed she had spent hours in that position, huddled in her seat, unable to move, or talk to Webber, or make any sense of her continued existence. Until the sunrise had released her.

"Over New Zealand," Webber answered. "You were out cold for about an hour. We've been flying for just over two."

"What happened to the *Illustrious*?"

"You know what happened, Cory."

She did. She just didn't want to believe it. Like Johnny. She straightened up cautiously in her seat, stretching her neck to relieve the cramp and look out at the ocean again. Long, slow swells rippled its sun-dappled surface. It wouldn't last. "Does anyone else know?" she asked.

"I picked up the 109th in Christchurch about thirty minutes ago. They know we're coming. I told them about the wave and they put through a Flash Alert to just about everybody. I'm still waiting for a response."

A half hour is too long to wait, and Webber knows it. Cory could see it now. The world would come to an end because of some military bureaucratic screwup. "When do we land?"

"About ten minutes."

"Is Christchurch inland?" Cory ran her fingers underneath the edge of her helmet. Her scalp itched maddeningly. She was glad she couldn't smell her hair. It could only reek of jet fuel, salt water, and vomit.

"No, but it's protected on the north side of a promontory."

"If it's not inland, it's *not* protected. That thing might be two hundred feet in open ocean, but when it starts coming up on the shoals and its wavelength changes, it's going to speed up, it's going to grow, and then it's going to break—like a mountain falling on its side. Nothing coastal's protected, Mitchell. Nothing."

Cory looked out over New Zealand again, saw the lush countryside coming to life in the dawn. She wondered if she and Webber would be the last people ever to see it this way.

CHRISTCHURCH

The New York Air National Guard 109th Air Wing operated runways associated with Christchurch's international airport. As instructed by ground control, Webber brought Clear Day One in on the runway farthest from the civilian operations. Past a stretch of tall scrubby grass, there was a forest, very little else. Two humvees and six personnel were on the tarmac to meet them.

As Webber popped the canopy, the sudden wave of moist warm air was a shock. In the eight days since he had cycled through Christchurch on his way to McMurdo, he had forgotten what it was like to be anything but cold. Two of the welcoming committee rolled a ladder to the side of the Harrier and Webber leapt down, surprised to see that they were MPs, not ground crew. Webber paused to make certain that Cory could negotiate the ladder as well, then turned toward the rest of the group waiting for him noticing that it consisted of two Air Force fliers in jumpsuits, and two more ANG military police. The MPs were checking what appeared to be photographs.

Webber put a hand out to help Cory down the last step, then spoke to the MPs by the ladder. "I told the air controllers I wanted to see the CO as soon as I landed. Where is he?"

The larger MP kept one hand on the exposed grip of his .45. "There are other matters to attend to first, sir."

Then the Air Force fliers stepped forward: a major, black with a rakish mustache, and a captain, lanky, with her long blond hair woven into an elaborate braid. Both wore sunglasses, making it difficult for Webber to judge their mood.

The major held out his hand to Webber. "Captain Webber, I'm Major Emmet Bardeen. This is my RSO, Captain Lou Rosinski."

Webber shook their hands but didn't understand their presence. "I made myself clear to the air controllers. We're in a situation where every minute means lives. Where's the CO?"

Bardeen held up his hands, telling Webber to slow down. "Captain, we're here to meet you under the direct authority of General Charles Abbott at the NMCC."

At once, Webber felt an enormous burden lifted from him. "Okay, all right, we're starting at the top."

"Hold it, what top?" Cory interrupted.

"National Military Command Center," Rosinski said. "The Pentagon." She showed a photo to Bardeen. "She's our Dr. Rey."

Cory grabbed the photo from the captain, then held it up for Webber. The photo trembled in her hand. "At least Hal and Johnny got the signal out."

Webber took the photo from her. It was a videoprint complete with scanlines and a CNNI logo, showing Cory speaking into a microphone on the deck of a ship. He handed the print back to Rosinski.

"What's the NMCC's involvement in this?" Webber asked.

Bardeen slipped off his sunglasses as if to make sure Webber could understand how serious the Pentagon was about the situation. "Thirty-five minutes ago, the Vice-President gave a news conference alerting the world to the existence of a tsunami, larger than any in recorded history, believed to have been generated by the collapse of the Ross Ice Shelf."

"*Believed* to have been?" Cory said, her face flushing with anger. "And what about the *bombs*?"

Bardeen looked sharply at Webber. "Captain Webber, we should have the rest of this discussion in a secure area."

Webber shook his head. "She's with me." He took Cory's hand and drew her up beside him. He squeezed her hand hard, in warning. She squeezed back, just as hard.

"Yeah, I'm with *him*."

Bardeen tried again. "I'm not authorized to discuss this with a civilian."

"Fine," Webber said. "I'll tell General Abbott you were unable to brief me. What are the evacuation plans? And how the hell did the Pentagon and the Vice-President get brought on board so fast?"

Bardeen glanced from Webber to Cory as if the briefing he had received had not anticipated this reaction from them.

Webber resented each lost second. "Major, get it straight—Dr. Rey saw this thing, she understands it, she's got the facts and figures we need to calculate the evacuation areas. And she is part of this."

"He doesn't go anywhere without me these days." Wisely, Cory said nothing more.

Bardeen was obviously keeping his temper in check with an effort. Webber sympathized, but held firm. "Captain, you might as well tell us both what's going on."

Bardeen looked at Rosinki, who shrugged.

"The evacuations are already under way," Bardeen began. "New Zealand is going to absorb the biggest impact. The thinking is the Polynesian islands and most of the Solomons are probably a write-off, but authorities there are moving their people to the northern sides of all the islands as rapidly as they can. They're expecting casualties, but the numbers should be low. The international relief effort is likely going to take at least a year."

"And . . . ?" Cory prompted.

When Bardeen didn't continue his list, Cory did.

"Hawaii?" she said. "California, Oregon, Washington, British Columbia? Taiwan, Japan, China—my God—for China, the Yellow Sea's going to concentrate this thing like a Venturi valve!"

Bardeen clearly disapproved of the intense emotion Cory displayed. He looked at Webber with a frown. "Dr. Rey, as I understand it, regular high-water alerts *are* going out all around the Pacific Rim. But the Vice-President said Hawaii, the West Coast, and Asia . . . they can expect maybe forty-foot breakers."

"*What?*"

Cory dropped Webber's hand and moved forward as if to threaten Bardeen.

"This is a *two-hundred-footer,* Captain! When it hits the shorelines it's—"

"*Dr. Rey!*" Bardeen's exclamation was a perfect imitation of a drill sergeant, and it stopped Cory dead. "*If* you have an issue to take up with the Vice-President of the United States and the science and military advisors who appeared with him on national television, I *suggest* you write your congressman." Now Bardeen brought his attention to bear on Webber like locking on a laser-guided bomb. "Captain Webber, if you insist on keeping this woman in your custody, I will expect you to have her behave in an appropriate manner. Do you understand, Captain?"

"Captain Webber is not my superior and neither are you!" Cory said.

And that's as far as Webber let her go.

He spoke quickly to the two Air Force fliers on Cory's behalf. "My apologies. Dr. Rey lost . . . someone . . . at McMurdo. She's had . . . a tough night."

As Webber had expected, Bardeen toned down his attitude. Proper command authority had been established. "I understand. We flew over McMurdo last night. There's nothing left." Bardeen nodded at Cory. "I'm sorry for your loss, Doctor."

But Webber wasn't interested in politeness. How had Bardeen and Rosinski managed to be over McMurdo *after* the wave had hit and reach Christchurch *ahead* of him? "What the hell were you flying, Major? The space shuttle?"

Bardeen smiled, showing all his teeth. "Even better. The Blackbird."

"Nice ride," Webber said. And that was all the time he wanted to waste with the pilot. "Did you happen to see the wave?" he asked, knowing that the SR-71 would have been flying far too high at night to find anything it wasn't specifically looking for.

"Not in flight," Bardeen answered. "Just the satellite photos from this morning."

"If it's not too much trouble, I'd like to see those," Cory said, her voice tense but civil.

"They're available on television," Rosinski said.

"Any word on who's claiming responsibility?" Webber asked.

Bardeen glanced at the closest MP, lowered his voice. "General Abbott has asked to speak to you about that. For the moment, this is being treated as a . . . natural disaster."

Cory's mouth dropped open. "There were nuclear—" Webber tugged sharply on her flight suit, interrupting her before she could say more.

"We're ready to talk to the general right away," he said.

Bardeen gestured to the parked humvees.

Webber lowered his head to speak quietly to Cory, as they all walked as a group toward the humvees. "First rule of combat: Save your ammunition for when it'll do some good. Bardeen's just the messenger, not worth a fight. General Abbott will give us a good hearing."

"You know this general?"

"Of him. He's a two-star on the Joint Staff. Came out of Special Ops."

They arrived at the humvees. One of the MPs held open a rear door for Webber and Cory.

"Cory," Webber warned, "whatever happens, no matter what you think of Abbott, don't lose your temper—"

"I never lose my temper. Just my patience."

The MP shut the door and hopped up into the back cargo deck. Bardeen got behind the wheel. *Odd,* thought Webber. *MPs drive majors, not the other way around.*

"Just do me—us—a favor, then, and don't lose your patience with him. He's a guy who can make a difference."

"What? And we can't?"

With a sigh, Webber settled himself as comfortably as he could on the hard bench seat, wondering if he might dare close his eyes for a few minutes. He'd been going at least twenty-eight hours without sleep, and the adrenaline rush of escaping the *Illustrious* had worn off at least an hour ago. That made him think of the leather case Captain Sofronski had entrusted to him. He decided he'd give the ship's log and the captain's letters directly to Bardeen, who would expedite their delivery to the British Embassy in New Zealand. Then Webber leaned back and closed his eyes, hoping by doing so to ward off further discussion with Cory.

"I hate it when you do that," she said.

The humvee rocked to a stop at another runway. Webber opened his eyes and looked out to see a gleaming, silver-skinned CF Galaxy transport beginning its takeoff. The lumbering aircraft's tail was painted bright red. Once, Webber knew, it would have been going to McMurdo. He wondered where it was going now, if it was involved in the island evacuations.

"Nothing's changed since we last talked about this, Cory," Webber said, raising his voice to be heard as the Galaxy rumbled past and the humvee trembled. "It's still cut-and-dried. The best way to keep the world free from . . . nuclear weapons and Chernobyls and . . . environmental disaster, is to work for the people who have the resources and the guts to take action against those things. That's what I chose to do with my life. That's why I'm with NEST. That's why I was in Antarctica."

The Galaxy lifted off and the humvee started up again.

"I was in Antarctica, too, remember?" Cory said.

"You want to hear something strange, Cory? When I thought about it, I wasn't even surprised."

"Why would you be? I was there to do the right thing—stop nuclear weapons. Not by working for the people—the *same* people, Mitchell—who make the damn things, but for all the rest of us in the world who don't want them, period."

"Oh, c'mon, Cory, nobody in their right mind wants nukes in the wrong hands. Think of it this way. Organizations like Earthguard are all on their own. But *I've* got the Pentagon behind me. That means I've got access to satellites and aircraft and scientists and soldiers. I can go after loose nukes and get them."

"Except your employer has a vested interest in *keeping* nukes around."

"Responsibly!"

"The Pentagon? Responsible? You're asking me to trust the Pentagon?"

Webber became aware of Bardeen watching them both from the rearview mirror.

"No, I'm asking you to trust me—and people like me."

Webber was surprised by the sudden intensity of emotion he felt as he waited for Cory's reply. But all she had to say was "Johnny trusted you."

Webber shot a glance, over his shoulder, to the second humvee behind them, an MP wheel, Rosinski and the second MP riding inside. He and Cory were being isolated. He didn't know why.

For the first time in his life, Webber wondered if Cory might be right about the Pentagon.

NINE

At the side of Major Bailey's situation panel were four phones: gold for initiating Flash Alerts, red for receiving them, green for internal calls, and a particularly ugly gray one for everything else. It was the gray phone Bailey used now to call San Diego, and she wasn't happy about it. She had been hoping to get her mother on the line—she was the early riser of the family—but her father had been in the kitchen and answered first. Unfortunately, her father was the marathon conversation champion of the entire family, and as she fiddled with the prepaid calling card she had used, she wondered how much longer the ten-dollar card would last.

"It sounds wonderful, Pops. Sausage stuffing is my favorite. And the yams, too. Is Mom down yet?"

Bailey sighed as her father launched into a new detailed description of her mother's hip operation, how she had lived in the living room for the first four weeks because of the stairs, how she was now handling the stairs, but slower than before, though she'd been getting better.

"I need to talk to Mom. Call her again, please?"

Bailey held the phone away from her ear as her father bellowed for "Woman" to get into the kitchen and talk to her daughter. A second later, Bailey heard her mother tell her father that he didn't have to yell, she was right there.

229

"Hello? Darlene?"

Bailey stared up at the distant ceiling of the control room. Darlene was her sister who still lived in San Diego. "It's Willie, Mom. I'm at work."

"But . . . aren't you supposed to be on your way by now?"

Bailey kept her eyes on the display screens above her situation panel. She finally had a realtime NOAA feed of the South Pacific on one, showing the wave closing in on New Zealand, an estimated ninety minutes from first impact. In another screen, she saw two of the sorriest-looking people she'd ever seen on an SVTS feed: survivors from McMurdo, now with the 109th in Christchurch. And on the screen beside them, she had Lieutenant Yoshii waiting for General Abbott to return so he could be patched into the Christchurch circuit. "That's what I was trying to tell Pops. I can't make it home today. I'm sorry, but . . ."

"Is it the wave, sweetheart?"

Bailey found it odd to hear her seventy-year-old mother refer in such a familiar way to what she herself saw on the satellite image, as if it were a new movie or hit song.

"Yeah, Mom. We're all tracking it here and a lot of people had already taken off for the holiday, so . . . we're going to be taking some double shifts." That was an understatement, of course, but Bailey knew that providing additional details might put her at risk of breaking security. She had never seen the control room with every observation console in use. Virtually all of the country's satellite resources were being directed toward the South Pacific. And with China's People's Liberation Army Navy having called off its war games near Taiwan in order to prepare for the high breakers expected, even the NRO's surveillance satellites were being retasked.

Bailey's mother began to whisper. "Willie, I know you're on a government phone, but . . . are we safe here?"

Bailey sighed. Her fascination with the secrets of the government and the military, and her desire to know more about them, had started at her mother's knee. But Bailey's parents lived in a wonderful, eighty-year-old frame house in La Jolla, a safe ten blocks up from the ocean. "Yeah, Mom. Just do what the Vice-President said, okay, and stay away from the beach tomorrow." Before her operation, Bailey's mother walked to the beach every day, but her doctors said it would be another few months before she could get back to that routine.

"The Vice-President told you that?"

Bailey rested her head in her hand. "Mom, he was on TV. Didn't you see him?"

On the NMCC feed, Lieutenant Yoshii began speaking. General Abbott had returned.

"Mom, I've got to go. I'll be home Saturday. Love you. Bye."

Bailey hung up quickly, not waiting for a response. If her parents weren't used to her work by now, they never would be.

Bailey activated the audio on the Christchurch feed. "Hello, Christchurch, this is SPACECOM. I have General Abbott online."

The two survivors straightened up in their chairs. They were both in Air Force flight suits, but only the man looked as if he belonged in one. Even though his face looked haggard, he had the proper military bearing, great shoulders, and the crisp short hair of a soldier. But the woman, who somehow looked familiar, Bailey thought, was obviously a civilian, and her short black hair was a real mess. Bailey didn't want to imagine what they had been through. The IR images of McMurdo had been haunting in their barrenness.

Bailey activated the NMCC audio. "Lieutenant Yoshii, Christchurch is online and ready for the general." Yoshii acknowledged and then Bailey added, "We're going to be doing a lot of jumping to hold this connection, so I'm going to stay online to monitor." So far, Falcon AFB had concluded that FLTSATCOM had lost five birds to the widespread EMP effect that had occurred when the Ross Ice Shelf collapsed. With all the preparations under way to provide relief to Polynesia and the Solomons, satellite communications, military and civilian, were close to overload.

Then the NMCC feed changed as Yoshii switched cameras to a shot of General Abbott. Bailey still found the camera's placement disconcerting. The general's uniform looked as if he hadn't worn it for more than five minutes, so she knew he must have had a spare in his office, probably two or three, but once again his head ballooned out of proportion to the rest of him as a result of the distorting camera angle. More engineers, Bailey decided, as she stifled a smile. Designing for efficiency and not effect.

The male survivor spoke first. "General Abbott, I'm Captain Mitch Webber, on detached service to—"

Abbott didn't let him finish. "That's quite all right, Captain Webber. I am well aware of your splendid service record. I take it the young woman with you is Dr. Corazon Rey?"

Bailey wasn't surprised by the female civilian's displeased reaction to being referred to as a "young woman," but she was surprised when Webber answered for his companion.

"Yes, sir."

"We all saw her on television."

The general didn't sound pleased and Bailey immediately placed the civilian. She was the Earthguard activist who had been broadcasting from the Antarctic through the Internet. Bailey had been impressed by the cleverness of the technique when she had heard how it had been accomplished by video compression over an ordinary satellite voice channel.

Neither Webber nor Rey responded to the general's comment, so Abbott continued. "Captain, I understand you have firsthand information about the possible use of nuclear weapons involved in the Shelf collapse."

Bailey watched Rey shift in her chair and knew it was a struggle for her not to speak for herself. Civilians always had a hard time adjusting to the way things were done in the military. But Bailey, as much as Abbott, believed that there was reason for proper procedure. It helped contain inappropriate reactions that got in the way of effective decision-making and action.

"Yes, sir," Webber answered. "But what we saw was a *definite* use of nukes. We both personally witnessed an atmospheric detonation minutes before McMurdo was destroyed by the initial displacement wave. That airburst was accompanied by the crash of two helicopters that had just taken off from the station, strongly suggesting EMP, and by a period of intense ionization that rendered the radar on my aircraft inoperable. Also, approximately four hours before the airburst, McMurdo experienced what at first was reported as an earthquake, but which Dr. Rey—and I—now believe was a series of underground, or deep-ice, nuclear detonations, perhaps as many as six, intended to separate the Ross Ice Shelf from the land so the shelf could be punched down by the airburst."

Bailey's sharp intake of breath revealed her surprise. No wonder Abbott was being so cagey. This wave wasn't an accident caused by a loose nuke. Its activation was deliberate.

"An intriguing scenario," Abbott said. Bailey recognized the phrase. It was the same one the general had used when he had

232

heard her suggest that an underwater detonation could have been the source of the wave that destroyed McMurdo.

Webber continued. "It's more than a scenario, sir. And from the precision with which the Shelf was separated and then accelerated into the Ross Sea, we believe that the wave propagated by that collapse is not a simple displacement wave."

Now Abbott seemed confused and Bailey *was* confused. The satellite images made it clear. The impossibly perfect curve of water radiating from the mouth of the Ross Sea could only be a wave.

"Well, then, what is it?" Abbott's fist tapped the side of his leg. The unconscious gesture seemed to Bailey to betray some inner agitation in the general. Bailey's attention sharpened as she waited for Webber's reply.

Webber started to answer, "It's . . . ," but he hesitated. He looked at Rey as if her turn had finally arrived.

As soon as Rey began to speak, she reminded Bailey of a racehorse that had just been released from the gate. "It's a soliton, General. A special class of wave first described in 1834 by John Scott Russell. The mathematics of the phenomenon were established in 1895 by Korteweg and de Vries, and are used today to describe the fundamental properties of quantum—"

"Get to the point," Abbott said.

From the general's abrupt manner, it was clear that Rey would not have long to make her case. Abbott and civilians were not a comfortable mix.

Bailey saw static rush across the feed from Christchurch and adjusted the frequency lock. She checked the countdown timer on her panel. In five minutes, she'd have to stand ready to switch Christchurch to the next DSCS on the horizon in case the interlink was lost due to the high demand for bandwidth.

"The point. The point is that a soliton doesn't lose energy. That's not water moving *across* the surface of the ocean. It's a pulse of energy that's traveling *through* the water."

Abbott's reply seemed condescending, even to Bailey. "Something that doesn't lose energy is a violation of at least one natural law of which I'm aware."

But Rey seem unsurprised by Abbott's attitude toward her. "Yes, it *does* lose energy. Of course it loses energy, but not at the same rate as . . . as a wave created by wind. And that's what your experts are telling everyone is going to hit New Zealand and the islands, an *ordinary* wave."

Abbott crossed his arms. "Dr. Rey, I would not call a two-hundred-foot wave 'ordinary.' "

"General, please, now you're missing the point."

"No, Dr. Rey, you are failing to make one."

Rey placed both her hands flat on the tabletop in front of her and took a deep breath. Bailey saw Captain Webber shake his head surreptitiously in warning at her.

"You want a point? Here's a point. That two-hundred-footer that's going to hit New Zealand is going to shoot up the west coast of North America like a scalpel. Only it won't be two hundred feet. It'll be three hundred, four hundred, hell, depending on the slope of the coast, you could be looking at a *six-hundred-foot wave* breaking over the Santa Monica bluffs and flooding the Los Angeles Basin! *That's* my point, General Abbott. And the longer you keep that from the people of the Pacific Rim, the more of them you're going to kill!"

"Holy shit," Bailey whispered. Commander Huber's favorite exclamation now seemed completely appropriate. On the Christchurch feed, Webber looked angry and Rey looked like a force of nature. On the Pentagon feed, Abbott's head was lowered, deep in thought. Bailey suspected—no, she was certain—that if anyone in uniform had dared to speak to the general that way, the firing squad would already be forming in the Pentagon's center courtyard.

"Dr. Rey," the general finally said. "Whatever you saw, and whatever your qualifications are for describing what you saw, you seem to be unaware of the simple scientific fact that no wave can be taller than . . . one hundred and ninety-eight feet, I'm told."

Rey leaned into the camera as if she were about to physically spring through the connection to get at Abbott's throat. "Which is why that thing in the Pacific *is* only two hundred—one hundred ninety-eight—whatever feet tall. *All* the energy from the collapse of the Ross Ice Shelf is traveling in the most efficient means possible, until something gets in its way, and then *all* that energy is released at once. Oh, God . . . how do . . ." Suddenly, the woman's eyes brightened, a look of inspiration, though Bailey knew the chances of her changing the general's mind were nonexistent. In fact, Bailey was amazed that General Abbott was letting Rey talk without interruption. Not that anyone of lesser status ever had a real discussion with a general. She wondered if she'd become like Abbott if—when—she became a general.

Rey continued with increased confidence. "General, bear with me one more minute. Have you ever seen those desk toys or whatever that demonstrate Newton's laws of motion? You know, five steel ball bearings hanging from string in a little wooden frame. You've seen those, right? And what you do is you pull up on the first ball at one end and you let it go and it swings down and hits the second ball and the second ball *doesn't move.* It just sits there, transferring the energy of the first ball's momentum to the next ball. And that next ball doesn't move, and the next ball doesn't move, but when all that energy reaches the last ball, it flies up! The Ross Ice Shelf was a seven-hundred-billion-ton ball, General. The ocean is all those other balls that just sit there passing the energy along. And when the ocean runs out and there's nothing left to pass that energy along to, *pow,* the full force of that ice-shelf collapse is going to explode in your face." Then Cory sat back in her chair and carefully crossed her arms just like Abbott's.

"Dr. Rey," Abbott said with the supreme self-control of the one truly in charge, "we will now end this part of the conversation. I will pass on your 'desk-toy' theory to the appropriate members of the Vice-President's Special Committee. But I would advise you to consider, since that committee consists of the top people in oceanography from both the Navy and the academic world, how is it that *you* are somehow the only expert to think of a soliton wave? Don't you think it is much more likely that the Vice-President's experts, with access to the constant data streaming in from the wave, have already considered the soliton explanation, and ruled it out?"

"Then let me talk to the top people!"

"I'm sure you'll have your chance." To Bailey, the general's voice suggested the opposite. "Captain Webber, I have a few more questions. I suggest Dr. Rey leave the room."

Rey glared at Webber as if daring him also to challenge the general's authority. But when he quite properly made no move to do so, she stood up so quickly that Bailey could hear a chair hit the floor. Someone in the background stepped in to right it again. Then Rey stormed off camera.

Webber folded his hands on the table where he sat. Abbott remained silent, as if expecting the captain to offer some apology for the woman's behavior, but Webber said nothing. Abbott ran out of patience first.

"Before we get into this, how did *she* manage to be the person you brought out with you, Captain?"

"Dr. Rey offered the Earthguard ship to help with the evacuation of McMurdo. I was heading out to it with her and . . ." Bailey studied Webber. It was evident to her that the captain was editing what he was saying, holding something back just as Abbott had. She wondered if the general would notice. "That's when the sea ice started to break up. I decided to take one of the Clear Day Harriers out of range of the volcano to her ship, and . . . just after we launched, there was the airburst and . . . the wave hit."

"Were any of the other NEST personnel able to escape?"

Interesting, Bailey thought as she observed Webber's face darken. That question brought the most emotional reaction she had seen yet from the captain.

"Sir—now that we're secure, I have to give you the full report. The commander of NEST Two, Nick Young . . . he is one of the people responsible for the detonations, and the collapse."

Bailey saw the shock register on Abbott's face, then change to stern graveness as he waited for the captain to elaborate.

"Young escaped after I located a Stiletto-class MIRV warhead being deployed into a borehole drilled into the ice. All members of both NEST teams, except for Young and me, were killed in the attempt to stop the warhead's deployment. NEST Two's engineer, Glendon Morris, was also working with Young. She was also killed. Young escaped from the deployment site by what I assume to be a Harrier." Webber glanced down at his wrist. Bailey could see that he wore two watches. "That was twelve . . . twelve and a half hours ago. He could be anywhere by now."

Abbott found his voice, clearly deeply affected by what Webber had recounted. "Young was a fine officer. Had to be, to be chosen for USURP—like you. Both of you . . . exemplary. Did . . . were you able to talk with him?"

"Sir, I have no idea why he was involved, or who was behind it," Webber said. "The only thing I can think of is that he sold out. But what the motives are of whoever he sold out to . . . well, by now I would have thought someone would have taken credit."

Abbott cleared his throat and Bailey saw that he had regained his composure. "Captain, our response to the events at McMurdo is being conducted as a SNAP BLUE alert. You understand that the scenario calls for us not to reveal that what has happened is a terrorist action, precisely so we can better judge the veracity of those who do eventually claim responsibility."

"Yes, sir."

"And I must share with you how deeply disturbed I am that someone from Young's background, naval aviator, SEAL, USURP pilot . . . his work at the Pentagon in setting up rapid response to chemical- and bacteriological-warfare terrorism . . . I am astounded."

"He was my friend, sir. I thought he was. I feel the same way."

Abbott chewed his lip, the first sign of actual personality Bailey had seen him exhibit that was not as precise and as predictable as the moves of a military marching band. "In addition to the Vice-President's committee, I have formed a Crisis Action Team here to deal with the classified issues of this matter. I'd like you to be fully debriefed by them here in D.C."

"Of course, sir."

"Very good, I'll expect you here in five hours."

Bailey appreciated Webber's momentary expression of confusion, soon replaced by the same look of enlightenment that had flashed across Rey's face.

"I take it you mean the Blackbird, sir."

"We have inflight refueling assets in Fiji and Hawaii, then Edwards will pick you up for the final leg."

A brief smile played on Webber's lips. Bailey understood. The Blackbirds were the sweetest ride in the Air Force. For now, at least.

"General, may I suggest that Dr. Rey accompany me, also for debriefing. She is—"

"Negative, Captain. I would like her contained at the 109th for at least the next twenty-four hours. Then she can—"

Abbott stopped as Bailey saw the bald Army major step into camera range, cover his mouth, and whisper something the audio pickup couldn't hear. Bailey had seen the major at Abbott's side off and on during the last ten hours. This time he was holding a red folder marked CLASSIFIED. He pointed out something in the folder to Abbott. Abbott nodded, then returned to Webber.

"Change of plans, Captain. We've just reviewed Dr. Rey's file, and . . . I would like her here as soon as possible. Bring her on the Blackbird."

While Bailey was wondering what the bald major had said to Abbott to make him change his mind about Rey, she saw a third party join the feed from Christchurch: the image of a good-looking black Air Force major with a troubled expression. "General, Major Bardeen here. I can't take two passengers."

"You won't have to, Major. Captain Webber is fully qualified in the SR-71."

To Bailey, Bardeen looked as if he had just been kicked where no man should ever be kicked. "Sir, that's my aircraft. The Black-birds, sir . . . they're all different, they all have their quirks, their—"

"It's the taxpayers' aircraft, Major," Abbott said. "And I need Captain Webber and Dr. Rey in D.C. in five hours. I will expect you to show him everything he needs to know about any quirks you believe significant."

Bardeen slumped like a deflating parachute. "Yes, sir."

"And Captain Webber," the general added, "again I remind you that you are not to discuss the involvement of nuclear warheads in these events, with Dr. Rey, or with any other civilian or military personnel. Is that clear?"

"Yes, sir."

"Have a good flight." Abbott gestured to the side and the NMCC feed went to STANDING BY.

On the Christchurch feed, Webber looked around at whoever else was in the room with him. "Where can I get some coffee?" he said. Then the screen went dark.

"You're all very welcome, and good night," Bailey said to no one. She closed off her connection to Christchurch, freeing up the signal path for the next transmission in line for the circuit.

Then, for the moment, her situation panel was clear, until the next communications request came through from Abbott. She rested her eyes by gazing across at the control-room wall display. Now it was a mosaic of television feeds. CNNI was the largest. A reporter in the cockpit of what seemed to be a LC-130 personnel transport was broadcasting live from over the Pacific, heading out to the wave to record its first contact with New Zealand. Other news broadcasts showed Royal New Zealand Navy Sea King helicopters winching up passengers from the decks of small craft not expected to reach shore in time. One lonely video window in the corner of the wall display showed highlights of the Macy's Thanksgiving Day parade. True to form, the *South Park* Kenny balloon had collided with a traffic light and deflated for the third year in a row.

"We got a hit!" Dominic Huber called out behind her, so loudly that Bailey was startled. She spun around in her chair to see him charge up the stairs of her platform. "Icefire!"

"Oh," Bailey said. She had almost forgotten. Other than determining what group had caused the Ice Shelf to collapse, there were no more mysteries left about what had happened in the Ross Sea. "So what was it?"

Huber shrugged and Bailey saw he wasn't carrying anything. "Don't know. But I got a reference. Here." He went to her panel and used the keyboard to access his own terminal on the floor. A series of data windows flickered onto the screen. One of them carried an NSA header. "Okay, so the knowbot went into the defense net, dropping queries about Icefire in every server it came to. One of them was the NSA's FILTER system."

"You can do that?" Bailey asked. FILTER, the Focused Intelligent Listening Terminal, was one of the largest brute-force computer networks in the country. Network nodes were installed at every major telecommunications switching facility, usually located in what appeared to be ordinary office buildings, noticeable only because of the surprising amount of security protecting them and their lack of prominent identifying signs. What the FILTER units did, essentially, was to listen in on every phone call made within the United States, as well as those originating elsewhere and ending in the country.

In a series of secret agreements reached between the government and the telecommunications companies in the late 1980s—related to the FCC's opening an unused spectrum of radio frequencies for a new generation of civilian phones, pagers, and other personal-communications systems—the major carriers voluntarily gave the government access to their networks: landline, fiber-optic, micro-wave, and satellite. First-amendment questions were considered moot because no human agent would eavesdrop on a phone conversation without cause. Instead, machines would. They were simple, low-power, purpose-built devices whose only function was to listen for specific words and word groupings used in conversation. These target words were strictly limited to phrases and contexts which should only occur over secure government lines. Use of them by any other person over unsecured telephone links was a strong indication of espionage or other federal crime. In order to preserve FILTER's effectiveness and secrecy, its capabilities had never been offered to any law-enforcement agency, and never would.

When a machine identified one of the target words or phrases, it contacted an NSA operator who would then listen to a digital recording of the entire conversation in order to judge how the target word had been used in context. Most of the time, the use was innocent, or the result of computer misidentification. However, those few times that incriminating conversations were detected, Bailey knew, had allowed major espionage cases to be developed and successfully pursued. No FILTER transcript had ever appeared in court, however. Another, legally acceptable reason for initiating each case was always quickly established instead. The best weapons were those the enemy didn't know existed.

Bailey also knew that the FILTER system was one of the key reasons why the government was so adamantly opposed to the introduction of unbreakable encryption schemes. The cost of replacing hundreds of thousands of FILTER processor boards with upgraded versions that could listen *and* perform high-level decryption in realtime would be horrendous, even for an agency like the NSA, whose budget was never broken down for Congress. The NSA had had a hard enough time keeping up with FILTER refinements to scan faxes and E-mail in the 1990s.

Given the system's importance and security, Bailey was surprised that Commander Huber had been able to access any part of it.

"FILTER has always been available to Space Command," Huber explained as he opened a downloaded file on the screen. "We use it for every launch. NASA, DOD, even civilian. Just in case someone's talking about shooting at a booster or something."

Bailey recognized the file format as a digital recording. "So you just typed in a request for 'Icefire,' and FILTER started listening for any use of the word?"

"Well, the knowbot added Icefire to the target list. FILTER found it and, since it wasn't classified, it forwarded the conversation to me to hear in context."

"And . . . ?"

"Get this," Huber said. He clicked the PLAY button on the screen. What came out of the panel speaker next was raspy, with the blurred sound of a recording that had been compressed, the equivalent of a low-resolution computer image.

First, Bailey heard a machine-generated voice. "Eight-four-two is not available. To leave a message, press one. For other options, press two." A beep sounded, the number-1 key on a Touch-Tone phone. And then a man spoke. His voice was deep, rich, and had a distinct accent. Russian, Bailey thought. "David, it's me. I saw the Vice-President's news conference and, well, you know what I thought. You're probably thinking it, too, yes? So, if I can be of service, if there is any part of Icefire that might be useful in studying this terrible, terrible thing, just call. I . . . I owe you so much. And Deborah says hello. Call me." Then a click, a dial tone, and the recording ended.

Huber smiled. "Now, that's a definite connection between the wave and Operation ICEFIRE."

"It is," Bailey agreed, "but maybe it's not *Operation* ICEFIRE. The man said, 'if there's any *part* of Icefire.'" She looked at Huber for interpretative analysis. Data was only the beginning of the process. "Does that make Icefire a device?"

"You mean a weapon?"

"A weapon to cause that kind of wave? Don't even think like that. It would have to be huge."

"Then maybe a process to hide what's happening. An EMP generator of some kind."

Bailey rubbed at the back of her neck. Almost two thousand feet above them, she decided the sun must be up. But down here in what was sardonically called the cave, there was only a constant flood of fluorescent light, no ebb and flow of a natural day, much less Thanksgiving morning. Pops had already been up for hours, fussing about the turkey he'd put in the oven hours before, for what he swore each year would be the best, certainly the slowest-cooked bird they'd ever eat. Her stomach rumbled and she quickly turned her attention back to the present. "What about that Greenland reference in the BOUNCEBACK report? What do Greenland and Antarctica have in common?"

"I looked it up. Not ice. Ice*bergs*."

Bailey didn't get it. "And the difference would be . . . ?"

"An ice shelf. Antarctica is ringed by ice shelves that grow from its glaciers, and when they reach far enough out to sea, they break up and form icebergs. Some of them can be more than a hundred miles long."

"Aren't there icebergs from the Arctic?"

"Your're on it. In the North Pacific, the only icebergs come from the piedmont glaciers in the Gulf of Alaska. And they're just a few. But over in the North Atlantic, more than ninety percent of all northern icebergs come from Greenland."

Bailey never enjoyed being in possession of more information than she required. So far all she'd learned was that Icefire was a government operation related to EMP over polar regions, *or* it was a weapon having to do with ice, *or* it was a process involving icebergs. None of the possibilities seemed to fit. Especially when she considered the most obstructive condition of all: It wasn't in the Cheyenne Mountain archives, which meant it probably had nothing at all to do with the government in the first place. "I'm stumped, Commander. If you've got suggestions, let me have them."

Huber's blue eyes sparkled with the audacity of youth. "Well, *we* might not know what's going on, but the guy who left that message does. Why don't we just . . . call him?"

Bailey couldn't help smiling as Huber leaned down to enthusiastically type in more commands on the keyboard. Data instantly scrolled up in the NSA window: the originating and receiving phone numbers for the call they'd just heard.

Bailey recognized the area code of the receiving phone number, 703—Arlington, Virginia. Same area code as the Pentagon. But she didn't recognize the code for the originating number. "What's eight-oh-eight?"

"Hawaii," Huber said.

Before she could suppress it, Bailey allowed a wistful sigh to escape her. "I've always wanted to go there."

"My sister lives there," Huber said. "Really nice place on the Big Island. Big guest house, too."

Bailey promptly retreated from that topic. She was too tired; her defenses were dropping. "I'll track this guy down. Why don't you—"

"Get you some tea?"

Bailey nodded gratefully. Every officer should have a mind reader as an assistant. But Huber didn't rush off right away as he usually did. Bailey looked up at him.

"You're not going to tell General Abbott about this, either, are you," Huber said.

Bailey shook her head. "Not yet." As far as she was concerned,

New Zealand would have had an extra hour's warning if she had just put through her Flash Alert directly to Falcon. Instead, she'd told Abbott what her suspicions were and he'd shut her down.

"Didn't think so." Huber smiled again, as if he really could read her mind. "And I'm guessing you know something else you're not telling me." Then he was gone before she could admonish him for his cheekiness.

"So does the general," Bailey said to no one.

Then she went back to work.

TEN

ANG 109TH AIR WING/CHRISTCHURCH, NEW ZEALAND

"Well, that's certainly the biggest penis I've ever seen."

At the entrance to the hangar, Webber turned to scowl at Cory. The unquestionably phallic silhouette of the Blackbird was behind him, a large sharp nose stretching out from short, set-back wings, each with a suggestively round, oversized engine. "Well, it is," she said.

"Don't let Bardeen hear you," Webber said. "We don't need any more trouble."

"Mitchell, I'm wearing a *space suit.* I have a urine collection receptacle stuck to my crotch with adhesive strips. And I'm being hauled off to the Pentagon against my will. Bardeen's the least of my troubles." Cory tried to put her hands on her hips, but it was too difficult a maneuver in the cumbersome orange pressure gear she wore. Just like the suits the shuttle astronauts wore for launches, Captain Rosinski had told her as she had helped Cory into it. Bardeen's reconnaissance officer had seemed to be about as pleased that Cory was going to fly in the Blackbird as Cory was—not at all.

"I *really* don't want to do this," she said as she surveyed the vaguely menacing aircraft before them. After the Harrier, she knew a little of what she'd likely be experiencing—and because Webber seemed to think a Blackbird was a big deal, it could be an even bigger deal for her.

Webber walked back to her, but stayed in the shadow of the hangar. The New Zealand morning sun was hot and Cory's orange suit was like a personal sauna. Rosinski had told her that the pressure suit wouldn't be air-conditioned until Cory was hooked into the Blackbird's pilot-support system. Apparently, the airfield didn't have the small air-conditioning suitcases that astronauts carried on their way to their craft because the 109th wasn't set up to handle the Blackbird. Rosinski had emphasized that she and Webber were lucky a Q-series fuel tanker specially equipped to handle Blackbirds had managed to land in time.

"I told you," Webber said from the shade, "if you stayed here, Abbott was going to hold you."

"On what charges?"

"He doesn't need charges."

Cory moved into the shade as well. The pressure suit was even more restricting than the multilayered cold-weather gear she had worn in McMurdo. Even to be able to look up and see Webber past the overhang of the white space helmet she wore, she had to bend her head back at an uncomfortable angle. "Have we suddenly become a military dictatorship? Or should I say, have we become *more* of a military dictatorship?"

"Look at it from his point of view."

"I just ate."

"Listen, I'm serious. What happened in Antarctica was at the very least an act of environmental terrorism. There is going to be a criminal investigation of this entire incident, more than one, by every country affected by the wave. And you and I are the only eyewitnesses. You hear what I'm saying?"

Webber's reasoning had just crossed the line from ludicrously self-deluded to surreal. "Abbott thinks *I* did it? Oh, my God, is that the caliber of brainpower running the Pentagon?"

The small area of Webber's face exposed by the black headpiece he wore under his helmet was moist with sweat. "Abbott doesn't think you did it."

"I bet you he does. He only wants to know the same thing that you do—how did Earthguard find out about the NEST deployment."

Webber gave her an odd look. "A conspiracy newsgroup on the Internet."

"*Johnny* told you?"

"He understood how serious the situation was. Unlike his sister."

At that, Cory reached up to her left shoulder and grabbed the black comm wire that ran from her helmet to her side. She started yanking on it. This stupid suit was coming off *now*.

Webber lunged at her. "Stop it!" But their struggle was ridiculous. Neither one could move quickly in their space suits, each action and reaction slow and clumsy. Webber's gloved hands couldn't keep a grip on Cory's bulky arms and shoulders. Finally, she just pushed against his chest with all her strength and half-spun around to collapse into a sitting position on the hangar floor, legs sprawled out, arms limp at her side, head bowed by the weight of the helmet and all that happened to her.

"I don't want this to be happening." Her voice sounded shamefully like a self-pitying sob, even to her.

She was aware of Webber's painfully slow attempt to kneel at her side, to raise her helmet so they could see each other again. "I know that, Cory."

Her nose was running, her cheeks were burning with tears of self-anger and frustration and raw grief. "How could *you* understand?" Once again, she felt Johnny's hand in hers and the terrible absence of it as he let go and dropped away from her. Overcome with fury at herself and her weakness, her failure to do something directly to change the odds for all the other Johnnys facing death, she was afraid to look at Webber. Afraid she'd begin to weep and never stop.

Enraging her even more, Webber made an awkward attempt to wipe away her tears. His glove was almost too big to fit through the opening of her helmet. But when his eyes met hers, Cory was startled to see that, somehow, Webber did know what she felt. That what she struggled with now, he had as well. But not in the time she knew him. Sometime after, sometime in the five years they'd been apart.

"As long as you're with me," Webber said as if he really meant it, "I can protect you from Abbott."

Though he would be the last one to whom she would admit it, Cory knew that Webber's solemn promise of protection was as good a guarantee as she would ever get from anyone. She also knew she would never give up responsibility for her life or her actions, nor would she ever relinquish control of her own thoughts and decisions. She still held Webber responsible for Johnny, of course, and when this was over, would have nothing more to do with him. But he could be trusted—at least to keep his word.

She held out her hand. Webber took it. Then, using her hand to brace himself, he got to his feet and, in turn, braced her as she stood up beside him.

"Two things," she said. "Then *I* promise not to fight you anymore."

Webber nodded.

"You help me make those assholes in the Pentagon understand what that wave is."

"Agreed."

"And then we get the guys who did this. Whoever they are."

"I want that, too."

"Even if it's Abbott who's responsible?"

Cory saw Webber's face go blank. He had obviously never even considered that.

"Mitchell, I *need* you to think how big this operation is. It isn't some homegrown militia building a dirty bomb out of baling wire and two-by-fours out in the barn. Remember what you told me? 'I've got the Pentagon behind me. Satellites and aircraft and scientists and soldiers.' Well, that sounds like a recipe to me. And don't give me that look."

"How can you even imagine the Pentagon would be involved in . . . in something this grotesque?"

"Oh give it up, will you? What about Hiroshima, and all those American troops marching through aboveground test sites just to see what would happen, and the Gulf War syndrome cover-up, and . . . and I could go on all day."

"Change of plans—let's *not* talk anymore." Webber turned away and stalked toward the Blackbird at the back of the hangar.

Cory hurried after him, as best she could, swimming in sweat within her suit. "I didn't say *you* did those things personally!"

Webber stopped by one of the Blackbird's wings. The wingspan was about half the length of the plane, and except for a few dark red numbers and lines, the skin of the plane was a dense, matte black. Seen from the side, where the plane's oddly flattened flares weren't as noticeable, Cory decided it wasn't quite as phallic as she had originally thought. Though it was still a long cylindrical object designed to penetrate enemy airspace. There was no escaping the military mind-set.

Webber turned back to her, infuriated. "Millions of American soldiers have died so that you can have the freedom to spout your bullshit. And dying is about as personal as it gets."

"I know you, don't forget. You can't lie. Are you willing to tell me that *no* commanding officer, *no* general in the history of the United States has ever made a mistake? Has ever undertaken an operation that was illegal? Grotesque? *Wrong?*"

"Of course it happens. But there are checks and balances. Command structure. The system is self-correcting."

"Eventually."

Webber forced his glove through his own helmet opening to rub his face. "You're doing it to me again. How can I fight with you when you end up agreeing with me?"

"If you agree with me, why fight?"

Webber looked incapable of speech. Which was fine with Cory. She still had a few points to make. "Face the facts, Mitchell. Abbott doesn't give a flying you-know-what about having me debriefed by his experts. He thinks there's a chance I had something to do with the wave, and all I want you to keep in mind is, he might think you had something to do with it, too."

"That's just stupid," Webber said.

But Cory sensed a crack in his belief system. "Then why does he want us in Washington in person? Especially when he has that teleconference setup we just used?"

"The power's going to be out in New Zealand for a couple of days."

"This place doesn't have generators?" Cory moved closer to Webber. Maybe she was finally getting him thinking. "Your trouble is that you're not paranoid enough. There's a lot of stuff going on that we don't know about. Maybe nobody knows about. And maybe Abbott does. That's all I'm saying." She held out her hand. "So, you protect me from Abbott, and *I'll* protect *you* from Abbott, too. Deal?"

Webber hesitated, then reluctantly held out his hand. Their gloves were too thick to shake properly, but she slapped her palm against his. "You're still insane," he said.

"As I recall, that's what made you fall madly in love with me."

"I was young and foolish."

"Well, now you're just foolish."

Webber stared up at the aircraft for a few moments, and Cory could see that he was definitely thinking something through.

"Okay, here's something to consider. Something that Abbott isn't—"

But he was stopped by a sudden shout from the front of the hangar. "Let's move it out!"

"Hold that thought," Corey said, wishing she knew what Webber had been about to tell her. Then both she and Webber turned to see Major Bardeen and Captain Rosinski striding toward them, sunglasses gleaming.

"She's not going to fly herself," Bardeen said, every word an apparent struggle not to reveal the resentment seething just beneath the surface. "You done your walkaround yet?"

"I was hoping you'd assist me," Webber said, every word an equally apparent struggle not to provoke that resentment.

"Follow me," Bardeen said, then marched toward the nose of the craft. Webber half-marched, half-shuffled after him.

Cory turned to Rosinski as the two men stopped to examine something under the forward tip of the plane. "So what's this, a male-bonding ritual?"

Rosinski wasn't much friendlier than Bardeen. "Pilots give their aircraft a visual inspection before every flight. At least the good ones do."

Webber and Bardeen continued around to the far side of the plane. "You ever flown one of these?" Cory asked Rosinski.

"I'm not the pilot."

Cory sensed a sore point and knew where to probe. "*Any* women fly these things?"

"Not yet." Then the captain went from defense to offense. "What's your flying experience?"

"Most recently? Harrier II," Cory said, trying to sound nonchalant.

Rosinski gave her a pitying smile. "Subsonic. Seven hundred miles, tops. Never gone Mach?"

Cory didn't like the sound of what that implied about the flight to come, shook her head.

"Well, honey," Rosinski said, "when those J60s hit ram speed, you better hope your adhesive strips are nice and tight, 'cause you're going to need 'em." Then she strode off to join Webber and Bardeen.

Cory felt there was little chance she was going to form a sisterly bond with Rosinski, so she waited where she had been left, unsure what to do next. She turned her attention back to the plane, noticing for the first time that stenciled on its side were Bardeen's and Rosinski's names. *No wonder they feel so possessive.* Close up to the aircraft, she did have to admit that it was impressive in its own testosterone high-tech sort of way. Then she noticed six very low-tech-looking pieces of equipment arranged beneath it: white buckets labeled JET FUEL, straight from a kid's cartoon. Hoses hung down from the plane as if they were draining into the buckets.

Webber had finished his walkaround and waved Cory over to the egress stairway rolled up at the side of the plane. She was grateful to see that this one had real steps and high handrails. "You're up first," he said.

Rosinski effortlessly swung up the stairs ahead of her, pulled on something at the side of the plane, and a section of the upper fuselage behind the cockpit swung up. It was mostly dark metal, or whatever the skin of the plane was made of, with a small rectangular window on each side.

Cory stomped up the stairway in her bulky pressure suit and looked down into a cramped cockpit slightly larger than the Harrier's. There were many more instruments clustered around the seat, including five large display screens, but no flight controls.

"Strap in," Rosinski said.

Cory stared at the straps in the seat. They looked different from the ones in the Harrier. "Okay, how do they work?" she asked as she backed into the cockpit and slipped down into the seat. At least there was enough room this time that she could actually sit down, not fall into her seat.

Rosinski leaned in and showed her how to latch the straps. *I was right,* Corey thought. It wasn't the same system as the Harrier had used. Then Rosinski connected her air hose and a blast of cool air, smelling like the ever-present stench of jet fuel, rushed through the helmet. Cory wiggled back and forth as she felt her suit shift all around her.

"Cooler?"

Cory nodded. Rosinski began deftly adjusting controls. Cory noticed that most of the control labels on the console were covered with duct tape. "What's with all the tape?" she asked.

"This is all classified surveillance equipment. No civilian should be in here. So don't touch anything."

"Like I'm going to tell anyone."

"I've heard that before."

Rosinski tapped a center display screen. "This will give you a forward view. Visible-light only." She looked over the cockpit controls, then checked a clipboard that she slipped out from beside the seat. "Any questions?" Rosinski was acting very much like someone who was glad to be finished with her work.

"Yeah, what are the buckets of jet fuel doing under the plane?"

"Blackbirds leak like a sieve. None of the fuel connectors seal until they get up to operational temperature and expand."

"What's operational temperature?"

"Classified."

"Thank you. You've been so helpful."

"Have a nice day." Rosinski slid Cory's helmet faceplate down with enough force to drive Cory back into the seat, and sealed it. Instantly Cory's ears popped as the suit was fully pressurized.

Then Rosinski stepped back and the top of the cockpit closed over Cory, sealing her as if in a coffin. The only sources of light were the two windows, one to either side. They were fifteen inches wide, about eight inches tall, and Cory couldn't see anything through them.

Except for the soft rush of the air, all sound was muffled. Cory could hear only scrapings and thumps, and guessed that Webber was getting into his seat up front. Unlike the Harrier, Cory saw, her section of the plane and Webber's were completely separate compartments.

That was when her first feelings of claustrophobia began to set in. She became acutely aware of the plastic shield only inches from her face. She tried to change position in her seat, but the straps were too tight. She could feel her breathing start to quicken. She wondered what would happen if her air hose twisted. Or if her air ran out. How could Webber do anything to help her?

Cory wanted to pound on the window. She needed to get out. Her breath began to fog the faceplate with each exhalation, making even the dim outlines of the cockpit less distinct. She had never felt so trapped, so confined. She raised her fist—

And the lights came on.

The instrument panels were studded with tiny shining lights, red, green, and white, that blazed merrily from the obscuring strips of duct tape. Five display screens lit up, two of them with a blue light so pure and flicker-free it was almost like seeing the sky. The other three contained incomprehensible technical data.

Having more light and something to look at took away some of Cory's anxiety. Then she saw the small red light in the upper left corner. The white letters on it said: PILOT HAS EJECTED. It shut off as she watched. She hoped she would never see it light up again.

Webber's voice suddenly blared into her ears. "You okay back there?"

"I was till you did that. Mind turning down the volume?"

A rush of static diminished. When Webber spoke again, it was much less painful. "How's that?"

"Better, I think." Cory felt the plane rock. "What was that?"

"They're just hauling us outside so they can start up the engines. We'll be taking off in about five minutes. Refueling about ten minutes after that."

"That soon?" Cory squinted as sunlight suddenly exploded through the left window, nearly blinding her. "What's this thing get to the gallon?"

"We take off almost empty," Webber said. "Makes it easier and safer. Then we'll refuel in the air two more times."

"Oh, great. You *are* trained to fly this thing, right?"

"You don't fly a Blackbird. You aim it."

Then a vibration built up in the plane as the huge engines fired. Cory tried to ask another question but Webber told her to wait until they were up. She busied herself in the meantime by methodically peeling off all the duct tape Rosinski had used to cover up her precious classified-instrument labels. She didn't learn anything, but the subversive action improved her spirits.

Then they took off. The engines roared and Cory was kicked back into her seat feeling like a bug about to be squashed. Because the Blackbird was climbing at such a steep angle, she missed the transition from the force of acceleration to the force of gravity pulling her back.

"Still alive?" Webber asked her.

"Clinically speaking," Cory said. "We should probably leave it at that."

"Bardeen said you'd be able to use the optical targeting scanner. That should be the large center screen."

Cory told him that it only showed a beautiful blue color and Webber talked her through adjusting the controls that brought up an image of what lay below the aircraft. Cory was stunned. It was like looking through a window. She couldn't figure out how the image was formed. She saw no evidence of television scan lines or of LED or LCD pixels.

The view was of New Zealand's South Island, slipping quickly beneath them as they sped north. The image brought her back to Earth.

"What's the time?"

Webber understood what she really meant. "About ten minutes to go. They've already lost contact with the outlying islands. Campbell, Auckland, the Antipodes, the Snares. It should hit Stewart Island and the East Shore about the same time."

"We're they able to evacuate everyone?"

"I don't know."

"Remember what you promised." She knew she didn't have to remind him. But a part of her needed the reassurance of hearing it again.

Webber, naturally, did the opposite of what she wanted by turning the question back to her. "Remember what *you* promised."

She nodded, though she knew he couldn't see her. "No more fighting."

"We're in this together now, Cory."

Mitchell, you'll just never get it, will you? Cory thought. They had always been together in the struggle to make the world safer. It was just that Webber had chosen the wrong side to fight on.

Still, Cory held out hope, just a little, for a different future for Webber.

But for New Zealand, like Johnny, there was none.

EVENT PLUS 10 HOURS

They were newlyweds, traveling by kayak, carrying all that they needed in the latest Eagle Creek backpacks, camping on beaches as they found them, bundling up in their new North Face sleeping bags, making love beneath the stars, making these first fourteen days of their marriage and their commitment a memory that would live in them for the rest of their lives. For that, they had no need of the rest of the world. They kept their radio turned off.

At Event plus nine hours, fifty-five minutes, they were on a small bluff, fifty feet above the shore, just north of Porpoise Bay, lying in each other's arms beside an outcropping of rocks where their campfire burned, grilling the perch they had caught that morning. They talked seriously of never going back to their jobs in Wellington. They talked about the children they would have. They kissed.

Pushed to sixty feet by the lessening depths of the New Zealand Plateau, the leading wave struck the beach below them.

The newlyweds thought a plane had crashed as they heard the leading wave sweep along the rocky shore and slam into the base of the bluff. A moment later they didn't know what to think, because they were drenched where they lay, their fire extinguished, as if an hour's worth of rain had fallen on them at once. They didn't notice that the rain was salty.

They looked at each other. They looked at the perfectly clear sky above them. They did what any young couple in love would do when faced with the absurd. They laughed as they stood up and looked down to the shore for their kayaks.

The kayaks were gone.

And so was the ocean.

The rocks of the shore extended past the waterline, into sand and silt and streamers of collapsed seaweed. Here and there, fish flipped and struggled, drowning in the air.

The water was gone.

But on the horizon, was a line. Thin at first. Getting thicker.

The ground beneath their feet trembled. They heard an odd sound growing so pervasive it soon felt as if it were part of them. A wind began to blow offshore, tugging at them, as if urging them to go forward to meet the line.

Hand in hand, they looked up to see a plane circling high overhead, sunlight glinting from its silver skin.

In seconds, the approaching line became a wall. Then the wall became a mountain 400 feet tall, trailing foam from its frothing crest as it rose, curled, blotting out the sky and the sun and the plane, to cast its shadow on two young lovers too astounded to move or to speak.

In the last instant, they turned away, toward each other, for one final embrace. And in that instant, they were gone.

The wave moved on.

The Foveaux Strait emptied next as if the ocean floor had split in two and drained the sea, only to be refilled by a tidal bore 300 feet tall that scoured Ruapuke Island and drove its debris into Bluff and Riverton. The backwash left Invercargill a swamp.

Up the east coast, the wave erased the shoreline of New Zealand. Because its water met the land at a 45-degree angle, the endless wave was always replenished, never expended.

For each mile of shoreline, it was the same. First, the ocean drew back to feed the monster that approached, and then it returned with the energy of the ice shelf that had fallen so far away. Depending on the depth of the shoals and how little or how much water there was to transport that energy, the wave that struck the land ranged from 200 to 500 feet tall. Now it moved up the coast, constantly falling and re-forming, churning up the seabed, launching rocks and cars and boats like missiles.

And where rivers emptied into the sea, torrents of high-pressure water now exploded up them and over their banks to ravage miles inland.

Depending on topology and drainage, the wave moved inland up to three miles on flatland, sometimes no more than a half mile on rough coast. But wherever the wave ran ashore, nothing and no one survived its touch.

Within 150 minutes, South Island's east coast was as if a shovel had scraped the edge of a garden; the forests were gone, as were the homes and cottages, roads and highways, a restaurant with an ocean view, and all the towns: Papatowai, Kaitangata, Oamaru, Timaru. Even Christchurch in the shadow of the Banks Peninsula was now flooded by the backwash, buried by the silt that was carried by the wave.

But the North Island had learned from the South Island's sacrifice.

The people of North Island moved even farther inland as the power and destructiveness of the wave was broadcast on realtime satellite images, and from news crews in planes and helicopters. Wellington and Lower Hutt, ghost towns before they were vanquished, were flattened as Port Nicholson emptied and then refilled. Again, the force of the wave was concentrated as if in a gun barrel.

It took four hours for the wave to pass. In its wake were 80,000 dead or missing, damage beyond estimate. What had been lost was now buried under eighteen feet of mud.

Yet New Zealand's devastation had created hope for others in the path—it had created a hole in the wave, a hole that would spare Australia's northeastern coast, the Great Barrier Reef, and the island of New Guinea.

But for Tasmania, Melbourne, Sidney, and Brisbane to the west, and the Solomons and Polynesia to the west and north, there was no escape from their fate. Their time would come in five more hours.

Hawaii was still twenty-one hours away. Japan, twenty-four. California, twenty-six.

But these lands had nothing to fear.

The Pentagon had told them so.

And the Pentagon was never wrong.

ELEVEN

NATIONAL MILITARY COMMAND CENTER/THE PENTAGON

"Why don't they move?" Like that of the other twelve people in the emergency action room, Lieutenant Ann Yoshii's attention was fixed on the big board and the MSNBC feed from New Zealand. The ANG 109th had sent a news crew up in one of their Hercules. It was flying at an altitude of 2,500 feet tracking the wave, and the nose-mounted remote-control camera had zoomed in on two people, a young man and a young woman, standing hand in hand on a small bluff overlooking the ocean that had vanished.

"Where could they go?" Abbott said with a frown. He had seen death before. Where some might say the military existed to cause it, he knew his mission was, instead, to prevent it. But those two people on the southern tip of New Zealand's South Island were beyond anyone's help.

The couple were like statues. At the last moment, they turned away from the wave, to each other, and embraced. Then there was nothing but a screen of out-of-focus darkness, blurred by speed. A few seconds later, the bluff was exposed again, resculpted, devoid of rocks and grass and trees, the man and woman gone.

"My God." Major Chennault sat down at the EAR conference table as if he could no longer support himself.

"Expand the NOAA image," Abbott said. He waited a few seconds as nothing on the board changed. "Lieutenant?"

"I'm sorry, sir." Yoshii forced her attention back to her workstation. Abbott could see she was shaken by what she had watched. He knew the lieutenant would soon realize that she'd have to get used to such events if she was to continue to serve here.

On the board, the realtime weather-satellite feed expanded to the size of the MSNBC live coverage. Abbott thought they might as well be looking at a child's tabletop model of the Earth, built of papier-mâché and flour, and that someone had dropped a large stone in the water, creating a single ripple. The image was that unreal, the wave that perfect.

"This is terrible," Chennault said.

"It is," Abbott agreed. "But it is also a challenge." He glanced with pride at the side of the board where Yoshii had opened a computer display window, constantly updated with site reports from Operation PACIFIC SHIELD. Abbott's response to what had happened in Antarctica was no longer a mere Crisis Action Team. It was one of the fastest major logistical operations ever mounted by the American military.

Before the wave died down to the level of intense, storm-driven breakers—somewhere around the equator, the experts had estimated—it would sweep past almost 14,000 islands in the South Pacific. With the exception of New Guinea, which would be protected in the "wave shadow" created by New Zealand, almost two million people were at risk. The larger, continental islands of Melanesia, such as New Caledonia, Vanuatu, and the Solomon Islands, would experience devastating economic loss as their southern shores were obliterated. But their mountains would provide height and shelter for the majority of their populations in the short term. In the long term, it was the armed forces of the United States, working with their Pacific Area security treaty partners of Australia and New Zealand, who would supply emergency food, shelter, and medical supplies and services over the long months of reconstruction that would follow.

The higher volcanic islands, such as Tahiti and the others of the Society and Marquesas islands, also would provide suitable shelter for their inhabitants, and their local authorities would become willing recipients of the emergency aid already being planned for them.

But the islands without mountains, especially the atolls of the Polynesia region, Tuvalu, Tokelau, the Tuamotu Archipelago, and most of the Cooks, were in immediate danger of total destruction.

They provided almost no high ground as protection from the wave's impact, so PACIFIC SHIELD was mounting an unprecedented air evacuation, calling up all available transports, including civilian airliners volunteered by their carriers, to take as many people as possible out of harm's way. It was an effort that could never completely succeed in the hours remaining, but at least, Abbott knew, a heroic effort would have been made. Among the at-risk atolls, some which were barely fifteen feet above high-tide levels, casualties in excess of 100,000 had already been projected. But up to 8,000 others would survive because of what he had begun in this room.

PACIFIC SHIELD's air evacuation also extended to American vessels in the South Pacific. All USN vessels south of the equator that were not within range of a protected port in advance of the wave's arrival were being abandoned. Their crews were being plucked from their decks by helicopters and taken to nearby islands in a nonstop convoy. Other less conventional means were also being used to rescue sailors at sea. Abbott had seen one report of a startled group of civilian crew and passengers being brought aboard the nuclear submarine U.S.S. *Dallas*, which had surfaced 200 feet from their windjammer cruise ship off Tonga.

Lieutenant Yoshii interrupted Abbott's study of PACIFIC SHIELD procedures with an update from SPACECOM. "Sir, Major Bailey reports that Captain Webber has completed his initial refueling and is beginning the first leg of his trip."

"Send the captain my regards," Abbott said. He checked his watch, specifically the counter in its digital window. Almost thirteen hours had passed since he had assembled his CAT. He suddenly remembered what day it was. "Happy Thanksgiving, Lieutenant."

Yoshii gave him an odd look. "Thank you, sir."

"Your shift was over several hours ago," Abbott continued. "If you have plans for today . . ."

"No, thank you, sir. I'd like to stick this one out."

Abbott smiled, pleased. He had suspected as much when Yoshii's shift replacement had arrived and she had put the new lieutenant to work coordinating communications through CINCPAC in Honolulu, but he appreciated having her enthusiasm and her dedication confirmed. It let him know he was doing a good job as a leader, and he felt it helped inspire the others under his command. Certainly, there was a gratifying sense of urgency and purpose in the

NMCC which Abbott had not seen since the electrifying reports of the Iraqi invasion of Kuwait.

The general took a moment to sit down beside Chennault at the conference table. In front of them lay two thick files: the personnel records of Captain Mitchell Webber and Captain Nicholas Young, complete with the results of all security investigations. Chennault had had them sent over from the DIA archives. Unlike Lieutenant Yoshii, the major was showing signs of burnout. "How about you?" Abbott asked. "Time to call it a night?"

Chennault shook his head wearily. "If I went home, I'd be doing the same thing I'm doing now. Watching the news."

Abbott looked back at the big board. On other Thanksgivings in the EAR, he had allowed the various football games to be displayed for the staff. But this year, quite properly, everything that was up there was because of the mission.

"There's George," Chennault said suddenly, pointing to the NBC feed. Just as suddenly, the image of George Lilley, the Pentagon's chosen spokesperson for PACIFIC SHIELD, multiplied across all the other news feeds. Behind him were the distinctive Pentagon logo and part of a large map of the South Pacific. Commodore Sam Drygalski, who was coordinating the movement of naval air assets from the United States to the northern Pacific, stood off to the side. Beside him was a civilian Abbot didn't recognize, a beefy individual in a rumpled sports coat, and with a wild fringe of white hair.

Young, clean-cut, always in his trademark blue tie, Lilley was a good man held in high esteem by the Pentagon. An effective representative for the military, he managed to put a human face on its sometimes impersonal bureaucracy, but there was never any question as to where his loyalty rested. Like a good soldier, he said exactly what he was supposed to say, no less and, most importantly, no more.

"Sound up, please," Abbott instructed Yoshii as he leaned back in his chair. It would be useful to see how the public was reacting to the crisis.

On the big board, the news conference taking place out in the A ring of the Pentagon began with Lilley reading aloud the latest updates based on the wave's first impact with New Zealand. He reported that the coastal evacuation of New Zealand was proceeding in an orderly manner and casualties were expected to be light. Thus far, the wave was behaving as Department of Defense experts had predicted, and once again the Pentagon was downplaying any fear that something similar might happen to the West Coast of the United States. "Just don't go surfing at Malibu," Lilley said at the end, quoting the Vice-President from earlier in the day. After the polite laughter had died down, he opened the floor to questions.

Pat White of the *Washington Post* was first. She asked what the President's reaction to the wave had been.

"The President is being kept informed of the situation and hopes that all Americans will join him this Thanksgiving Day in offering their prayers for the affected countries and island nations. When he returns home on Sunday, he will introduce an emergency-spending bill to facilitate relief efforts in consultation with Australia and New Zealand, and with the South Pacific Forum."

Abbott and Chennault exchanged a look of commiseration. The real story was that when the Secretary of Defense had spoken to the President eight hours ago and told him what had happened, the President's first response was to ask if the wave would affect the United States. When the Secretary had assured him it would have no greater effect than a hurricane, the President had ended the call in less than a minute and gone out to a state dinner with the other leaders in Berlin. No one had been in touch with him since. To Abbott, the man's lack of interest and responsibility was appalling.

Eric Zamir of the *New York Times* was up next. Abbott had no doubt as to what the dangerously left-leaning reporter would ask.

"Mr. Lilley, in light of the fact that the collapse of the Ross Ice Shelf would require an unimaginably strong force, and in light of the fact that the Earthguard organization, as we have all seen on television in a mysteriously truncated live broadcast, has claimed evidence that the United States has deployed nuclear weapons in Antarctica, how do you respond to charges that the United States is in fact responsible for the deliberate creation of the wave?"

Lilley looked as outraged by that question as was Abbott. Judging from the outburst in the pressroom, most of the other members of the media shared the general's reaction as well.

Lilley leaned forward, hands at the side of his podium like a fire-and-brimstone preacher. "That question has been dealt with in the release handed out this morning. The Department of Energy deployed two units of the Nuclear Emergency Search Team to Mc-

Murdo Station as part of an exercise." Zamir tried to interrupt but Lilley held firm. "Mr. Zamir, you'll have a chance for a follow-up. Let me answer the question. As you know, from 1962 to 1972 Mc-Murdo Station was the site of a small nuclear generating plant which provided electricity for the facility. At the end of its operational life, that generator was shut down, disassembled, and shipped back to the United States, along with fourteen thousand five hundred cubic yards of slightly contaminated soil and rock. By 1979, the site on which it had rested was declared decontaminated, and it was that same site, which had been exposed to precisely measured quantities of radiation over a known time, that the DOE chose for testing a new generation of specialized equipment designed expressly to keep America secure from the threat of terrorist nuclear weapons."

Chennault grunted in approval, "He's good." Abbott agreed.

Lilley continued. "Again, for the record, the United States categorically denies that it had shipped to Antarctica any type or quantity of nuclear material other than ordinary isotopes used in common mineralogical tests, nor do we have knowledge of any type or quantity of nuclear material in Antarctica as the result of the actions of another party. The NEST teams on site were there for an exercise and only an exercise. As for the fact that their deployment was a secret, for obvious reasons it is DOE policy not to reveal the activities of NEST at any time. Just as obviously, Earthguard learned of the deployment through questionable means and instead of checking their sources—as I know the reporters in this room do at all times—they acted in their typical and precipitous manner, adding an unnecessary and regrettable air of confusion to what is undoubtedly the greatest natural disaster of modern history."

"Follow-up!" Zamir shouted over the clamor of the other reporters.

Lilley nodded at him with strained politeness.

"If nuclear weapons were not involved, then how do you account for the collapse of the Ross Ice Shelf?"

Lilley looked up from his podium as if beseeching aid from an authority even higher than the Joint Chiefs of Staff. "Mr. Zamir, look at the satellite images. Mount Erebus is erupting more powerfully than has ever been recorded. We are picking up underwater lava hot spots all around Ross Island. Seismic stations around the world are reporting a cluster of unusual seismic disturbances centered on the Ross Sea—disturbances which preceded the collapse by approximately four hours.

"Though it will be many weeks, perhaps months, before conclusive results can be obtained, the action of subglacial volcanic activity has long been a concern in the western Antarctic." Lilley looked over his shoulder and waved the white-haired civilian forward. "Dr. Casey, perhaps you could take this one."

The civilian looked bemused as he approached the podium and Lilley introduced him. "Dr. David Casey is with the National Oceanic and Atmospheric Administration. He has specialized in studying the meteorological effects of Antarctica on the world's climate and he is a member of the Vice-President's Special Committee. Dr. Casey . . ."

The white-haired man looked out at the reporters before him as if he had never seen so many in one place in his life, but then began to speak with the assurance of an expert. "Since 1993, we have known that there is considerable volcanic activity underlying the WAIS, that is, the West Antarctic Ice Sheet, of which the Ross Ice Shelf comprises, or did comprise, about twenty percent. Our concern, in the climate business, has been that these eruptions might generate enough heat to melt the undersides of the ice sheet, you see, forming water that could mix with the volcanic ash most of the ice sits on, creating what we could call a lubricant layer, a volcanic grease. So, instead of a glacier advancing a few meters in a season, giant sections might slide off into the sea in a matter of weeks, even days.

"Now, this is still early, but based on the preliminary data I have seen, it is entirely possible that this is what has happened to the Ross Shelf. Volcanic activity, heat, slippage, and, in a sense, the calving of the largest iceberg in history."

A reporter shouted out above the tumult, "Dr. Casey, if the volcanic activity continues, is it possible that more of that western ice sheet could slide into the sea? And if so, that sea levels could rise by sixty-five feet around the world? That continental outlines would change, and whole countries could disappear?"

Abbott was impressed that despite the topic, Casey tried to keep the reporters calm. "Oh, no—we're certainly not predicting that. And sea-level rise from the collapse of the Ross Ice Shelf will be nowhere near as catastrophic as that. *Catastrophic* isn't even the word to use. Now, we haven't been able to get accurate measurements of the actual amount of ice that has separated, but . . . based on earlier studies I've seen, I would think we will see a sea-level rise of no more than a meter. Say, two . . . two and half feet. Remember, a great deal of the Ross Shelf was already in the water, already displacing it, which is why this terrible wave will slowly decrease in energy as it nears our shores. It is a tragedy, just an immense human tragedy, but . . . we will learn from it. And, I am hopeful that, as we are once again reminded of how fragile our planet is, it might even draw us closer together. That's all I have to say."

Casey stepped back and Lilley was instantly barraged by questions concerning the fate of American personnel in Antarctica and the ongoing evacuation of the most seriously at-risk islands.

But Abbott ignored the news conference, fascinated by something Casey had said. He turned to Chennault. " 'Earlier studies'?"

"I was thinking the same thing. And he is just down the hall."

"Good idea," Abbott said. "Lieutenant Yoshii, send someone to the pressroom to escort Dr. Casey here. I'd like to speak with him."

Yoshii got on it right away. Abbott stood up, then looked down to check his uniform and smooth his jacket. He only had one more fresh uniform in his office. To get another, he would have to phone his house. It was much too early to expect his wife and daughter to answer. But Sam would be home. And that was a conversation that could wait until the end of the weekend. With luck, it wouldn't take place until the drive to the airport.

To avoid that call and the ensuing disruption in his concentration, Abbott decided he wouldn't change until just before the next major news conference. Lilley had asked him to take part in a sum-up after the wave had done the worst of its damage and passed Western and American Samoa, about thirteen hours from now. Of course, Abbott reconsidered, he could always send a driver to the house to pick up a fresh uniform.

"General?" Insensitive as always, Chennault had broken his concentration.

"Yes, Major?"

Chennault was on his feet, but his posture sagged. He looked troubled as well as tired. "Do you think it might be a good idea to let the Vice-President's experts know that nuclear explosives *were* involved in the collapse?"

"Other than compromising a tested scenario for identifying the actors responsible, what would that accomplish?"

Chennault didn't seem to notice Abbott's sharp rebuke of his reasoning. "Something Dr. Casey said. The idea that an ice shelf might collapse over days. That the Ross Shelf was already in the water when it collapsed. Those two conditions seem to have something to do with his estimate of how powerful the wave will be, which is far less than Dr. Rey's estimate. And she knows nukes were involved."

Abbott's jaw tightened. Chennault's dedication to the mission wasn't what it should be. The major's equivocation about revealing the existence of SHAARP had been annoying and had added delays to the CAT's reaction time. But what he was suggesting now was even worse. "That Earthguard woman is not a credible source. I still consider her a suspect."

"But she seemed . . . awfully sure about her soliton theory."

"Try fanatical. That type always is, Major. No discipline. No desire to work constructively within the system. Her kind only wants to tear down traditions and institutions that have served this country for generations. I'm all in favor of change, provided it brings improvement, not anarchy." Abbott read the objection in Chennault's expression. "And I can see you don't agree."

"Then why would someone like Mitch Webber have been seriously involved with her, before all this?"

Abbott reached down to the table and picked up Webber's personnel file, flipping it open to the same sheet Chennault had shown him during the teleconference with Christchurch. A photograph of a younger Dr. Corazon Rey looked back at him. She was in a bathing suit, two abbreviated pieces, not a type that Abbott would ever let his daughter wear, one arm around Webber, both of them smiling foolishly at the camera.

"There, Major. That answers the question of Webber's attraction. She was good-looking, and obviously available."

Abbott dropped the thick file with the results of Webber's security investigations back on the conference table. The DIA had never uncovered the slightest hint of irregularity, but for those operators like Webber who were involved in ongoing classified work, they were an annual rite of passage.

"Webber's involvement with Rey wasn't a fling, sir. According to this, they were together for almost two years." Chennault had a faraway look, as if caught by a memory. "I was stationed in San Diego when I was an operator—about Webber's age. He'd have had other opportunities, but he chose to stay with her. I think that means there's more to Dr. Rey than you're giving her credit for."

Abbott decided he'd have to spell it out for Chennault. This was no time to psychoanalyze the enemy. The moral equivalent of a war was being waged in the South Pacific. What Abbott had done was the only correct strategy—take the enemy out of the game. "Major, I'm not a fool. As soon as you showed me this, that's when I ordered Webber to bring Rey back here."

Chennault looked confused. "I thought you made that decision when I showed you her CV. She *is* highly qualified as an oceanographer *and* in fluid mechanics. If anyone understands that wave, it'll be her."

Abbott felt his patience being strained to its limits. He spoke forcefully, as if by his doing so the major would finally understand what was so clear to him. "Her academic background isn't important. And the reason why Webber might have stayed with her so long is simple. She and her group needed access to someone in the military, so she lied to him. She became something different, hid her true beliefs from him, didn't talk to him about Earthguard and saving the spotted owl. She probably ate steak, went to the shooting range, and watched John Wayne videos with him. Women do that, Major. They lie to get what they want. I know."

"Then why exactly did you ask Webber to bring Rey?"

Abbott decided to give Chennault one more chance to get back on the right side. "Understand, Major. I am trying to give Captain Webber the benefit of the doubt. But it is clear to me that because of their past association, we must consider Webber and Rey as a team."

"*What?*"

"Now, now, I'm not suggesting that Webber is an active member of Earthguard. I want to believe that he doesn't know how he was being used. But the fact is that Webber was part of a classified NEST deployment, and Webber's girlfriend somehow found out about it. That convergence of events demands explanation."

"NEST hunts nukes," Chennault said. "So does Earthguard. The only thing that's surprising is that they haven't run into each other before this."

That was Abbott's point and he was glad to see that Chennault was finally getting it. "Exactly. How can we be sure they haven't?"

But Chennault wasn't in agreement after all. The major flipped the file to the follow-up report of the investigation that had identified Corazon Rey as Webber's romantic interest. "Sir, it says here they split up five years ago."

"An old girlfriend would never call up an old boyfriend and suggest a drink, talk about old times, catch up on things? I've seen this happen so many times in the past, Major. Honey traps, the Soviets called them. Webber wouldn't even know he was giving up classified information."

"I've read Webber's file. He is not naive."

"That's too bad, Major. Because if Webber is *not* naive, if he has not inadvertently passed on classified information to this Rey woman, then the only other explanation is that he is in deliberate collusion with her, and that *he* is the one who's been leading a different life." Abbott smiled, to ease the tension growing between him and his junior officer, but he resented being placed in the position of justifying what he had done.

Chennault picked up Nick Young's file from the table and waved it at Abbott. "General, *this* is the soldier who lied to us all."

Abbott then responded by doing something he rarely did. He raised his voice. "According to whom, Major Chennault—*Webber!* And where is Nick Young? We don't know. According to his close friend Webber, Young escaped in a conveniently placed Harrier jet—and there *are* no missing Harriers in our inventory. And all the other witnesses are just as conveniently dead!"

Abbott was intensely aware of everyone in the EAR staring at him. He lowered his voice as if he and Chennault were but two old warriors clearing the air, nothing out of the ordinary. "Major, I'm not saying Captain Webber *has* done anything wrong. I'm simply keeping myself open to all possibilities until a full investigation has been conducted. You have to admit there are a great many unanswered questions."

Chennault hesitated, unsure how to respond to Abbott's abrupt change of attitude. Then the main doors opened and two white-helmeted MPs entered, flanking Dr. David Casey. Not only was the rumpled, white-haired scientist beefy, he was huge, at least six-eight.

Abbott held up his hand to the doctor. "Dr. Casey, I'll be right with you." Then Abbott looked at Chennault, waiting for his acknowledgment that their confrontation was over.

Chennault dropped Young's file back on the table. He made no attempt to hide his own troubled emotions from the other personnel in the room. "General, my fear is that those questions are unanswered because you will not allow them to be asked."

"I believe in the system, Major. I am trusting in the scenarios."

Chennault looked at the big board and the weather-satellite image. The wave ate at New Zealand like an acid wash, the destruction visible even from 300 miles in space. "There is no scenario for that," he said.

That was when Dr. Casey brought the business of the emergency action room of the National Military Command Center to a halt. "But there is," the scientist said. "And I've read it."

TWELVE

On the immense SPACECOM wall display, Major Wilhemina Bailey saw New Zealand torn apart three times over. In one image window, from a NOAA satellite, the wave was a gray scalpel slicing across a ragged gray shore in low resolution and an extreme wide angle. Beside it, in another window, she saw the wave in full color, rippling with atmospheric distortion, at a magnification that made it appear she was only a few hundred feet above it. That image was from a newly retasked Lockheed Big Bird photoreconnaissance satellite that yesterday had been tracking the PLA Navy off Taiwan. And beside that, perhaps the most disturbing image of all: a three dimensional geo-elevation composite created from the Big Bird's optical data and the radar returns from a Trumpet MSI—multispectrum imaging—satellite. By blending the two data sets, the computer had developed a reconstruction of the wave's shape as seen from ground level. Because of the processing time required, the computer image was running eight seconds behind the real wave's advance, but it offered a disturbing simulation of what those two on the bluff must have seen in the last moments of their lives.

Then one of the small displays on her situation panel chimed, and Bailey looked away from New Zealand with relief. On her middle screen, a completely different image appeared: a Hawaiian

269

driver's license, courtesy of the Defense Intelligence Agency's UNIIC system.

UNIIC, invariably pronounced "unique," was the Uniform Identity Confirmation system, and was patterned after similar computer databases used by the Immigration and Naturalization Service at airports and border crossings. High-security federal facilities, such as Cheyenne Mountain, sometimes admitted civilians under controlled access. Rather than have to submit every visitor to an exhaustive security check, UNIIC offered a quick method of confirming identities, often without the visitor knowing that a check was being made. UNIIC was not a database itself, but made inquiries of other systems, usually state Departments of Motor Vehicles and phone-company records, with options including access to Veterans Affairs computer archives, and passport records. As a commanding officer at ESC, Bailey had simply accessed UNIIC and asked it to confirm the identity of an individual called NO NAME GIVEN, who had provided the phone number Huber had obtained from the NSA. The process had taken less than five minutes.

Bailey leaned forward to see the name printed beside the photograph of a burly Caucasian with dark curly hair, a thick ragged beard, and, oddly enough, a huge, lopsided smile. "Hello . . . Anatoly Cerenkov," Bailey read aloud. "You great big Russian guy, you." Six-one, 260 pounds, the license stated. Fifty-five years old with an address in someplace called Manoa Valley on Oahu. Without a doubt it was the man she had heard on the answering-machine tape. She wondered why he was smiling so broadly. It was just a driver's-license photo.

Bailey picked up the green phone and punched in Commander Huber's extension. "I got our Russian." Huber said he would be right up. Then Bailey's screen chimed again and another window opened over the driver's license. UNIIC had called up Cerenkov's passport-application file from the Department of State. In the photograph in this window, his hair was brushed back and his beard was more neatly trimmed. But he had almost the same outsized smile. *He must really like Hawaii,* Bailey thought. She began to read the rest of the information.

In case of emergency, the Russian had requested contact be made with Deborah Cerenkov at the same address. *Married an American,* Bailey concluded. Deborah didn't sound like a Russian name. Up until his 1998 renewal, a child had been included on the passport,

Betsy Paullina. *Betsy Ross? A name from each parent's heritage?* The child would be twelve by now. Then the kicker: Cerenkov's occupation was listed as Professor, University of Hawaii at Manoa, Faculty of Earth Sciences.

Bailey heard Huber rush up the stairs behind her. "What would you say Earth Sciences are?" she asked him.

Huber leaned past her to read the screen himself. "Geology, meteorology, oceanography, all sorts of things. But I thought you said this guy's a Russian."

"Look at his name."

Huber tapped the screen. "Yeah, but look at his place of birth."

Bailey squinted. After fourteen hours on duty, her eyes were getting tired. Then she saw what Huber meant as she read it on the screen. "Tucson, Arizona?"

"His parents could be Russian," Huber suggested.

"You heard that accent. That wasn't second-generation. That was someone whose first language is other than English." Bailey looked around for her tea mug. It was empty. "Something isn't right here."

Huber essayed a scenario. "He was born in Tucson to Russian parents, they moved back to Russia, he moved back to the States when he was old enough?"

Bailey rejected that out of hand. "Look how old he is. Russians in the Southwest in the fifties? I don't think so. And what I really don't like is that Captain Webber said he found a Russian warhead being deployed in the ice."

"Holy shit." Huber regarded Bailey with excitement. "You think the Russians are behind this?"

"They've got their right-wing fanatics same as we do."

"That still doesn't explain what Icefire is."

Bailey leaned back in her chair, reached up to her left shoulder, and rubbed. All this sitting around was stiffening her up. She caught Huber's eye and for an awful moment thought he was about to offer to rub her shoulder for her. Involvement with an officer under her command was not on her agenda. Ever.

"So what do you think about this guy?" she asked Huber. "Regular joe or spy with a secret?"

"We've got his phone number, and he mentioned Icefire on an unsecure line. It couldn't hurt to call him."

But Bailey wasn't so sure. Cerenkov might have called from an unsecure line, but the number he had called was another matter. It was an Arlington exchange, but it was unlisted. *Unlisted* unlisted. Which meant even UNIIC couldn't access it. And that meant it was a number unavailable to the public phone system. And that meant only one thing—the government.

"So this is what we've got," she said to Huber, thinking aloud as much as she was updating him. "A deliberate act of environmental terrorism, caused in part by a Russian nuclear weapon, which may or may not be connected to a U.S. government operation or project called Icefire, which is something which is known to an American who has a Russian name and accent."

"We've also got General Abbott," Huber said, "who's not telling us everything he knows."

Suddenly, every instinct in Bailey told her to drop what she was doing right now. Put it in a report. Pass it up through channels to the commander-in-chief of SPACECOM. She was a senior intelligence officer for Earth Surveillance with expertise in technical systems, satellites, and electronic data, not conspiracies and secret knowledge.

The bottom line, though, was that she wasn't willing to let this one go yet. Not without answers. "Oh, what the hell," she said.

"You're going to make the call?"

"Yeah," Bailey said, feeling good to be doing something on her own initiative instead of just responding to other people's orders. "But not the one you think."

ARCHANGEL FOUR

At 80,000 feet, traveling at 2,000 mph, the SR-71's enormous J60 Pratt & Whitney turbines had ceased to be ordinary jet engines. They had become ramjets. The rarefied air of fifteen miles above the Earth entered the engine intakes at Mach 2.5, and through a diffuser system, was slowed to subsonic speeds. The result was a staggering increase in air pressure within the engines' combustion chambers that vastly increased efficiency in converting the plane's exotic fuel into kinetic energy.

When the ramjet switchover had occurred, Mitch Webber had grinned with pleasure as the sudden acceleration slammed him back into his ejection seat and the Blackbird soared to 102,000 feet and

Mach 5.2. The only drawback was that the plane could hold enough fuel to maintain that speed for only forty-five minutes before another slowdown for in-flight refueling was required. Still, Washington, D.C., was only three hours away.

"You going to tell me what that was?" Cory's voice was breathless over Webber's helmet speakers.

"We've switched over to ramjet operation. Just over nineteen miles in altitude, just under four thousand miles per hour velocity."

"Well," Cory said. "Now I know why I'm wearing the urine-collection receptacle."

Webber tried not to laugh. "Next time I'll warn you. How's the view?"

Even Cory sounded impressed. "It's like looking down from the space shuttle. Any idea what kind of a screen I'm looking at? It doesn't look like a television display."

"Classified info," Webber said. "So don't even mention it when we land."

Webber had a much better view than Cory, because he could look out through thick quartz windows that had actually been heat-fused to the plane's titanium frame. Before him, the long nose of the Blackbird was no longer black; it was a rich blue, a color change brought on by the heat of atmospheric friction in excess of 3000°F. The blue seemed the perfect transition color between the bright color of the sky below, and the darkening indigo of space above. In the unnatural smoothness of flight in a region of the atmosphere where the air was not dense enough to create pockets of turbulence, this was a moment of perfect freedom, and it brought Webber peace.

Then again, he thought, *it might be the drugs.* After more than thirty hours without sleep, he had been in no condition to risk flying anything, let alone a Mach 5 spyplane. Before he and Cory had suited up, the flight surgeon at the 109th had given him a traditional "long-haul" cocktail, a combination of stimulants developed for fighter pilots to keep them alert on long flights, without pushing them into a fearless state of mind in which high-risk actions might begin to seem reasonable. Webber only felt as if he had had one cup of coffee too many, but knew that meant he'd be tireless for the next twelve hours. After that, however, he'd need to sleep for days.

"So how often do you fly something like this?" Cory asked him. He was surprised that he didn't resent her sudden intrusion into his moment of reflection. He knew how unusual it was for them to be experiencing together a part of his world that he'd never dreamed he'd be able to tell her about, much less share with her.

"Not all that often. Part of my training is to qualify on as many different aircraft as possible. I can't fly this with the precision Bardeen can, not for pinpoint surveillance. And I wouldn't last long in a dogfight in a fighter I hadn't spent a hundred hours in. But I can get most anything off the ground and I can land them. That's enough for what I have to do."

"You ever get planes confused?"

Webber smiled. "Nervous?"

"I'm getting over that. Looks like practice works for non-SEALs, too."

"I'll let you in on a secret. But you can't—"

"The old 'classified' again."

"Nope. But you won't make any friends with pilots if you let them know I told you. The Harrier's like a cross between a helicopter and a jet. The changeover in vector thrusting is real tricky. So it's actually *harder* to fly than this plane."

"Yeah? Why?"

"The aerodynamics of planes like the Blackbird, the Stealth fighter—almost any of the new-generation high-performance fighters—they're too unstable for human reflexes to manage. Bardeen wouldn't like me for saying it, but no human pilot can actually fly them. The only thing that keeps them in the air are computers changing flaps and thrust hundreds of times a second. It's called fly-by-wire. In the old days, the pilot would move the flight stick, and that would actually pull cables connected to the wing flaps. Every type of plane was different, had a unique feel. What worked on one model might make another veer out of control.

"Today, the pilot moves the flight stick, and it's like a joystick in a computer game. Nothing's actually moving. Instead, the computers interpret the movement as the pilot's request for action. So they send out thousands of commands to dozens of different motors that perform the actual control-surface adjustments. Under most conditions, that makes it extremely difficult to put the plane into a turn or dive that's outside its capabilities—the computers will ignore or override those commands—so there're fewer pilot-error crashes. Anyway, the long and short of it is when you get into the cutting-edge stuff, like the Blackbird, basically, you only have to know how to fly one kind of plane. An F-14 Tomcat."

"So what's so special about a Tomcat?"

Webber wondered if Cory really wanted to know all this, or if she was just getting him to talk until he said something she could later use to her advantage. But even if she did, he found to his surprise that he didn't care. It was a relief to finally talk freely with her, without arguing.

"When the engineers develop a new plane, they like to give the pilots something familiar to work with, so they adjust the computer controls to feel like a plane the pilots already fly and like. The Tomcat's one of those jets. Solid, dependable, every test pilot's flown them. So every new fly-by-wire plane feels a lot like a Tomcat."

"I'm not going to be able to tell anyone about this, am I?"

Webber understood that they were no longer talking about aircraft. The resignation in her voice worried him. It didn't sound natural, not from her. "I don't know, Cory. I'm going to guess that they'll take a couple of days to debrief you, find out exactly what you saw, and how much of that you understand. Then they'll probably give you a list of things they'll ask you not to talk about."

"Ask?" With that one word, some of the old challenge returned to her voice.

"They can order me, but they can't order you. There'll be some negotiation involved."

"Negotiation. You mean threats."

"Cory, I said I'd protect you from Abbott, and I will. When we land, you go where they tell you, and you sit down and tell them *everything* they ask. And then, don't sign anything or agree to anything until you've spoken to a lawyer, and to me. Okay?"

"C'mon, Mitchell. You really think they'll let me do that? You know how these people operate."

"Cory, I *am* these people."

"You don't have to be."

Webber kept his mouth shut. He wanted to say that *she* didn't know how the military operated, but that would just start the spiral into another argument. He'd end this one before it started. If she'd let him.

"You still up there, Mitchell?"

Webber saw the communications display flash into life as he

275

heard a hiss of static. "Archangel Four, this is Space Command, do you copy? Over."

"Just a second," Webber told Cory. "I've got an incoming message."

"Very convenient," Cory said; then Webber cut her out of the circuit.

"Space Command, this is Archangel Four. Go ahead. Over."

Webber heard the distinctive voice of Major Wilhemina Bailey, the ESC officer who had set up the teleconference feed between Christchurch and the Pentagon. That he was receiving a communication from her didn't surprise him. But what she said did.

Alone in her separate cockpit, Cory Rey reflected on what she had learned during these strange hours with Webber. With the exception of three bouts of unconditional terror—takeoff, the unexpected loud thumps of in-flight refueling, and the stomach-churning switch to ramjets—her flight in the Blackbird had been exhilarating. She envied Webber his view of the world she had been trying so hard to protect. Now she knew why he had never been able to share his world with her. She'd had to be *in* it to understand.

But then, there was the other part of his world: witness Webber's knee-jerk reversion to his Rambo persona at the slightest criticism of the military. Like that bogus incoming call. He'd still do anything to avoid admitting that what she believed was right, and that he was wrong.

Then a click in her helmet told her she was back in the circuit.

"Uh, Cory," Webber said. "It's for you."

Cory shook her head, as best she could in the space helmet. It only reminded her how badly she wanted to scratch her nose, and how impossible that simple act was. "Yeah, right."

"Dr. Rey?" a voice asked.

Oh my God, he's serious. "Who is this?"

"Major Bailey, U.S. Space Command. You might have seen me on the STVS screen at Christchurch."

Cory remembered her—the woman who had the unflappable air of someone in complete control. "Yes, of course, Major Bailey. Uh, what can I do for you?"

"To get to the point, I was wondering if you have ever met, or know of, a man named Anatoly Cerenkov."

The name was familiar to Cory. At least, she had read it some-where. "He's an oceanographer? San Diego?"

"Hawaii, actually. So he is a specialist in waves?"

Cory was puzzled by the odd series of questions. "I think he's in climate. I'm pretty sure he was one of the speakers at the Global Warming conference I was at last year. But I don't know him. What's this about?"

Bailey seemed to take a longer than usual time to respond. "Captain Webber, are you still on the circuit?"

"I'm here, Major."

"We're trying to run down any background Department of Defense studies that might have been done regarding appropriate response to giant, uh, tsunamis. We've come up with a reference to something called Icefire. Does that mean anything to either of you?" Both Cory and Webber said it did not. Bailey continued. "This Professor Cerenkov seems to have some connection to it, and we were wondering if it was an avenue to explore."

Cory had no idea what Bailey was talking about, but she was certain the major knew more than she was saying. There was just something in the way she hesitated between words. "How could we help you with that?" Cory asked.

"I heard what you said to General Abbott. You seem to be very knowledgeable about waves. I thought perhaps you might know if Cerenkov was also an expert. In case he was someone we could contact."

Cory liked the idea that Major Bailey thought of her as an expert. But considering the fact that General Abbott was holding her virtually incommunicado, she still had no idea why Bailey had come to her with this question. "I thought General Abbott already had all the experts he needed."

Another long silence from Bailey followed. When she spoke again, Cory could hear how cautious she was being. "Dr. Rey, I know General Abbott already asked you this, and I don't mean any offense, but do you have any idea why the experts on the Vice-President's committee haven't considered your idea of the wave staying as strong as it is now when it reaches the States? I mean, all the networks here are giving it full coverage. We've got live shots of it chewing up New Zealand. We're feeding full satellite data streams directly to the Pentagon, the White House, NOAA, you name it. So everyone knows exactly what the wave is and how it's progressing."

Cory had no idea where this was going, but she took the major's question seriously. "Science is not a matter of opinion, Major. If qualified workers have access to the same data, they usually arrive at the same conclusion. So if all information is being shared the way you say it is, I have no explanation for why they can't see it's a soliton wave, and not an ordinary tsunami."

But then Webber cut in, and Cory had never heard him speak the way he did, deliberately, like a teacher leading a particularly slow learner. "Cory, would I be right in thinking that the difference between you and the people in Washington is that you saw how the wave formed?"

"Seeing it makes no difference. I mean, as long as they know how—" Cory felt a sudden knot of tension twist up inside her. "Major, is television reporting that the collapse of the Ice Shelf was caused by nuclear explosions?"

Cory knew she had hit it even as Bailey began to answer. "No, Doctor. No specific cause has been publicly identified, though I have seen a news conference in which it was suggested that volcanic eruptions under the ice shelf caused it to—"

"*God damn them!*" Cory shouted. "Abbott's experts think they're dealing with a displacement wave! They think the Ice Shelf just sort of *slipped* into the ocean with a little splash and we're looking at a ripple or something. Listen to me—someone has to tell them it was caused by a high-speed impact of the entire shelf. *That's* the energy expenditure you need for a soliton. No wonder they don't see it. What is Abbott thinking?"

Again Webber spoke slowly and deliberately. "Major Bailey, I am under orders not to discuss the circumstances which led to the wave's creation. Could you explain to Dr. Rey the significance of a SNAP BLUE alert in relation to a terrorist use of weapons of mass destruction."

"What's going on, Mitchell?"

"Cory, trust me. Just listen to the major."

"Dr. Rey, I think I can help you out here." Cory noticed that Major Bailey's calm voice had the same odd deliberateness about it as Webber's. "SNAP BLUE is a DOE scenario which is to be fol- lowed when a rogue nuclear weapon has been detonated. According to this scenario, even as emergency support services begin, the government will not confirm that a nuclear event has taken place. This is to permit the more accurate evaluation of claims of responsibility."

Cory exploded again. "That is outrageous! By withholding the truth, innocent people are put at risk."

"Dr. Rey, I'm not arguing with you. But the government's position is that by withholding the truth for a day or two under these circumstances, it will be easier to apprehend the parties responsible."

"A day or two? How many millions do you think are going to be dead in a day or two when that thing hits the West Coast? Your General Abbott is a monster. And if you go along with him, you're monsters, too."

Now when Webber spoke, it was with extreme politeness. Cory found the flat tone unsettling. "Major Bailey, would it be possible for you to pass on to General Abbott Dr. Rey's concerns about informing the Vice-President's committee about the nature of the wave's creation?"

Bailey replied with the same even control. "Captain Webber, I am not sure that will be an efficient use of the general's time. For example, earlier today I informed General Abbott about some initial conditions which suggested the possible involvement of nuclear weapons in the McMurdo region. Instead of allowing me to proceed with a full investigation, the general requested that I refrain from contacting any other facility, until he had investigated from his end. I believe that resulted in at least an hour's delay before word of the wave reached New Zealand."

"I understand," Webber said.

Cory pounded her fists against her thighs in frustration, the only movement she dared make in the cramped cockpit that might not cause something vital to malfunction. "What is wrong with you people? Abbott's sentencing millions to death and you sound like you're at a tea party! If you won't tell Abbott, then pick up the phone, Bailey! Call CNN! Call the newspapers! Let the people know!"

"Dr. Rey, that would be the first thing I would do, *if* I were a civilian. Don't you agree, Captain?"

"I agree. If I were a civilian, that's what I'd do, too."

If Cory could move, she would have kicked the side of the cockpit. "I'm a civilian! I'll make the call!"

But Bailey quashed that idea. "Dr. Rey, the general has asked me to arrange all aspects of your flight from Christchurch to Washington. Per the general's instructions, I have arranged for you to be placed in custody upon your arrival."

Cory's cry of fury almost deafened her in the helmet she wore. "Don't you people understand what you're doing?!"

That was when Webber lost his temper completely. "Yes, we do, goddammit! Now be quiet and let us do our jobs!"

Then Cory heard the click that told her she had been cut out of the circuit once again.

She wasn't the only one who needed protection from Abbott. She'd been joined by all the countries who now believed they would escape the wave.

She finally had proof that the Pentagon had lied.

But General Abbott would not release her until her knowledge no longer mattered. Even more people would die.

Unless she could change Mitchell Webber's mind about the Pentagon *before* they got there.

THIRTEEN

NATIONAL MILITARY COMMAND CENTER/THE PENTAGON

Abbott spun the dial on the third and final lock of the green door sealing the Tempest room, then checked the active status display above it. No electronic surveillance measures were detected. The room was secure.

"All right, Dr. Casey. *Now* you may continue."

Abbott returned to the gleaming wood table in the center of the small, windowless room. David Casey had precariously settled his bulk into a chair never intended for a giant. Major Chennault sat at the side of the table, in the same position he had chosen late yesterday evening, when he had discussed the origins of Operation SHADOW FORGE.

But this time, General Abbott took the head of the table, establishing his control. This was no longer a conversation among warriors. This was an integral briefing for PACIFIC SHIELD. And perhaps, he suspected, something more.

Casey's chair creaked as he rocked forward to rest his arms on the table. "Start at the beginning?" he asked.

"This is not a colloquium, Doctor. Keep it brief."

Casey winked at Abbott. "Hence, *briefing*, hey? Okay, short and sweet. J. Tuzo Wilson. Ever hear of him?"

"He established the theory of continental drift," Abbott said. "Continue." He could see that Casey seemed impressed that a sol-

281

dier knew of a geologist. But in Abbott's view, how could a soldier preserve his culture if he did not understand and embrace it?

"Wilson's also the same guy who came up with the idea of subglacial heat—heat generated by the internal processes of the Earth radiating up through the Antarctic landmass, creating meltwater that forms a lubricating layer that makes it possible for the ice to slip. This was, oh, back in sixty-four or thereabouts. He thought he was coming up with an explanation of where ice ages come from."

Abbott tried to hurry the scientist along. "But they're now linked to subtle changes in the Earth's orbit."

"Right. Anyway, Wilson was talking about gradual processes. Didn't get it quite right, but subsequent work in Iceland has shown that he was pretty close. Turns out you get the same slippage effect from subglacial volcanic activity. It's just more dynamic." Casey bobbed his head at Chennault inquiringly, making sure the major was having no difficulty keeping up. When Chennault asked no question of him, Casey continued. "Anyway, that's what I was going on about in that news conference."

"We both saw you," Abbott said.

"Okay, getting back to the sixties. It's the Cold War. It's suspected that heat from the Earth can do something catastrophic to the climate. How about heat from nuclear weapons? That's when I'd say it started."

"Where?" Abbott said.

"Institute for Defense Analyses. Right across the river in D.C. They did a study of what would happen if . . . *someone* . . . you know, they never did say Russia back then . . . just *someone*, you know, as if Canada or who knows who else was going to come after us all of a sudden."

"If you please, Dr. Casey. I am needed back at my post."

Casey nodded, unperturbed, but he began speaking more rapidly. "Okay, so the IDA developed a scenario in which nuclear explosives would be inserted through deep boreholes down to the surface of the rock, and we're talking up to nine thousand feet here, to create enough heat and physical motion to shake the ice caps loose. They figured if the ice could get moving at about a hundred meters a day, the resulting tsunamis would wreck coastal regions around the world. Even up in the Northern Hemisphere."

"And the IDA called this study Icefire?"

"No, no. This is way before Icefire, General. But this is where

Alex got the idea." Casey clarified his reference before Abbott had to ask. "Aleksandr Rykov. He's the fellow who thought it up."

"A Russian?"

"Soviet back then. But a Russian, yeah. Look, here's the basic concept. Blowing up the ice in Antarctica makes no sense. It affects everything. Ruins the whole planet. Probably would start another ice age. But in, oh, let's say seventy-seven, the National Science Foundation, they're the boys who run the U.S. Antarctic Program, you see, they get all upset because all of a sudden they're thinking the big ice shelves down there are in danger of cracking off. Not just WAIS, but all of them. They were talking sea-level rises of twenty feet. What was that movie with the guy who played Robin Hood?"

Abbott rapped sharply on the table. "Dr. Casey, make your point."

"That is the point. That's what made it all come together. You don't blow up the *whole* ice cap. Counterproductive. But, let's say you could break off a *particular* section of ice that'd create a surge directed straight at the enemy, and only the enemy? Now, that's a weapon. Sick, isn't it? But, I mean, Alex never thought they would seriously consider it."

" 'They'?"

"The Kremlin, of course. Their advanced-concept war college. Took Alex three years to work out the whole thing. He even over-wintered in the Russian Vostok Base. You know, the Pole of Inaccessibility. From what I remember, his plan called for detonating about a dozen small nuclear charges around the edges of the Ross Ice Shelf. Specifically where the Shelf was anchored to the land. If you look at where that shelf is on a globe, it's like the mouth of a cannon pointed right up the Pacific to the North American West Coast."

Casey now began using a flurry of hand gestures to demonstrate the stages of the Icefire scenario. "The way Alex had it, the charges were to be set pretty deep within the Ice Shelf itself. Alex did soundings and satellite mapping to locate the key connection rises. Soon as they went off, those charges would cut the Shelf away from the land, and then I think it was four more bombs would go off in the atmosphere above the Shelf. Three of them were down low to punch the Shelf into the water all at once. And the fourth one, and this was incredibly diabolical, was set off at the same time, only extremely high up, so the electromagnetic pulse would blind all the nearby satellites. That way, no one knows the shock wave's coming, you see."

Casey stared up at the ceiling. "And there was something else. . . . Oh, yeah, they were going to do something to the high-altitude bomb. Wrap it in iridium. So when the site was studied, we'd pick up the iridium signature and think it was a meteor that had hit. We'd never realize the whole thing had been a setup. Lord, what a horrible time in history that was."

Abbott was aware that Chennault was staring his way, his face tight with recrimination. But he ignored the major. For all his exasperating digressions and confusing gestures, Casey was providing invaluable intelligence.

"You said you had read the Icefire scenario, Doctor," Abbott reminded the scientist. "Where exactly?"

"Well, I evaluated it. For you boys. I do consulting work for the DOD through NOAA. Weather warfare, things like that."

"When did you read it?"

"Well, let's see, that'd be eighty-four, eighty-five. When Alex defected."

For the first time, Chennault spoke. "Are you saying the man who created the Icefire scenario is in the United States?"

"Has been for twenty years. Icefire is what brought him here. I mean, according to him, when the Soviet Union was in the midst of self-destructing, there were some old-style generals there who were actually taking a second look at the idea. I mean, it was just a thought experiment for Alex. It was never meant to be taken seriously, you see."

Abbott knew that was untrue, no matter the country. A weapon was a weapon, especially if it could be so precisely controlled and targeted. "Do you know what it was about the plan that prevented its being seriously considered for implementation, in Rykov's estimation?"

"How about, it was insane."

"That alone wouldn't have stopped the Kremlin, especially if they believed their country to be at risk."

Casey made a face that indicated his distaste for what he said next. "I believe the term you use in your business is 'collateral damage'—i.e., the surge created by the Ice Shelf's sudden collapse would not only devastate the West Coast of the United States, which is what Alex's plan called for, it would also have affected Canada,

New Zealand, all the islands of the Pacific, *and* China, Korea, and Japan. Even the Kremlin wasn't crazy enough to alienate the entire world. You see, in the end, I believe, Icefire wasn't so much a military weapon as it was an economic one."

Then Chennault asked the question whose answer most interested Abbott. "Dr. Casey, in your opinion, how is the wave we see today similar to the . . . the Icefire 'surge,' you called it."

"It's completely different, thank God. As I told the reporters, what we're seeing of this wave is much more like what the National Science Foundation feared in the seventies: a natural collapse of the Ice Shelf creating a tsunami. An absolutely nightmarish situation for New Zealand and the South Pacific islands, but little more than a bad storm for us, China, and the other countries of the North Pacific. In fact, since the breakers that reach us won't be combined with high winds and rain, and will be of relatively short duration, I suspect the damage will be less than we might see in a hurricane. Oh, the subsequent rise in sea level will cause more damage in the long run, but that will still be manageable."

Before Chennault could go on to ask what must be asked next, Abbott regained the initiative. "Dr. Casey, what exactly is the difference between the wave we see today, and the Icefire surge?"

Again the scientist could not be content with a simple answer. Once more he acted out his various descriptions with his hands. "Well, the wave today was created by displacement, as if you *waved* your arm through a swimming pool. I'm estimating there's a physical transport of water involved. That's energy-intensive. There will be a rapid drop-off in the total energy of the system, so the waves that eventually hit us will be nowhere near as energetic as the wave hitting New Zealand. But the Icefire surge, because the Shelf would be slammed down into the water all at once across its whole area, well, that creates a different kind of wave, you see. It's what we call a soliton." Casey hesitated, puzzled, as he saw Chennault's bitter look of recognition. He began to speak more slowly. "A soliton means pure energy transport. . . . According to the Icefire projections, it would hit Alaska with about eighty percent of the energy it had when it hit New Zealand. . . ." An expression of alarm appeared on Casey's face as he looked from Chennault to Abbott. "Hell's bells. This isn't a natural collapse, is it?"

Chennault shoved back his chair as he stood up to face Abbott. "General, we've heard enough. We have to take this to the Vice-

President right away. We have to get this on the news. Let the people know."

Casey stood, too, his face almost as white as his hair. "If you boys think that's a soliton out there . . . I read the damage projections. In 1984, they called for *six million dead* in the United States alone."

But Abbott wasn't ready to let anyone dictate to him. He remained seated, as if by force of will he could keep both Chennault and Casey from bolting. "Where is the Icefire report now?"

"It was twenty years ago." Casey's huge frame vibrated with nervous agitation. "I don't know. I mean, it's classified up the wazoo, isn't it? You boys should have it somewhere."

"Where's Rykov?"

"In Hawaii. He got the works. New identity. Citizenship. He teaches . . . General, I demand to know if what's chewing up the Pacific is Icefire."

"You can't waste any more time, General," Chennault urged. "You heard Webber. Nuclear weapons were used in Antarctica. And Dr. Rey was right about the soliton. Someone has activated the Icefire scenario!"

"Both of you, sit down. Neither of you is to leave this room. Major, that's an order. Dr. Casey, I will be posting guards outside."

"But the wave, General . . . if it *is* Icefire, that's just the beginning."

"I will not have either of you spreading panic through the nation with wild accusations that have not been verified. Now *I* am going out there to obtain a copy of the Icefire report, and to contact Aleksandr Rykov."

For Abbott, that the Icefire scenario was under way had not been in question since the moment Casey first described it. The question that now concerned him was *who* had set it in motion?

With a sense of inner peace he had not known in years, General Abbott was certain he knew the answer.

All that remained was to move out onto the watch floor and direct the hunt for the evidence. And then, when he had the proof in hand, he would make history as it had never been made before.

FOURTEEN

"Cerenkov's a defector."

Huber dropped a sheaf of printout pages on the chart table behind Bailey's situation panel. Bailey sat at that table, reading Captain Mitchell Webber's service record. There were so many gaps in the version she had been able to download from the DOD's central records archives that she was certain he was heavily involved in black ops. It was the only explanation. Navy fighter pilots didn't suddenly become SEALs. And what kind of pilot is rated for helicopters, Harriers, Blackbirds, and the list of all the other aircraft included in the file? There were three in it she had never even heard of before. And the Delta Clipper was a spacecraft, for pity's sake. And how did that kind of expertise qualify someone for NEST, which as far as she had been aware had begun as an emergency response team of *civilian* weapons designers and engineers?

Reading between the lines of Webber's file, Bailey had the feeling she had stumbled upon one of those shining souls whose worth to the country was pure gold. They became the soldiers who could do what no one else could do. The ones who truly could make a difference. The only part she couldn't figure out was why in God's green earth a man like that would drive a Volvo station wagon. Yet there it was, a handwritten comment in the additional-remarks category. Even the personnel officer had found it unusual.

"You interested?" Huber asked.

Bailey pushed back from the table, wedged her fist against the center of her spine, and cracked her back, relieving the strain. Self-chiropractory and instant gratification. She was a believer in both. "If he's a defector, just don't tell me he's a war criminal," Bailey said. She had been juggling all sorts of different possibilities for the past hour, and she kept coming back to Cerenkov. He was someone outside the system, which meant he might be safe to approach.

"No sign of military service at all," Huber said. "But his background's a fabrication."

"And how can you tell that?"

"First clue, he became a fully tenured professor of environmental science at the University of Hawaii at the age of thirty-five—"

"That sounds reasonable."

"—*without* ever having published a single paper."

Bailey turned the sheets around so she could read them herself.

"The guy doesn't even have a doctoral thesis. But one of his academic credits is a PhD."

Bailey flipped through the pages until she found the credit. From the University of London, twenty-five years ago. Those records wouldn't be available online, so there would be no quick way to check them. She skimmed the list of Cerenkov's publications. Huber was right. Cerenkov had authored dozens of scientific papers over the past twenty years, many of them with collaborators, but none before the time of his appointment to the university's staff. The list of titles revealed a clear, unifying theme: "GPS Measurements of Rock and Ice Motions in South Victoria Land"; "Antarctic Marine Geology and Geophysics"; "High Latitude Geomagnetic Pulsation Measurements"; "Planetary Waves in the Antarctic Mesopause Region"; "Volcanic Record in Antarctic Ice—Implications for Climatic and Eruptive History and Ice Sheet Dynamics of the South Polar Region." She handed the pages back to Huber. "I agree. This is our guy. He knows what's happening down there."

"And check this out," Huber said, flipping to the end of the list to one particular publication title he had circled: "Rayleigh and Sodium LIDAR Studies of the Troposphere, Stratosphere, and Mesosphere at the Amundsen-Scott South Pole Station."

Bailey looked up at Huber. "Project SHAARP."

"At the very least, he's a consultant. Which gives us a Russian national with a false American birth certificate, no past, yet has academic acceptance at one of the top fifty universities in the country, involvement in a classified DOD project, *and* we caught him on tape mentioning Icefire in a call to a secret government number. I smell CIA all over this. He's a defector who's been given a new life."

The big smile in the ID photos, Bailey thought. The reason for that smile was obvious, now. *From Moscow nights to Waikiki weekends.*

"So what do we do?" Huber asked.

Bailey knew she was approaching one of those career-defining moments of decision. It was time to set up the firewalls and protect her people. "*We* do nothing. This is going to be up to me."

"No way."

"Commander, I'm giving you an order. Go back to your workstation and return to your normal duties."

Huber stood to attention, the formality of his bearing and words aging him the ten years that divided him from Bailey. "With respect, Major, I have no normal duties. I was replaced at the last shift change and have been assisting you on special assignment ever since."

Bailey stood up so she could speak in a quieter, more private way. "Look, Dominic, what I'm thinking of doing could backfire."

Huber looked straight ahead, not at her. "It is our job, Major, to defend this country from enemies foreign and domestic. And that wave is our enemy." Then he paused, giving her a sideways glance, and spoke more naturally. His real concerns apparent. "General Abbott doesn't seem interested in stopping it."

"The general's being cautious. Command prerogative, Huber. Plus, he very likely has access to intelligence we don't." But even Bailey did not find her explanation fully convincing.

Huber pointed to Bailey's situation panel. "Major, ever since Falcon handed off the first DSCS transmission to you, everything the general knows has come through that panel and he hasn't acted on any of it. There are people *dying* in New Zealand now who might have lived if he hadn't stopped you from investigating the EMP. Major, this wave is fast. The only way to beat it is if we're faster."

Bailey looked out over the control room to check the wave's progress on the wall display. The wave was nearing the end of New Zealand's North Island now. There hadn't been a live news report from the small island country for at least an hour, except by satellite phone. The damage had been more extensive than any of the experts had predicted. In a few areas, the wave had struck more than three miles inland.

"Whatever you want to do, Major," Huber's open, freckled face was grim, "I want to help."

But Bailey was an Air Force officer and a leader. She would not, and could not, allow someone under her command to take an unnecessary risk. "I'll give you a choice, Commander. You can stay on duty and help me field General Abbott's communications requests. Or you can be dismissed. But you will have no part in what I am going to do. Make your decision, or I'll make it for you."

"I'd like to help you handle General Abbott."

That wasn't quite how Bailey had put it, but she accepted Huber's choice. She moved to her situation panel, followed by Huber, and cleared all open circuits to the NMCC—those on standby and those in use—so they could be monitored from a third station. "There," she told him, "you've got three video feeds, five audio channels, and thirty-two data streams to the emergency action room. Keep an eye on them, make all the connections Abbott requests. You'll be dealing with Lieutenant Yoshii, and she's good. She can read the general's mind. If you run into anything tricky, I'll be up here."

Huber nodded. "Can I get you some tea?"

Bailey shook her head. "No. We're going to do the rest of this by the book. You go to your station."

"Good luck, Major."

Bailey smiled at the expression. She appreciated Huber's loyalty, if not his sense of what was appropriate.

Then her situation panel chimed. She had an audio signal coming in.

She sat down at the panel, toggled the channel open, becoming aware that Commander Huber was still standing behind her. According to the control-room display screen, the incoming signal was being passed over automatically by Falcon. It was from Archangel Four.

Bailey checked the time display on her panel. Webber was checking in as he had said he would. A little over an hour ago, when she had first contacted the captain and Dr. Rey at General Abbott's request, she and Webber had both verified to one another, and to Rey, that neither could take official action outside the chain of command. Webber had suggested that he would report to her when the second in-flight refueling of the Blackbird was completed. Then he had asked if Bailey could confirm that Wheeler Air Force Base on Oahu could support the SR-71, just in case any problem developed with the aircraft.

Suspecting Webber's line of thinking, Bailey had accessed Wheeler's status on one of her screens and discovered that a KC-135Q Stratotanker was permanently stationed there. She knew that, unlike other 135s, the Q-series were specifically designed to handle the exotic, low-volatility fuel used by the Blackbirds, 30,000 gallons of it. Bailey had then confirmed to Webber the base's ability to handle the SR-71. As soon as she had relayed that information, Webber had signed off.

The major looked over her shoulder at Commander Huber. "It's Webber. He'll be reporting that he just finished his next refueling. You can go."

Webber's voice hissed over the panel speakers. "SPACECOM, this is Archangel Four."

Bailey pointedly waited for Huber to leave before she replied. "This is Major Bailey, go ahead Captain Webber." She could hear Huber clomp heavily down the stairs, back to the control floor.

"I have completed my second in-flight refueling."

"Copy that. I have your ETA Washington at 13:55. Can you confirm?" Bailey held her breath. Now she would find out whether she and Webber had analyzed the situation, and its opportunities for creative, independent action, the same way.

"Uh, no I can't, SPACECOM. I've got an SER warning light on my hydraulics. I am requesting clearance to divert to Wheeler."

Bailey released her breath. Webber was as smart as his record implied. If there was anything wrong with that Blackbird, Bailey would eat it. Webber was making sure Rey was not going to be whisked away by Abbott's people. The captain had said he was under orders not to discuss the nuclear explosions in Antarctica. Bailey could not talk about anything that passed through her station except with the express permission of the commander-in-chief, SPACECOM, or General Abbott. But as a civilian, Rey was under no such restrictions—at least until the DIA began debriefing her.

"Copy that, Archangel Four. I will alert Wheeler you are inbound. Do you have a revised ETA Oahu?"

"I'll be keeping the speed down," Webber said. "ETA forty-two minutes."

Knowing that everything they said was being laid down on spools of magnetic tape in three different NSA storage facilities, Bailey continued with her part of the plan they had jointly developed, each without expressly speaking of it. "Do you want me to advise General Abbott you will be delayed for your debriefing?"

"That won't be necessary, Major. If Wheeler's standing by with a ground crew, we should be able to turn the aircraft around fast enough to let me make it to the general's meeting. I'll advise you of my status when I'm on the ground."

"We'll stand by. SPACECOM out."

The speakers stopped hissing as the channel cut off. Emotionally, Bailey suffered a twinge of guilt, but intellectually was confident that she had done no wrong, or harm. Technically, she had not disobeyed orders or broken procedures. After all, Webber was still on his way to Washington. And Rey was with him. Bailey had simply used her own initiative to set various options in place, and it had been up to Webber to unilaterally decide to act on them. But the next option was one she would have a difficult time explaining if an investigation was called. If it were not for the communications confusion caused by the incredible efforts of Operation PACIFIC SHIELD, she doubted she would have the nerve to try it. The only condition that made it possible for her to even consider what she planned to do next was that she was certain that no one would notice her making a simple, personal call.

Bailey reached into her pocket for her ten-dollar calling card, hoping her father hadn't exhausted it with his description of her mother's hip surgery. She picked up the dull gray phone, then dialed zero and the number she had written on a scratch pad. She entered the phone-card number at the prompt.

The call went through. It was answered on the third ring. A young girl.

Thinking of every old war movie she had ever seen, Bailey hit the beach running. "Is this Betsy?" she asked.

The girl, twelve to thirteen years old, sounded more world-weary than Bailey could ever imagine being, even at her own age. "Betsy Paullina. I'm Paullina."

"Oh, I'm sorry. Is your father home?"

"Just a minute."

Bailey heard the phone being held to the side. Music was playing. She could hear laughter. A party. Then she hear Paullina shout, "Hey, Dad! It's for you!"

Bailey watched the seconds counting on the timer display. She wondered what the holiday rates from Colorado to Hawaii were and how long the card would last. Captain Webber's SR-71 was costing $350,000 an hour to operate. That she knew. But long-distance rates were something else. Her job might help her oversee the whole world, but it certainly didn't keep her in touch with it at street level.

Finally Bailey heard the phone receiver being handed over. Paullina's muffled voice issued a stern warning: "Don't talk long. Daryl's calling."

A voice with a Russian accent said, "If he wants to marry you, he has to talk to me first."

"Da-aad!"

More shuffling of the phone, then a booming voice exclaimed, "Happy Thanksgiving!" *Here goes*, Bailey thought.

"Professor Cerenkov?"

Cerenkov's voice remained friendly, but it was clear he didn't recognize her voice. "Yes. Do you need instructions?"

Bailey was caught off-guard. "For what?"

"The Orphans' Thanksgiving! Are you a student? Even if you're not, you're invited!"

"Well, thank you, Professor. But . . . I'm calling on behalf of Dr. Corazon Rey. She was one of the speakers at the conference—"

"On global warming. Yes, yes, I know her. Know of her, I should say. What is on her mind?"

Bailey felt her hands go cold. "She would like to talk to you about Icefire."

Cerenkov's good humor was instantly replaced with guarded caution. "Are you with David Casey's office?"

David. That was the name Cerenkov had used in his message. Bailey saw her opportunity and took it, bluffing wildly, glad Huber was not close by to hear her. "David Casey, yes. You left a message for him earlier this morning."

Cerenkov seemed to relax. "How is he?"

"Very busy. But that's why he'd like you to talk with Dr. Rey."

"Then I would embrace the chance."

"Good. She'll be arriving at Wheeler Air Force Base within the hour."

Again, a long silence on the other end. "Are we discussing the same Corazon Rey who was broadcasting live from McMurdo Station yesterday evening?"

"Yes, sir. That would be her."

"And she will be in Hawaii in . . . less than an hour you say?"

"Yes, sir."

Cerenkov laughed heartily. "Very impressive, indeed. Tell me, would *she* be interested in joining us for Thanksgiving dinner?"

"I don't think that would be possible, sir. She's on her way to Washington."

"I understand. Well, I'm glad to think that some good might come from my early work. I trust it's helping plan the evacuations."

"That will be something Dr. Rey will want to discuss with you, I'm sure."

A beeping tone started on the line. Bailey's card had one minute remaining. "Professor Cerenkov, that's . . . the White House. I have to go."

Cerenkov accepted her second impromptu falsehood at once, as if he often talked with people who were interrupted by the White House. "Of course, of course, yes, by all means. Wheeler Air Force Base, one hour. Tell Dave I said hello. And to Michelle, say hello to his wife for me, please."

The beeping speeded up. Thirty seconds. "I will, Professor. Thank you." Bailey hung up.

She stared at the phone. She had the worst feeling that whoever David Casey was, he wasn't married to Michelle or anyone else. But there was no time to dwell on what she couldn't remedy. She called up a DSN—Defense Support Network—access node, logged onto Wheeler AFB's internal directory, and created a security-pass request for Cerenkov. But her request was flagged as redundant and not processed. Cerenkov already had access to the base as a civilian instructor. The system didn't identify what kind of instructor he was.

Guiltily, Bailey logged off, half-expecting the green phone to ring at once, with her C-in-C calling her up to the command floor to have her listen to a playback of that last call. She wondered if it would be wise to figure out a way to call Cerenkov again in ten minutes to see if he was actually on his way to the Air Force Base, or if he had decided to ignore her because of the slip about David Casey's wife. She regretted that the one thing she couldn't do was tell Rey and Webber that Cerenkov might be there to meet them when they landed. But it would be too risky to mention the professor again in a conversation she knew would be recorded. Rey and Webber knew Cerenkov's name, and they might even remember the term Icefire. Past that, Bailey would have to trust in their own good sense.

Bailey's attention returned to her panel. She studied the status lights. She hadn't heard from Abbott or anyone from the NMCC for a long time. According to the status lights, almost all the channels she had assigned to Huber were in use, so Abbott was involved in something having to do with satellite communications. But what?

Then Huber came dashing up the stairs and on to her platform again. "Abbott's up to something," he whispered, breathless and concerned.

Bailey wheeled herself back from her panel as Huber began calling up the NMCC feeds. The first thing Bailey noticed that was odd was that none of the visual channels were of the wave. In fact, Abbott wasn't watching the Pacific at all, even though he had set PACIFIC SHIELD in motion.

And what he *was* watching was baffling.

Abbott was tapped into an NSA data stream from a Block 5D-2 DMSP satellite. Ostensibly part of the Defense Meteorological Satellite Program, the standard weather-sensing systems on board the birds were augmented by additional, and classified, high-resolution MSI sensors. With twelve of the satellites in orbit, almost every part of the planet, except the poles, could be viewed at least once every hour.

And the region of the Earth that General Abbott was so interested in right now, to Major Bailey at least, made no sense at all.

NATIONAL MILITARY COMMAND CENTER/THE PENTAGON

Abbott stood with his hands behind his back, gazing down on Moscow. He was in the Russia, Eurasia, and Ukraine section of the NMCC watch floor, and this collection of cubicles was as quiet as the Russian capital itself. It had been that way for years, since the collapse of the Soviet Union.

The DMSP image on the high-definition gas-plasma display before him showed a sleeping city. His point of view was as if from an aircraft at 5,000 feet. He recognized the spiderweb pattern of the main city streets radiating out from the Kremlin at the city's center. A few cars—ghostly white smears in the SAR image—traveled along them. It was 4:00 A.M. there, and the city was being blanketed by a late-November snowfall. But the heavy clouds Abbott peered through meant nothing to the Synthetic Aperture Radar sensors of the satellite.

The military academy in Lefortovo Park was dark. Savelov, Riga, and Yaroslav Stations were without movement, and only a single train pulled out of Kiyev Station. The beast that had for so long threatened the security of the United States had been slain, more by its own actions than those of its opponents. In the peaceful cityscape spread before Abbott, there was no sign of it reawakening.

But then, Abbott had expected no less. If he had been a Russian general leading a military coup against the failing government, he, too, might think to attack the country's enemies as a diversion. But such an attack on foreign soil would also be matched by preparations within Russia herself. And even though the Cold War was long over, the watchful eyes of America regularly scanned the enormous country, looking not only for the sudden solitary launch of a single missile fired in madness, but any appreciable repositioning of the country's domestic troops.

Yet, on this night, Russia remained dormant. In another generation, it would be lobbying for entry into the European Union, changed from a transforming force in the history of the last century, into a footnote in the history of the new.

"Thank you," Abbott said to the lieutenant charged with observing Russia's military installations this shift. "Carry on."

Then Abbott walked through the cubicles of the watch floor, passing by South America, the crammed sections of the South Pacific where PACIFIC SHIELD continued at a furious pace, and then around the corner to Asia.

Five cubicles were on his right. Three were devoted to satellite monitoring. Two were focal points for ELINT—electronic intelligence—collected and filtered by the NSA before high-priority transmissions were relayed here for further study. To his left were four offices. Unlike most offices in the Pentagon, their front walls were half glass, so the occupants could remain connected to the observers in their cubicles outside. Only one office was occupied this holiday—Milton Harrap, senior analyst, DIA. Abbott knew that the analyst was responsible for preparing the preliminary assessment of the intelligence gleaned from the tracking of the recent Chinese war games off Taiwan.

Abbott, however, was no longer convinced that the maneuvers had been mere war games.

Harrap's door was open. Abbott knocked on the frame. The small civilian, distinguished by a well-trimmed and waxed mustache, looked up from his keyboard. "General. Happy Thanksgiving." Harrap was an expert in divining the political currents of the PRC, legendary for having correctly forecast Jiang Zemin's last two replacements months before the Pentagon's other analysts had reached the same conclusions.

Abbott gave a perfunctory smile. His Thanksgiving would come later. Perhaps as early as Sunday. "Mr. Harrap, I could use your assistance."

Harrap was out from behind his desk at once, quickly pocketing a box of candy mints on his way to the general. "I'm all yours. With the way those war games ended, I find myself with some extra time." Abbott knew that was true. But he also knew that Harrap enjoyed any chance to spar with him about the future of China. Where Abbott was convinced of the inevitability of military conflict between the People's Republic of China and the United States, Harrap foresaw the country's eventual dissipation and Balkanization, its fate a mirror of that of the former Soviet Union. At least, Abbott acknowledged, Harrap, in contrast to most civilian experts, approached his position from knowledge and thoughtful consideration. He was wrong, but he was not ignorant.

Abbott led the analyst to the China DMSP cubicle. That constellation of satellites with their MSI sensors had their orbits arranged so that there were always a minimum of two passing over China at any time. With each satellite having a scanning area of 1,400 miles, no part of the huge country was ever out of observational range for more than an hour, and, when necessary, Trumpets and Big Birds could be employed to keep any sections that were not already covered under constant surveillance, 24 hours a day.

Under usual peacetime operations, all satellite data streams were examined on a realtime or near-realtime basis by interpretation specialists of the National Reconnaissance Office, the National Security Agency, and the Central Intelligence Agency. Some data, like those from the older series of Landsats, required up to forty-eight hours to be processed, first through the Goddard Space Flight Center, and then through the Earth Resources Observation System Data Center, in South Dakota. With the sporadic coverage of Antarctica and the holiday weekend adding to the delay, Abbott knew that the first detailed satellite images of the Ross Sea since the collapse of the Ross Ice Shelf would not be available for study until late Monday evening at the soonest. By then, Abbott knew, it would all be over.

Should some security issue arise, the vast bulk of data obtained from military surveillance satellites went into the archives for comparison with later scans. The returns from those satellites whose missions were primarily directed toward instant alert of possible missile attacks on the United States or her allies, such as the warning component of the GPALS constellation—Global Protection Against Limited Strikes—were also monitored, by computers and people, in realtime at Cheyenne Mountain and its mirror sites.

But scans of those areas of the globe of immediate strategic concern to the military composed only a few percent of all available data, and it was those images which were relayed directly to the Pentagon for continuous study by intelligence analysts. In Asia, the regions under constant surveillance included areas surrounding Beijing, Taiwan, and the border between North and South Korea. And it was specifically Taiwan, and the adjacent Chinese coastline of Fujian Province, less than 100 miles away, in which Abbott was most interested now.

Abbott and Harrap entered the cubicle, drawing a nod from the naval lieutenant who observed the gas-plasma display. During duty hours, no formal acknowledgment, such as a salute, was required. A second plasma display, smaller and on the lieutenant's desk, presented a still image of a Chinese warship clear enough for them to see the sailors standing at the rail on the upper deck. It was a radar image, so no painted markings were visible. Abbott could see that the lieutenant, a young woman with a cap of curly brown hair, was attempting to determine the ship's identity.

Abbott told the lieutenant that he was going to interrupt her work for a few minutes, and she put her displays at his disposal.

"Show me the port in Quanzhou," Abbot said. The coastal city was located at the mouth of the Jin Jiang River just across from Taiwan, and though it was not a PLA naval station, its sheltered harbor had been an unexpected staging area for some of the war-game naval exercises. The lieutenant began typing in the command codes that would change the sensor positions on the satellite in order to bring the required coordinates into view.

"I must admit I'm intrigued, General Abbott," Harrap said. "Are you after something particular?"

"I just want to get your impression of something. Have you been following China's reaction to the wave?"

Harrap popped a candy mint into his mouth and offered one to Abbott, who accepted. He made a point of doing the little things that built connections between people. "They've begun a well-organized evacuation of low-lying coastal areas. It's part of their regular tsunami-warning network, like we have in Hawaii. But it is working with remarkable efficiency. And the government reaction has been the mirror of our own. They deplore the loss of life, and they're standing by to take part in whatever international relief efforts are arranged in the next few days. They have also sent private offers of aid to Taiwan, South Korea, and even Japan. No strings attached." Harrap smiled like a parent seeing a child go off to school for the first day. "China's growing up. And the more involved they become with the rest of the world, the more difficult it will be for the country to remain cohesive. Witness what happened to the Soviet Union."

Abbott wasn't here to continue their traditional debate. "Are they conducting any evacuation of their naval units in the South Pacific the way we are?"

"No. They were very fortunate. The PLAN's been operating under severe fuel shortages for the past few months, so the fleet isn't far from home. Most of their assets were involved in the war games, so they're steaming toward protected shipyards. This would involve only about a hundred twenty, a hundred thirty ships."

Abbott slowly worked the mint with his tongue. Harrap was confirming his expectations. "A severe fuel shortage seems an odd time to run a war-game exercise."

Harrap yawned, then covered his mouth and excused himself. Abbott was not holding his interest. "General, the editorials in that Taiwanese paper were extremely provocative. The People's Army really had no choice but to respond. It's been a long-established policy for them."

Abbott watched Harrap carefully. "Any chance those editorials could have been planted?"

Harrap frowned. "By the Taiwanese government? Not a chance. They don't have to probe the PRC's thinking on independence. It's a subject Taiwanese only make a commotion over during elections. And then, usually, it's only by the side most in danger of losing. The Taiwanese would be foolish to attempt formal independence and they know it. Better to wait out the Communist rule of the mainland." Harrap shook a finger at Abbott. "Which will happen, and you heard it here first."

"Could the editorials have been planted by Beijing?"

Harrap's forehead creased, the analyst not just surprised, but startled. "In heaven's name, why?"

"To provide an excuse for the war games." Abbott saw the image on the gas-plasma screen snap into focus. The satellite, now locked on to the coordinates of the Quanzhou harbor, was north of the target area, moving south, at an altitude of 390 miles. But the magnification and motion-blur adjustment made it seem as if the image were coming from a helicopter hovering less than a thousand feet from the ground. It was 11:00 A.M. local time and the dark water in the harbor shimmered in the bright sunshine as tendrils of gray and black smoke twisted from hundreds of smokestacks. "Move in," Abbott told the lieutenant. "I want to concentrate on the shipyard."

Harrap gave Abbott a sly look. "You're playing a game with me, General. You're leading me along so when you finally tell me what all this is about, I'll be in a box and forced to agree with you. What are you getting at?" He shook the box of mints invitingly.

Abbott held out his hand for another mint. "Answer my question first." It was a brusque demand but it had been asked in a friendly fashion. This conversation wasn't between warriors, it was between students of history.

Harrap tapped out a mint from the small packet. He looked like a chess player who has just uncovered his opponent's ruse and was enjoying the promise of a new level of complication. "Very well. Yes, if Beijing felt it needed an excuse to stage war games off Taiwan, it would certainly be within character for it to arrange for the publication of provocative editorials in the Taiwanese radical press.

As Sun Tzu said, 'All war is based on deception.' And the poet Tu Mu, in his commentaries on *The Art of War*'s thirteenth chapter, points out that inside agents 'can as well create divisions between the ruler and his counselors, so that they are not in harmonious agreement.' Spreading foment in Taiwan is quite in keeping with present-day China's plans for it." Harrap gestured grandly at the screen, now showing the portion of Quanzhou's sheltered harbor that had been set aside for the People's Liberation Army Navy. "But there's a major flaw to your argument."

"I haven't made it yet."

"What did the war games accomplish? Nothing. They were called off, on account of the wave. If China wanted to invade Taiwan under cover of war games, I say their timing was fortunate. The wave allows them to save face. Because there *is* no way China could pull off an invasion. The Taiwanese Air Force is superior in every way. The PLA has yet to demonstrate the command and control necessary to coordinate a full-scale land, air, and sea assault. And with the sheer number of vessels—military and civilian—they'd have to assemble to get a credible ground force to Taiwan, we'd have ample lead time to get half the U.S. Navy there to provide logistical support. No, General, your theory simply doesn't hold water. No pun intended, of course."

Abbott remained undisturbed, and undiverted. "That wasn't my theory."

Harrap looked at him sharply. "Why hold diversionary war games if they're not a diversion for an invasion?"

"I didn't say that, either. You're jumping to too many conclusions." Abbott pointed to the screen. "What do you see there?" Abbott had seen it right away.

"Besides the obvious . . ." Harrap stared at the screen, then looked questioningly at Abbott. "The dry docks?"

Abbott nodded. "They're all full. Now look beside them, those patrol boats, they're on dry land."

Harrap saw it but didn't fully understand. "They're preparing for the breakers."

Abbott shook his head. "Mr. Harrap, that is a protected harbor that reaches almost ten miles inland. And it's sheltered from the open sea by Taiwan itself. Forty-foot breakers are not a concern."

Harrap was quick, which was why Abbott tolerated him. "Then they're expecting bigger waves?"

Abbott gave him the only conclusion possible. "No. They're expecting *the* wave."

The general saw that all Harrap knew about the wave was what he had heard on television. "I don't understand," the analyst said. "It's not supposed to get that far."

"What's the disposition of the PLA? After the war games?"

Harrap seemed thrown by the change of topic. "I believe ten Group Armies took part. The Fourth, Seventh, and Ninth were deployed to Zhejiang Province to the north. The Eighth—"

"I'm not interested in the farmers with their pitchforks. Where're the elite troops? The Rapid Deployment Forces? The Marines?"

"Well, three divisions of the RDF were stationed in Fujian Province."

"How many are normally there?"

"Two."

"How many RDF divisions are there in the country?"

Harrap was looking worried. "At least twenty."

"So what you're saying is that China's People's Liberation Army just conducted a full-scale naval war game that involved most of its assets, but which wasn't supported by more than a handful of the troops who would take part in a lightning invasion." Abbott saw the first of the perfectly aligned dominoes begin to topple. It was a perfect plan.

The civilian analyst was defensive. "I had noticed that, General. It's in the report I'm working on right now. These war games were hastily called."

"Hastily enough that the army couldn't take part but the navy could?" It was so transparent to Abbott, so beautifully conceived. "The objective of the exercise wasn't Taiwan, Mr. Harrap. It's *Beijing.*"

Abbott pushed Harrap aside and stepped into the next cubicle. The image on the gas-plasma display was a crisp optical view of Tianjin, near the shore of Bo Hai Bay and the ports that served Beijing. Beijing itself was a safe ninety miles inland. "Lieutenant—drop the optical and go to SAR and infrared," Abbott said to the startled officer at the controls. "Call up the ETEM on Beijing, hundred-mile radius, then overlay moving heat sources and traffic. *Now!*"

The lieutenant was typing rapidly on his keyboard as Harrap rushed up behind Abbott. "General, what is it?"

"You watch," Abbott said. "You watch and tell me what you see." He clapped the lieutenant on the shoulder. "As soon as you've got it, son, you throw it over to the big board in the EAR. Got that?"

Still typing, the lieutenant nodded, lost his place, began typing again.

Abbott stepped out of the cubicle, moved resolutely through the congestion of officers and aides in the South Pacific, then around the corner past South America, the Russia, Eurasia, and Ukraine section, and across the watch floor to the emergency action room. As soon as he was through the side doors, he ordered the room cleared out, except for Lieutenant Ann Yoshii and . . . he looked around, trying to find someone he could trust. . . . "You, Captain Woolman. I want you to stay."

In thirty seconds the room was empty except for three people, two of whom were confused.

"Lieutenant Yoshii, you're about to get a satellite feed from the China section. Push the PACIFIC SHIELD display to the side. I'm going to want to see detail."

Yoshii made the adjustments and the ETEM map of the South Pacific, studded with realtime satellite images of the wave, shrank to the upper-left-hand corner of the big board. Abbott tapped his hand against his leg, glad that Yoshii and Woolman knew better than to disturb him. They'd understand soon enough.

Yoshii's phone rang. Abbott waited, expectant. It would be the lieutenant setting up the internal feed.

"No, I'm sorry," Lieutenant Yoshii said. "The general is very strict about that." She listened, then hit a control on her phone without hanging up. "General, I apologize, but your wife says she has an emergency and needs to talk with you."

Abbott did not vent his anger at Lieutenant Yoshii. She was merely a conduit, no different from the phone she held. "My son is home for the holiday. He can help her. And tell the switchboard that it is my *order* that no other personal calls are to be put through." Abbott turned back to the almost empty big board, not caring that Woolman was covertly staring at him. Abbott knew the Air Force captain couldn't have any understanding of how his wife was continually and maliciously doing all she could to damage his career, to punish him for imagined wrongs. The woman knew better than to call at a time like this, when he was so close to proving himself to the Joint Chiefs and to the country.

Yoshii nodded briskly. "Yes, sir." Then she repeated into the phone what he had said, but with considerably more emotion than he had allowed himself to display. She did her job well.

As soon as the lieutenant hung up, her phone rang again. Abbott looked at once to the big board, knowing it was not another assault from his insubordinate spouse. The chain of command could be counted on in the military. Eagerly he watched as the big board began flickering with a tremendously detailed map of Beijing and the industrial sprawl and countryside surrounding it.

"There's the ETEM, sir," Yoshii announced. "Second layer coming up. . . ."

The map turned pale green as a realtime infrared scan was combined with the stored imagery. Thousands of white hot spots appeared, small and large—the heat signatures of everything from smokestacks to burning buildings to car engines.

Yoshii spoke again. "Filtering for movement, sir."

Fully eighty percent of the white spots suddenly disappeared from the map. Of the ones that were left, all were moving, most confined to the highways and roads converging on Beijing and the outlying towns. A few random moving dots were most likely aircraft.

"Oh, yes," Abbott said softly, vindicated, as he sought out and found exactly what he was looking for. "Captain Woolman. Do you see those?" The general pointed to the amorphous blobs of white that indicated inbound traffic slowing on the main freeways, fifty miles from Beijing. Where they bunched up in the greatest concentrations, they suddenly winked out, indicating regions where all traffic stopped.

"What are they, sir?"

"Roadblocks." But only for the inbound roads. Outbound traffic continued unimpeded.

"Lieutenant Yoshii, ask the name of the lieutenant in the China cubicle."

Yoshii did. "It's Moffat, sir."

"Tell Lieutenant Moffat General Abbott says he's doing a damn fine job. Then ask him to add the SAR layer. I want it tuned to show hard metal objects only."

Yoshii passed on the compliment and the command.

Woolman stepped closer to Abbott. "Permission to ask a question, sir."

Abbott's attention remained fixed on the board. "Go ahead."

"May I ask why Beijing is so important?"

The ETEM display flickered again as a blue layer of imagery from Synthetic Aperture Radar was integrated with the infrared signal. Again, the main roadways were clearly outlined as metal car bodies were detected, moving and stopped.

Abbott held up his hand, indicating he wasn't to be disturbed. The answer to Woolman's question was better demonstrated than spoken. "In a moment, Captain." Without taking his eyes from the board, he called out, "Lieutenant Yoshii, ask Lieutenant Moffat to adjust infrared selectivity. I want all sources, moving or stationary, registering between eighty-eight and one hundred eight degrees Fahrenheit only."

That was a simpler request, which did not involve sending commands to the satellite. The temperature values could be filtered where the signal was received in the Pentagon. The response on the big board was almost immediate.

The cars and other traffic disappeared, along with hot spots from factories, generators, and fires. But millions of pixels, the smallest possible resolution that could be displayed on the board, wavered in and out of view, showing white clusters around town centers across the map, and along roadways in Beijing. Groups of people, Abbott knew, their detection at the very limits of the map's sensitivity.

Then he found the next artifact he had been searching for. "There," he told Woolman, pointing to large concentrations of pixels, entire masses of blurred white, concentrated approximately ten miles north of Beijing, in the Jundu Shan highlands.

Abbott read out the coordinates from the map. "Lieutenant Yoshii, I want maximum magnification on the heat concentrations, same temperature range, at approximately 116° east, 40.3° north. Now."

"Why that particular temperature range, sir?" Woolman asked.

"Human beings," Abbott said, "plus or minus ten degrees for observational error and atmospheric distortion."

The ETEM map rippled as it expanded, zooming in on the coordinates Abbott had given, followed by a matching expansion of the infrared layer, then the SAR. The unusual angled line at the top of the map was part of the Great Wall.

The concentration of human heat signatures had expanded to fill the center of the board, but was still one amorphous blob. Humans. Tightly assembled. "All right, Lieutenant. Ask Lieutenant Moffat to drop the infrared and the SAR, and switch back to optical, maintaining this magnification."

It took less than a minute. Then even Woolman got it.

"Troops," the captain said with a frown as an aerial image of what could only be bivouac camps appeared. Abbott could make out small vehicles driving along dusty roads, rows of parked transports. Helicopters. Tanks. APCs. And soldiers in parade formation. "But there's no army base there."

"It's a staging area," Abbott said with pride and relief. He had found the missing Rapid Deployment Forces. If he had the time, he was certain he would find similar troop concentrations outside Shanghai, Hong Kong, Tianjin, and Canton.

"What are they doing there?"

Abbott turned to Woolman. The moment had come. "Captain, I am placing you under my direct command. Henceforth, everything said between us is privileged. You will not report to the Secretary of Defense except through me. Is that understood?"

Woolman had no choice. He stood at attention, sensing the seriousness of what Abbott was saying. "Yes, sir."

"Lieutenant Yoshii, tell Lieutenant Moffat he is to use all available satellite assets to prepare a complete description of the troop concentration we've located. Mr. Harrap is to help him. I want the Trumpets and the Big Birds to give us images that will let us read the division numbers and insignia on those vehicles. I want to see the unit badges on the soldiers' uniforms. Harrap is to then provide me with the command structure of each division, including the generals who are responsible for armor support. I want to know who we're dealing with."

Yoshii started speaking quickly into the open line with Lieutenant Moffat.

Abbot turned his attention back to Woolman. "You asked what those troops are doing there."

Woolman nodded. His respectful manner showed Abbott he had picked the right officer.

"They are preparing to take control of Beijing, the State Council, and the National People's Congress."

Woolman's eyes widened. "A coup?"

"That's one name for it."

Woolman seemed genuinely shocked. "They're exploiting the wave, aren't they sir?"

But Abbott knew the truth with a certainty that was almost religious in its intensity. "No, Captain. They're not exploiting it. The generals in command of those troops, they *caused* it."

Woolman was speechless.

"Absolutely brilliant," Abbott said with true admiration. "By taking a single action ten thousand miles from home, they have taken control of their country, and strengthened it immeasurably."

"Strengthened it?" Woolman said, with no trace of admiration. "How?"

Abbott quoted from Sun Tzu. " 'The acme of skill is to subdue the enemy without fighting.' In other words, Captain, when that wave hits *us*, we will be subdued."

Woolman was rigid with emotion. "How can you stand here and take that, sir?"

Ah, Abbott thought, *indignation. Much better than anger.*

"I have no intention of 'taking this,' Captain. This is what we're here for." Abbott felt alive as he had never felt before. His eyes brightened in expectation of what was to come. "This is war," he said.

FIFTEEN

Jack of all trades, Mitch Webber thought as he brought Archangel Four in on its final approach to Wheeler. *Master of none.*

Webber was well aware that the problem with flying for any length of time at altitudes of 100,000 feet or more was that the pilot lost the ability to judge distance. He had only been flying the Blackbird for just over two hours, but after almost thirty-five hours without sleep, he knew that his reflexes were suffering, even with the Air Force-approved drugs in his system. He was also coughing a great deal—a reaction to the dry pressurized air being fed to his space suit, and most likely a complication from the cracked rib he had had taped at Christchurch. The dull throbbing from the back of his head where Glendon Morris had swung an ice auger at him was now merely something in the background, to be tolerated. Its demands on his attention had been superseded by more recent irritants. *Sort of like Cory*, Webber thought, smiling at his own joke. But even smiling hurt. Sometime during the past day and a half, he decided he must have been in another fight. He just couldn't remember when or with whom.

"Archangel Four, you're three hundred feet below optimum glide."

Webber concentrated on adjusting his descent. Wheeler AFB wasn't trusting the Blackbird to mere flight controllers. The wing commander had dispatched an F-15 Eagle to serve as Webber's wingman and keep him on the proper flight path. The fighter was about two-thirds the length of the Blackbird, and could hold its own at speeds up to Mach 3. In the Gulf War, it had also established a kill ratio of 26:0 against MiG-29s and Mirage F-1s. The pilot of this particular F-15, call sign Mother One, did not sound pleased to be Webber's baby-sitter. Blackbird pilots weren't supposed to need hand-holding. Webber read between the lines and deduced that Major Bardeen, Archangel Four's primary pilot, might once have been stationed at Wheeler.

Webber watched his cockpit's central monitor screen, where analog images of the critical landing instruments were displayed, and brought the Blackbird back to the proper glide path. Mother One was having him come in from the west to avoid traffic into Honolulu International Airport. Hawaii was the most militarized state in the Union, and fully twenty-five percent of Oahu was owned or controlled by the military. So other air approaches were not hard to plot.

"How's it going up there?" Cory asked from the RSO cockpit behind him.

Oh, yeah, Cory. He'd almost forgotten she was still with him. He had to admit he was truly surprised by the change that had come over her on this flight. He knew the Harrier legs of their journey had been rough on her. Not to mention the Blackbird takeoff and that first kick to ramjets. *Not many civilians get a chance to throw up in a Harrier at government expense. She'll have bragging rights in the most exclusive pilots' bars when we get . . .* Webber realized that his concentration was drifting off again. Remembering how much Cory had needed to be in control of her life in the past, he marveled at how well she'd put up with a situation only he could direct. Somehow Cory seemed different up here. He recalled how, after the second refueling, she had asked him to give her a countdown for the next switchover to ramjet operation, and when the acceleration boost had come, he could swear he had actually heard her whoop as if she found it as thrilling as he did.

He knew how she felt. The jump from 2,000 mph to just under 4,000 mph made all those years of flight training worthwhile for him. Not even shuttle astronauts had that kind of visceral experience of speed, even as they gradually sped to Mach 25 and escape velocity.

"Less than two minutes," Webber told his passenger. "You know what you have to do when we're down?"

"That's an affirm," Cory replied, doing what he supposed she thought was an impression of a pilot. As soon as he had signed off in that first contact with Major Bailey, Webber had been able to explain to Cory what he and Major Bailey had actually been discussing. Virtually every in-flight radio transmission made by a jet of any nation, and all transmissions by U.S. military craft, were recorded by the NSA as a matter of course. That's why, he had told Cory, the major couldn't come right out and say that Webber should divert in order to give Cory a chance to reach the media and warn the rest of the Pacific Rim nations that the wave would not diminish in energy. The diversion to Wheeler had to be Webber's decision. Just as the announcement to the media had to be Cory's. He felt confident that Cory was prepared for what she had to do when the Blackbird landed.

Surprising him with her calm, reasonable attitude, Cory had simply asked Webber if he didn't consider his and Bailey's subterfuge another example of how the military was out of touch with reality. She'd pointed out what she thought was a problem in most bureaucratic systems—the lack of incentive for independent thought and encouragement for creative problem-solving.

Webber had tried to help her see it from the military's POV. He'd explained that the whole point was not to have to count on being creative or independent in a crisis. Creativity and inspiration were for peacetime. Strategies that were developed had to be able to be followed by anyone, so that in a crisis no conscious thought was required. The *system* went into action, without delay, and without fumbling. In a crisis, he'd told her, the military was *designed* to function instantly, *without* leadership. He'd left himself wide open with that "without leadership," but incredibly, Cory let it pass without comment.

"Archangel Four, this is Wheeler," ground control radioed to him. "You are number one on one-mile final."

Webber dropped the airspeed even more, slowing to below three hundred. At that speed, the Tomcat-feel left the computer-mediated controls and the aircraft became an unbalanced teeter-totter, threatening to rear nose-up at the slightest inattention.

"Here we go," Webber told Cory.

Nestled among the lush tropical growth of the island, Wheeler looked like a nondescript base as Webber closed on it. But that was what made it valuable. Few would suspect the level of classified projects that operated from here. With the headquarters of the largest U.S. strategic military command in the world—CINCPAC, Commander-in-Chief, Pacific—located less than ten miles to the south, the DOD required a local airfield that was not as exposed to public eyes as was Hickham AFB, right next to Honolulu International.

The runway rushed up at Webber faster than he anticipated and he hit hard. He felt a sudden lurch that told him one of the plane's nitrogen-filled, powdered aluminum-impregnated tires had blown. Adrenaline and pride helped Webber keep the runout straight and he easily reversed thrust, bringing the aircraft to a perfect stop by the designated crash truck, humvees, and ground crew.

Webber glanced out the forward windows to see if he spotted any telltale white helmets belonging to military police, but saw none. *Good.* That meant Bailey had not yet informed Abbott of his landing at Wheeler. And with all the other activity in the South Pacific, it was unlikely that Wheeler's wing commander had bothered to report the unscheduled landing.

"Ugh, I still feel like we're moving," Cory said.

"Well, stay put until the ground crew gets you. And don't touch the outside of the plane. It's still a couple of hundred degrees."

Webber went through the shutdown checklist, then confirmed with the ground crew that all systems were off or powered down. The first airmen rolled the stairways up to both sides of the Blackbird, ready to go to work the moment the pilot and RSO had left.

Since the aircraft's skin was still hot, SOP called for Webber to pop both cockpits, instead of making a maintenance worker fumble with a heat-resistant glove on the outside releases.

"I've got someone at my window telling me to open up," Cory reported to him.

"I'll do it," Webber told her. He lifted the cover on the canopy-seal override switch, toggled the switch on, then pulled back on the lever that released the canopy clamps. Even inside his suit, he heard the rush of air. Then he unlocked his visor at the side of his helmet and slipped it up. Instantly a mixture of scents assaulted him— machinery, fuel, the burning plastic odor of the Blackbird's scorched skin, and as an undercurrent to it all, the moist green scent of tropical jungle.

There was also heat. Not the gentle warmth of New Zealand. But blistering, high-altitude, Hawaiian heat. Webber knew that he and Cory had to get out of their space suits fast.

The ground crew was efficient and practiced. They helped Webber step out of the cockpit, keeping well away from the lip of the plane. He looked back and saw two other airmen almost lift Cory from her separate cockpit. He could see that her legs were wobbly. An understandable reaction for a novice.

As Webber climbed down the open metal stairway, he felt distinctly dizzy. The constant changes in pressure, temperature, and movement he had been subjected to were building a residue of confusion in him. His body was beginning to rebel.

At the bottom of the stairway, an Air Force colonel suddenly appeared, having stepped out of the humvee by the crash truck. The colonel's name badge read Lightfoot and Webber realized that the wing commander himself had come to greet him. That was unexpected. Webber regarded him warily, wondering if Lightfoot had been in contact with Abbott after all.

Awkward in his suit, Webber saluted at once. Colonel Lightfoot returned it with a practiced nonchalance. "Aloha, Captain Webber. Major Bailey of SPACECOM has requested we show you the full hospitality of the base, and we would be delighted to do so."

Webber smiled, hiding his relief. He had calculated the odds were fifty-fifty that he and Cory would both be taken into custody when they landed, just as Abbott had planned if they had reached Washington. "Thank you, sir. But I really won't have time. Dr. Rey and I are due in Washington to meet with General Abbott as soon as possible."

But even as Webber spoke those words, he knew the Blackbird wouldn't be cleared for flight for hours. He was prepared to tell the ground crew that the SER warning light had winked out when his airspeed had dropped below Mach 1.6. He knew that would make the hydraulics system almost impossible to check without disassembling parts of it and heating them on a test bed. It could be as late as tomorrow morning before the crew determined there was nothing wrong.

In the meantime, seeing the F-15 had given Webber the idea of requesting one so he could continue on to Washington himself— the jet was only a single-seater. With one refueling over the Rockies, the F-15 could make it from Wheeler to Washington in just under three hours, following Abbott's orders to the letter, while leaving Cory free in Hawaii.

The roar of a C-17 Globemaster shook the air. The stubby cargo plane was taking off, no doubt part of PACIFIC SHIELD. Colonel Lightfoot waited only until the sound had slightly diminished before he began speaking again. "We'll certainly do what we can to get you on your way. Almost all our planes have been sent south, so our maintenance crews have an open schedule."

Suddenly, Webber was knocked almost off-balance as two eager young airmen attached a portable air-conditioning unit to his air hose. The sudden rush of cool air through his suit revived him almost immediately. Cory was now at the bottom of her stairway, also being attached to an air conditioner. A third airman fiddled with her helmet. Her visor still wasn't open.

"We'll get you two cleaned up and fed, then," Colonel Lightfoot said, "after you've had a chance to meet with Dr. Cerenkov. He's very eager to see you."

Webber hadn't even thought of Cerenkov since Major Bailey had mentioned him. What was he doing here at Wheeler? And how had he known that he and Cory would be here, too?

"I'm sorry?" Webber said, at a loss to say anything else.

"Anatoly Cerenkov. He said you'd be expecting him. Someone called him from Dave Casey's office. At the CIA."

Webber wasn't sure what was going on, but his first guess was that it was something Bailey had arranged. "Oh, right." Webber hoped he sounded convincing. "Dave Casey set it up."

Colonel Lightfoot gave him an understanding smile. No one, Webber knew, could be unaware that he was in need of sleep and food. The colonel's smile broadened as Cory waddled toward him in her orange suit, unscrewing the sealing rings of her gloves, her helmet finally open. "Aloha, Dr. Rey. Welcome to Wheeler."

Cory had a bemused expression. Like Webber, she had been ready for any welcome except that. "Uh, aloha," she answered.

Webber caught her eye. "Colonel Lightfoot says Dr. Cerenkov is eager to meet with us."

Cory caught on fast. "Oh, good," she said casually, as if arriving by Blackbird at a military base in Hawaii for a meeting in which she would be dressed in an astronaut-like pressure suit was routine procedure for her.

"Limousine's over here." Colonel Lightfoot waved at what Webber had thought was a crash car—a vehicle intended to provide emergency medical care to pilots foolish enough not to land perfectly. Webber thought its presence had been an indication of how Wheeler AFB had assessed his flying skills.

But the vehicle was an air-conditioned pilot transport, like those used for astronauts at Kennedy and Vandenberg. All it was missing was a large NASA logo on the side. Considering the types of vehicles they had flying here, and the fact that many of the pilots would have to wear full pressure suits, Webber decided that in Hawaiian heat such a vehicle was a necessity, not a luxury.

The colonel said he would check in with Webber and Cory at the officer's mess, then excused himself as an airman opened the transport's back doors. Another welcome rush of cold air spilled out on them, though Webber could only feel it on his exposed face.

A large man already seated in the passenger compartment of the van stood up. He threw his arms expansively apart to greet them as the ground crew hefted Webber and Cory into the van. "Captain Webber, I presume. And Dr. Rey."

The man was tall, built like a television wrestler, with deeply tanned skin showing through a luxuriant beard and long black hair. He was also wearing one of the loudest tropical-print Hawaiian shirts Webber had ever seen—hula dancers, fantasy fish, and palm trees in a kaleidoscope of clashing colors, none of them restful.

The man's identity was unstated, but obvious.

"Dr. Cerenkov, I presume," Cory said. She thrust out her ungloved hand to shake his, but instead he turned it palm down and swept it up to his lips for a kiss.

"Dr. Rey, *enchanté*. I admired your broadcast with immenseness, and I am delighted to see that you survived what must be a terrible tragedy." He indicated the bench seats behind him. "Please, please, sit down, make yourself at home. Colonel Lightfoot, a dear, dear friend, has insisted that you are properly taken care of."

Webber and Cory fell back onto the seats as the transport took off. Cerenkov took a seat facing them.

"I take it you've spoken to Major Bailey," Webber said.

"Ahh," Cerenkov replied mysteriously. "This is where it gets interesting, yes? I have no idea who Major Bailey might be. The woman who called me was not forthcoming about her identity. And more to the point, I have no idea who you are, Captain Webber, or why either of you should want to talk to me. And yet—" He held

314

up his hands to prevent Webber from interrupting. "—and yet, you have somehow become aware of a message I left for a most intimate friend, on a secure phone to which only one other party might have access: the CIA. So you see, I am quite at the loss to understand why I am here, why you are here, and why someone felt it was necessary for us to meet in such a way."

"We're not CIA," Webber said. He looked at Cory to confirm that his next statement was true for them both. "And we don't know Dr. Casey."

Nodding agreement, Cory began her own approach. "Major Bailey told us that you knew something about a study called Icefire that relates to the wave."

Cerenkov nodded, a shadow of anxiety dampening his natural ebullience. "And the woman who called me said you would want to discuss it with me." He leaned forward. "You can tell me. Are you NSA? DIA? Men in Black, though you're both wearing orange?"

Webber shook his head. "None of the above." He found the locking clamps on his helmet, released them, and took off his helmet.

"So what is Icefire?" Cory asked, as Webber started unfastening the clamps on her helmet.

Cerenkov sighed heavily and leaned back against the wall of the passenger compartment as if he needed support. "A bad dream from another age. A youthful scientist's game. A thought experiment. A fantasy."

Webber lifted Cory's helmet off. Then both of them began to compulsively rub at their faces and scalps.

"That doesn't answer the question," Webber said.

Cerenkov sighed again. "Americans—no poetry in their souls. Very well. Icefire was a war-game scenario whose results are much like the starting conditions of this wave. The collapse of the Ross Ice Shelf, and all that that entails."

"War game," Cory said. "Did it involve the use of a series of nuclear weapons to collapse the Ross Ice Shelf? To create such a powerful impact that it would produce a soliton wave?"

"Ah," Cerenkov said, "then you *do* know of it. I thought perhaps this was a ploy to get me to break my security oaths."

For Webber, the jumbled pieces flying around in his tired mind were starting to fall into position by themselves. "We don't know anything about Icefire. But . . . Cory, you have to tell him." Webber still felt constrained by Abbott's orders not to discuss what he had seen at McMurdo.

Cory picked up the story. "Dr. Cerenkov, we know about the nuclear weapons because we were there. We saw them. We saw what they did."

Webber had no explanation for the change that came over Cerenkov then. He seemed to lose his tan, his body sagged, and then he flushed with anger. "No. It's not possible."

"The wave that's coming toward us is a soliton," Cory said. "It's not going to lose energy at the equator. It's going to continue into the North Pacific, to hit Hawaii, the West Coast, Asia, the whole Pacific Rim."

Cerenkov sounded as if he were being strangled. "But . . . that's ridiculous. No one would ever implement the Icefire scenario."

"Someone did," Webber said, anger building in him as well as he thought of Nick Young and the lives that betrayal had cost, and would cost. "That wave is real."

Cerenkov's hands fluttered. "No, you don't understand. Certainly you can *create* the soliton wave from the forced collapse of the Shelf. That's simple physics. It's *all* simple physics, because—" The Russian straightened up in his seat. He beamed in nervous relief. "No, believe me, my friends, what you're suggesting is *not* possible. If that *were* the Icefire wave bearing down on us now, the Navy would already be out at sea, readying their defense. No evacuation would be necessary. No need for panic where there is no threat.

"You see, more than twenty years ago, when I created Icefire, I worked out *all* the details. And I know for a fact why it is of no practical use as a weapon to anyone. Because as easily as the Icefire wave can be produced, I assure you both, it can also be stopped."

The silence in the passenger compartment of the pilot-transfer van was absolute. And in that silence, Mitch Webber understood that the game had changed again.

The wave was no longer something to run from.

It was something that could be attacked.

And anything that could be attacked could be defeated.

ICEFIRE

FRIDAY NOVEMBER 26
SATURDAY NOVEMBER 27

EVENT PLUS 23 HOURS

Nine hours after the wave struck New Zealand, all but a stubborn handful of the 42,000 inhabitants of the principal island of American Samoa gathered on the northern side of their forty-five-square-mile homeland, protected from the wave's southern approach by the island's central highlands, and well away from the northern shores.

Then, on a sparkling clear day, hot and humid, no different it seemed from any other, the wave bore down on the island.

It took nine minutes to reshape Tutuila.

Still propelled by the energy of the collapsed Ice Shelf so far to the south, the wave climbed the shoals that sloped up to the island. Just as in New Zealand, the wave once again gained in height and speed as the waters before it were drawn back into its curve.

As the ocean receded from the exquisite shores of Pala Lagoon and the harbor of Pago Pago, they took with them the freighters filled with canned and processed tuna that were bound for the United States. As the boats were rolled onto their sides and dragged, metal shrieking, across the exposed sand and rock of the harbor, their cargo containers tumbled free like the cars of a wrecked freight train. The sound of the freighters' ordeal was almost loud enough to eclipse the growing roar of what approached.

Almost.

In a minute that destroyed a century of investment and construction, the wave exploded into Pago Pago Harbor, scouring shoreline beaches to rock in seconds. Fagaitua Bay was obliterated, smaller harbors filled with silt and debris, and new channels were gouged instantly in the fragile rock and coral shores. Within the minutes following, the wave erased whole villages, forests, roads, until it was as if time had been reversed on Tutuila and the lifeless land of Earth's earliest days had been restored.

But the wave took fewer than one hundred lives.

As the wave now moved on to the north, beyond Tutuila, side waves converged to create choppy waters with energetic, fifty-foot-high sprays. The survivors, whose homes and livelihoods had been destroyed, but who had evacuated as ordered, now cheered as the wave moved on. They had been spared as they'd been told they would be.

Then the top seventy-five feet of their island's central mountain blew apart in an eruption worthy of Krakatoa. Tutuila's Matafao Peak was the first Pacific volcano triggered by the energy release of the wave. It would not be the last. Except for the coral atolls of Rose and Sain, all the islands of American Samoa were volcanic in origin.

Steaming ash and lava spray now rained upon the survivors. Billows of poisonous gas rolled down from the hills and choked them. Rivers of lava cut through roads and power lines and trapped them. Then the island's dense tropical growth ignited in the blazing heat of molten rock.

There was no escape. The island's only airport had been at Pago Pago, and Pago Pago no longer existed. The silt- and debris-filled harbors were devoid of docks and boats. And even if ways off the island had still existed, there were no roads left to follow to those exits.

Of those who had survived the wave, 38,000 more died on Tutuila.

In the nine hours since the wave struck New Zealand, more than 300 eruptions occurred. There were 25,000 islands in the waters of the South and North Pacific, more than half of recent volcanic origin. And more than two-thirds of the Pacific still remained before the wave.

Hawaii was twelve hours away now. Japan, fifteen. California, seventeen.

As some had planned and others now knew, the wave was only the beginning.

ONE

In his dreams, Nick Young rode a white horse through the Arizona buttes. Red rock, red sky, a six-gun in each holster, no end to the trail ahead. That had been when the true glory and promise of America had shone, more than a century ago, when her people had embraced the adventure of discovering their own lands, carving their own place in their own part of the world.

But with the closing of that last frontier, something had become twisted in the American psyche. Their system had begun to corrode from within, and the populace had turned away from their soul-stirring anthem of "We, the people." Lacking the discipline to accept her limits, America had begun to strike out like a cornered tiger, no longer intent on bettering the world, as was each person's duty, but only concerned with dragging others down with her as she descended into the pit.

Nick Young knew his analysis of the corruption of America was correct. Had the America of the past existed with the China of today, there would be no tension between them. American leaders of the present could somehow not accept that, unlike the United States, China had never maintained her armies in regions beyond her own borders, except in self-defense, of course. China had no belief in or need for a manifest destiny that would lead her to world domination. America of the past had been much the same.

321

But America today seemed to exist only to homogenize the entire planet into one vast American town, where human dignity was trampled by eating fast-food swill, watching televised pornography on MTV, and working only to provide comfort for the parasites of the corporate elite.

That was not what the creators of the Constitution had had in mind two centuries ago, Young knew, when the farmers of America had thrown off the yoke of imperial aggression. How the descendants of those heroic, proletarian, American revolutionaries could not comprehend China's people's revolution today was something that Young had never been able to comprehend himself.

But, wisely, he had never discussed his puzzlement with any of his American friends, especially Mitch Webber, who had never bothered to find out how his "best friend" really felt about things, only accepted unquestioningly the convenient stories he was offered. Instead, Young had simply continued his studies on his own, examining the history of both his countries—China, the place of his birth, and America, the battlefield where he had gone to ground with a false identity at the age of eight, waiting for his moment to serve.

It had taken almost twenty years for that moment to arrive, but twenty years compared with 5,000 carried no more weight than a dream.

"Colonel Wei?"

The voice that woke him from that dream spoke in Chinese, called him by his real name, his real rank, and for a moment, Nick Young battled confusion born of exhaustion.

His eyes fluttered open, and he half-expected to see the cockpit of the Floating Dragon jump jet he had flown from the Ice Shelf to the staging camp near Roosevelt Island—a staging camp that no longer existed, lost as planned with the breakup of the Ross Shelf. The subtle pitch of his cabin reminded him of piloting the HST suborbital transport from the Shelf to the rendezvous site less than 200 miles from America's shores, where he had boarded the *Sun Tzu*, undetected, again as meticulously planned.

But what Young felt now was not the vibration of flight, it was the deep currents of the sea. His journeys had ended. All that remained now was to wait, just in case the impossible happened and someone realized what a fragile thing the Icefire wave could be.

"Colonel Wei," the mate said again, "your uncle calls."

322

Young sat up on the side of his cot. There were only five such sleeping berths aboard the *Sun Tzu,* short, narrow, little more than sheets of canvas stretched between wooden poles, with folded clothes as pillows. The designers of the tiny craft had reduced the crew size to its absolute minimum to compensate for the complex technology that made it invulnerable. The five cots served the ten crew members in alternating shifts. Though no one would be sleeping now. Not so close to the culmination of three years' worth of flawless preparation.

"Has it begun?" Young asked the mate.

"Soon," the mate replied. He stepped back to give Young more room to stand in the cramped crew cabin. The ceiling was only five feet here—a thin panel of pale brown plastic covering the plastic pipes and fiber-optic waveguides that wove through the pressurized crew compartment.

Head bowed, Young rubbed lightly at his chest as he stood, easing the tightness there. When he had put on his pressure suit for the HST flight, he had been startled by the blue-black mottling of bruises across his skin, caused when Mitch Webber had fired the submachine gun while Young lay across it in the cabin on the Ice. Only the bloody scalp wound and swollen lump at the side of his head, courtesy of Mitch Webber's boot, hurt more.

But no physical discomfort could compare to the pain of being separated from his true family and home for thirty years. Nor was it in his nature to complain. Young straightened his shoulders, ignoring his compromised chest muscles, then stepped out to greet his crew.

All of the *Sun Tzu*'s life-support areas were on one deck at the center of the craft, and when Young left the sleeping cabin, he passed through a narrow alcove with a small, fold-down mess table on one side, a head without a door on the other, and then into the control room itself. The largest open area on the craft, sixteen feet by twelve feet, with a six-and-a-half-foot ceiling, the control room was so crowded with glowing instrument consoles and open equipment-access alcoves that the overwhelming impression was of entering a half-assembled, room-sized computer. Running aft, opposite the crew cabin, only a half-height corridor provided access to the engine, the two missile bays, and the four torpedo tubes. There were no shower rooms, no medical facilities, nothing superfluous.

The eight crew members in the control room stood to salute

Young as he entered. He returned the salute, then waved at them to sit down. In such impossibly tight quarters, military protocol was counterproductive.

But the crew had no doubt that this would be their nation's greatest moment of triumph, and Young could not begrudge them their enthusiasm and their pride. If the American soldiers he had met in his lonely posting had shown half the spirit of the lowest member of the PLA, China would have good reason to fear America's armies. As it was, it was only American technology that China was wary of. Though that wariness diminished with each passing year as the others like Young, the little fish swimming along the currents of the West's military and technology-based industries, quietly passed on to their homeland the secrets that America and her allies, in their insular arrogance, did so little to protect.

Young's Floating Dragon jump jet was simply the Chinese version of the Harrier, built from British Aerospace's own engineering sheets. The HST suborbital transport had cost China only a few tens of millions of dollars for its construction, and not the almost four billion dollars Japan had spent to develop it. Even the *Sun Tzu* and her sisters had their beginnings in the corridors of the Pentagon.

Karl Marx had once said that capitalists would gladly sell Communists the rope with which the capitalists were to be hung. But today, Young knew, the American capitalist system, so fatuously self-assured, and so ignorant of history, seemed dedicated to *giving* that rope away.

Fortunately, the peace-loving people of China had no desire to hang the Americans. Their only goal was to reintroduce the concept of limits to the American leadership. What Americans chose to do within their own borders was their right. But all their grandiose plans to force their perverted American "ideals" on the rest of the world must end.

Nick Young knew that, in part, it was because of him that those grandiose plans would come to an end within hours.

The radio operator offered Young the chair at his station and Young took it. Like most every other structure in the control room, the chair was made from slender tubes of black plastic composite. Even the crews' uniforms had no metal. In the whole vessel, fewer than 500 pounds of metal could be found, and most of that existed only in the nuclear warheads of the torpedoes and missiles.

The radio operator handed Young a small headset and he slipped it on. As in the other controls on the vessel, volume was adjusted by pressing on a touch-sensitive plastic surface that changed the modulation of light patterns under the surface, then transmitted them through fiber optics to the photonic computer that was the *Sun Tzu's* heart. Young held his finger on the marked spot until the hiss of static in his earphone was at a tolerable level. Then he spoke into the small plastic tube that served as a microphone. "Colonel Wei here."

The static instantly ended as a digitally processed signal was received. Another radio operator, somewhere outside of Canton, Young presumed, asked him to stand by for the general. Then, a moment later, Young smiled broadly as he heard his uncle speak. It had been years since they had been able to talk directly to one another like this.

"They tell me we awakened you," General Wei Jincheng said.

Young heard no amusement, as he might have expected, in his uncle's voice. It sounded instead as if he were being reprimanded. He kept his own tone crisp and military. "I am here, now, Uncle."

"Then remain alert. We expect you will be called to action."

Young tensed in surprise. The *Sun Tzu's* presence off the Mexican coast was merely a contingency plan against a highly improbable scenario.

"Uncle, a few hours ago I heard a radio news report. The Pentagon has announced that the wave will bring little more than heavy breakers to the countries of the North Pacific. The Americans have no idea what they are facing."

Wei was not someone who wasted words. "Naval Captain Mitchell Webber is alive."

Young coughed involuntarily as the skin of his chest compulsively contracted. "Uncle . . . I flew over him in the Floating Dragon. I incinerated his helicopter. And even if he survived all that, the only place he could have reached was McMurdo."

"We have intercepted his encrypted transmissions from an American Blackbird spyplane."

Only the implication of Wei's news was stunning to Young, not that his uncle could intercept encrypted American military transmissions. The Chinese military used the same decryption equipment and programming techniques the Pentagon used, helpfully provided by the endless stream of doctoral students who studied in America, then returned home to China trained in the latest advances. "A civilian is with him," Wei continued. "She has quite forcefully described the wave as a soliton. The Air Force major with whom they conversed used the code name ICEFIRE. Do you understand?"

Young's head pounded, as if Webber were still beside him, still kicking at his temple. He looked at the time display on the radio board. "Uncle . . ." He reconsidered. "General Wei, they have less than seventeen hours to prepare their defense."

The general made no attempt to hide his fury. "Our studies showed it could be done in *six* hours."

But Young had read those studies, too. "Not on Thanksgiving, General. You forget how soft these people are."

Wei's voice was an explosion in Young's ear. "You have lived too long among them! *You* are the one who has gone soft. This is a war of the twenty-first century! A war of information! Your mission was to prevent *any* information from leaving McMurdo. You failed because you could not kill your 'friend.' "

Young had no words to defend himself. For almost thirty years he had lived a lie in the United States, pretending to be an American among Americans. *Your life is a sacrifice,* his true parents had told him. A sacrifice that would lead to unimaginable rewards.

As a child, he had gone to sleep without his family, dreaming only of the day he would be accepted in his own country, hailed as a hero. As an adult, he had worked only for the day he would show everyone he was a true son of China. And now his own uncle was telling him the sacrifice of his entire life hadn't been enough.

"I did kill him," Young said, and even as he said it he knew how unsatisfactory that obviously false declaration was. "I . . . wanted to kill him."

"Answer us this," General Wei demanded. "Are you Chinese? Or are you American?"

Young could imagine no worse insult. "I am Wei Quanyou," he said defiantly. "I am Chinese."

"Then prove it by your actions now," Wei commanded.

Young's breath came in sharp exhalations. He was thankful that only he could hear his uncle on this side of the conversation, and he was mortified to think that others on his uncle's side might be listening in. With a fury matching the general's own, he replied, "I await my orders, General."

Wei seemed to step back, as if his point had been made. "We

must assume the enemy will attempt to mount a defense against the wave. Do you understand what that means for you?"

Young wouldn't think of that. Couldn't think of that. But his answer was immediate just the same, the product of a lifetime of conditioning. "General, I am prepared to die for my country."

"We hope that is true. And we hope when the time comes, you will die not as you have lived, but as a Chinese warrior."

"You have my word."

There was a long pause. When Wei spoke again, he was almost conciliatory. "Things here are well, and on schedule. Whatever happens, China will be renewed."

"I am glad, sir."

"This is the last time we will talk until the new government is formed and you return home."

Young covered the microphone tube as he sighed. His journey still had seventeen hours to go. And he could no longer be certain what lay at the end of it.

"Good luck, Uncle."

"We have no need of it, nephew. See that you do not, either."

Young heard a click in his earphone, and the hiss of static returned. The conversation was over. A third of the way around the world, his uncle was preparing to go to war. Deep beneath the ocean's waves, Nick Young knew that was his duty, as well.

He handed the headset back to the radio operator, not caring what the crewman might have made of his half of the conversation. There would be time enough for that over the next seventeen hours.

Young made his way back to the mess alcove to make green tea. As he sipped it, he tried not to think how much he would prefer coffee, or even a Coke. America had given some good things to the world, he knew. Coca-Cola was one of them. The dream of the Old West was another.

He closed his eyes as he inhaled the weak fragrance of the tea. As if he were twelve years old again, he forced himself to see the buttes of Arizona. They would escape the wave, Young knew. But he no longer was certain that he would.

He was surprised to discover how much that thought bothered him.

That made him open his eyes.

To be afraid of death was to think like an American. And the last thing Nick Young wanted to be was like Mitch Webber.

He gulped his tea, scalding his tongue, erasing the memory of Coke and coffee from it. Then he returned to the control room. If Mitch Webber had helped the Americans stumble upon the defense for Icefire, as unlikely as it seemed, then it was up to Young to make that defense useless.

Fortunately, the *Sun Tzu* had been designed to do exactly that.

For a moment, Nick Young wished his own purpose could be so easily defined. Then, as he had learned to do in BUD/S, he banished all doubt from his mind.

Nick Young had been taught by the best. Now it was up to him to show the SEALs and Mitch Webber just how well he had learned his lessons.

TWO

UNIVERSITY OF HAWAII AT MANOA/PHYSICAL OCEANOGRAPHY CENTER

"I will now pull the plug from the Pacific Ocean."

Cory watched as Professor Anatoly Cerenkov pressed a large blue button on the panel he had unlocked. There was a gurgling noise, and suddenly the water began to drain from the eight-foot-wide relief model of the Pacific Rim. "Voilà," the professor said as the rush of the water grew louder.

Cory caught Webber looking around the three-story atrium of the Manoa campus's newest research facility and library, almost as if he were planning an escape route. An occupational habit, she supposed. The teak woodwork of the interior space was rustic and Hawaiian in texture and color, but startlingly modern in design. Every line in the open area, from the railings of the open library floors above, to the edges of the sunken conversation pits around them, brought the eye to the raised center dais on which the three of them now stood. And the focal point of the dais was the stunning three-dimensional map installed at its center. A meticulously modeled simulation of the landmasses that rimmed all 63,838,000 square miles of the Pacific Ocean Basin.

Now the Plexiglas-covered model was proving even more impressive as its hidden pumps siphoned off the water, tinted a deep cerulean blue, to reveal that the three-dimensional structure of the map continued beyond the shorelines. The model also served as a detailed map of the ocean floor's topography. Compared with the map scale, elevations had been exaggerated so that one inch equaled a thousand meters. That meant that the deepest part of the Pacific, the *Challenger* Deep in the Mariana Trench, was recessed just over eleven inches, while a few feet to the north, Japan's Mount Fuji soared to just under four. There was more unexplored terrain beneath the Earth's oceans' surface than there was on the whole of Mars, Cory knew.

As the water level dropped, she recognized the unusually straight line of the Hawaiian ridge, bearing off from the islands at ten o'clock, and the sinuous S shape of the Kuril-Kamchatka Trench snaking along the western edge of the Pacific Basin, from the Bering Sea to almost the tip of New Guinea. The model's receding waters revealed the alligator-skin-like texture of the fracture zones extending from North and South America as a somehow separate and distinct region unlike the rest of the basin floor. When the last of the water trickled through tiny screens set in the deepest parts of the basin, the visual impression created in Cory was that of two pieces from two different jigsaw puzzles that had been forced together along the mid-Pacific ridge, with a pattern of swirls and whorls on the left, and regular crosshatching on the right. The two halves of the Pacific floor did not look as if they belonged on the same planet.

Webber adjusted one of the two watches he wore, apparently setting the digital one to local time. "Professor," he said, "Hawaii has twelve hours before impact."

Cory had become aware that Cerenkov was a man at war with himself, and Webber's constant time reminders were not making control of that battle any easier for the Russian scientist. Shortly after Cory and Webber had convinced the professor that they had been witness to the Icefire scenario as it had begun in Antarctica, it was as if a long-suppressed and troubled personality had arisen within him. Before he had left the pilot-transport van at Wheeler Air Force Base, the scientist had somberly agreed to assemble all his research to show them what must be done.

When they had stopped before a flight-prep building on the base, Cerenkov had slipped away as soon as the van's back doors had opened. A female airman had escorted Cory to a changing room and helped her peel off the three layers of her space suit, which lacked only the additional micrometeorite- or radiation-protection layers to be true astronaut's garb. But before Cory could treat herself to the shower she so desperately craved and needed, Webber had been pounding on the door, telling her they had to go. With no time to visit the quartermaster with a list of appropriate sizes, the female airman assisting her had found and apologetically handed over a baggy set of gray, government-issue underwear, and a clean flight jumpsuit that was almost small enough to fit properly, but not quite. Cory's latest outfit was completed by a pair of overlarge heavy black boots. Quickly throwing on the new clothing, Cory had paused only long enough to be sure the carefully folded letter she had carried from the *Illustrious,* the final message of Cadet Andrews, was still safe in the plastic bag she had scrounged for it in Christchurch.

The moment she had emerged from the changing room, back into the Hawaiian heat, she had been bundled into a humvee, which then sped across the base to a helipad.

There waiting for them, its rotor slowly spinning, had been a white helicopter with a red, white, and blue horizontal stripe painted on its side, the top of its nose black. The craft was designed for ferrying passengers, not soldiers or cargo, and to Cory that meant the seats were, for once, comfortably padded.

Cerenkov, already in the helo, informed them that Colonel Lightfoot was having them flown to Manoa campus.

The flight took less than ten minutes, and they set down in a parking lot next to the Physical Oceanography Center. Because of the Thanksgiving holiday, the university grounds were deserted.

Cory resisted the impulse to wash her face and hair in the cascading fountain by the center's main door. She was beginning to wonder if she would ever feel clean again.

Cerenkov had hurried into the center to lead them up the interior stairway to his office on the building's third floor. He then spent five minutes in his office loading a disk he took from a locked drawer into his computer. Setting several files to print, he next guided them back to ground level, to the model of the ocean's floor. The Russian scientist was clearly anxious to show them how the Icefire process worked and, more important, how it could be stopped.

As they watched the real water drain from the simulated ocean floor, Cerenkov, grim, told them that it was already too late to save Hawaii. "The people, yes, if we keep them away from the southern

331

shores and the volcanoes. But not the cities, not the ports, not the beaches."

"What about North America?" Webber asked. "Cory estimates we've only got four hours after Hawaii before the wave starts up Baja." Cory was positive that Webber was already selecting and ranking strategies that might help them proceed most efficiently, but she couldn't help wondering how many of those strategies would involve her, and how many would involve the Pentagon.

Cerenkov turned to her, touchingly earnest in his desire to respond to Webber's urgency, but equally adamant that they truly understand what they would need to know to defeat the wave. "Dr. Rey, it is not time that's important. I assure you, the soliton can be collapsed in . . . no more than a minute. The critical factors are distance and geography. And Hawaii has run out of both." He twisted two locking bolts at the edge of the model and started to lift the framed Plexiglas that covered the map. "I will need both of you to assist me."

Cory and Webber helped Cerenkov slide the cover to the floor. Then the professor leaned in from the west side of the map and placed his finger at a point in line with the northernmost tip of Australia, directly south of the Hawaiian Islands. Cory judged the distance to be about 2,500 miles.

"Here," Cerenkov said, with anguish apparent in his voice. "*This* was where Hawaii could have been saved. The Samoa Basin, just north of the Cook Islands." He shook his head in despair. "They'll be gone by now. All of them."

As Cory studied the undulations of the ocean bottom, her attention on the oceanic region to the south of Hawaii, Cerenkov's eyes caught hers. "The fracture zones in this basin are the only true east-west trenches south of Hawaii."

That isn't right. Cory reached out to trace on the map the Penrhyn Basin just below the equator, and the trenches at the top of the Line Island chain. *All due south of Hawaii, and all east-west trenches, so—* She froze, and looked up at the Russian scientist. The hair on her arms bristled as she realized what his plan must have proposed. *He can't have been serious.*

As if reading her mind, Cerenkov added, "I am not talking about the *stable* trenches, you understand. But about *instability*—here in the Samoa Basin. Two mechanical triggers—here and . . . here—" He tapped two spots on either side of the basin. "—give us a coordinated release of pressure, and whoosh, the seafloor in between drops."

Even as Cory caught her breath at the professor's incredible solution to the wave, she saw Webber lean in closer to inspect the map. She wasn't sure, but his interest seemed to have been sparked by the Russian's use of the term *trigger*. "The timing would have to be perfect," she said.

Cerenkov rocked a hand back and forth. "Of course, with the wave advancing at two hundred miles per hour, there would only be a minute, plus or minus thirty seconds—a total window of perhaps ninety seconds. Well within the range of technical possibility."

"I'm not sure I understand exactly what you're suggesting we do, Professor." Webber's attention was still focused on the ocean-basin model.

Cory shook her head at Cerenkov, telling him he didn't have to respond. Lately, with practice, Webber had gotten better at following her explanations, though she wasn't quite certain yet just why that was. "Mitchell, it's just like an oscilloscope."

In the air before her, she moved her finger to describe an up-and-down pattern moving to the side. "For a steady frequency, the oscilloscope shows a perfect sine wave, right?"

"It can." Though Webber's grasp of where she was going with her explanation seemed tentative, Cory felt encouraged enough to continue.

"So, in a system with a wavelength of x height, what happens when you overlay a second signal that's perfectly out of phase?"

Webber obviously knew the answer but just as obviously wasn't sure how it applied. "Interference," he said. "And if the two signals are *exactly* out of phase, they cancel each other out."

"That's it," Cory said, rewarding him. "The wave traveling toward us, because it's a gravity wave, self-sustaining, it's also a perfect sine wave. It deforms the *top* layer of deep-water ocean by making the surface rise two hundred—more or less—feet. So if we deform the *bottom* layer of the water by an equivalent amount, in effect generating an out-of-phase signal, the two deformations will cancel and the wave will flatten. And since the water really isn't moving, once the energy's gone, the wave's just . . . over."

Cory looked at Webber. Surely the magnitude of what they were contemplating would be as staggering to him as it had been to her. But then, as Webber turned to Cerenkov and rephrased what she'd told him, he demonstrated less than perfect comprehension. "You're proposing we can stop the wave by dropping the floor of the Pacific Ocean by two hundred feet."

"No, no, Captain," Cerenkov said. "The absolute measurement of height is not relevant. It's the amount of *energy* that's introduced into the system that matters, not the distance of the displacement."

Cerenkov snapped his fingers several times in frustration until he came up with an example that he felt would work for a layperson. "Here, up here on the map." He indicated the Alaska Panhandle, where the state reached down into the Canadian province of British Columbia. He squinted at the section of the coastline like a man who had forgotten his glasses. "Ah, here, you can see it. This bay above Baranof Island. I used this location in my original calculations." To Cory, it seemed as if the professor were getting more and more agitated the more their discussion forced him back to a time and a place he had thought was behind him forever. On the short helicopter journey from Wheeler to the campus, Cerenkov had told Cory and Webber that after he had defected he had found a new life, with a new wife and then a young daughter born in America. Cory hoped their new home was located on high ground.

Cerenkov stared intently at Webber, and Cory was glad to see Webber return that look seriously. "July 9, 1958," Cerenkov began. "The Fairweather Fault gave way. In terms of its displacement, the total, absolute measurement of distance was twenty-four feet. That was it, twenty-four feet, no more. But, my friend, the displacement wave generated by that paltry twenty-four-foot displacement . . ." Cerenkov spoke each syllable slowly. "One thousand, seven hundred and twenty feet! The headlands were wiped clean. Millions of trees washed away. Twenty-four feet of displacement created one thousand, seven hundred and twenty feet of wave. And that is almost four hundred feet *taller* than the World Trade Towers. It's the energy release that counts, not the distance.

"Tsunami are like that," Cerenkov added. "I live here, so I know. A tsunami from an offshore earthquake that causes a seafloor subsidence can travel across open ocean with a height of *four* inches." He held up four fingers and waved them at Webber. "Only four. That's all. But when those four inches hit the shore, we have waves ten, twenty, sometimes *thirty* feet high. Energy. It all comes down to energy."

Cerenkov looked back at the seafloor model. "If we drop a section of the seafloor only a *few* feet—in the right place at the right time, mind you—the wave is canceled. Icefire means nothing."

Webber looked to Cory for confirmation and she nodded. "The Ice Shelf wave was only two hundred feet on the ocean. When it hit the shoals in New Zealand, it was six hundred feet."

Webber waved his hand across the Pacific's expanse. "In the time we have, how can we drop enough sections of the seafloor to stop the wave over this entire area?"

"We can't," Cerenkov agreed. "But we don't have to." He placed his hand near the northern edge of the Pacific and then moved it down as he began to talk more and more rapidly. "Here, where the wave becomes focused on the Bering Sea, the Aleutian Trench is like a brick wall. A checkerboard of slippages here, here, and here, and the wave becomes nothing more than what the shore would receive during a bad storm. Plus, after all this distance, it will already have lost twenty percent of its energy just through friction. And if it hits some real storms along the way, so much the better."

Cerenkov moved his hand toward the eastern Pacific rim. "For China, Korea, and southern Japan, the Ryukyu Trench forms the barrier. Now, I tell you right away that it will be impossible to collapse the entire wave front as it strikes this region." Cerenkov looked at both Cory and Webber almost beseechingly as he continued. "But only a few critical areas really need to be protected. Long stretches of shoreline on both sides of the basin are not developed, so all they require is evacuation.

"You *must* concentrate on the population centers. You begin here, at the southernmost tip of Ryukyu, to protect Taiwan; then, three hundred miles north, a subsidence in this area will protect the Yellow Sea." Cerenkov patted the relevant area near the Chinese mainland on the map. "Another three hundred miles north along this line will spare Kyushu, Honshu, and, most importantly, Tokyo-Yokohama."

"But those aren't east-west trenches," Webber said. Cerenkov agreed, but he explained that the wave front would not be approaching directly from the south in these regions. Because it was spreading out like a ripple, it would be coming in from the southeast. The key to selecting which trenches and fracture zones could stop it was to be sure they were within five degrees of being perpendicular to the wave's advance. The answer seemed to convince Webber. Cory could see that he was being won over by the detail of Cerenkov's planning. *Cold, hard facts and figures, those are what Webber always understands.*

The Russian scientist took Cory and Webber through the rest of the key locations in minutes. It was clear to Cory that Cerenkov had once been obsessed with his project. The exact latitude and longitude of each potentially useful target zone was still within his memory, especially those off the coast of North America. South America did not seem to have been of much concern.

"For the land south of Baja California, the angle of attack from the mouth of the Ross Sea is too oblique," Cerenkov said, "and the wave front will begin to fragment from internal stresses as it curves to follow the Earth's surface. At the farthest points south, Chile will see higher than usual tides. Farther north, Peru, Ecuador, Central America, these countries will experience the forty-foot breakers the news describes, but the breakers—they will arrive in sequential pulses over two or three days. Mexico will be in a transition zone— small wave pulses to the south; the chance of one strong set of waves, perhaps fifty or sixty feet high, to the north. And there will definitely be heavy flooding within the Gulf of California."

Now Cerenkov indicated the long, narrow sliver of land that ran along the west coast of Mexico, beginning almost at the U.S.-Mexico border. "But starting here, just south of the tip of the Baja peninsula where the breakers will become concentrated, the rest of North America has barricade after barricade of potential subsidence zones." Cerenkov jabbed a finger at them, the deep, parallel fracture zones that ran from the West Coast into the Pacific at almost regular intervals of three to four hundred miles. Cory was fascinated to hear the Russian recite the names of the fractures as if he were moving bead by bead along a rosary chain.

"The Clarion Fracture Zone for Baja; this transverse fault, the Socorro, between the Molokai and Murray Fracture Zones for San Diego and Los Angeles; the transverse fault between Murray and the Mendocino Zones for San Francisco and the coast beyond; all this distance up to Oregon where the Cascadia Basin has hundreds of potential subsidence zones that can protect Victoria and keep the wave from flooding the Georgia Strait. And that brings us back to Alaska and the Aleutian Trench."

Cerenkov placed his hands on the edge of the model, his lecture at an end. "In all, twelve key spots, Dr. Rey, Captain Webber. If you collapse these fracture zones, you will protect the major population centers of the North Pacific. And as the wave front stretches out— to rejoin the sections disconnected by the regions of collapse—it will lose at least another fifty percent of its energy, reducing even further its impact on the areas not directly protected."

"You've worked out the coordinates of the twelve target sites?" Webber asked.

"I spent eight months in the most awful base in Antarctica," Cerenkov said bitterly. "I calculated more than fifty key points where the Icefire wave could be broken." He paused for a moment as if a new thought had occurred to him. "Though most of them were in the South Pacific." But then his own sense of urgency surfaced again. "But the twelve I've told you about, they are the risky ones. If the timing is not exact, within that ninety-second window, there are no second chances. And if the timing is too far off, the subsidence could even accelerate the wave. You will need absolute and ongoing measurements of the wave's speed and height at all times."

"Why didn't you come forward with this when the story broke?" Webber spoke as if he still didn't trust anything Cerenkov had said. Cory was embarrassed. Why did Webber always have to attack people and their motives? Why couldn't he just look at Cerenkov, sense the man's torment, and *know* that everything he was saying was the truth? The way she could.

Cerenkov threw up his hands, running out of patience. "My calculations were for the Icefire wave. A soliton. The news reports said this was a displacement wave. In that case, I knew the energy would be too spread out, not a sine configuration. Seafloor collapse would not make a difference. As for casualty estimates and evacuation plans, I remind you that I did call David Casey the moment I learned about the wave. And that phone call, which you two somehow learned of, is what brought you to me, yes?"

Cory was out of patience, too, but for another reason. "Mitchell, we've heard all we need to know. We have to get this to the media."

But Webber showed no sign of moving. "The media can't do anything with what we've heard." Webber looked across the map at Cerenkov. "You used an interesting euphemism, earlier. One worthy of my bosses. 'Mechanical triggers.' What kind of triggers? Or should I ask, How many megatons?"

"*More* nuclear weapons?" Cory asked in shock. "Set off in the ocean?"

With an apologetic glance in her direction, Cerenkov turned to Webber. "Two megatons, Captain. Underwater bursts. Fifty meters above the ocean floor. That allows the full fireball to develop and transfer the most kinetic energy to the active faults. For most target sites, I allowed for two impacts, one each at the outer edges of the sections of the faults to be activated. If you use my calculations, I suggest you allow for three impacts in the Aleutians and along the Ryukyu. My plan called for forty detonations in all. Eighty megatons."

The Russian scientist turned to Cory, profound sadness in his eyes. "Both my former homeland and yours—now mine—have tested single bombs with yields far greater than those forty combined."

Cory found it hard to breathe. *What would eighty megatons do to the ocean?*

"The terrible irony for us all, Dr. Rey, is that this time we will be using nuclear weapons to *save* the world, not destroy it."

Cory was beyond caring about irony. She took a deep breath. She was about to act against all that she had lived to protect. She saw no choice. "Okay, Mitchell. You're the bomb guy. Can we make this happen?"

Webber's attention was still focused on the relief map. *Seeing those mind pictures again,* Cory thought. *For once, Webber's ability might be used for the forces of good, not the Pentagon.* "Too many variables to be certain," he said slowly. "It'll depend on where the Pacific fleet is. We'll need subs and destroyers. Aircraft carriers. Anything that can launch nuclear-tipped torpedoes or POPDOWN Tomahawks." He looked up at Cory, the irony plainly not lost on him, either. "There's just one problem. Of all the ships we'll need out there, except for the carriers, maybe a few of the subs, none of them carry nuclear cruise missiles. We might have disarmed ourselves to death."

Then he checked one of his watches, and looked quickly around the atrium. Breaking into a jog, he took off for an alcove where a sign pointed to the rest rooms.

"Mitchell! Where are you going?"

Webber kept running as he answered her. "I've got to call General Abbott." Then he was gone.

Cerenkov sighed as he leaned forward against the edge of the exposed map display. "It was just a fantasy, you know. I thought if I could do the calculations that would tell me how such a thing could be made to happen, it would help me understand how nature might arrange it."

Cory's mind spun as she contemplated the additional irony that while they now knew *how* to stop the wave, there was no time for them to fight the bureaucracies that lay between the solution and the implementation.

"Professor, do you have any idea who might have done this?" she asked.

Not taking the offense that she feared he might, the Russian shook his head. "My countrymen would never think of it. It was well known the plan was flawed, precisely because it was so easily defeated."

"But only if people knew what was coming."

"Twenty years ago, perhaps no one would know of the wave until it was too late. But there are no secrets in this world any longer." Cerenkov looked up, waving his hand in a circle. "So many satellites now, everyone watching everyone else. I believe that is a good thing. Fear comes from the unknown. And if we have no secrets from each other, then how can we be afraid?"

Cory touched the empty basin of the Ross Sea. "This makes me afraid."

The professor shook his head again. "The people who did this, the people who would bring Icefire to life, *they* are the ones who are afraid. There is desperation in this action."

"Are you really sure it couldn't be someone in Russia? Someone trying to bring back the Cold War? The Russian mafia? A general who wants to restore lost glory?"

Cory regretted her insensitive persistence as she saw the Russian scientist seem to wilt before her eyes.

"You forget, Dr. Rey. I am a defector. Under communism, my country died a long time ago. It had no glory to lose."

Then Cory heard Webber swearing and the slam of something hitting the floor hard as he charged angrily out of the alcove.

"Don't tell me," Cory said. "Abbott didn't believe you." She wasn't in the least surprised. The Pentagon wasn't known for its ability to accept unconventional and inconvenient ideas.

"How the hell should I know," Webber said. "No personal calls!

Abbott's shut down his whole section. And all the people I know in the building . . . it's Thanksgiving! They're not even there."

"I don't know why you even tried," Cory said. "The Pentagon can't turn on a dime."

Webber started running for the main doors. "Maybe not. But I know who can."

THREE

NATIONAL MILITARY COMMAND CENTER/THE PENTAGON

As the unparalleled press conference unfolded on the big board, General Abbott allocated a part of his attention to Major Prospero Chennault, standing across from him in the emergency action room. Each minute that passed appeared to be reducing Chennault's anger. Abbott took that as proof that he had assessed the man correctly and properly manipulated him.

On the board, the press conference was being carried on every civilian television feed. But this time, it was Pentagon spokesperson George Lilley who waited in the background as Dr. David Casey held forth, now in the midst of answering the first question since he had made the startling statement with which the conference had begun.

"Remember," the scientist said, "under usual conditions, it can take two days to receive satellite data from Antarctica. The last major mapping survey of the ice there took sixteen days of measurements, then another five months to correlate the data into a map we could read. The speed with which we're receiving data from down there now is only because of the extraordinary cooperation of the Pentagon."

Abbott nodded approvingly in his role as conductor of the greatest choir ever to sing America's praises. Casey had been aggravating in close quarters but was acquitting himself well now, in response to an appropriate incentive from Abbott.

"So," Casey continued, "that is why I *don't* believe it has taken too long to determine the true nature of the wave. We've accomplished in hours what normally might have taken weeks. I think we should be proud of the extraordinary technological expertise the Pentagon has demonstrated."

"Follow-up!" an unseen reporter shouted. Lilley stepped forward to assist Casey and pointed to the man.

"Dr. Casey," the reporter said from offscreen, "how does the revelation that the wave is actually a, uh, soliton—meaning a wave that will not lose energy as it travels across the ocean—affect the Pentagon's earlier statement that the collapse of the Ross Ice Shelf was a natural event, and not a deliberate act of ecoterrorism?"

For this answer, Abbott watched the television feed carefully. The "live" broadcast was actually being transmitted on a ten-second delay, and Captain Woolman was in the pressroom with his hand on the main circuit breaker. If Casey deviated from his agreement with Abbott, the screen would go dark and America would never even know the question had been asked.

But Casey knew how to play ball. Abbott had correctly read him. For all the scientist had seemed dedicated to the ideals of truth, the opportunity Abbott had offered, which was guaranteed to put Casey into the history books, had been too tempting to resist.

"All the data we have received to date, including the reports I've received since the last time we spoke, have confirmed that the Ice Shelf collapse is the result of subglacial volcanic activity. This *is* a natural event."

That had been the masterly compromise Abbott had negotiated with Major Chennault and Casey. In accordance with Department of Defense policy, the fact that the Ice Shelf collapse had been a deliberate act had to be withheld for the present. However, Abbott had agreed with Chennault that the people of the North Pacific should be warned in time to evacuate their coastal regions. Thus, if Casey would agree to keep the origin of the collapse classified, Abbott would clear him to make the historic announcement that would save literally millions of lives. A Presidential Medal of Honor was a certainty, along with appearances on *Nightline* and *20/20*.

George Lilley stepped up to the podium as the packed pressroom reverberated with the din of shouted questions.

"Ladies and gentlemen," the spokesman said. "We'll take one more question. Then, as Dr. Casey has said, at 4:30 West Coast time,

FEMA will be activating the emergency broadcast system throughout the affected states—that's Hawaii, California, Oregon, Washington, and Alaska. Everyone will receive full and detailed instructions about who should evacuate, and how far you should travel from the coast in each region." Lilley looked around, then pointed. "Jackie, go ahead."

The camera angle changed as an older woman in a bright blue dress and a flamboyant Thanksgiving corsage stood up. "Jackie Cassell, Associated Press. Dr. Casey, have the governments of the other affected countries been informed? And who informed them?"

Casey leaned down to the podium microphone again. "As soon as we realized that the wave was self-sustaining, and that was literally less than fifteen minutes ago, General Charles Abbott, who has been in charge of the Pentagon's response to the wave, and Operation PACIFIC SHIELD, from the beginning, immediately set up a task force to communicate with the affected countries at once. I can't tell you who the actual individuals are, though I know they're officers and Pentagon staff who are trained in these matters, and I understand there are long-established emergency channels in place. These channels are in use now, as they have been from the first detection of the wave."

Lilley pushed past Casey to add on to the answer. "I'd just like to say that all American armed forces stationed in or near the affected regions have been committed to full evacuation and relief efforts by the President. He is cutting his Berlin trip short and will be arriving back home tomorrow morning. His first order of business will be to travel to the West Coast, and we should see him there by early Sunday morning. Disaster-area declarations for all the affected states have already been drawn up, and he will be signing them immediately as damage assessments come in. The President has promised the American people that there will be absolutely no delay in aid."

The Pentagon spokesperson looked out over the reporters like a preacher assessing his flock. "As we saw in that interview from Berlin, the President has called this disaster America's first defining moment of the new century, and he is determined to make it our finest moment. And, in the President's words, with God's help, we will."

Abbott was surprised that even the jaded Pentagon press core applauded at the repetition of the President's empty platitudes. Like much of America's civilian population, they too, were blind, he decided, and ignorant of history.

After the applause died down, Casey looked determined to have the last word and leaned back down to the microphone. "And if I could remind everyone again, this is not going to be like a hurricane battering our coast for days on end. As we saw in New Zealand, the wave will come in, it will do its damage in a matter of minutes, and then it will move on. We're not dealing with rain or high winds, so relief efforts will be fast and unhindered."

Lilley waved off the other shouted questions. "Ladies and gentlemen, that's it for now. We're going to cut it off so all West Coast residents can pay full attention to their local EBS announcements. We expect to be back with the next update within the hour. Thank you."

As Lilley escorted Casey and the requisite senior officers from the dais, Casey couldn't resist adding a "Thank you" of his own. Then the networks and news channels all switched back to their local anchors.

"Sound off," Abbott told Lieutenant Yoshii, and the audio from the television feeds faded out. Abbott walked over to Chennault, determined to restore the rapport that earlier had been damaged. "You see, Major, it all worked out. Security has been maintained. The DIA's investigation isn't compromised. And we have a full twelve hours to move a few million people three miles inland. That is not an overwhelming task."

Abbott could see that the major was still upset by having been put under the equivalent of house arrest in the Tempest room, though Chennault's mood was nothing like the self-indulgent fury he had allowed himself to show when Abbott had returned to present his offer. Now, somewhat more in control of himself, Chennault turned away from him to pick up from the EAR's center table the thick document that had been delivered an hour ago from the Pentagon's Digital Document Center. Beneath the red security cover, the title page was printed in both Cyrillic and English: ЛЁДОГОНЬ at the top, and ICEFIRE, the translation, beneath it.

Chennault hefted the scenario study in his hand. "But nothing you've done addresses yet who dug up a Soviet war game and decided to put it into action."

Abbott's demeanor betrayed nothing. He, the China analyst Milton Harrap, and two lieutenants filled with the fear of God and courts-martial, were the only people in the West who knew who the true enemy was. Abbott intended to keep it that way. For now.

"The security of our country comes first," Abbott said with absolute sincerity. "The guilty parties can be hunted down tomorrow as easily as today."

"What I want to know," Chennault said sourly, "is why this document didn't show up on any of our searches for related scenarios. I say it's because we're too damned obsessed with secrecy. No one knows what the next department is doing."

"Major, have you read the Icefire abstract? It's pure science fiction. I've read three separate Rand Corporation studies commissioned under Reagan detailing war games that were run to test this country's response to an invasion by extraterrestrials." Abbott did not have to exaggerate the indignation he had felt when he had learned that the taxpayers' money had been spent on such nonsense, let alone that the Chief Executive had asked for and authorized them himself. "You're not going to find those reports cataloged in the archives, either, Major. They're in a locked filing cabinet in the chairman's private library, where I trust they will stay."

Chennault placed the Icefire document back on the table. "So, how did we do?" Abbott looked at him inquiringly, unsure as to what the major meant. "Against the extraterrestrials?" Chennault explained.

Abbott took the opportunity to share a joke with the man, and laughed. Humor, in measured doses, of course, was another way in which to bond with subordinates. "We lost. All three times."

Yoshii interrupted the conversation with the announcement that Major Bailey at Space Command wanted to speak with the general. Abbott instructed her to put Bailey through.

The SPACECOM shift supervisor looked tired as she appeared on the board. She had been on duty a few hours longer than Abbott, and he mentally saluted her determination.

"What can I do for you, Major?"

"Sir, I have Captain Webber on a FLTSATCOM channel wanting to speak only to you."

Abbott checked his watch. Webber and the radical Earthguard activist were due to land in Washington in less than an hour. DIA agents were already at Bolling AFB, ready to escort them directly to the Pentagon. Abbott sincerely doubted that Webber had been involved with the Chinese generals plotting to take control of their country, but he held open the possibility that Webber's paramour had been duped by Chinese agents into providing unwitting support for their implementation of Icefire. A "little fish," she would have been called, the Chinese intelligence term for the thousands of innocuous spies, some with ties to China, some merely misguided idealists, who had infiltrated America, some not to be contacted or activated for years, perhaps decades. For now, and in the truly defining days ahead, Webber and Rey were too dangerous to be allowed to remain at liberty, whatever the investigation into their activities would eventually reveal. Protective detention was the only reasonable, no, prudent—Abbott smiled—alternative.

But rather than put Webber on guard, the general decided the best strategy was business as usual. "Put him through, Major."

Bailey made some adjustments and Webber's voice hissed over the room's speakers. Abbott acknowledged him, then added, "I don't know if you've been keeping up with developments down here, Captain, but we were able to follow up on Dr. Rey's theory about the wave being a soliton, and it seems she was right. Our latest satellite data show that the wave will not be diminishing in power as it crosses the equator. Just two minutes ago, we announced that to the country, and FEMA is implementing a full coastal evacuation plan."

"That, uh, is good news, sir. And I think I have even better news."

"I look forward to discussing it with you," Abbott said. He didn't have much time to spare to keep Webber from becoming suspicious. A nuclear strike could take hours to set up, and he wanted to have the preparatory arrangements already in place when the time came. "We should be meeting within ninety minutes."

"Actually, sir, I'm not en route to Washington. I'm in a helicopter in a parking lot at the University of Hawaii."

To Abbott, the location made no sense at all. "I think an explanation is in order, Captain. You appear to be in violation of your orders."

"Sir, I had a malfunction with the Blackbird. I had to divert to Wheeler and . . ." Then, apparently deciding against getting involved in a long excuse, Webber jumped ahead. "General Abbott, what it comes down to is that Dr. Rey and I, since we last spoke to you—while we've been in Hawaii—have learned that the wave is the implementation of an old war-game scenario. A Soviet scenario."

Abbott's temper flared. What he had to do in the next few hours required that there be no unexpected developments. Silently damning Webber and Rey and anyone who had helped them make their discovery, the general spoke quickly. "I know that, Captain. Icefire. I have the report in front of me. Now, I want you to get back on the Blackbird, with Dr. Rey, and—"

"Sir, I'm sorry. We have no time for that. Dr. Rey and I are with the man who created Icefire. And, sir, he knows how to stop it."

The general saw the sudden excitement in Major Chennault and Lieutenant Yoshii, but the only thing he could think was, *If the wave is stopped now, it will ruin everything.*

USSPACECOM/EARTH SURVEILLANCE CENTER/CHEYENNE MOUNTAIN

The instant Captain Webber delivered his bombshell, Bailey flipped the green phone into the air and dialed Commander Huber. "Get up here, now," she told him. "You won't believe what just hit the fan."

On the SVTS feed on the leftmost screen of her situation panel, Bailey watched General Abbott pick up a thick document that reminded Bailey of the ones behind her on her worktable. "Captain Webber," the general said, and even Bailey could hear how provoked he was, "I have the Icefire report in my hands now. I am looking at the section titled 'Defense.' And, Captain, the only defense strategy listed is evacuation. I do not understand why you would choose to disobey my orders and attempt to disrupt an evacuation that will save millions of lives, and frankly I don't like the conclusion I'm seeing."

Webber was on a much-relayed audio feed. It was being routed from his helicopter, to Wheeler, to FLTSATCOM, to Falcon, to Bailey's station at SPACECOM, and from there to the Pentagon. But even if the four levels of encryption-decryption did affect clarity, digital processing kept the feed static-free. "General Abbott," the captain said, "I want you to speak directly to Professor Anatoly Cerenkov. He's the person who created Icefire."

Yes! Bailey thought in triumph. *Captain Webber put it all together. He knew what to do.*

Then Cerenkov's familiar accented voice came over the speakers. "General Abbott? This is Cerenkov."

"I don't know who the hell you are, but the name on the report is Aleksandr Rykov."

"And that is also me. My name before I defected. If you are at the Pentagon, I know you have the capability of confirming this. You may even talk to my resettlement officer, Dr. David Casey. Do you know him?"

Bailey found General Abbott's brief, fierce grin unsettling. It reminded her of a predator about to capture lunch. "As a matter of fact, sir, he is in the building. Tell Webber to keep this channel open. Major Bailey, don't lose this connection."

"No, sir," Bailey answered. Then she watched as the audio feed from the EAR was shut off, and the general went to a telephone on the conference table.

Huber ran up onto Bailey's platform and Bailey quickly filled him in.

"Has Abbott said anything about China?"

"Why would he?"

"I've been tracking the satellite data streams that've been going through to the EAR. Infrared, SAR, extreme optical. As far as I can tell, what Abbott's most interested in is that half the PLAN's been taken out of the water, and there's a serious concentration of troops outside Beijing."

Bailey tried to figure out why those things should be happening. Taking ships out of the water was a good idea in the circumstance. But the troops? "Are the soldiers there to protect the city from looting after the wave hits?"

"Beijing's inland. Way inland. The wave won't get anywhere near it."

Bailey's back was aching again. She shifted in her chair, trying to ease the pressure on her spine. "We could be looking at another police action, except with the way they lock up their dissidents, there hasn't been any major civilian unrest in China for years. Or else they're staging troops to help with the disaster relief."

"Then why's Abbott so interested in it? I mean, he's calling for opticals that're identifying unit patches on uniforms. That's a lot of money he's spending to take the Big Birds off their regular scanning runs."

Before Bailey could respond again, in the video feed on her situation panel General Abbott hung up the telephone receiver and gestured to someone offscreen. A moment later, the audio feed returned. "Major Bailey, is Professor Cerenkov still there?"

Bailey checked and he was.

General Abbott addressed Cerenkov. "Very well, Professor. Dr. Casey has confirmed your identity and your name change. And the question we both have for you is, *if* there is a defense for Icefire, why is it not in your report?"

To Bailey, the Russian scientist sounded depressed, with no trace of the vitality she had sensed on the first tape she had heard, when he had left his message for Casey.

"I wanted to be an American, General. I wanted to sit on the beach in Hawaii and drink rum from a coconut. So, I . . . edited my résumé. Took out the parts that might make it less appealing. I needed the CIA to believe that Icefire was sound. Very . . . Madison Avenue of me, yes?"

The bald major appeared on the feed beside General Abbott. "Everyone's got an angle," he told the general, and the disgust in his tone was apparent even to Bailey. "Everyone's got a secret."

General Abbott cut him off without even the courtesy of looking at him. "That's enough, Major." Staring into the teleconference camera, he said, "What is the nature of this defense you came up with?"

Cerenkov told him—the fracture zones and transverse faults, the need to match the energy of the wave, not the height, while still remaining precisely out-of-phase. And he described the twelve key underwater target sites and the nuclear explosions that would be required.

Bailey was overwhelmed by the complexity of what Cerenkov was suggesting, but she saw the general taking careful notes. When the Russian had finished, General Abbott's only question was "And you have the coordinates of each of these target sites?"

"Based on your own U.S. Geographical Survey's GLORIA side-scans from sixty-eight to seventy-one," Cerenkov said. "We obtained all your data from . . . friends within the Royal Australian Navy."

"What form are the coordinates in?"

Bailey heard Webber break back into the circuit. "General Abbott, the professor has printed out his complete Icefire file. I have an appendix with all the target-site coordinates listed."

"Captain Webber, in your opinion, is . . . this scheme at all practical?"

Bailey heard the hesitation in the captain. But she also heard the hope. "Sir, a lot will depend on the disposition of our forces. But our nuclear Tomahawks each have a two-megaton W-80 warhead and a thirteen-hundred-mile range. We can hit at least some of the targets, sir. And the way I see it, we have to at least try."

Bailey watched as the general drummed the table with his pen. "What does your . . . what does Dr. Rey say about the Navy detonating nuclear warheads at the bottom of the Pacific? As I recall, Earthguard was one of the more vocal groups to lobby President Bush to order our warships to submit to nuclear disarmament."

"We talked, sir, and I believe she understands that sometimes . . . sometimes sacrifices have to be made for the greater good."

Bailey saw General Abbott nod his head at that, though there was something sad about the gesture. "Yes, Captain. I do believe that's true." The general stood up from the conference table. Then he turned and walked toward his lieutenant's workstation, the automated camera tracking him. "Captain Webber, I have a change of orders for you. I want you to return to Wheeler, with Dr. Rey and Professor Cerenkov, and locate a secure fax machine. Then I want you to fax the target coordinates directly to me. Lieutenant Yoshii, do you have that?" The lieutenant read out a phone number. Bailey noted that it had a New York area code. That wasn't surprising. Most secure lines into the Pentagon could not be identified by area code or exchange.

"I then want you all to remain at Wheeler for further contact. If I'm going to deploy nukes, I'm going to have to make one helluva case to the President to get his authorization to use them, and I'm going to want Cerenkov, especially, to be standing by. Are there any questions?"

There were none.

"Very good, people. I commend your initiative, if not your methods. Contact me as soon as you're back at Wheeler and ready to fax. Until then." The general gestured and the feed ended.

Bailey spoke quickly before Webber could sign off. "Captain, Major Bailey here. I just wanted to say, good job."

"You gave me all the pieces of the puzzle, Major. It was pretty easy to put them together after that."

"We're going to beat this thing yet, Captain. I'll be waiting to hear from you. SPACECOM standing by."

Webber's channel clicked off and Bailey treated herself to a luxurious stretch, leaning back and accidentally catching Huber in the stomach. "Sorry, Commander," Bailey said instantly. She was startled by the contact because she had forgotten he was there. And she was even more startled by how firm his stomach was. There wasn't an ounce of fat on that boy. But she had seen him put away the sloppy joe and the fries and the chocolate milk *and* the two double-fudge cupcakes. *He* must *be a mutant,* she thought, envious.

"Don't worry. It'll be our secret." Bailey understood Huber meant that as a joke, but there was that undercurrent again. For a brief, unprofessional moment, she wished she had been paying closer attention when her fingertips had brushed against him.

But Commander Huber had moved on, even if her thoughts hadn't. He was staring at the blank screens of her station, apparently ignoring the displays that showed the latest satellite update of the wave's progress. The northernmost curve of it was just reaching the equator. Twenty-foot breakers had begun to hammer at the shores of Chile, and Australia was cleaning up the damage to its east coast, where a section of the wave had propagated south of New Zealand and into the Tasman Sea. Casualties so far were estimated at 130,000, though the total count was not yet in for the number lost in the smaller South Pacific islands. Before the wave had entered its third day, reporters were already stating its death toll would eclipse the more than 300,000 deaths attributed to the horrific tidal wave that had hit Pakistan in November of 1970. There was a chance it might even surpass the death toll of the greatest natural disaster of all time: more than 830,000 killed in the earthquake that struck Shensi Province in China, January, 1556.

"Are you all right?" Bailey asked Huber. Huber had been pulling the same hours she had since that first news from Antarctica. His exhaustion was beginning to show.

"Well, *you're* standing by for Webber's next contact. . . ."

"Yes . . ." Bailey said, wondering what the commander was leading up to.

"Why isn't Abbott?"

Bailey looked again at her set of screens. Huber was right. The

SVTS link to the NMCC was no longer on standby as it had been for more than twenty-four hours. It was shut down.

Then Bailey understood why. "He's contacting the President."

"The President's either in Berlin, or on board Air Force One by now. So doesn't Abbott need to access the DSCS to get him?"

"That's right," Bailey said. Once again, Huber was correct. There was no sign on any of her status displays that the DSCS was being used to establish a link with the President.

"So what's Abbott doing?"

She took a wild guess. "Preparing a report? Some kind of briefing?"

Huber leaned past her to bring the other NMCC channels online.

On one screen, they watched an overhead view of two soldiers leaning against a Jeep-like vehicle, sharing a cigarette. The image rippled, then closed in on the hood of the vehicle and the soldiers' heads. There were Chinese characters, a Red Star, and the vehicle-designation number on the hood. For a few seconds, the image swam as if seen through the heat of a desert mirage. But then the speckle-interferometry software went to work. The soldiers froze as the image locked, and then began to increase in resolution as more and more data points were added to it.

In the end, it was as if Bailey were looking down on the two soldiers from a stepladder. The vehicle number was easily read, the D's clearly distinguished from the O's. Then Bailey saw a selection box appear on the shoulder of one of the soldiers.

"What did I tell you?" Huber said.

The selection box expanded, enlarging the image of the soldier's unit patch within it. Then a cursor tugged on the corners of the selection box to change its perspective so that the unit patch angled up and to the side, as if Bailey were looking at it head-on. More data points fluttered across it, and suddenly the image of the unit patch was perfectly clear. She could even see the thread stitches that held it to the soldier's shirt.

"So here's my question," Huber said as Bailey marveled at the display of technology that had just been presented to her. "In fifteen hours the West Coast is going to get smacked into next week, and just when Abbott should be talking to the President to save us, he's more interested in learning the order of battle for troops outside of Beijing."

"That's not a question," Bailey said.

"Unless you're an academic, the only reason you need to know the enemy's order of battle is if you're going to engage the troops you're studying. And right now, it seems to me that our general is more interested in getting ready to kick some Chinese butt than he is in defending our country."

Bailey's stomach seemed to drop out of her, as if she had just gone over the top of a bottomless roller coaster. *Unless,* she thought, *he thinks that by going after the Chinese, he is defending our country.*

"I don't want to believe it, Major, but that wave might not be what we should be worrying about anymore."

Bailey didn't want to agree, but it seemed Commander Huber was right for a third time.

Perhaps they should be worrying about General Abbott.

FOUR

EASY FIVE FIVE/OAHU

"I never said that," Cory said.

Webber had angled himself against the bulkhead in the airliner-style seat at the back of the personnel-transport Huey, and had closed his eyes. But Cory wasn't letting him off that easily.

"Said what?" Webber asked. He sounded maddeningly half-asleep.

"That sacrifices have to be made for the greater good. That was a terrible thing to say."

"You have to believe it though. Look who you work for."

"That's not the point, Mitchell. I never said it. And I certainly never said it in the context of turning the Pacific into a radio-active cauldron."

"Cory, I needed to convince Abbott that you supported Cerenkov's plan."

Cory slapped the back of her hand against Webber's arm, meaning it to be read as a gesture of annoyance. At least it made him open his eyes. "Why the hell would he care what I think about anything?"

Webber sat up and adjusted the small headset he wore, as did Cory, so they could be heard over the helo's engines and rotor rush as it sped back to Wheeler AFB. "Because the military mind you hate so much operates on consensus." He started to settle back in his seat.

354

Cory had no intention of letting him sleep. "I've talked with Abbott. He only operates according to his own ego."

"Cory, the man's a two-star general. He's on the Joint Staff. He's earned the right."

Cory folded her arms across her chest, enjoying the irritated flush that was coming to Webber's cheeks. He had always seemed more interesting when he was provoked into passion. She'd realized, almost as soon as they had first met, that if she could work him up into a state where he let his emotions guide him, he would become more open to communication. Otherwise, he'd slip back into that infuriating reserve with its air of smug superiority. And she knew exactly where that state of mind, that ignorance of the heart, would lead. To a future in which she and Webber could never . . . She brought herself back to the present, and reality.

"If Abbott had been doing his job properly, we'd be hours ahead of the wave, instead of where we are now." Cory felt another wave of inexpressible loss hit her. "Maybe McMurdo wouldn't have had to happen. None of it."

Webber surprised her by taking her hand. "I am sorry," he said. "For Johnny, for my team, for everyone who died at McMurdo . . . all those people in New Zealand . . . but what you have to understand is that I'm not going to be able to keep everyone safe, and neither are you. No one can."

Cory pulled her hand away from his. "I *tried* to save Johnny. Why didn't you?"

"I *did*. You know I did. And ask yourself what would've happened if Johnny *hadn't* sacrificed himself."

"What Johnny did wasn't a sacrifice! You made him commit *suicide!*"

"Cory, no. I couldn't hold you up. Johnny sacrificed himself so you wouldn't go into that crevasse with him. Johnny died and you lived and he knew it would happen that way. He wanted you to help me tell the world."

"You can't know that."

"I *do*. Cory, I was going to let go." His eyes told her the truth. "I would have lost both of you."

Webber settled back with a sigh. "Don't kid yourself, you and I were *supposed* to die back there. Everyone was. The satellites were supposed to go blind. Whoever bought Nick Young counted on it being Thanksgiving, on no one noticing when a few check times

355

were missed. What do you think would have happened to New Zealand if we *hadn't* been able to get out to make contact with SPACECOM? How far along would the evacuation plans be now? And do you honestly think Abbott would have done his about-face and told the world that the wave wasn't getting weaker? Johnny saved more than your life by his sacrifice. He saved millions."

The helo swung about to begin its descent to the helipad at Wheeler.

Cory hugged her arms close to her chest as she stared out the side window. She felt colder than she had in all her time in Antarctica. Webber had just confirmed what she had known from the moment they had escaped across the ice. She would never understand him, never know what had caused him to become who he was. But at least she knew what he was.

Through the window, Cory saw the ground rush up to them. From the presence of the humvees and the pilot-transport van, it appeared that Colonel Lightfoot had arranged another welcoming committee.

"Murderer," she said.

"You should think about what I said, Cory. Sometimes . . . sometimes sacrifices have to be made. For the greater good."

"And just what gave *you* the right to make that decision, Mitchell?" This might be the last moment they would be alone together, and it was suddenly important to her that Webber understand that he had become just like his Pentagon, accepting of tragedies that benefited some vague, greater good for the group.

As the helo settled, Webber actually answered her, and it was if she were hearing his confession. "Because this wasn't the first time." He held his hands out before him and stared at them as if they belonged to someone else. "The last time . . . I *didn't* let go. I wasn't ready to be a soldier, and my failure cost lives. Johnny was a soldier. His death saved lives."

Cory studied him, puzzled. Was this what she had sensed in Webber when they had had their argument in Christchurch, when Webber had promised to protect her from Abbott? Something— some terrible, classified military operation that somehow still drove him to do what the military ordered him to do, no matter what it cost others?

Then the helo's rotor slowed and the pilot and copilot slipped out of their seats and through their own doors as the ground crew slid open the port passenger door. Nothing left to say to one another, Cory and Webber clicked open their two seat belts and the straps slithered into their reels.

Webber stepped stiffly down from the helo. In one hand he clutched the thick envelope Cerenkov had given them, the Icefire report. The Russian scientist had remained at the university, collecting the equipment he said he'd need to measure the wave when it came. When Cory had last seen him, he was telephoning his family, to tell them he'd be home a bit late.

Cory stepped down from the helicopter behind Webber. She felt as if she and Webber had lived several lifetimes in the last thirty hours. The extreme highs and lows of their traumatic reunion had done what five years of separation from each other had not been able to achieve. *It's finally over,* she thought. *We'll never see each other again.*

That was when the MPs that met them drew their guns.

Colonel Lightfoot stepped forward and took the envelope away from Webber. Only the sweat stains ringing the underarms of the base commander's shirt revealed his discomfort. Cory blinked in surprise as he turned to address her formally. "Corazon Maria Rey, you are hereby placed in protective custody on this base until you can be turned over to the FBI for arrest."

Then, before Cory could even proclaim her innocence of any wrongdoing, Lightfoot had signaled to the MPs who seized Webber's arms from behind and forced a plastic tie around his wrists, tightening it with a sharp tug.

Over Webber's protestations, Lightfoot recited the rest of his charges. "And you, Captain Webber, are hereby placed under military arrest."

"For what?" Webber demanded, while Cory watched, speechless.

"The charge," the colonel said, "is treason."

WHEELER AFB

Had Mitch Webber been in another place, and this another time, the MPs would have been dead by now and Lightfoot would have been facedown on the tarmac, answering questions.

But since this was the United States, and friendly territory, Mitch

Webber merely stood in silent resistance as he felt the bite of the thin band of the plastic restraint around his wrists.

When the senseless charge against him had been stated, he had only one question. "On what possible basis, sir?"

Colonel Lightfoot looked down at the envelope he held in his hand, a package with three years' worth of calculations that could protect the North Pacific against the wave. "General Abbott's been conducting a full investigation of you. Apparently there's reason to believe you've been cooperating with the people responsible for what's happened. A deliberate attack against the United States, and millions of innocent people in—"

"*Are you* all *crazy?*" Cory exclaimed, and made a move as if to rush at the colonel. Before Webber could use the distraction to begin to move forward, the two MPs behind him yanked back on his restraint even as a third MP, a woman, grabbed Cory and held her in place.

The carefully constructed puzzle Webber had assembled in his mind flew apart, all the pieces spinning. Only in the center did one key element remain motionless, the one to which all the others must somehow connect. General Charles Quincy Abbott.

Though he was simply standing beneath the intense Hawaiian sun, in no physical danger, Webber's body responded as if a firefight had begun, with bullets spraying around him, explosions jarring his vision and assaulting his ears. And as always happened in battle conditions, Webber felt the calm of combat settle over him. Now everything was at a distance. All elements could be studied, controlled, and manipulated. It was simply a matter of knowing the terrain and choosing his first target.

"Did General Abbott tell you what was in that envelope?" Webber asked the base commander.

Colonel Lightfoot held the envelope to his side. "I'm under orders not to open it. It is to be held as evidence against you."

"Did the general tell you what Cerenkov's involvement in this is?"

"I explained that Anatoly was a friend, and a trusted civilian employee here. The general merely wishes to have him brought in for questioning."

"Colonel Lightfoot, Cerenkov devised the scenario that created the wave."

Lightfoot whipped off his sunglasses. He was livid with anger. "I have never met a man who is more loyal to the United States!"

"He never intended it to be implemented. It was his job when he worked for the Soviets."

The base commander motioned tightlipped to the three MPs. "Take them to detention." A fourth MP opened the back doors on the pilot-transport vehicle.

As he and Cory were strong-armed toward the open doors, Webber shouted back at Colonel Lightfoot. "Colonel—that's Cerenkov's work in there! It shows how the wave can be stopped! If Abbott won't let you read that material, then he *wants* the wave to hit. You have—"

The van doors slammed shut. He and Cory were now locked in the back of the transport, in the company of two hard-eyed MPs, a wiry sergeant with his billy club already loose in his hand, and the female master sergeant who had been given responsibility over Cory.

The MPs pushed Webber and Cory onto facing bench seats on opposite sides of the compartment. The sergeant with the club sat at the back by the doors on Webber's side. The master sergeant sat by the front of the compartment on Cory's side. Webber assessed the arrangement. Someone had told them that he was a SEAL. Any attempt he made to attack one MP would be an invitation to get cracked over the head by the other.

"How can you be a party to this incredible fiasco?" Cory had apparently decided to take on the female MP. "You're nothing better than a puppet of a fascist regime, right here in the democratic U.S. of A. And that goddamn wave's going to tear apart the West Coast, *and* China, *and* Japan, *and* who knows how many other countries, and your idiot leaders aren't even interested in stopping it!"

The master sergeant replied by the book. "Please keep your voice down, ma'am. You'll be able to explain everything you're upset about to your lawyer."

"Lawyer, my—the Pentagon's going to take us out into a field, shoot us in the back of the head, and set fire to us."

The master sergeant raised her eyebrows at what she considered evidence of Cory's unbalanced mental state. "Ma'am, this is the United States. That kind of stuff doesn't happen here."

"Or else someone knows how to do it so well, no one ever finds out about it." Cory glared back at the sergeant with the billy club.

"What about you? When your kids ask, What did you do to stop the wave, Daddy, what're you going to tell them? Well, kids, I killed the only two people who had a clue how to stop it?"

Very calmly, the sergeant said, "Keep your voice down or we will be forced to gag you."

"Why? Are you afraid someone who *isn't* stupid will hear me? I wouldn't want to be you when you see all those bodies on CNN and—"

At the same instant the sergeant slammed his club against the wall, making an explosive sound as he yelled, *"Shut the fuck up you bitch or—!"*

The sergeant took a threatening step forward. Webber stood up slowly. The sergeant raised his club. "You better sit right back down, motherfucker!"

Webber allowed his shoulders to slump forward, the next ten seconds of his life already planned and mentally rehearsed. Now that Cory had set them up for him, the MPs didn't have a chance. "Give me a break, man. I had a real bad carrier landing. I think I broke my tailbone. Just let me stand, okay?"

Webber's unthreatening plea helped the sergeant regain control of his temper. Now he could do something positive for the prisoners, to make up for his earlier loss of control.

"Yeah, yeah," the sergeant said. "Just don't move." He shot a glance at Cory. "Is she always like this?"

"Usually," Webber said, getting into the rhythm of the moving transport, "she's worse."

The sergeant laughed.

Cory's reply brought his attention back to her with a snap. "Stupid *and* bigoted."

Webber whirled, with his left leg raised so that his flight boot struck the sergeant's jaw at the same instant the sergeant noticed the movement.

At once the master sergeant launched herself forward, her billy club now out and already descending in an arc for his unprotected head.

Just then Cory twisted and fell heavily off her bench seat, legs out to trip the master sergeant at the ankles.

The female MP sailed forward, momentum driving her down to the floor of the van, a mere three feet from Webber. The impact claimed her breath in an explosive grunt, and then Webber's boot kicked her neck, directly targeting her trachea.

Hands at her throat, the master sergeant rolled onto her back as she fought to pull air into her lungs. But Webber was not finished with her. He dropped to the floor beside her, his back to her body, and then he leaned back, tight against her face. His bound hands sought her throat, his fingers expertly located her carotid arteries, and he applied the necessary pressure. Three seconds later, the MP stopped struggling.

As Webber rolled off her body, he saw Cory's expression. "She's dead," she said in horror.

"Not yet. Just missing a little blood in her brain. She'll be conscious in two minutes." Then he told Cory where to find the restraint cutters—a folded pair of blunt pliers—in the small woven leather pouch on the MP's belt. As soon as she'd cut his restraints, he went to work, pulling four more sets of restraints from the unconscious sergeant's belt to bind the MP's arms and legs. Then, for good measure, he ripped the sergeant's shirt into strips to make gags.

The master sergeant was just waking up as Webber used two more plastic restraint loops to tie both MPs to the support legs of the bench seats. Then he stood with another strip of shirt fabric in his hand. It had been less than two minutes since he'd stood up to confront the guard. Cory stared at him in unabashed awe.

"Nice distraction moves," Webber said.

The transport stopped.

"Is that what I was doing?" Cory asked.

Webber nodded. "Good timing, too." Then he held a finger to his lips as he heard the back door handles being turned.

The van's driver had less than one second to react before Webber grabbed him by the shirt collar and hauled him up into the passenger compartment. The driver fought hard, but Webber's hands, now crossed at the wrists, gained purchase on the man's collar. Then Webber simply twisted his wrists ninety degrees, to form a V-shaped clamp across the front of the driver's throat. The man was down in two seconds as his brain ceased functioning from lack of oxygenated blood.

Webber dragged the driver to the back of the compartment and began to swiftly gag and bind him.

"How do you do that?" Cory asked.

"I'll be happy to show you," Webber said as he finished securing the driver. "Later, okay?"

Then he moved to the partially opened doors at the back to check on their immediate situation. They had stopped in front of an administration building. *Good. No other MPs.* The colonel's security had severely overestimated their own abilities.

But Webber knew that he and Cory only had a few minutes before the base commander realized his prisoners hadn't been taken to detention.

"Well, Sundance, what's the plan now? Do we go out and surround them?" Webber didn't blame Cory for her negative assessment. There were at least twelve hundred personnel on the base, and in less than five minutes the sirens would sound and everyone would be hunting for the two escaped prisoners.

"Look," Webber said, "we can't let them get us before we can warn Cerenkov and have him get that targeting information to someone who can use it."

"Oh, yeah? Like who?"

"CINCPAC." He saw the question in her eyes. "Commander-in-Chief, Pacific. That's Admiral Browne at Pearl Harbor Naval Base."

"Pardon me, sir, I'm just a civilian, but I know my geography. Pearl Harbor opens to the south. In ten hours, there won't be a Pearl Harbor."

Webber was stunned that he'd slipped up on terrain, but CINC-PAC was still the only option available in Hawaii. "Rear Admiral Sweetman. Commander, SUBGRU 5. The sub base at Ballast Point, San Diego. He knows me. He'll listen."

"Be serious, Mitchell. How will we get to him? There's no way we'll get out of this base."

"Not on foot." Webber studied Cory for her reaction to his next question. "Are you up for another ride?"

Cory shrugged. "After the Blackbird, I can survive anything."

Webber pulled Cory out of the van and started to run.

"Don't be too sure," he said.

FIVE

WHEELER AFB/RECORDS STORAGE/HANGAR FIVE

There was a mirror in the pilot's shower room, but Cory was reluctant to use it. Just looking down at what she was wearing told her she wasn't going to like what she saw. She didn't like trusting everything to gravity.

"Ready?" Webber asked.

Cory turned to face him. So much for modesty. "So when did *Playboy* start designing uniforms for the Air Force?"

She was enclosed in what Webber had told her was a PPG—a Class Four Permeable Pressure Garment—but she might as well have been wearing dark blue Saran Wrap. The fabric, or plastic wrap, or whatever startlingly clingy material the suit was made from, had about the thickness of nylon hosiery, though it was at least more opaque. And it was a full-body bodystocking. The gloves were connected seamlessly to the arms, as were the foot coverings. In fact, Cory had not been able to find a seam anywhere. The only disruptions of the fabric's slick finish were a series of raised disks, each an inch in diameter, that ran up either side of her torso, from her hipbones to her shoulders. She had pulled on the PPG first by following Webber's instructions to strip off everything else, including the gray Air Force skivvies, then simply stepped through the stretchy neck opening and wiggled her way into it. A pair of light, pull-on outer boots were the only separate part of the final outfit, again surprisingly thin, though they had a reinforced, tougher heel and sole. The end result was that Cory felt she was standing in front of Webber in a pair of slippers and a coat of paint. A very thin coat of paint. The only thing that mitigated the embarrassment of the experience was that Webber was wearing the same type of outfit. Cory had to admit he didn't look as if he'd gained an ounce or lost any of his major attractions in the past five years.

"This is just *part* of the protective gear," Webber said, politely keeping his eyes above her neck.

"Good." From Cory's point of view, the gear didn't offer either of them nearly enough protection. She had a hard time imagining that ordinary, macho fighter pilots would be caught dead in outfits like these. But then, so far, every part of her experience with the world of high-tech military aviation had been surprising and very different from what she'd imagined it to be, as an outsider. *Not to mention smelly*, she thought. Something else she'd been unprepared for. "So where's the rest of our 'gear'?"

"In the plane." Webber pointed to the door at the end of the changing room. "You ready?"

"I'd feel a whole lot more comfortable if I could put the jumpsuit on over this."

"Sorry, no time," Webber said. "Once we're out that door, we're going to have to move fast." He gave her an encouraging look. "For what it's worth, these things haven't been made for women yet, and . . . you look great."

"A compliment," Cory said as she followed him toward the far door. "It *must* be the end of the world."

By the door was a series of open shelves, each containing a flight helmet, or what Cory thought was a flight helmet. The helmets all had a solid ring at the base and an opening where the visor would go in a space helmet, except there were no visors. She also noticed that the back part of each helmet included a smooth, upward projection that looked almost like the tip of a soft ice-cream cone that had started to melt.

Webber handed her one of the helmets. The name stenciled across the visor opening was PIKE. Webber took one marked HARRIMAN. He slipped it on, then, from inside the helmet, pulled down a fringe of dark blue fabric and pressed it to the neck of his PPG. Cory frowned as she saw it adhere without wrinkling or bunching.

"Is that magnetic?" she asked as she pushed back her by now flat and stringy hair and pulled on her own helmet.

"It's like Velcro," Webber said as he helped her connect the fabric from her helmet to her PPG. "But microscopic. The connection strength is a hundred times more powerful."

"Then how the hell do we take them off?"

But Webber didn't answer her. He was already holding the door open. "Okay, now, just walk right up to it as if you own it," he told her. Then he strode away from her, into an enormous, dimly lit hangar. It was just then that the base's sirens sounded.

Acutely aware of what must be happening all around them, Cory concentrated on keeping her own pace controlled and deliberate, to match Webber's. Someone at the administration building must have finally found the MPs bound and gagged in the back of the transport vehicle. It had been fifteen minutes since Cory had run flatout after Webber until they had reached the unguarded, nondescript building whose sign had read RECORDS STORAGE. She knew the rescued guards would realize that too little time had elapsed for their prisoners to have run off the base, so the base most likely had been sealed. Now the entire base population would be looking for them.

Yet Webber was walking right up to the nearest airman, who was holding an ominous rifle in his hands—not just carrying it slung on his back—as if he did this sort of thing every day.

What do I know? Cory thought. *Maybe he does. After all, stealing aircraft is his job.*

"Captain Harriman?" The airman crisply moved his rifle so it rested on his shoulder, and he gave Webber a salute that Webber promptly returned. The airman's salute wavered as his gaze settled on Cory and then moved down her body.

Whatever Webber did to the armed guard, it was so fast even Cory didn't register it. One moment the airman was goggling at her, the next Webber's open hand was coming away from the airman's face and the young guard's knees were buckling.

Webber caught the rifle just as another guard ran into view and immediately aimed his own weapon at Webber.

What happened next made Cory feel she had stepped through the looking glass.

Webber pulled Cory behind him and then took careful aim with his captured rifle, not at the second airman, but at the plane.

The plane.

Cory had walked fifty feet through the hangar and this was the first time she had noticed that there was something sitting in the middle of it. Something which she now knew she must assume was a plane, though from its shape and appearance, she couldn't be exactly certain what it was.

Webber said to the airman, "It's not going to be much good to anyone with a hole in it, kid."

But the airman didn't take his rifle sights from Webber. He was a soldier following orders and Cory could tell that nothing was going to stop him from doing his duty. "You can blow it up for all I care. But you are not taking that craft from this hangar."

Webber lowered his rifle slowly. "Okay, you win." By now, Cory knew that was far too reasonable a move for Webber. There must be some way she could help him to distract . . .

"You, too," the airman said to Cory. She moved out from behind Webber, slowly, letting the airman get a good look.

A half second's distraction was all Webber needed.

Webber swung up the rifle and shot him dead center in the chest. A full burst.

The airman's shirt disintegrated as he flew back several feet, even as Cory cried out at Webber to stop.

Webber ran for the airman's body. Cory ran after him, enraged, disgusted.

As soon as she caught up with Webber, Cory noticed the airman's chest was encased in a black vest. Webber had already torn off the airman's belt and was using it to rapidly tie up the body.

"Body armor," she said.

"It was obvious. No matter what you think, I won't kill an American soldier." Webber looked up at her. "Unless I have to."

Then he had her pull the other airman across the hangar to the wall while he dragged the one he had shot. As they both ran back to the plane, Cory got her first chance to see it in detail. At least, as much detail as she could make out, which was astoundingly little.

Its shape was like that of no other form of transport she'd ever seen. From the stern of the craft, she could see that it resembled a wide flattened ring, though it would have been a ring shaped by the sculptor Henry Moore. Extending forward from the stern, the body ended in an elevated nose that reminded Cory of the unbroken curl of a wave.

As they moved closer, Cory could see, in fact, that the craft's body was like that of a doughnut resting on its side, with its top surface pulled out like taffy to form a forward fuselage. The doughnut's toroid was flattened, with the leading edges of it faceted like a cut jewel. To Cory, it seemed as if she were looking into the maw of a jet engine twenty feet across and ten feet tall, except that there was nothing inside it.

"Is this the plane?" she asked.

"Some people call it the Aurora, or the Skybolt, but the code name's NEVADA RAIN." Webber then added quickly, "But real code names never mean anything, of course. They're just two words a DOD computer pulls up at random. It's an HST—a hypersonic transport plane."

"It has no wings."

"Neither does a rocket."

Like a lamb to the slaughter, she followed him to the back of the craft, where a steep aluminum stairway ascended to a small hatch. The hatch was located where the fuselage emerged from the flattened ring. Cory squinted at the plane, puzzled by how distinct the hatch opening seemed, and by how blurry every other part of the plane was, in contrast.

"I'm guessing there's a reason it almost looks like it's . . . invisible."

"Try three billion dollars' worth of reasons," Webber said. He started up the ladder. With a sigh, Cory followed.

The hatch was only about four feet tall and Webber had to duck down to crawl in the opening. Cory took a moment to run her gloved hand over the plane's exterior surface. The skin seemed to be made from a series of hexagonal tiles of an indeterminate, muddy gray color. It felt glassy smooth, but looked rough and unfinished, like badly sanded plywood.

"What's this thing made of?"

Webber motioned her inside. "It's a composite plastic, like the leading edges of the Blackbird, but this one's etched by a particle beam. The idea is to create microdiffraction gratings about the same thickness as wavelengths of sunlight."

"Why?" Cory asked as she crawled in to join him.

Just under six feet in height, Webber was almost able to stand up in what Cory decided must be the plane's cramped cockpit. "It's called optical stealth technology. Light hits the plane's skin and is absorbed in places, refracted in others, and normally reflected from still others—but this is all at the microscopic level. That's what creates the illusion of a rough surface and optical-interference pat-terns. The very expensive end result is that the farther away an observer is from the aircraft, the more the light from it diverges randomly. That makes the shape impossible to make out, let alone focus on. Cameras with autofocus, they can't even get a shot of this thing. And even if you try tracking it by eye, under most lighting conditions, it's as if you're looking at it through fog."

As strange as the plane was, the cockpit was reassuringly familiar to Cory. Two seats framed by metal tubing were arranged side by side. To the front, above, and to either side of the seats were dozens, probably hundreds of dials and readout displays. And there Cory noticed the familiarity ended. There were far too *many* dials and instruments. "Um, where's the windshield?" she asked.

"Doesn't have one." Webber sat down in the pilot's seat and Cory saw the material bulge up and around him, as if it were a jelly-filled sack. Then he folded a solid section of the seat's base up to his chest. Once the front of the seat had locked in position, press-ing tightly against him, Webber lifted a curved mirrored visor from a pocket on the side of his seat, snapped it into place, then pointed to the chair beside him. "That's yours. And remember—"

"Don't touch anything," Cory completed for him.

"Except for the VAD—the Virtual Attitude Display." He tapped the visor now attached to his helmet.

The experience of sitting in the seat was odd, and somewhat rude. Folding the solid section up—it was also lined with jelly bags—gave Cory the impression that she was being intimate with an alien whale.

Another disturbing element of the cockpit was that Webber didn't have a flight stick. Instead, there were two half-spheres angled out from his seat arms, and inside each Cory could see a joystick-type control. Webber had his left hand on one, and with his right hand was checking off a flight checklist on the closest computer-display screen. Cory had the same half-spheres on the arm supports of her seat, but was careful to keep her hands clear of them.

Then Webber slipped his right hand into the second half-sphere and settled back in his seat. "You lock your helmet by pushing back."

Cory leaned back and felt her helmet's protrusion lock into place. The seat suddenly seemed to grip her with even more strength—a not uncomfortable pressure applied evenly all around her.

"Okay, here we go. Just like the simulators."

"Simulators? I thought you'd flown everything?"

"Only six people have flown this bird. You and I are seven and eight."

"Lucky lucky us."

"Use your VAD when you want to look around," Webber said.

Then the cockpit seemed to thrum, not with the thrust of a jet engine but with the vibration of an electrical circuit. Cory was suddenly aware that the Nevada Rain was hovering in place.

As she felt the plane slowly pivot, Cory fumbled with the VAD visor at the side of her seat, slipping it from its pocket, then snapping it into place on her helmet. The visor covered about half her field of vision, allowing her to look down, as if through bifocals, to see the controls in front of her. *As if the controls made any sense.*

For a few disorienting seconds, all she saw in the visor itself was a wide, green-bordered black box, with a number of smaller boxes arranged beneath it, each with a three-letter acronym inside. There was no strain at looking at something she knew was only a few inches from her eyes. And from the three-dimensional appearance of the small labeled boxes, she decided that each of her eyes must be receiving a slightly different image, allowing her to focus as if she were looking at something ten feet away. It was a curiously comfortable system, with only one problem.

"What exactly am I supposed to see with this?"

"Down to the left," Webber answered—and now she could hear his voice in her helmet speakers, just as she had heard him in the Blackbird and the Harrier—"there's a selection box labeled OPT for 'optical.' Look at that and blink twice."

Feeling foolish, Cory followed Webber's instruction, and suddenly she was floating in the center of the hangar by herself. She held her breath, trying not to blink again in case a third blink would cause something irreversible to happen.

Cory released her breath in a rush as she realized that she was still in her seat in the so-called plane. Her VAD visor was displaying a wide-screen virtual reconstruction of the Nevada Rain's immediate environment, as sensed through visible light. The effect was unbelievably true to life, with no sense of scan lines or computer graphic artifacts at all. She moved her head as much as she was able within her immobilized helmet and the image before her changed smoothly, tracking perfectly with her eyes.

"Okay, this is it," Webber said. "I've got their base communications feed, and they know we're in here."

The Nevada Rain started forward.

From her you-are-there POV, Cory watched the hangar door loom closer. Then it split in two before her and began to slide open.

The thrumming in the cockpit increased and she felt the vibration pass through her, intensified by the jelly sacs that kept her in place, connecting her with the very act of floating above the ground. "Oh, my God, Mitchell. This is incredible."

Before her, she saw airmen and MPs running back and forth, scattering before the Nevada Rain. She saw the wind effects of whatever kind of thrusters were holding the plane up and moving it forward. The uniformed base personnel held on to their hats and helmets and turned away to shield their eyes.

Then Cory looked left and right and saw no walls at all. They were clear of the hangar. "What if they scramble their jets?" she asked suddenly, worrying, remembering what Webber had told her about not being able to fly dogfights in the craft he knew how to steal.

"They won't," Webber said. "Nothing can catch us. Look at the box in the center marked REV and blink twice."

Cory did. Suddenly she was looking to the rear. Humvees were driving toward her between other hangars, airmen with rifles standing on the running boards.

"Time to fly," Webber said. "*Really* fly."

And then the airmen and their rifles, the humvees, Wheeler Air Force Base and the jungles surrounding it, and all the roads leading toward it, fell away from Cory as she gripped her seat and her seat gripped her and the Nevada Rain soared to 50,000 feet in less than thirty seconds, already hitting Mach 2 by the end of its ascent.

Cory couldn't even draw breath because of the pressure on her chest. She was convinced that only the seat applying equalizing pressure to her sides was keeping her from blacking out. Amazingly, she was awake, alert, and maybe because, she realized, she could sweat through her exotically thin PPG, she felt cool and comfortable for the first time in days.

"Mach two point five," Webber reported. "Ramjet switchover."

Cory gave a whoop as the Nevada Rain leapt forward, driving her back into her seat even as her seat worked to support her. Her heart raced, not from fear, but through sheer exhilaration. Only ten minutes ago, she and Webber had been defeated, surrounded on an air base, no chance of escape.

And Mitchell had the answer, Cory thought. *He* always *has the answer.* But then she remembered the crevasse and Johnny. There would never be an answer for that terrible moment. No matter what Webber said. She refused to accept that what had happened had been necessary. Her brother deserved more than that.

A steady, distinctive whine, muffled by her helmet, now filled the cockpit. The Nevada Rain in ramjet mode sounded a lot like what she remembered of the Blackbird in steady flight. She knew now, from experience, that what she heard was the sound from the engine vibration that traveled through the aircraft's frame. The actual sound of the engines was lost behind her, unable to reach the plane's cockpit as it drew away faster than sound. As Cory looked down, the VAD display angled to show her the green gemstone of Oahu shrinking in the distance within the stunning clear blue of the Pacific. She found the selection box marked FWD, looked at it, blinked twice.

The VAD dutifully showed her the forward view again. She pierced clouds rushing by her, as the sun gleamed on distant waters below. She was suspended in flight, aware of nothing man-made around her. There was no resistance from the atmosphere. No buffeting, no fear.

Only movement, only speed, and the thrill of absolute freedom.

It wouldn't last, she knew. The wave was still below them, gaining on them, no matter how quickly they flew before it. But at least for this moment, up here beside Webber, she could almost delude herself into believing there was hope.

"Mach five point five," Webber said. Cory could hear the excitement building in his voice as well. "Switching to HST scramjet."

Scramjet? Cory wondered.

And then a sound unlike any other traveled through her as a series of jarring, rhythmic thuds violently shook the Nevada Rain. The sound was different even from the advancing roar of the wave, deep and low and pulsing so slowly she could count a peak with every heartbeat. As it intensified, Cory no longer heard the sound— she *was* the sound.

And as the sound expanded and rushed ahead through the thinning air around her, that sound lifted her and carried her with it, until only she and Mitchell Webber and their delusion of hope rushed forward, together.

SIX

"He stole what?"

Major Bailey could barely believe it herself. For the past ten minutes, she had been monitoring an incredible barrage of communications between Wheeler AFB and Groom Lake, Nevada, America's legendary birthplace of cutting-edge aviation technology, also known as Area 51.

"The Nevada Rain," she said. "Webber stole it right out from under their noses."

Commander Huber put down two mugs in the cup indentations on the foldout tray of Bailey's situation panel. Herbal tea was a thing of the past. Bailey had gone back to coffee five hours ago and her bloodstream, she was sure, was an equal mix of caffeine and adrenaline.

"I can't even get away with parking in the wrong lot topside," Huber said. "How could Webber even get close to its hangar?"

Bailey wasn't sure, but it had to have something to do with all the missing gaps in Webber's service record. *A test pilot who became a SEAL?* "I bet the government trained him to do exactly that," she said. The Nevada Rain was operating out of Wheeler, so it was prepped and ready to go on scramble. If the base commander had put the standard level of security on it, nobody could have driven

372

within fifty miles of the place and half the people on Oahu would have known something was up. But once Webber got on the base, their internal security was probably nonexistent. They didn't have a chance.

Huber pulled up the chair he had carried in from a conference room. He had been working at Bailey's side since they had begun to track General Abbott's sudden interest in Chinese troop movements. Bailey hadn't wanted anyone on the floor below to see what was being displayed on Huber's workstation.

"Any idea where he's taking it?" he asked.

Bailey sipped her coffee, double double, the way she liked it when she was in overdrive, especially the brake fluid that came out of the coffee machines in SPACECOM. "Let's see, Commander. The plane has the radar cross section of this coffee cup. It circulates its cryogenic fuel beneath its skin so it can turn atmospheric friction into kinetic energy and erase its infrared signature at the same time. Above a hundred thousand feet, it doesn't leave a sonic boom. And from what I hear, if you were looking straight at it, you'd be seeing what was on the other side."

"Optical stealth?" Huber said. "Holy shit."

"Offhand, I'd say Webber could take that sucker anyplace he wanted and we'd never know it." Bailey was suddenly overcome with a sense of loss. She had liked Captain Webber. She still didn't understand how, after seeing the devastation firsthand, the captain could have remained a double agent for whatever terrorist group had collapsed the Ice Shelf. But in this world, she supposed nothing was certain. Even though she wasn't usually that wrong about judging character. "I thought Captain Webber was one of the good guys. When he started talking about stopping the wave with all those Tomahawks, I really believed him."

"Me, too," Huber said.

Bailey clinked her coffee mug against his. Whatever else this past day and a half had brought to the world, she was thankful for the pleasurable bond she had developed with Huber. She caught herself staring at him thoughtfully, and so did he.

"Something the matter?" he asked.

"Absolutely nothing." *I was just wondering if you were going to be making the Air Force your career for life,* Bailey thought. She believed in the Air Force regulations covering fraternization, so if Dominic Huber were to end up in the civilian sector, it would make life

much easier, and much more interesting for her. But all she added
was "You know, I think I'm ready to start dozing off."

Huber checked the time on the panel. "We need an energy fix.
They've got a special turkey plate coming up on the menu this
shift. Gravy. Sausage stuffing on the side."

Bailey couldn't take it anymore. "Huber, where do you put it all?
You're scrawny as a fence post." And then she thought, *What did I
just say?* She had to cover, fast. "But I like scrawny. I mean lean. I
mean . . . it's not like there's anything wrong with that, but . . ."
She felt the hole getting deeper with every inane thing she added to
the original offense. "Commander, I have no idea what I'm saying. I
apologize."

Huber sipped his coffee for a few moments; then he put his mug
down and smiled, not at her, but at his coffee mug. "It's funny
how things balance out. Being scrawny—" The way he said the
word Bailey knew he had taken no offense from it. "—myself, it
kind of makes me appreciate the more . . . substantial things in life."

A column of heat rose instantly within Bailey. She wanted to
wave a hand at her whole body to cool herself off. Hell, she wanted
to put Huber in her briefcase and take him home for Thanksgiving
dinner. But instead, she simply nodded sagely and said, "Hmm.
Interesting." And then, because she was a professional, and an officer, she saved herself from further impossible, insanely complicated
thoughts by turning her attention to the distant wall of information.

The wave was now plotted on the main satellite display, nine
hours from Hawaii, within half an hour of crossing the equator.
Originally, the major knew, that was where its intensity was supposed to have been downgraded to the level of a bad squall. But
as the Pentagon had finally announced, the wave was something
different from what they had first thought, and first hoped.

The latest measurements, obtained as realtime ocean-topography
data from the TOPEX/POSEIDON Jason-III satellite, indicated that
the central wave arc heading for Hawaii had so far lost only about
five percent of its energy in the open sea. In the western arc, when
the wave had slammed through the Solomons, triggering more than
fifty-seven volcanic eruptions, it had lost considerably more energy.
The Polynesian islands still awaiting their turn were expected to
further reduce the wave's energy by cutting down the force of the
fragmented eastern arc sections, until they were nothing but violent
breakers when they eventually reached Mexico and Central America.

But the western arc of the wave front was still barreling toward the Caroline Islands at eighty-five percent of the wave's initial strength. The Pentagon's experts were predicting that it was going to reach the Yellow Sea and Japan at just more than seventy-percent strength. The computer projections that took into account the depths of the coastal shelves in the shoreline areas of those regions agreed on a wave 980 feet tall ripping through the Yellow Sea at 200 miles an hour.

In Japan, the experts now predicted even greater heights for the wave arcs that would become concentrated in the narrow, southern-access harbors of Kōbe, Nagoya, and Tokyo, and tear through, at the same time, the Seto-naikai channel north of Shikoku island from the east and west.

The Pentagon's PACIFIC SHIELD team had issued warnings that Tokyo itself was facing the certain prospect of a 2,000-foot wave that would destroy every building within two miles of the shore, and shoot through the city streets to cause extensive damage at up to five miles' distance. Bailey had seen the reports: The train and traffic jams created by Tokyo evacuees were already horrendous, and world markets had announced that they would remain closed on Friday, and for at least the next week, in order to give the world financial community time to assess the mind-boggling, *trillion*-dollar losses expected in Asia alone.

Even American banks were not expected to open tomorrow in order to prevent a run on cash. North America's biggest shopping day before Christmas was predicted to be the worst on record because everyone would be at home watching the wave's progress. Some financial news networks had begun discussing the inevitable world depression that would follow in the wake of the expected catastrophic losses, not only because of property damage, but lost industrial capacity, workforce disruption, and relocation pressures.

On every channel Bailey had had a chance to flip through on her screens, the ramifications of the wave were being discussed, not only on a global scale, but on the local. California insurance companies had labeled the wave an act of God, so no claims would be allowed—an interpretation that would be applied to any freak weather or earthquake damage that followed within ninety days of the wave's impact. In that forward-looking state, lawsuits had already been announced and would be filed tomorrow, enjoining the insurance carriers from enforcing their unpopular decision.

Globally, the amount of particulate matter ejected into the atmosphere by the hundreds of volcanoes set off by the wave were predicted to have a profound cooling effect on the world's climate over the next three years. Growing seasons would change. Rainfall patterns would shift. The phrase "Wave Winter" had been coined and was gaining currency the more it was used.

Within a week, sunsets around the world would be noticeably redder. The disruption of the nutrient-rich Antarctic waters was expected to cause a massive whale die-off at one end of the food chain, and cause a severe depletion in the algae that provided ninety percent of the world's total oxygen production at the other end.

And still to be determined was the condition of the Ross Ice Shelf. If it was in millions of pieces, shipping in the South Pacific would be at risk for the next two years as the icebergs filled the sea-lanes. Also, as the ice drifted northward, it would reflect more of the sunlight reaching the planet and again a new source of climate cooling would add to the volcanic contribution. Without question, summers and winters in New Zealand and Australia would be much colder. In the long run, fishing off the west coast of South America—which fed tens of millions and employed tens of thousands—was expected to collapse for at least ten years until the deep ocean currents disrupted by the wave had reestablished themselves. And none of these dire predictions had even yet been able to include what might happen if volcanic eruptions were triggered in the Northern Hemisphere at the same rate they had occurred in the Southern, or even what the long-term effects of the seismic strains might be.

Some experts were saying it could even be possible the Earth would enter a century of unprecedented volcanic activity in which the Pacific Ring of Fire would become exactly that. And whether the subsequent infusion into the atmosphere of millions of tons of volcanic gas would create a runaway greenhouse effect or edge the world into a new ice age, not one expert agreed with another.

And almost all of it could have been avoided, Bailey thought, *if Captain Mitch Webber had been who he said he was, and who I believed he was.*

"If I had money to invest," Bailey told Huber, "I'd put it into churches. When the world wakes up after this, that's going to be the biggest growth industry of the decade."

About the only thing she had to be thankful about this weekend was that she had managed to get through to her parents again, and by now they were in the car with Darlene, the two cats, the three birds, and the goldfish, heading inland. Fifty miles, she had told them, then find something nice and just wait till she caught up with them.

Huber seemed to sense her mood. "We'll get through it," he told her.

When he said it, she almost believed it.

Then her FLTSATCOM alert lit up. It indicated an incoming transmission, directly to her station.

"Finally," she said as she leaned forward to activate the channel. "General Abbott's checking in." She toggled the switch. "This is SPACECOM, go ahead."

Then she nearly jumped from her chair as she heard Mitch Webber's voice. "Major Bailey, whatever you do, stay on the channel."

"It's not as if I have a choice, Captain. The whole U.S. Air Force is out looking for you. I hear you've got yourself on quite the joyride."

Bailey's fingers flashed over her board as she began isolating the transmission source. It was coming in on DSC Satellite V, transponder eight. According to the DSCS orbital tracks, that put Webber over the Pacific, no more than 2,000 miles east or west of Hawaii, somewhere between 48°N and 12°S. It was nowhere as close as a GPS fix, but at least if she measured the Doppler shift in the signal over the next few minutes, she'd be able to establish his current speed and heading. What she didn't understand was that Webber must also know that option was available to her.

"What have you heard, Major?"

Bailey knew that technically she should be reporting this contact to General Abbott or Colonel Lightfoot. But to confirm the speed and course data necessary to track the Nevada Rain, she'd need to keep the channel open for at least three minutes. *It couldn't hurt to talk to Captain Webber for that long.* Which is why she waved her hand and shook her head at Huber, who had already picked up the gold phone to send out a Flash Alert.

"Here's the story, Captain. General Abbott read the riot act on you and Dr. Rey to Colonel Lightfoot. He said everything you had said about collapsing the wave with Tomahawks was disinformation, intended to deflect blame from you."

"Blame?" Webber said. "For what?"

Bailey took a deep breath and let it out slowly. She hadn't enjoyed hearing this. She wasn't looking forward to repeating it. "The general has evidence that you and Dr. Rey are members of the terrorist group responsible for dropping the ice shelf."

"That's not true!"

"Then I suggest you return to Wheeler, turn yourself in, and let the lawyers fight it out. Otherwise, Captain, you and your lady friend are on the run for the rest of your lives."

"I am not his 'lady friend.' "

Bailey and Huber exchanged interested glances. Bailey had wondered where Corazon Rey might be.

"Hello, Dr. Rey. No disrespect. It's just that when I saw you two on the video feed from Christchurch . . . well, never mind. You've got to make the call, Captain. I've read your service file. I know you'll make the right one."

"If you've read my file, you know that Abbott's lying."

Bailey didn't want to hear that. It was true she had serious questions about what General Abbott was involved with, but that was the nature of her job. When she had a need to know, she would be told. Until then, all she had to do was follow orders. The whole chain of military command rested on that precept. "No, sir, I do not know that."

"Dammit, Major—you were the one who put us in touch with Cerenkov. You heard him tell the general what had to be done. You heard the general confirm his identity with Dave Casey. And then as soon as we were in the helicopter back to Wheeler, you must have heard him tell Lightfoot to put us under arrest."

"That is incorrect, Captain." The words left Bailey before she had had time to think about them. But Webber was right *and* wrong. She slowed down, trying to fit General Abbott's actions into a pattern that made sense. "Actually, the general had arranged to have you taken into custody when you arrived in Washington. He arranged that after you had left Christchurch."

"But that's where we told him the wave *wasn't* going to lose energy," Rey said.

"The Pentagon reversed its stand on that," Bailey reminded them. "So he did listen to you, Dr. Rey."

"Then why arrest us, Major?" Webber asked. "Why listen to us in Christchurch and not in Hawaii?"

"You'll have to ask the general that. When you land."

"Major Bailey, you've read my record. Do you trust me?"

Bailey checked her watch. She had almost had Webber transmitting long enough. "Trust has nothing to do with the situation at hand. You can end it by landing. It's as simple as that."

"I trust you, Major."

Bailey waited, not knowing what the captain was trying to say.

"How long have we been talking?" Webber asked. "Long enough for you to get a Doppler fix on the Nevada Rain, correct?"

He knew all along, Bailey thought.

"So ask yourself this, Major. Why the fuck would I go to all the trouble of stealing an invisible plane, and then *tell* you exactly where I am? Is that someone who's hiding something? Is that the act of a terrorist?"

Bailey knew that the captain was making sense, as far as he went. But what kind of mind could conceive of unleashing the Icefire wave on the world? Who really knew what kind of person she was speaking with?

"Captain, you're putting me in a difficult position."

"I bet you've been watching television, Major. What kind of casualties are they calling for now? Even with the evacuations?"

Bailey felt sick as she contemplated the numbers. "Immediate casualties . . . four to five million."

"Those are the people in a difficult position, Major. Those are the people we can help by stopping the wave."

"Then *land*, Captain. Fax those calculations General Abbott wanted to see."

"We can't!" Bailey was startled by the unforgiving rage in Webber's voice. "Colonel Lightfoot took the report from us. He told us the general had ordered him not to even look at Cerenkov's figures. Abbott already has those calculations, no matter what he's told you."

Now Bailey had the course information she needed. She knew she had to bring this to an end.

"Charles Abbott is a general in the United States Army. He is on the Joint Staff. He is a man of honor." Bailey's finger was over the END TRANSMISSION button. "Nevada Rain, this is SPACECOM. Out."

"Wait! Did the general call the President?"

Bailey hesitated, the button not yet pushed.

"Did he?"

Huber leaned over to whisper to Bailey the explanation for Gen-

JUDITH & GARFIELD REEVES-STEVENS

eral Abbott's lack of action. She passed it on to the captain. "The general only told you he was going to call the President to make you feel secure about returning to Wheeler. He never had any intention of making that call."

"Bullshit, Major! Think about it! If we were the terrorists, why would we risk going back to Wheeler after being with Cerenkov at the university? And if Abbott really believed he had captured two of the greatest criminals in history, don't you think he'd call the President immediately?" The rage was gone from Webber. Instead, Bailey heard only extreme exhaustion, and frustration. "He lied to us. He lied to you. You know it, Major. You have to."

Bailey also heard truth in the captain's voice. Whether he was actually right or not, she knew he believed in what he was saying.

She could feel Huber staring at her in concern as she took her hand away from the cutoff control. "Then give me a reason, Webber. *Why* would someone like General Abbott of the NMCC be lying to all of us?"

There was a long stretch of silence. Bailey checked the signal strength to be sure the channel was still open. "Are you still there, Captain?"

"Misdirection," he said at last. "It's the only reason that makes sense. Abbott is telling you we're the terrorists because he wants to distract you. Because he knows who the *real* terrorists are. Because he knows who started the Icefire wave and he doesn't want anyone else to know."

"Ho—ly—shit, Major Bailey." Bailey followed Huber's line of sight to stare where he was staring, at the middle display screens above the panel, the ones that tracked all the satellite data streams General Abbott was accessing in the NMCC.

The answer had been right there, all along.

It was China.

SEVEN

NEVADA RAIN/OVER THE PACIFIC

In the Nevada Rain, at 160,000 feet, and at a velocity of more than 7,400 mph—an incomprehensible Mach 9.8—Corazon Rey looked out through her VAD visor and clearly saw the curvature of the Earth.

That meant San Diego was less than twenty-five minutes away, though Webber had explained they would have to allow extra travel time, first to accelerate to maximum velocity, and then to shed that speed as they came in to land. Still, she and Webber would have traveled from the island of Oahu to the coast of California in less than one hour. At Mach 9.8, Webber had told her, they could have circled the world in three hours and twenty-two minutes.

Cory understood that whatever would happen to them when they arrived in San Diego was riding on whatever Major Wilhemina Bailey did next. And for now, Major Bailey seemed to be doing nothing.

"Are you still there, Major?" Cory heard Webber ask from his position beside her in the Nevada Rain's cockpit. Webber still appeared alert in his pilot's seat, more encased by its unusual design than actually sitting upon it. The mere act of flying had seemed to revive him. To Cory, caught between overstimulation and bone-deep fatigue, her own seat was beginning to feel like a vertical waterbed, though without the tendency to rock.

Finally, Bailey responded. "I'm here, Captain. I'm . . . thinking about what you said."

Cory didn't know how to take herself out of the communications circuit. Unlike the Harrier or the Blackbird, the PPG and helmet she wore had no visible wires to connect or disconnect. Given the equipment's level of technology, she suspected any wires were embedded in the fabric itself, or that there were wireless ports built in to her helmet. But without something physical to adjust, she had no way to say something that only Webber could hear. So she did what she did best. She spoke her mind aloud.

"You have something on General Abbott, don't you?" Cory asked. It was the most obvious reason for Bailey's reticence. The major wouldn't want to believe her commander could be at fault.

Cory was convinced that her conclusion was correct when she heard the edge in Bailey's answer. "I will not show disrespect to my commanding officer."

"Why is that?"

"Because he *is* my commanding officer."

Webber's voice was louder in Cory's helmet than Bailey's. The internal cockpit signal, however it was transmitted, was stronger than the radio transmission from Cheyenne Mountain. "Cory, let me handle this."

"I will not. I want to know. All you people in uniform go running around following orders without ever asking yourself if those orders are *worth* following."

"Orders *have* to be followed!" Bailey insisted.

"Okay," Cory said. "I give you that. I understand. Otherwise you don't have your sacred chain of command. But then why aren't you asking yourself if the *person* giving those orders deserves your loyalty? Do Abbot's orders *deserve* to be followed?"

Cory saw Webber angling his head in his rigid helmet to look down past his VAD, trying to get her attention. "Cory, rank can't be questioned."

"Don't give me that! *Everything* has to be questioned! You're not robots or pack animals! If someone tells *me* to do something without giving me all the facts I need to make up my own mind, I damn well want to know I can trust that person. That I'm not being misled."

Webber flipped his VAD visor up from his face, leaving it attached to his helmet like the brim of a baseball cap. Cory hoped the plane had an automatic pilot because now there was no way for Webber to see outside. "You're confusing what we have to do here! The major and I have to work within the system!"

"Thank you, Captain," Bailey said.

"And as soon as you start questioning it," Webber continued, "the system breaks down."

Cory flipped up the VAD on her own helmet so that now no one in the plane could see where they were going. *What is it about uniforms?* she thought. *Do they cut off the flow of blood to the head?* "Listen to yourselves," she said. "If the system breaks down simply because you question it, *it's not a system that deserves to exist!* We're not talking about going on night patrol or writing reports or marching around a damn army camp—we're talking about saving millions of lives! For God's sake, Major Bailey, if you don't *question* authority, you'll never know if the orders you're given are *worth* being followed. Otherwise, how can you call yourself a thinking human being?"

Cory angled her head to look at Webber. Webber was furious, and she had no doubt that his fury was all directed at her. He mouthed silent words to her. *Thanks. We just lost her.*

But Cory knew Webber was wrong. Webber saw only the rank or the insignia. But Cory had listened to Wilhemina Bailey long enough to gamble on the sort of person she was.

That's why she wasn't really surprised when, after a long pause, Bailey finally said, "Captain Webber, Dr. Rey, I have General Abbott on the circuit."

NATIONAL MILITARY COMMAND CENTER/THE PENTAGON

The wave would not be stopped. That was the only thought in Abbott's mind as he agreed to Bailey's request that he speak with Webber and Rey.

He wasn't even too concerned about the location of the Nevada Rain. It functioned as a stealth craft at microwave, infrared, and optical wavelengths, even eluding American technology. But the craft was intended for simple there-and-back surveillance missions. According to the elapsed-time counter on Abbott's watch, the Nevada Rain had been under way for thirty-five minutes. Within another forty minutes, its fuel would be diminished enough that it could no longer cryogenically cool its outer skin, making it an infrared beacon easily detectable by satellite surveillance assets that were intended to spot the launch of enemy missiles. And in fifty minutes, the exotic craft would be out of fuel entirely. Certainly, Webber could set the plane down anywhere in its hover mode. But by then, a SKYFALL retrieval team would already be on its way.

To Abbott, all that mattered now was keeping Webber and Rey away from the media. The general could handle the military, just as he could control the level of the retrieval team's response. Once this distraction was dealt with and the plane recovered, the Nevada Rain could return to duty. But Webber and the good doctor would not emerge from preventive incarceration for years. If at all.

When Major Bailey had contacted him, Abbott had cleared the EAR of everyone except Woolman, Chennault, and Yoshii. Of those, only Woolman knew of the China connection to Icefire. He and Pentagon analyst Milton Harrap had already developed enough intelligence from the satellite imagery of the troops north of Beijing that Abbott had a list of the five PLA generals who without question had to be involved in the projected coup.

Three of those generals—Xinsheng, Zhenhuan, and Jian—were old-school hard-liners who had solidified their careers under Deng. Given their constant though low-key criticism of China's ongoing push for modernism, and the resulting spread of Western-style morality and crime—which together were an anathema to Chinese traditions—those three had been obvious suspects as instigators of any attempt to reform the government.

But the two other participants had been a surprise to Harrap—Wei Jincheng and Che'en Huan. They were younger generals, part of the next generation of Chinese warfighters, notable because they were among the new military leaders who had been children when Mao had died in 1976, and to whom the cultural revolution was something that had taken place only in textbooks.

In Abbott's estimation, the presence of the younger generals among the coup leaders only proved his interpretation, not Harrap's, of the Pentagon's Chinese Question. China would *not* grow conciliatory in the years ahead. The leaders who would wage the inevitable war with America were already ascending through the ranks, preparing for the coming conflict.

But, Abbott knew, if he kept to his plan and his convictions, the Chinese Question would be answered before the weekend was over.

He faced the big board, smiling confidently at Major Bailey and the commander at her side. "Any time you're ready, Major," he said. "Are you there, Captain Webber?"

Webber's answer was remarkably static-free. "I'm here, General."

Abbott didn't waste time, and he was intent on leaving a clear statement of purpose on the tapes the NSA would be making of this conversation. "I'm sorry it's come to this, but you've left too many questions unanswered. The best thing to do is to land your craft at the nearest U.S. base and allow yourself to be taken into custody."

But instead of from Webber, the next response came from Rey. "Hi there, General. I'm crashing your tea party. I don't care how many rules these other people have to follow. Captain Webber and I know how to stop the wave. And if you don't help us do that, millions of people will die needlessly and everyone will know you killed them."

Abbott reminded himself of all the people who would hear this conversation someday, students and historians, perhaps even ordinary citizens listening to snippets played in museums and libraries, a collection of the moments leading up to America's boldest action in defense of her freedom. For the sake of all those for whom he fought, especially those unborn, he would not lose his temper. He would set the record straight from the beginning. As was any person driven to greatness, General Abbott was sure of his place in history and had contemplated it often.

"Dr. Rey, let me assure you, all affected countries have been warned about the nature of the wave, and evacuations are under way," Abbott said clearly. "The only 'killers' are the people who set the wave in motion. And from where I stand, from what I know at this moment, you, Dr. Rey and Captain Webber, are most certainly suspects."

"Help us out, Bailey." Abbott was startled to hear Rey call on the major for support. "We're practically in orbit up here, but you're right in the middle of it. Remember distraction. He knows something he's keeping from all of us. What is it? Why's he—"

"Major Bailey," Abbott cut in, "you will end all communication with the stolen aircraft and forward its location and course to

NORAD for interception. In enemy hands, the Nevada Rain could be a significant threat to—"

"Think, Bailey," Rey urged. "Do his orders *deserve* to be followed? You're the only one who can decide that."

Abbott didn't know what kind of discussions Bailey had been having with Rey, and he didn't want to know. "Major Bailey, I *order* you to shut down communications *now*."

On the big board, Abbott watched the video image of Bailey as she hesitated, actually *hesitated*, even though she had been given a direct order. "What is your problem, Major?"

Bailey's voice was unexpectedly soft. "My problem . . . it's China, sir. With PACIFIC SHIELD under way, with all that's happening because of the wave, why are you studying Chinese troop movements so closely?"

Abbott went cold. "Are you questioning *me?*"

Bailey looked as shocked and as apprehensive as Abbott felt. "Yes, sir. I suppose I am."

"Major Bailey, you are relieved of duty."

"No, sir, I am not. Not until you answer my question."

Abbott felt as if the air had rushed from the room. "I am your commanding officer!" He was aware that Major Chennault and Captain Woolman were on their feet staring at him. Lieutenant Yoshii sat frozen in position at her workstation.

On the board, Bailey glanced at the young commander sitting beside her. "Then why aren't you protecting this country, sir? Why are you squandering time and resources on something that doesn't have anything at all to do with the threat we're facing?"

"It has everything to do with what we're facing!" Abbott regretted those words the moment he said them.

Webber was next to speak. But he didn't address himself to Abbott. "Major Bailey, exactly what kind of troop movements is the general watching in China?"

"End communications now!" Abbott shouted.

But Bailey said again, "No, sir, I will not."

Abbott's fist slammed down on the EAR's center table. All of his dominoes were falling, but not in the directions he had planned.

NEVADA RAIN/OVER THE PACIFIC

Webber flipped down his VAD visor and scanned the sky ahead. There was no point to doing so, really. He and Cory were traveling at more than two miles each second. Human perception and reflexes were useless in these realms. Technology had long ago outstripped human limits of command and control.

But in three more minutes, he would have to commit to his landing trajectory at San Diego Naval Base. Before that happened, he had to know what would be waiting for him there.

Major Bailey's voice was calm and deliberate as she answered his question. "As near as I can tell, Captain, there are significant troop concentrations north of Beijing. General Abbott has been using the Big Birds to identify the units and divisions."

"Bailey!" Abbott's voice thundered over the radio. "You are in violation of your orders! I want that aircraft's location now! Webber has to be stopped!"

Since Bailey didn't seem dissuaded by Abbott's commands, Webber also ignored them. "Please continue, Major. Is this part of an ongoing program for the general? Is there any reason why the NMCC should be concerned with China's internal troop movements at this time?"

"No. This is something new. All this interest started just before the Pentagon's announcement that the wave wasn't losing strength. General Abbott pulled up realtime surveillance imagery of Russia, then of the Chinese coast, then of Beijing. And that's where it's been ever since."

For Webber, that was all it took. The pattern was complete. "Thank you, Major. I can tell you what the general's doing. When he found out the wave was caused by a deliberate act, he went looking for the bad guys. Anybody would have done the same. It was the right move. And since it was an old Soviet plan, and I had seen an old Soviet warhead, he checked out Russia first. And he didn't see anything."

Abbott's outrage flooded the circuit. "You are all traitors! Bailey— I *demand* the coordinates of that plane!"

But once more Bailey did not respond and so Webber kept going, describing for her the puzzle pieces, with Abbott at the center, holding everything together. "So then the general checked out the second most obvious choice: China. And he did find something. Something suspicious on the coast. Was that it, General? Evidence that China was better prepared for the wave than it should be, as if the Chinese navy knew what to expect? Something like that?" But Webber didn't wait for Abbott to answer. The details weren't important right now. He had sixty seconds to his go/no-go point for San Diego.

"It's a classic Chinese strategy, isn't it, General?" he continued. "Make yourself strong by making your enemies weaker. Win a war without fighting a battle. Commanding those troops outside Beijing, we're probably looking at a handful of old generals wishing for the good old days of the Red Guard. They dug up Icefire—maybe in a fire sale from the Kremlin archives—and updated it, using better technology, and then they set it loose. They wanted a global economic meltdown that'd make Korea and Japan and Taiwan irrelevant, that'd devastate America's industrial base, and leave the world with only two power centers—the European Union and China."

For Webber, it was the perfect answer. All the pieces fit.

But then Major Bailey objected. "That can't be right, Captain. China's going to get hit by the wave just like everyone else in the Pacific."

"Of course they'll be hit!" Abbott said quickly. "That proves Webber's lying."

"I'm not lying, Major. The wave is a *high*-tech weapon. It's going to take out industrial centers and manufacturing and banking systems . . . but *China?* China's still *low*-tech. Even they admit they're thirty years behind us. That wave's going to hit them, but it won't hurt them. Not the way it'll hurt Japan and California. More than any other country, China's got enough land and people to overcome anything the wave can do to her."

"Major Bailey," Abbott said urgently, "if Webber is allowed to spout this fantasy to the media, some people are going to believe him. Can't you see what he's doing? He's trying to push the world into war!"

Webber could tell that Abbott still seemed to have some power over Bailey. She was on the fence, not yet fully convinced. *Maybe she's never been in combat,* Webber thought. *Maybe she can't see how clear-cut the choices are when the weapons are loaded and aimed, and the threat is personal.*

388

"What *about* the troops, Captain?" Bailey asked. "Why are they outside Beijing? And why does General Abbott care?"

Webber knew the answer, though he wasn't sure how to explain it. But as he paused, Cory stepped in, having no compunctions about how and where to place the blame.

"Major, no offense, but Icefire is something so appalling it could only have been put into play by the military. Not real people. You're part of the system. You know how generals sit around talking about 'acceptable' losses. No sane government would allow this kind of indiscriminate attack on innocent people. The Chinese generals know that, too. So they're getting ready to change their country's government. It's the only way they can get away with it."

"She's right," Webber said. "Those troops are waiting for the wave to hit the China coast. In the confusion, they'll move in and install their generals as the new, official government. And with everything else the world will be going through after the wave, nobody's even going to notice for at least a month. And by then, nobody's going to care."

Webber read the coordinates printing out along the bottom of his VAD's visual display. It was time to commit to landing. There was only one question left: Was Major Bailey willing to commit as well?

USSPACECOM/EARTH SURVEILLANCE CENTER/CHEYENNE MOUNTAIN

Bailey was in conflict. When she had entered the Air Force, all her initial training had been directed toward war fighting. But over the years, as the world had calmed and she had moved into intelligence, the emphasis of her mission changed—from the waging of war to the management of peace.

Yet here she was, forced to consider the Icefire wave as the first strike in a conflict that could change the world and weaken her country.

In the SVTS window on her situation panel, Bailey saw General Abbott raise a hand to her, as if in appeal. "Major, no more orders. I'm not a general commanding my troops. I'm an American. And I'm trying to save my country from what Webber and Rey want to do to it. Think it through. If *I* thought China had done this to us,

don't you think I'd be talking with the President right now, setting up a counterattack?''

"Don't listen to him," Webber radioed. "You know politics. If we stop the wave, Abbott can't attack. That's why he wants to stop *us* instead. He *wants* the wave to hit. He wants the whole country to see those damage reports and casualty figures. Because then he can launch everything we have at China, and the world and the U.S. will say we are justified in what we do!"

"Give me their location, Major. This is the last time I will ask."

"Major, you can't let Abbott destroy this country just so he can destroy another."

Bailey felt poised on a precipice. Her hands trembled, but it wasn't the coffee. Her job was to quickly weave connections at the center of a vast communications hub, as the business of the nation's defense ran smoothly, all by itself.

It was not her job to make decisions. Yet with the general on one side and the captain on the other, a decision is what she would have to make.

Aware only of Dominic Huber's presence beside her, the only human presence in this cave of technology, Bailey felt herself hesitate, uncertain, unsure.

On the display wall, the wave moved on, relentless in its advance. Hawaii in less than nine hours. Japan in less than twelve. California, less than fifteen.

The moment was now, and all her training had not prepared her for what she must do.

Then a determined female voice came over the speakers. "Major, have you ever heard the story of Pearl Harbor? How Roosevelt knew the attack was coming. And how he chose not to act, because he believed the rage of the American people was necessary to take this country into war? Do you remember what happened at the end of that war?"

Bailey did. *Hiroshima. Nagasaki. Three generations of unspeakable fear and a spectre of terror that grew larger every day.*

"I don't know if that story is true," Corazon Rey continued. "And we can't second-guess the actions of the dead. But today, Major, here and now, we're better than that. If any of the wars this country has fought in the past are worth anything, we *have* to be better. If you believe there's no more need for such acts in this world, then you know what you have to do. You just have to know."

Bailey felt Huber's hand on her shoulder, nothing more to it than a confirmation of his presence. Of his support.

Major Wilhemina Bailey saw no choice.

She was a major in the United States Air Force, sworn to defend her country against all enemies.

Foreign *and* domestic.

She did the only thing she could, the one thing that history now demanded of her.

Major Bailey pressed a single button on her panel.

And shut down the Pentagon.

EIGHT

NATIONAL MILITARY COMMAND CENTER/THE PENTAGON

Abbott stared in disbelief as, one by one, the video windows winked out across the big board. The SAR of Beijing disappeared. The extreme optical study of the bivouac of General Wei Jincheng's 2nd RDF Division. The harbor of Quanzhou in infrared. Then the ADEOS-III satellite imagery. The TOPEX/POSEIDON realtime feed showing the wave surge across the equator, pressing the attack.

Lieutenant Yoshii turned to him, her mouth opening in shock. "Sir?"

"No . . ." he said as his hydra's heads were severed. "No . . ." as the doors of history closed.

But in the end, all that remained was the top layer of the ETEM map, showing the world without borders, and a single video window with the East Coast feed of CNN International. The small insert screen beside the news readers had more information about the wave than he, the officer in charge of the NMCC, could command now.

"Is it true?" Chennault asked.

Abbott didn't answer. He was already busy, working out strategies, preparing a counterattack for which he had no scenarios.

"General Abbott," Chennault persisted. "Is it true? Did you know about the Chinese involvement? Were you waiting for the first strike so we could respond in force?"

Woolman stepped to Abbott's side. "It's true."

Chennault stared at Abbott as if he were gazing down into an endless crevasse. "Why?"

Abbott straightened his shoulders, tugged down on his jacket to smooth the wrinkles. He was an officer. A leader. "I wanted to win." He met Chennault's gaze squarely, warrior to warrior, sharing the camaraderie of the battlefield. "And I still can," he said.

Abbott turned away from Woolman and Chennault. "Lieutenant Yoshii, are any satellite communication channels available to the NMCC?"

Yoshii's voice cracked as she answered from her workstation. "No, sir. The only open channels are in use by PACIFIC SHIELD. We've been locked out."

Abbott nodded. He had expected as much. "How about land-lines? Fiber-optics?"

Yoshii checked something at her station. "Those are still open, sir. We just won't be able to access satellite repeaters. I have no idea how she's managed this."

"That's quite all right, Lieutenant. We can work around Major Bailey. Get me Elrey Boyd at the NSA. We don't need a satellite for that."

Chennault pulled on his shoulder, trying to turn him from the board. "General, let it end."

"I will not let the Chinese get away with this."

"You heard them! It's not the Chinese. It's a coup, a cabal, at most a group of tired old soldiers who refuse to let the world change."

Abbott pushed Chennault away from him. "The world will *not* change, Major. That is what we are here for and that is what we will do. To preserve the country as it is."

"Our job is to defend our country, not to control it."

A video window opened on the board. Elrey Boyd, in need of a shave and a clean shirt, appeared on it. His desktop was littered with foam coffee cups.

"You can't do one without doing the other," Abbott said to Chennault. Then he smiled at Boyd's tired face. "Good day, Mr. Boyd. I have an assignment for you."

Boyd chewed his lip. "PACIFIC SHIELD is eating up most of our capacity, sir. If there's any way we can put off something new until—"

"I need you to get me the President."

That got Boyd's attention. The youth straightened up at his desk. "Uh, sir, you're at the Pentagon and he's on Air Force One. You can pick up a phone and DSCS routing will get him for you within thirty seconds."

"We have lost DSCS ability."

Boyd shook his head as if to clear it. "What happened?"

"Mr. Boyd, the United States is about to come under attack by hostile forces. Those forces have compromised the satellite communications abilities of the Pentagon. I am relying on the NSA to put me in touch with the President at once. Have I made myself clear?"

"You mustn't listen to him!" Chennault shouted.

In the video window, Boyd looked alarmed as on his own monitor he saw Chennault rushing forward to block Abbott.

But Woolman grabbed Chennault, clamped one arm across his chest and the other across his mouth, and pulled him back.

"This nation is at a crossroads, Mr. Boyd. Get me the President."

Boyd nodded, showing no understanding of the situation he was witnessing. He began to type on his keyboard. "Opening the channel," he said.

Yoshii confirmed it. A third video window opened on the board. When the static faded and the President appeared, Abbott remained expressionless. It was difficult to do, because the nation was about to go to war, and the Chief Executive, a man not fit to command a Boy Scout troop, was wearing a sweatshirt with WILLKOMMEN BERLIN printed on it. The man was a disgrace.

"Good evening, General," the President said.

Abbott cleared his throat. He was under no illusions. This President was his enemy. But China was the bigger threat. So he would use the lesser against the greater. It was a reasonable compromise. One he could live with.

"Mr. President, I must tell you our country is facing the most serious and immediate threat to its security since the worst days of the Cold War."

"I quite agree," the President said.

Abbott stumbled over what he was about to say next. The President was not supposed to agree with him. Not yet.

"I've just been having an interesting conversation with some people you might know. A Major Wilhemina Bailey, Captain Mitch Webber . . ."

Abbott stared at the video feed.

394

" . . . an oceanographer, Dr. Corazon Rey, and a friend of yours, I believe, at Pearl, Admiral Browne. Commander-in-Chief of the Pacific Fleet. Any of them ring a bell?"

"Sir . . . they're all lying. . . ."

The President looked down upon Abbott with pity.

"I haven't even told you what they said."

"China . . . has attacked us, sir. . . ."

"General, let's cut the crap. You're a military man. Are you familiar with the work of Sun Tzu?"

Abbott stared blankly, bleakly. Of all the names that might ever have passed from the President's lips, he would never have expected to hear that name.

"I studied it," the President said. "Hell, I memorized it, just so I could understand the challenges that our country and China will face together. Near the end of the book, Sun Tzu says, 'If you are not in danger, do not fight.' And I assure you, it is not to our interests, or anyone's, to put China in danger and they know it.

"Then this Sun Tzu, he says, 'A ruler cannot raise an army because he is enraged, nor can a general fight because he is resentful. For while an angered man may again be happy, and a resentful man again be pleased, a state that has perished cannot be restored, nor the dead be brought back to life.' "

The President's eyes were those of a man who has won a great victory. " 'Therefore,' Sun Tzu says, 'the enlightened ruler is prudent'—that sounds like someone we both know—'and the good general is warned against rash action. Thus the state is kept secure, and the army preserved.' Good advice. One smart guy. If you read the thing all the way to the end, you realize he should have called it *The Art of Peace*."

Abbott was in a state of shock. There was nothing more for him on the board. He had heard the words of Sun Tzu quoted by a man he despised. There was no honor left in this world. No glory. And no hope.

"Pack it up, General. As Commander-in-Chief, I relieve you of duty. I've got Norbie Morrow coming in from Florida. He'll take over."

Abbott tried to say one more thing, but the President held up a finger, a parent admonishing a child. "I said you were relieved. It's over, General." The President reached for a control on his desk. "You're history."

The President hit a switch on his desk and his image disappeared.

At the side of the emergency action room, Woolman let go of Chennault.

"We haven't been able to keep up," Chennault said bitterly. "There's too much information out there, not enough communication. But when you read the casualty lists on Sunday, General, I want you to ask yourself, how many of them are there because of you and your secrets?"

Chennault pushed past Woolman, through the main doors, and was gone.

Woolman couldn't meet Abbott's eyes.

"General," Lieutenant Yoshii said, almost hoarse. "Shall I . . . shall I call your car, sir?"

Abbott nodded. There was nothing left for him here.

"Where shall I say you're going, sir?"

Where else could someone go who had lost the world? But Abbott could barely get the word out, so seldom had he said it in the past.

"Home."

NINE

"Are we ready?" the President asked.

Major Wilhemina Bailey had gone past nervous and was well into giddy. She had pulled the plug on the Pentagon, and she was not in a jail cell facing court-martial. Instead, she was talking to the *President*. Because *he* had asked for *her*.

Bailey studied her situation panel, making sure all the circuits were patched together, all the appropriate lights were lit. They were.

She looked at the President on the middle display screen of her station. He was still in Air Force One over the North Atlantic, just passing Iceland, but the satellite reception was perfect. "Yes, sir, we are ready." Bailey glanced away from the board to find Huber. He was at the edge of her platform, smiling at her, sharing her excitement, and staying out of camera range. He gave her a thumbs-up.

"Then let's go over it one more time," the President said.

Bailey had the list at her fingertips. She had had to draw a diagram to keep it straight. "Okay, first, when you hold the red button down, everything you say will be heard by the Premier, Ambassador Roth, the Premier's translator, your translator, Mr. Harrap and Secretary Bannock at the Pentagon, Admirals O'Malley and Sato at Yokohama, and Admiral Browne at Pearl. When you let go of the

397

red button, you'll only be heard by everyone on this side of the call—nothing will go through to the Chinese."

"And you're standing by with the . . . what was it, the SLAM-SHIFT transmission?"

"I've got my finger on the button, Mr. President."

"Better you than me, Major." The President laughed and Bailey was transfixed by his smile, even on the tiny screen. It made her wish that she had voted for him.

"I'm putting through the call now, sir." Bailey closed the circuit, and instantly seven channels from two continents, plus Japan, Hawaii, and a 747 over the North Atlantic, converged on three satellites orbiting 19,300 miles above the Earth, each of which transferred the connections to Falcon AFB, and then, through an EMP-proof fiber-optic landline, to Major Wilhemina Bailey's situation panel.

The first thing that told Bailey it had all worked out was the electronic chirp of a ringing phone. The full power of the United States's military electromagnetic communications network had been used to connect to a simple landline that was part of the People's Phone Company, in a small town house in Mentougou, about fifteen miles due west of Beijing. Bailey heard the click of the phone being answered.

"Hello?"

Here goes, Bailey thought. "I have a call for Ambassador Martin Roth."

The phone was passed over. Bailey could hear rustling, then, "This is Roth."

"Ambassador Roth, this is Major Bailey, U.S. Space Command. I have the President of the United States for Premier Changzhi." Bailey couldn't help it—a wave of goose bumps rushed over her arms and up her back.

"The Premier is standing by," Roth said. "He also has his translator, Mr. Pin, and his military advisor, Admiral Chen Jijun. We are encrypting on this end with a Chinese system, so there might be a bit of a delay."

"Just a moment, please," Bailey said.

"Who's the general?" the President asked. "He's not on the list."

"Mr. President, Milton Harrap here. Admiral Chen Jijun is commander of PLAN submarine operations. I think his presence is a good sign that the Premier is taking your call seriously."

"What do you know about him?" the President asked.

"Married, one child, a daughter. Took part in an exchange semester at Annapolis in 1980. Speaks English. A moderate."

"Ready or not," the President said. "No, wait. Let's make this good. Is the television on in the house?"

Bailey checked the board. The town house in Mentougou was the Chinese Premier's private retreat, and she had overheard enough frenzied conversations in the past hour to know that there would be considerable political fallout from the revelation that the CIA knew where to find the Premier when he was taking his usual, every-other-Friday retreat with his mistress. The town house was undistinguished from the outside, but outfitted with enough optional extras to make it into *Architectural Digest*, including an indoor swimming pool, a Jacuzzi from the States, and a light-up dance floor, just like the one in *Saturday Night Fever*.

Bailey checked the screen that showed the EM emission graph from the house as registered from the SLAMSHIFT satellite now passing slowly over the region. They would have a thirty-minute-long window of opportunity for this operation. Milton Harrap had said it would be long enough.

The emission screen showed that a television set was in operation in the town house, in addition to five computer-monitor displays. Bailey typed her inquiry for the SLAMSHIFT database. If she had requested it, SLAMSHIFT could have uploaded screen images of whatever was being displayed on the computer screens in the house. But all she had asked about was the television. It was a Mitsubishi, forty-inch direct view, on the second floor. It was connected to a satellite receiver, and the station it was tuned to was . . .

"Mr. President, the Chinese Premier is watching MTV."

"God bless America," the President said. "Put me through."

After another minute, when it had been firmly established by Premier Changzhi's staff that the President was on hold for the Premier, the conversation began. The President got right to business.

"Mr. Premier, that wave is coming down the pike on both our countries, so I won't waste words or time." He paused, letting Changzhi's translator keep up. "First, we know what caused the wave. Second, we know how to stop it. Do I have your attention?"

The Chinese portion of the conversation was muted, but Bailey could hear the increase in tempo. She didn't have to know the language to know that the President's approach had worked.

"All right," the President said. "Let's get to it. I understand you like MTV." Bailey made out the words "Kenny G" in the Premier's reply. Fortunately, the President did not pick up on the reference. "Well, I'll tell you, sir, if you've got a VCR set up, I'd turn it on to record. Don't change the channels though. I want to send you some tapes we made off our satellites this past hour. Can you see the screen? Okay, you stand by, now. Here it comes." There was a click on the line—the President letting up on the red button. "Okay, Major, do your stuff."

Bailey started the video feed. A signal went from the NRO to the DSCS system, then was transferred to the SLAMSHIFT ELINT counterintelligence and propaganda satellite. It broadcast a narrow-beam video signal directly to the Premier's television, overriding all other inputs with the strength of its signal. The transmission carried highlights of General Abbott's recent surveillance of China, all recorded courtesy of the NSA.

"Here's the deal, Premier. You recognize these generals?" The President read off the names of the Chinese generals suspected of being involved with the coup. He was asked to repeat one of the names, and Bailey hoped the translator was correcting the President's pronunciation. "You got those? Well, those troops you're looking at, they're all camped out north of Beijing." The President paused until the translator came back to him with a question. "That's right. Now, I'm not going to tell you how to run your country—except the way I usually do, in a campaign speech—but my intelligence services say that you're looking at a coup. Am I making myself clear?"

The line clicked off on the Chinese side. "All the circuits are open," Bailey reported as she checked the channels on her panel. "They're just using their red button to have a private conversation."

"How're we doing for time?" the President asked.

Admiral Browne at Pearl gave the countdown. "Hawaii in six hours, Mr. President. Japan in nine. California, twelve."

Bailey had been monitoring the news coverage of the monstrous traffic tie-ups on the West Coast. Police had shut down all west-bound lanes to double the capacity of the freeways. She prayed she had given her parents and sister enough of a head start to get out of San Diego.

The line clicked back to life and Bailey heard the translator say that the satellite images were intriguing, but what did this have to do with the wave?

The President explained the prevailing theory, that the generals he had named, the generals in charge of the troops near Beijing and five other key government cities, had unleashed the Icefire wave to diminish China's enemies while they took advantage of the confusion to take over the country.

Bailey heard shouting as that was translated. The translator replied that the Premier was outraged that America would think China was responsible for such a barbaric act of international banditry.

"I did not say that at all," the President stated forcefully. "Believe me, Mr. Premier, if I thought the wave had been started as a deliberate tactic by the government of the People's Republic of China, in the first place, we would not be having this conversation, and in the second place, there would no longer *be* a People's Republic of China."

The line clicked off again.

"Um, Mr. President," Harrap said timidly, "it might not be productive to be quite so forceful with them. The Chinese don't respond well to threats."

"That wasn't a threat, Mr. Harrap. That was God's own truth."

The translator came back. "How do you propose stopping the wave?"

The President's line clicked. "Okay, what the hell is that supposed to mean? Did they buy into it that fast?"

Harrap spoke up first. "If I were in their position, I'd be dispatching aerial surveillance assets to confirm what is on the satellite tapes. They won't believe anything you say or commit to anything you ask for until they have that confirmation. But by advancing the conversation, they're acknowledging that time is short. I'd keep up with them, sir. They won't agree to do anything soon, but when the time comes, they're making sure they'll be prepared."

"Fair enough," the President said. He clicked his line back on. "To stop the wave, we're going to have to get technical, and I'm going to pass you on to my specialists." The President introduced the two American admirals and the Japanese admiral who were standing by. "The important thing is that we have the target coordinates of key spots on the seafloor where nuclear charges will have to be detonated."

The translator came back at once with the objections of the Premier. "Right now, sir, I don't give a good rat's ass about the treaties. We're going to be hitting the target sites on our side of the ocean and we can all argue about it next week. Now here's the important part. China is the only nuclear power in the region. We're going to need your help to stop the wave from hitting Japan."

Bailey had heard the discussion about this part of the President's message. China and Japan had a long history, little of it good. Harrap said there was little chance that China would go out of its way to aid Japan, even at the most minimal level.

"For that part," the President said, "I have people standing by in Yokohama, ready to give targeting support."

The translator asked a blunt question.

The President gave an equally blunt reply. "Not only do we know where each and every one of your thirteen nuclear subs is located, we can tell you which ones are running hot."

Another delay. Another blunt question.

But the President already had his reply worked out. "You tell Admiral Jijun that I know he wants his daughter to grow up in a world that's a helluva lot safer than the one he and I grew up in. You tell him that what I'm about to do, I'm doing for his daughter, and my son, and maybe someday the two of them can get together and complain about their old fathers.

"So here goes: If the admiral checks with PLAN headquarters, he will learn that his Xia-class, ballistic-missile, nuclear-powered sub, *Long March*, has been station-keeping at 21° 14 minutes north, 124° 3 minutes east for the past eight days, without taking part in the war games off Taiwan. It is at a depth of eight hundred twenty feet. And according to the United States Navy—which is the best naval force in the world—when the crew of the *Long March* last conducted a torpedo drill, the number-five torpedo door did not open. "

The line clicked off on the Chinese side again.

"How'm I doing, people?" the President asked.

Admiral Browne broke in from Pearl. "If I were Jijun, I'd be shitting my pants about now. They're going to know we wouldn't let them know our surveillance capabilities without a good reason."

"But is it a good enough reason?" the President asked.

Not even Harrap had an answer for that, and this time, the delay on the Chinese side lasted four minutes. When it ended, the translator expressed the Premier's regrets, but explained that he had been forced to leave to investigate claims of a disturbance outside Beijing. In the meantime, the translator said that Admiral Jijun would appreciate the chance to speak with the President's admirals, and the Japanese admiral, if they would just give him a few more minutes to get his technical staff to join him on the phone call.

"You tell the admiral that the United States Navy is standing by to work with the PLA Navy whenever he's ready."

There was a long pause on the Chinese side before the translator said he would pass that message on. Then the line clicked on hold again.

"Okay, people, listen up," the President said. "It sounds to me as if we just preserved the stability of the PRC, and are getting ready to help save Asia. Only problem with that is that those folks can't vote in the next election. So let's get off our butts and save America! Are you with me?"

Bailey couldn't believe it, but the answering chorus from across the globe was as rousing as any political rally. There was a reason why politicians were politicians, she decided, and soldiers were soldiers.

And now that the politicians had done their job, it was time for the soldiers to do theirs.

TEN

SUBGRU 5/BALLAST POINT, SAN DIEGO

Captain Mitch Webber was in a fog of confused sensation. Each time he closed his eyes, he saw ice or ocean or sky so dark it was no different from space. If he leaned back in his chair, the floor pitched as if it were a helicopter, or a speeding snowmobile, or the Nevada Rain kicking into its wave-pulse mode, burning its fuel on the outside of its fuselage to propel it at speeds no contained engine could match for efficiency and control.

And then he forced open his eyes and it was as if his Volvo had come to a sudden stop and nothing moved. He was in the quiet, air-conditioned situation room at Ballast Point, the San Diego Naval Base, protected deep within the solid stone of Point Loma, surrounded by the command staff and technical specialists of Submarine Group 5.

They were the ones tasked with saving the West Coast from San Diego to San Francisco. SUBGRU 9 in Bangor, Washington, in cooperation with Canadian naval forces, would handle the Icefire target sites protecting the coast from San Francisco to the Gulf of Alaska. And a combined flotilla from SUBRON 1 and SUBRON 7 based in Pearl Harbor and on patrol in the North Pacific, were already moving into position to hit the target sites in the Aleutian Trench. For the first time since he had seen three hostile figures in red parkas walk toward him from out of an Antarctic storm, Mitch Webber felt the situation was under control. For once, all he had to do was sit back and watch.

The security doors opened and Cory walked in, a newfound bounce in her step. She was in another jumpsuit, but this one, finally, was her size, crisply pressed, and set off by a new *Sea Wolf* baseball cap—one of the souvenirs they had been given when the Nevada Rain had put down. At the time of the landing, with the craft straight down in hover mode, Webber had looked to the ground through his VAD visor and had seen at least ten MPs waiting at the side of the tarmac. His first thought was that his conversation with the President had meant nothing. But when he saw the flatbed truck near the MPs, loaded with rolled tarpaulins, Webber realized what the soldiers were there for—not to arrest him and Cory, but to secure the top-secret aircraft. Within two minutes of landing, the Nevada Rain was little more than a mound of canvas sheeting, surrounded by ten armed guards under strict orders to forget what they were guarding.

Cory paused to take in the room. It was like a relaxed version of NASA's mission control, with a dark gray carpet, pale blue walls, a seating area with conference tables set at the back under a low ceiling, then a forward area with ten monitoring consoles, each staffed by two sailors. On the far wall, the one that all the consoles faced, there were three large gas-plasma display screens arranged in a triptych. On them, the location of every USN ship and sub was tracked, along with the positions of ships from all other navies.

It was a secure room, Webber felt, nothing haphazard or temporary about it. The SEALs might be the upper echelon of the Navy's battlefield warriors, but the submariners were the pinnacle of its sea-based forces. If the business of this room had been anything other than war, he knew Cory would have found it comforting.

To maintain a calm mood himself, he was making a point of not watching the television screens that had been set up near the tables at the back. The wave was fewer than ten minutes from the Big Island of Hawaii. And almost as an afterthought, some networks were passing on reports of fighting breaking out between military units in parts of China.

Cory saw Webber sitting at a table near the back of the room, and came toward him.

"Did you get any sleep?" she asked. It had been two hours since they had seen each other. More than five hours since they had landed and briefed . . . just about the whole world, it had felt like to Webber. Starting with the President while in transit in the Nevada Rain, after Bailey had finally put an end to General Abbott, then working their way through the Joint Chiefs of Staff and the top officers of the USN, the Japanese Self-Defense Force, and the PLA Navy.

But Webber hadn't tried to sleep since then. "I'm afraid if I close my eyes, I won't wake up till Christmas." He noticed that her hair was different. It had a clean shine and curled attractively at the nape of her neck. "You look better. I mean, good. You know."

Cory took no offense. "I found the showers." She sat down two chairs over from Webber. They both stared ahead at the three displays, not at each other. "I think I used up all their hot water."

Webber looked over at one of the flat television screens. There was a graphic of China onscreen, showing stylized explosions near Beijing. The caption read AIRSTRIKES. But the sound was turned off. He didn't care. Not when he felt this tired. "So are we actually going to be able to do this?" he asked her.

Cory raised her eyebrows, as if not wanting to tempt the fates. "We've run Cerenkov's calculations, and the fracture zones and thrust faults he calls out are where he says they are. The Tomahawks all have GPS navigation, so hitting the right coordinates won't be a problem. So—if we get the speed and height readings we need in the next hour—there's no reason why we can't get the timing right, too." She held up both hands, fingers crossed.

Webber looked at her, seeing her as she had been five years ago, seven years ago, carrying a sign, handing out leaflets, keeping him up till dawn, sometimes by talking endlessly about the human assault on the environment. More usually, by other methods. Even when things had been at their worst between them, he had never once asked himself how it was he had fallen in love with her in the first place. But Cory then and Cory today were no longer part of the same continuum to him. "Even in my wildest dreams, I never imagined you helping the Navy call in nuclear strikes."

"Yeah, well, this is no dream, Mitchell. It's the nightmare your friends gave us."

So maybe she's not that different, Webber thought. Then the left-hand screen on the far wall ahead flashed a close-up thermal image of the south shore of Hawaii. Beside the MSNBC logo at the bottom of the screen, a countdown display showed 00:02:33 to contact.

"Can you believe the media? They're treating this like New Year's Eve," Cory said. She stood up. "I'm going to check out the readings." She started toward the monitoring consoles between them and the wall screens. But Webber knew the heart of the Navy's southeastern submarine command was not Cory's natural domain. So, though every muscle in his body protested his decision, Webber pushed himself up from the conference table and followed her.

One of the wall screens up ahead now showed the view from a remote camera that had been left at Ka Lae—South Cape—the southernmost part of Hawaii, and of the United States. Webber had seen the same shot a few minutes earlier. Then, ocean waves had been pounding large dark rocks.

Now, he saw only large dark rocks.

The ocean was gone.

It was time for the wave.

EVENT PLUS 35 HOURS

First came the winds. For 7,000 miles, a layer of air had been pushed ahead of the wave, laden with moisture, absorbing energy, serving as herald to the beast that followed.

On the southern tip of the island of Hawaii, the largest of the chain, that wind found the Kamoa Wind Farm. The flailing arms of the Mitsubishi windmills at first embraced the growing breeze, transforming it into power which no longer had users. The southern shores had been deserted by all except the lost, the deranged, and a dozen true believers in God's mysterious will who felt the promise of the millennium had finally reached them.

But then the windmill arms had reached their design limits and been hurled through the air like javelins, driven into the ground, shattering trees, and stampeding a small herd of frightened cows abandoned on the scrublands.

By then the ocean had retreated from the shores, leaving only the tide pools full and undisturbed.

The roar was louder here than it had been in Antarctic waters, amplified as it was by the warmer, moister air. And it grew louder still as the wave scaled the abrupt underwater slope of the Big Island.

For a moment, to the remote-control camera, to the carefully placed scientific instruments left by a Navy Sea King helicopter, and to the deluded believers who knelt and prayed, the wave seemed

408

to pause as it hung over the island. As if God had once more changed his mind.

But the steep angle of the underwater slope was such that at that southernmost tip of land, and only there, the full 200-mph fury of the climbing wave was deflected almost entirely into vertical movement.

A mile from shore, the wave was 300 feet high. At half a mile, it was 600 feet. And when the believers on their knees looked up, wondering why their God had forsaken them, their necks craned back to see the frothing edge of a wall of water more than 1,200 feet above them.

That wall collapsed so quickly they never saw it fall, the brief remainder of their lives a timeless moment of awe.

But to the east and west the wave did not pause. The shores of the island were like the wedge of a ship's prow and the wave curled away from either side, accelerating to 380 mph, pushing ahead of the arc to the east, moving toward the next islands in the chain.

On Hawaii's eastern shore, the wave raced inland and up Highway 11, leaving South Kona a memory. It plunged into petroglyph caves with such force that the rock walls exploded.

On the western shore, Papakolea Green Sand Beach vanished in the time it takes to speak its name. Kaalualu and Kaalela lost every building, every roadway, every clue that once two villages had ever existed at their sites. Civilizations had always clung to the edges of Hawaii, and now all traces of all the people who had made the shores of the island their home were erased for all time.

And just in case the evacuees to the north, or those who had found vantage points almost a mile up the slopes of Mauna Loa, thought they might escape the beast from the sea, the goddess Pele now awakened.

Less than eight minutes after the wave made landfall, Mauna Loa and Kilauea erupted together, spewing 100 million cubic yards of molten rock in the first half hour. Hawaii Volcanoes National Park became, simply, a single volcano as all the calderas within it filled and joined as one. Even Devastation Trail could not survive its own devastation. And the people and evacuees in Hilo, the Big Island's largest city, sheltered from the wave in a north-facing bay, soon learned that they were not sheltered from lava or fire or poisonous smoke.

The Big Island had taken thirty million years to rise above the waters of the Pacific.

The wave took twenty-three minutes to destroy it.

Honolulu and Pearl Harbor were 200 miles farther north than South Cape. But when the wave was finished with the Big Island, Honolulu and Pearl Harbor were only thirty-eight minutes away.

Farther east, Japan had three hours left. California, five.

The wave moved on.

ELEVEN

SUBGRU 5/BALLAST POINT, NAVAL SUBMARINE BASE, SAN DIEGO

Cory knew their last chance was the NASA tracking station at Hawaii's Kaena Point. It was two-thirds of the way up the southeastern shore of the Big Island, and the staff there had the expertise to deploy the ranging gear, both laser and Doppler, that she needed to complete Anatoly Cerenkov's calculations.

Three hours ago, the station crew had set up the two pieces of equipment, which looked little different from standard surveying instruments, on weighted tripods, aimed according to Cory's GPS directions. They had also left a small video camera, which transmitted an extreme-wide-angle view of the station, slightly ahead and to the right. The crew hoped that in its last second of operation, the camera might transmit a close-up record of the wave's impact with the station and its three massive satellite dishes. The record was to help determine the wave's full force on land—the next calculation that would have to be made.

The NASA staff had carefully checked out and tested the radio link between the camera and the ranging equipment to the station's main transmitter, then headed off on their evacuation run across Puna to Hilo.

The Kaena Point instruments had been providing constant, though unnecessary, data ever since. The essential readings that

411

Cerenkov's plan needed would come in the thirty seconds before the wave actually hit. So far, the camera showed only the typically choppy seas off the point. The station's white walls and white dishes were so bright in the sunlight, little detail showed.

When the wave had reached South Cape, the southernmost point of Hawaii, Cory and Webber stepped up behind the two sailors monitoring the Kaena tracking-station signal on one of ten monitor consoles in the forward section of the Ballast Point situation room. The news was not good. The South Cape ranging instruments set up and left there by Navy crews were down, toppled at least two minutes before impact by the unexpectedly high winds generated by the wave. For the want of a minute and a half's survival time, the instruments provided no data.

The TOPEX/POSEIDON readout on one of the three main screens on the wall facing the consoles gave the wave's initial impact speed, measured by the Jason-III satellite, at approximately 400 mph, plus or minus five percent. That meant the actual speed would fall within a 40-mile spread between 380 to 420 mph.

Cory frowned. She had to trim that range of observational error. The Navy had given her detailed maps from the U.S. Geographical Survey which supplied the exact numbers she needed for the depth of the water at every critical point along the wave's path to the shore. And the satellite-based infrared sensors the Navy used to search for enemy submarines had given her the vital sea-temperature readings she needed to determine the water's density in the key regions.

But on their own, those precise depth and temperature measurements were useless to her. She had to know the wave's speed to within two miles per hour—plus or minus 0.003 percent—and its height to within one foot. Without that critical level of accuracy, she would never be able to determine the wave's total energy content. And without that, she would *not* be able to plot the wave's approach off Japan and the U.S. West Coast with the accuracy Cerenkov required to confirm that his plan for stopping the wave would work. The data had to come from Hawaii, because the Hawaiian chain of islands were the last major landfall before Japan, and would be the first operational test of the plan.

As the Russian scientist had told Cory and Webber, their window of opportunity to precisely drop the seafloor at each key fracture-zone site was, at maximum, ninety seconds. He had emphasized to them both that there was no room for error. If the Navy set off their nuclear charges at the target sites too soon, the wave would accelerate as it gained energy from the tsunami caused by the seafloor drop. And if the charges dropped the seafloor too late, the wave would move on, unchanged, undiminished, toward the land.

Before Webber's brute force saved the world, Cory knew she would have to provide the numbers that would guide that force. The loss of the South Cape instruments meant the NASA station instruments at Kaena Point would have to come through. There wasn't enough time left to set up another pair of rangers to get the confirming data they needed.

Six minutes after South Cape was hit, the monitors began to show signs of a disturbance at Kaena Point.

A tense mood of anticipation now infected the command staff and technical specialists of Submarine Group 5, now Cory and Webber's allies against the wave. Cory couldn't help feeling the oddness of being in the camp of what she'd considered for so long the enemy. But these men and women who moved about the room in so purposeful a manner had accepted her presence and done all they could to assist her. Cory knew that she was changing and that, like it or not, Mitchell Webber was the agent of that change.

"Here it comes," one of the sailors said. Cory set aside personal reflections and concerns to concentrate on what she knew best, her work. *Just like Webber*, she thought, before focusing all her attention on her monitor.

One of the two sailors manning the console made an adjustment that put the video signal up on the large, right-hand display screen on the far wall of the situation room, and printed out the constantly updated stream of wave height and speed readings. For now, the wave height was at five feet, the velocity at ten miles per hour.

"This is going to work," Cory said, willing it to happen. Her hands gripped the back of the chair of the sailor in front of her.

The image of the tracking station suddenly vibrated. Webber leaned forward. "Is that wind?"

"Ground tremor," Cory said. The palms weren't moving. "Look at the trees." She knew the instruments' tripods were braced by sandbags and rocks. *A little bit of shaking is tolerable. I can correct for that.*

Then the palms began to flutter.

"This is it," Webber said.

Cory's nails dug into the chairback.

One of the sailors began to call out the change in ranging data. "We've got a wave speed of . . . *minus* forty miles an hour. Wave height of three inches."

Webber looked questioningly at her.

"Drawback," Cory explained. "The wave needs water to make up its mass. It's drawing it from the water ahead."

"What happened to the precursor wave? The little one?"

"That only happens in open ocean, where there's no friction—no obstacles. The surface water rides on top of the thermocline. Around these islands, the seabed slows the little wave down so the main event catches up."

"Hold it," the sailor said. "Wave speed of zero miles."

"End of drawback," Cory said. She could feel tension rise in the situation room as the Group 5 staff clustered around the monitors. "Here we go."

The rate of increase was astounding. The numbers on screen blurred as they advanced.

"Look at the acceleration," Cory said. "Two hundred miles. Two twenty . . ."

"Cory, the palm trees," Webber said. "The wave is going to—"

Cory saw it happen on screen, without believing it was possible. Two palm trees were uprooted at the same, precise instant. One tree flew out of range of the camera, the other cartwheeled madly past the camera to careen into one of three huge satellite dishes, each about forty feet across.

Knocked backward by the impact, the dish then rebounded with a snap that sent it sideways into the dish in the center of the array. The center dish, which had caught the growing gale like a wind sock, suddenly spun around to collide with the third.

The third had been aligned so it was facing almost straight up, like a giant bowl. Now it shuddered and then trembled, and then lifted off the ground like some alien mothership, and it skipped through the air directly toward—

The screen went dark and all data ended.

"*Shit!*" Cory didn't even need to play back the tape to know that the speed and height figures had not reached their maximum values.

At the other nine monitors, heads turned at Cory's reaction as she slapped the chairback in front of her, startling the sailor whose chair it was. He glanced back nervously, then hunched forward as if to put his back out of range.

Webber touched her shoulder. "Cory, Admiral Browne knows how critical these measurements are. He has helicopter crews at Pearl, ready to hang in front of this thing and get you the readings you need."

Cory stood, rigid, her hands fists at her sides.

"Not good enough. I need readings at impact. On the shore. And that's suicide."

Then Webber amazed Cory by having one of the few good ideas of his life that could make a difference in hers. She almost kissed him in her relief as she heard it. "So we ask the Admiral for *two* helicopters. They both land on the beach. The first crew flies back with the second. And they leave the first helicopter there with the ranging equipment for the wave."

Webber looked at her expectantly, obviously anticipating her praise.

"What are you waiting for?" she said. "Do it!"

Webber saluted her.

She punched his shoulder—it seemed the soldierly thing to do.

USSPACECOM/EARTH SURVEILLANCE CENTER/CHEYENNE MOUNTAIN

Bailey hadn't a clue what she was running on anymore, nerves, caffeine, or sheer momentum. The President had finally told her that she should take a break and turn over the rest of the communications links between the five navies—U.S., Japanese, Chinese, Canadian, and British—to Falcon.

The President also said he wasn't needed anymore, at least until he reached California, so there was no need for a middleman, i.e. Bailey. "I'm taking a break, Major. As your commander-in-chief, I'm ordering you to take one, too."

But for the second time that day, or days, or shift, Bailey had refused to obey an order, the first time from a two-star general, this time from the President—she was moving up in the world. Instead, she had gone off to the standby crew station, washed up, had a sandwich, then stretched out on a cot and closed her eyes.

For about five seconds.

All she could think was that she had been there for the beginning, so she was going to be there for the end. And if the President didn't like it, well, she'd just not vote for him again.

When she returned to her workstation less than an hour after leaving it, she found Huber there, filling out the shift reports.

"You really think that's necessary? Everything that happened here tonight—today?—was on CNN."

"I don't want to go home, and I certainly can't sleep," Huber said.

"Then how about I get you some tea?"

"You're my commanding officer."

"All right," Bailey said. "I'll make it coffee and chocolate cupcakes."

Huber put up no resistance.

Two hours had passed since then, with little to do but to catch up on paperwork and keep track of the wave's progress. Huber shared his concern about his sister on Hawaii with Bailey. None of his calls could get through the system. He told Bailey that his sister worked at the observatory at Mauna Kea, elevation 14,000 feet, one of the highest points on the island, so he was counting on her being safe. Bailey tried to reassure him by saying that if she had worked there, that would be where she would go during an evacuation. She gave his hand a squeeze then, returning his earlier gesture of much-appreciated support. *There was nothing more to it*, she emphasized to herself.

Then, together, they had watched the reports from the Big Island of Hawaii as the wave finally reached it. For Bailey, New Zealand had been bad enough, yet somehow easier to comprehend—one shore, one wave. But now the wave ripped along both sides of Hawaii, and then backsplashed on the northern shores. Bailey was beginning to think of the wave as a giant, voracious amoeba engulfing defenseless land and people as its prey. New Zealand had put up a fight and resisted, so it was damaged but victorious. Hawaii was simply swallowed and spit out like a stony pit.

And when the first aerial shots from the Air Force observation planes had come in, showing the eruptions beginning, Huber's pale, freckled skin had become even paler. Bailey knew what was tormenting him: There was no way to know if Mauna Kea was among the reborn volcanoes. There was no way to know what terrible price his sister might have paid to live in paradise.

It was after the wave had moved away from the Big Island, and just as it rolled across the Alenuihaha Channel toward Maui, that Bailey saw her alert-status light flash. The last person to contact her through that circuit had been the President. At once, she switched over to the DSCS satellite transponder, expecting to hear his voice again.

But, instead, she heard the deep, vibrant voice that had started her in all of this, as startling and as welcome as if an old friend had called. "Professor Cerenkov! How are you? *Where* are you?"

"Major Bailey, a pleasure to speak with you again. At the moment, I am in a rather noisy helicopter over a ghost town with empty streets, like a city of the dead, but instead it is Honolulu." Cerenkov was speaking too loudly, as if he were having trouble hearing her. Bailey pictured him in an ungainly flight helmet with a small microphone too far away from his face. "Captain Webber has requested you patch me through to him at SUBGRU Five— have I said that properly? SUBGRU Five? San Diego."

"I know the joint." Bailey hit the FLTSATCOM switch that took her from the twelve channels reserved for Air Force Nuclear Forces Command and Control to the ten channels reserved for Navy Operations. It was an automatic response, and as she made it, she checked the time display. "Professor, I hope you've got a full fuel tank. Honolulu is twenty minutes from wave contact."

"Ah, yes, but I am also only five minutes from the COMSUBPAC silo. I have little reason to worry."

Bailey had to agree with him. The complex of underground tunnels and blast doors that stretched deep beneath the Pearl Harbor Naval Reservation was the equal of Cheyenne Mountain's. The headquarters of the Pacific Command was considered so secure that it was the one key U.S. command and control center for which no mirror site existed. Even a direct nuclear strike against Pearl Harbor would not compromise the safety and security of the staff and equipment burrowed more than a thousand feet into the volcanic rock. America had been surprised at Pearl Harbor once. The lesson had been learned.

Bailey got an active receipt from SUBGRU 5, and an access inquiry from a communications specialist. "This is Major Bailey, U.S. Space Command, with a transmission for Captain Mitchell Webber." Webber was added to the circuit in seconds, obviously having been waiting for the contact. He was as pleased to hear Bailey as she was to hear him.

"Hey there, Major. I think we've got a lot of the old beer-drinkin' and bullshittin' to do when this is over."

Bailey would look forward to that. They had all done a lot of good work these past hours and days. "Only if the President is buying, Captain." But there was still more work to do before the mission was over. "I've got Dr. Cerenkov for you. He says he's in a helo over Honolulu. Is that right?"

Rey was on the circuit, too. "This is news to us, Major. Honolulu's our last solid-ground site for getting open-ocean speed and height readings on that thing. We asked for a Navy crew to go out, but the professor's not supposed to be with them. What's he doing there?"

"You'd better ask him," Bailey said. "Patching you through. Go ahead, Professor. You've got Dr. Rey and Captain Webber standing by."

"Dr. Rey? Are you there?"

"I'm here, Professor. But where are you?"

"I am over Fort Kamehameha." Bailey and Huber smiled at each other, hearing the Hawaiian name said with such a pronounced Russian accent. "We are setting the helicopters down on the runway built out in the sea. Do you know it?"

For her own reference, Bailey called up an ETEM of Honolulu on one of her displays. The city stretched along the entire eastern half of the southern coast of Oahu. Pearl Harbor was a trident-shaped indent at the city's eastern edge, right in the middle of the coastline. The runway Cerenkov referred to had been constructed for use by Honolulu International Airport. It ran east-west in the Keehi Lagoon, and would be hit dead on by the wave in . . . eighteen minutes. The professor was cutting this tight.

"I've got it on a map," Rey radioed back. "But you still haven't told us why you're out there."

"The crew needed the equipment I brought from my university. It is not quite the same as what you requested, so I will make the proper adjustments."

"But you've got two helicopters, right?" Webber asked.

"I have been told exactly what to do, Captain Webber. I have also been told that the main helicopter-silo blast doors at COMSUB-PAC are on standby. Thirty seconds after we land, we are to be untouchable."

"Copy that," Webber said. He sounded reassured and Bailey

418

knew why. Like the Cheyenne Mountain blast doors, the first level of aviation-asset protection at Pearl were three-foot-thick silo covers.

Now Rey came back. "Well, just keep it moving, Professor. Tell the pilot to set down anywhere on that runway, aim the rangers due south, and get the hell out."

"No need to worry, my dear. From this height, I can see the wave on the horizon. Quite distant. A striking dark blue line, from edge to edge."

"Just land, will you? And let me know when you're down," Rey said.

Bailey heard Cerenkov grunt and complain. Then, after about a minute had passed: "I am now down. The wind is picking up. It is a bit rough."

"Is the helicopter oriented so the ranging instruments are facing south?"

Bailey wasn't certain how difficult or time-consuming the professor's task was supposed to be, but she could hear the urgency building in Rey.

"The copilot is opening the side door," Cerenkov said. Then the background noise changed. Now Bailey could hear wind cutting in and out of the microphone's threshold level. "The door is open. I am activating the scanners." Bailey heard the scientist breathing hard, as if he were turning something, operating equipment. "Doppler ranging is on . . ." More heavy breathing, more grunts of exertion. "Laser is on and aligned. Are you receiving data?"

Bailey waited, as eager for Rey's response as was Cerenkov.

"Negative, Professor. There are no readings. Are the power leads hooked up?"

Cerenkov sounded baffled. "Yes. I double-checked everything before we loaded it onto the craft. Power leads, backup batteries, VHF antenna, lens cover, tripod brack—"

Bailey cut in. "Doctor, am I reading this right? You're trying to transmit instrument data on VHF?"

"*Da.* Yes. I use these in the field all the time for tracking surface currents."

Bailey saw the problem, even without being able to see it. "Professor, *where* are you broadcasting to?"

"There's a tall tower at the airport."

Bailey found it on the ETEM map. "If your instruments are facing the water, and the receiving tower is behind you at the airport, the helicopter fuselage is blocking the signal."

Webber joined in. "She's right, Professor. I should have seen it. You're using line-of-sight equipment. Bailey—is there any way he can patch his gear through the helo's HF and use the exterior antenna?"

Bailey felt the first intimation of panic. "Captain, there's always a way. But we're fourteen minutes from impact. I don't know his equipment. I don't even know what kind of helo he's in."

"Professor," the captain said quickly. "Haul those instruments onto the runway and set them up so you can see the tower behind you."

"No!" Rey said. "They have to be anchored. Otherwise, we'll lose them like at Kaena Point."

"Dr. Rey," Cerenkov said. "My pilot is showing me heavy equipment boxes. They're metal. We can use them to brace the equipment." Bailey again heard the sound of strained and irregular breathing. She could visualize the series of actions he must be making: jumping down from the landed helo, hoisting and setting down boxes, lifting up and carrying his equipment. Then his audio went dead.

"Major Bailey?" Rey asked. "Is Dr. Cerenkov still there?"

"I'm guessing he's switching over to the second helo, Dr. Rey. We've still got twelve minutes. He's probably in a Sea King or a Huey, so worse comes to worst, his pilot can chop up to five thousand feet and hang tough till the wave passes. They've got a good safety margin there."

"Hello? Major Bailey? Dr. Rey? Can you hear me now?" the Russian scientist asked.

"Fill us in, Professor," Webber said.

"I have the equipment braced in line of sight of the tower. I'm switching it on . . . yes?"

"Yes!" To Bailey, Rey's response was so abrupt, she sounded as if she had been shot.

Then Rey continued. "I've got it, Dr. Cerenkov. Range *and* speed."

"Very good." Bailey could tell that something had startled or excited the professor. He seemed to be very out of breath now. "I can see the wave on the horizon now, from ground level. It is quite a—"

Webber cut in. "Get *out* of there, Professor. We can watch it on the news."

Cerenkov's increasingly labored speech and impaired breathing told Bailey the professor was quite properly taking the captain's advice. "I'm getting into the second helicopter, now, Captain." His next words seemed to indicate that he was talking to the helo crew. "That goes there? All right. I'm in."

Bailey heard static building that made the professor's continuing on-the-spot coverage hard to hear. "Dr. Rey, Captain Webber, I am strapped in. We're starting up the helicopter. Oops. Big bump. And we're up!"

Bailey heard cheers and clapping. *Probably from the San Diego base.* She smiled over her shoulder at Huber. Confirming her guess, Rey then added, "Good work, Professor. I'll talk to you when—*oh, God, not now!*"

Webber's question was the same as Bailey's. "Cory, what is it?"

But Cerenkov answered, his agitation evident as he spoke to all of them, and his pilot. "I can see it. The force of the rotors . . . we have knocked over the rangers. Go down! Go down! This will just take a minute! I can see how to brace it!"

"Eight minutes!" Bailey said, raising her voice. "Professor—tell the pilot he'll have to climb! There's no time to make it back to Pearl!"

"I'll tell him! We're down again! Very windy!"

With the professor's breath coming and going in noisy bursts, Bailey realized he must already be out of the helo and running full-out across the tarmac. She covered her microphone with her hand and turned to Huber. "Get to another station. Tell COMSUBPAC the helo won't be back until after the wave has passed. They've got to shut the silo or they'll lose half the base!"

Huber was a streak of light heading for the first available work-station on the floor.

"Talk to me, Professor," Bailey said.

But as soon as she did, she heard an odd flatness in his voice, all the tension of the previous exchanges gone from it. "I am afraid there is no longer much to say."

"Professor! What'd you find!" Rey was almost shouting.

"One of the cases slipped, my dear. The tripods are broken. They were only wood."

Bailey saw the time readout. Five minutes. She spoke sharply, decisively. "That's it, Professor. Get on that helo now! Tell the pilot he's only got five minutes to get you to five thousand feet."

No answer. "Professor?" Bailey repeated, wondering why she wasn't hearing anything from Rey or Webber.

"I would consider it a personal favor, Major, if you would tell the authorities that I was the one who instructed my helicopter pilot to take off now."

"I'll do no such thing! Now you just get on that helo yourself, Professor!"

"I cannot, Major Bailey. Dr. Rey and Captain Webber must have these readings, or they will never know if my plan will work."

Bailey was stunned. Four minutes. "Dr. Rey! Captain Webber! Tell the professor to get back on the helo!"

But the only voice she heard was Cerenkov's. "Are you receiving the data, Dr. Rey?" His tone was gentle, not urgent at all, as if he had all the time in the world.

Now Bailey could hear tears thickening Rey's voice. "Yes . . . I am . . . they're exactly what we need. . . ."

"Ah, good," Cerenkov said. "I see the helicopter taking off. As I am unable to move my hands to wave, you will tell them thank you for me, please?"

"Webber here, Professor. I've already told them."

Bailey stared up at Huber as he returned to her platform. The professor had been left behind, alone, on the runway. There was nowhere he could go. No way he could escape.

Three minutes.

"I would like you all to know I have enjoyed America very much," Cerenkov said. For Bailey, there was no fear in that quiet voice, only acceptance and determination. No indication that a dead man was speaking. "Sometimes, I do not think those of you who were born here can appreciate it the way I do."

"You're right," Webber said.

"How am I doing, Dr. Rey?"

". . . perfect . . . perfect . . ."

Cerenkov continued as if he were just making conversation, under no time pressure at all. "Talking to the President today, that was a very good thing. Will you tell Betsy Paullina that? Sometimes . . . sometimes I think she is embarrassed by me. But that is always the way for old fathers and young daughters. You let her know that I told you that. That I understand. That I love her. And her mother. Deborah. Let her know that . . . of everything this country has given to me . . . she is what I treasure most. . . . Dr. Rey? Are you still receiving?"

Bailey felt the sting of her own tears.

Ninety seconds.

". . . still receiving . . ."

"I can see it at Diamond Head. The spray is . . . I can't see where it ends . . . I . . . I don't know if you can hear anything, but there is a most unusual sound building. Subsonic, I believe. Major Bailey, you must have special equipment for such things. Can you register subsonics?"

"I'm . . . I'm not set up for that."

"No matter. But look into it. It's very large now. More than three hundred feet is my estimate. Accelerating, too. The sound is quite remarkable . . . and . . . do you have the readings, Dr. Rey?"

"I have them, Professor."

"There's an enormous drawback now—to my right. I believe it's—yes—I can see enormous ships rolling over in the water! I believe Pearl Harbor is being drained! I just felt a tremor in the ground now. It feels like a . . . sound . . . I can't quite hear. Something I've heard before? There's the wall! Oh, how can I tell you? The face of it—almost completely vertical—rivers of water moving *across* water . . . the *color* . . . it's getting higher . . . I had *no* idea . . . it's so—"

There was no fade out. No static.

Just an end.

Webber's voice was barely audible. "Did you get what you needed?"

Rey's sounded even fainter. "I got it."

That was when it all caught up to her. Bailey put her head down on her table and wept. With the death of Anatoly Cerenkov, the deaths of more than one million people before him suddenly had become very real.

She felt Huber's presence behind her. His firm hand on her shoulder. She raised up her hand to his.

He took it, covering hers completely with his.

If it was more than a gesture of support, she no longer cared if it offended propriety.

For this moment, whatever it was, it was just what she needed.

EVENT PLUS 36 HOURS

For the second time, Pearl Harbor died.

Once it had been a refuge, a safe harbor for America's warships to protect them from storms and winds and enemy action. Then in one day in 1941, six of those ships had been sunk, twelve others damaged, almost 350 planes destroyed, and 3,581 fighting men and women killed or injured. On that day, the attack had come from the sky.

On this day, it came from the sea itself.

First, the harbor began to empty. As if low tide had come and would never stop, the harbor's water was caught in the violent drawback that fed the wave, turning it into a focused torrent that sliced through the banks of the entrance channel where it emptied into Mamala Bay.

The first casualties were the abandoned glass-topped boats that served the tourists, their slender ropes and cables snapping one after another as the pleasure craft were swept up in currents moving at speeds of up to eighty miles an hour. Most of these lesser vessels collided with each other or with sections of small docks torn loose when their moorings had buckled. Most would never make it to the open sea except as splintered bits of wood and fiberglass.

But after the terrible lesson learned at Pago Pago, the large ships had been well secured. Emptied of cargo so they would ride high, freighters had been turned to decrease the area of the sea's grip, and to offer the least resistance to the flow of the water. And the warships had been evacuated and were now grouped in the shelter in Kaneohe Bay on Oahu's north shore.

One warship, though, remained behind. It had not moved for more than sixty years. Until this day, when it was liberated by the wave that pulled at it, stirred it, and called it back to the sea.

Pearl Harbor drained and, as those new and terrible currents rose, the U.S.S. Arizona rose with them from her grave, threw off the alabaster memorial that straddled her, and with her dead still aboard her, one more time, one last time, she set out to sea where she belonged.

That battered, corroded, but still proud ship was buffeted in the channel, being carried south by the last surge of the drawback, when the wave reached the offshore runway of Honolulu International Airport and claimed its creator.

Three-tenths of a second later, the wave—this time known to be traveling at 403.6 miles per hour—met the harbor surge, and the spray from that collision climbed more than 2,000 feet into the blue sky, carrying with it the spinning, glistening shards of the shattered Arizona, her long-delayed voyage at last at an end.

Pearl Harbor had drained in just under three minutes. But now, it refilled in less than forty seconds. And still the wave did not stop.

It pulsed over the narrow confines of the channel to strip the hangars of Hickham Air Force Base from their foundations. Next it sprayed across the Naval Reservation, exploding white wood-frame buildings as it scooped away the gardens. Then it pounded on the hidden blast doors of the Pacific Command Center with such power that, in the air of the tunnels and chambers sealed behind them, a pressure wave was born.

At the same time, the wave also found the underwater doors that led to the sub pens of Pearl Harbor, built in the forties, expanded in the fifties, hardened against nuclear war in the two decades following.

And, in all that time, nowhere in their specifications did the designers of those pens imagine the double attack that now imperiled them. Like Cheyenne Mountain, the facility had been built to be sealed. Thus, as the second pressure wave formed at the other, underwater end of the buried command center, there was nowhere for the air within the center to go.

From opposite ends of the sealed center, the two pressure waves rushed toward each other. And the result of their meeting was as if two depth charges had exploded simultaneously on either side of a submarine deep in the sea.

The walls of the Pacific Command Center remained intact. By deliberate design, not even a nuclear bomb could destroy them. And that rigidity now allowed a concussion wave to pass through the center, bursting the eardrums and rupturing the alveoli in the lungs of every person who had sought safety there.

The wave was finished with Honolulu in less than ninety seconds. It was finished with the island of Oahu in less than five minutes.

But by that time, every person in the U.S. Navy Pacific Command Center had died, gasping, flailing, suffocated by the explosive collapse of their lungs. The death toll within those unbroken walls was 4,800 naval personnel, and their families.

Japan would be next in two hours, twelve minutes.

California, two hours after that.

Another lesson had been taught.

The wave moved on.

TWELVE

SUBGRU 5/BALLAST POINT NAVAL SUBMARINE BASE, SAN DIEGO

"They've made it official," Cory said. "They've lost CINCPAC."

Webber was numb. He heard that pronouncement as if it had something to do with someone else, somewhere else. At dawn, 1.3 million people had lived in Hawaii, awakened the morning after Thanksgiving wondering what the day would bring. Now, when the satellite images of the altered shorelines had been assessed, when the volcanoes had been counted, when the wave had passed . . . the unofficial estimate was 400,000 dead.

Four hundred thousand people. Families. Children. Civilians with lives still to live. Civilians who believed their government knew how to protect them, that their navy knew how to fight for them. Who believed they would be *safe*.

Cory had found him in the study off Admiral Sweetman's office, two of its walls lined with bookcases, the other two paneled with oak, antique naval prints the only decorations. Old Ironsides, cannons blazing. The *Monitor* and the *Virginia* beneath fiery clouds, squaring off. A simple three-rigger, cresting a wave, a splendid sunrise captured in the spray from her bow.

"Mitchell?"

Webber opened his eyes. Cory was standing beside him, by the sturdy brown leather couch where he lay stretched out. He had

427

turned off the harsh overhead lights, leaving only the softer, amber glow of wrought-iron floor lamps that had probably served in some admiral's office in World War II. But the door to the corridor was half-open behind her and she was framed against the brighter light.

Webber gazed up at her, at her silhouette caught that way. He thought of the sunrise in the old-fashioned print.

"You okay?" Cory asked.

Webber sat up too quickly, rubbed at his face. "Sure." He swayed back slightly, still feeling the floor move as if he were on board a ship or airborne. "Everybody?" he asked. "At CINCPAC?"

Cory sat sideways on the high arm of the couch, the fingers of one hand stroking its smooth surface. She didn't look at him directly. "Bailey's working on it. As far as she can tell, all the lines of communication are open and the automated systems are still working. But it doesn't look like there's anyone moving down there. I think there's a video feed from one control room. It's showing bodies on the floor. Pressure burst, they're calling whatever killed everyone. Something to do with concussion."

Webber leaned forward to put his head down lower than his knees. He'd need a clear head to deal with the rest of this mission. "What did Tom Brokaw say the record was? Eight hundred and thirty thousand in some earthquake in China? We must be getting close to that."

"This isn't a natural disaster."

Webber's jaw tightened. *No argument there*, he thought. It still was almost impossible to conceive how anyone, let alone someone like the Nick Young he'd known—thought he'd known—could deliberately set in motion something that would kill so many civilians. Webber lifted his head to look at the coffee table before him. On it he had laid out the photos of the five dissident Chinese generals who had revived Cerenkov's plan. Dossiers were clipped to each photo. CNNI had already reported that three of the generals had been killed in the unexplained fighting that had broken out in China. A fourth had been arrested as soon as the fighting had stopped. Only one was still missing.

Beside the photos, to one side, was Nick Young's file, Nick's photograph on top of it. Admiral Sweetman had asked Webber to check it against those of the generals. Nick's mother had been Taiwanese, and Sweetman said she was being investigated, along with every other piece of information in Nick's file, to try and find the point at which his life intersected with the generals'. The Pentagon, in particular, wanted to know how and when Nick's loyalties had changed. Sweetman had asked Webber to study the generals' faces, to see if there was anything . . . familiar.

Webber had flagged the photo of Wei Jincheng—the one general who was yet to be captured. The man was too young to be Nick's father. But was there some resemblance there? An uncle? A brother? Could the answer be so simple?

Webber suddenly remembered that while he'd been occupying himself with the causes of the wave disaster, Cory was still focused on the consequences of what Nick Young had begun in Antarctica. "Are the numbers working?" he asked her.

"We'll know for sure in about an hour, but they fit the satellite data, so I'm confident I . . . he . . . got us what we needed."

Webber considered Cory's downturned face in the half-light from the corridor, the warm light of the study. More than the world had changed in these past two days. And like the world, some things would never be returned to what they had been before.

It had been less than forty-eight hours since he had walked into the infirmary at McMurdo Station and found Cory there, wrapped in her blue blanket like a diminutive Caesar, the last person he expected in the last place he ever expected her to be. But the way he felt now, that meeting could have happened in a lifetime lived a century ago.

"Are *you* okay?" he asked. The best defense was always a counteroffense.

Her dark eyes were shadowed, unreadable. "You would have done the same thing, wouldn't you?"

He didn't answer. She knew the answer.

"Stayed on the runway like that," she went on. "Steadying the equipment. Making sure we got the numbers. Watching it come for you."

"Cory, why are you asking me this?"

"Those sailors out there, all those people in the situation room, why did they sign up to *die* for their country?"

"It's part of the deal they chose to make. They found something worth dying for."

"That still doesn't explain Dr. Cerenkov, or—" A sob caught in her throat, unexpected, quickly suppressed. "Why did he choose to die?"

Webber looked again at the photograph of Nick Young. "Maybe to save something he believed in so much he was willing to do anything to keep it safe. That wave was Cerenkov's monster, and it threatened everything he loved."

"So what about you, Mitchell? Don't tell me anything that's classified. I just want to understand your deal. When did you decide which side to fight on?"

Webber held his hands out before him, checking himself as he might after combat, looking for blood, assessing his condition. Then he lowered his hands until they rested flat on the table before him, just touching Nick Young's file. Something inside him relaxed. Somehow it was the right time.

"A couple of years ago, there was a . . . a country that was not our friend. And it was getting weapons, jet fighters, from . . . someplace we just couldn't figure out. Good fighters. With the right pilots, they could take out ours, one to one.

"So we decided we were going to get one of those fighters. Sneak in, hotwire it, bring it back home. When we took it apart, we'd be able to tell who was building them. Then we could cut off the supply."

"And you were the pilot."

Webber nodded. "The SEALs had tried things like that before. Half the time the pilot got killed before he reached whatever asset they were after. So the Navy started putting some pilots through SEAL training. Cut their losses considerably. Only a quarter of the SEAL pilots died."

Webber studied his hands. He remembered the desert heat. Even at night, it had been 110°. "There were six of us. All SEALs. Two of us, pilots. Came ashore from a sub. Took us two days to get to . . . to where the plane was. The third night, we got rid of the local clothes, bypassed the wired fence, got into the compound. We could see the planes there, the fighters, in concrete bunkers. Just waiting for us.

"And then this guard got me. She put a gun in my back." Webber shook his head at his innocence that night. "I was standing *up*, using a nightscope to figure out which one of the fighters was more likely to be ready for takeoff.

"So I turn slowly, hands up, knowing I know twelve different ways to drop whoever it is thinks they've got me. And I see this skinny kid. A girl. Fifteen, tops. Foot shorter than I am. Her rifle's got sand on it. It probably won't fire. And then—it all goes so perfectly—it's as if I'm in a dream where everyone else is stuck in tar and I'm the Silver Surfer flying through space.

"The back of my left hand deflects the rifle to the left as my right hand comes in under her chin, I'm shifting my weight as if I'm in slo-mo and . . . her gun hits the tarmac, doesn't even go off. She's down so fast, she doesn't even get a chance to shout for help." Webber saw every move again.

"You killed her?" Cory asked.

"No," Webber said. "I . . . pull my right hand back, my left drops to my knife, and her . . . wrap, her burnoose comes off and I have it in my hand and she's lying flat on her back on the tarmac, eyes wide, scared out of her mind, and I look at her and I realize there's no way this kid should be out here. Some guy she couldn't even vote for put her out on that airfield. She still has to finish school, have boyfriends, a job, kids, and . . . I'm thinking all this even as I hear the rest of the team move up behind me.

"And I figure, the hell with my training. I'll just cut off her air, knock her out, tie her up, and then go get what I came for.

"And then the captain's beside me and he says, Cap her. And while I'm putting my knife back in the scabbard I turn to him and I say, Already got it covered.

"And then the kid pulls out this huge forty-five and she shoots him right in the face." His memory replayed the flash of the gun, the explosion of blood.

"I was next," he said. "I saw her eyes. She didn't care who I was or why I hadn't killed her, she was going to pull that trigger."

"Nick was the other pilot," Cory said.

"He shot her straight in the mouth. Guaranteed destruction of the brainstem, he said. Stops the nerve impulse from tightening the finger on the trigger even after death."

And that's where Webber's picture-perfect memory ended. What followed had been panic and confusion, the terrible knowledge that he'd compromised the team, the mission. The other guards had heard the gunshots—there was a firefight. Lieutenant Estevanovich, Lieutenant-Commander Pantigoso—they didn't make it off the airfield. "But I got away with the Fulcrum . . . you didn't hear that—the fighter jet. Forty minutes after the kid was going to kill me, I was back in friendly territory.

"Our radio operator got his leg shot off. Nick carried him four days across the desert, through enemy patrols. Told me they ate scorpions for their water content."

Webber paused to rub the tops of his thighs, to ease the stiffness in his leg muscles.

"Everything was different after that. I was different." Webber looked over at the *Monitor* and the *Virginia*, the two ironclads trapped in their eternal battle on the print. A battle that neither had won. "But you already knew what I was like. That's why you gave me that ultimatum: Quit the Navy or quit us."

The silence seemed endless to Webber. Then Cory said, "I only knew you and I were different, Mitchell." She reached down and took both of his hands in hers, pulling him to his feet. "If it had been me hanging on to you and Johnny, I wouldn't have let go, and we'd have died with everyone else at McMurdo. No one would have known the wave was coming or what it was until it was too late." She looked at the photos on the coffee table. "And the wrong side would have won."

There was a knock on the door. A young commander stood there, leaning tentatively through the study door. "Captain Webber?" the young woman asked. "Dr. Rey? They've made contact with the *Red Dawn*, and they're ready for you."

"Think it's time to see if we can do the right thing, together?" he asked Cory.

"Mitchell, that's something you knew a long time ago."

THIRTEEN

SUBGRU 5/BALLAST POINT NAVAL SUBMARINE BASE, SAN DIEGO

When she entered the situation room, Cory was surprised by the number of people packed into it—the seating section at the back now had extra chairs and each one was filled. Then her attention was caught by the number of men she saw who were wearing civilian suits, along with a few women in ordinary business outfits. The naval technicians were all in uniforms—dark slacks or skirts, white shirts with rank insignia. The officers were easy to identify because they all wore jackets. But who the civilians were, Cory had no idea. So she asked Webber.

"Spooks," he said. "We're about to see what the actual capabilities of the Xia- and Tzu-class boomers are." He anticipated her next question. "Those are the two types of Chinese nuclear submarines that the PRC government has committed to this. The suits are defense analysts, engineers, war gamers . . . people who want to know if their estimates of the subs have been correct."

Cory didn't bother to say anything. She knew Webber could read the look on her face. At this moment, in an unprecedented act of international cooperation, five navies had combined their forces in the defense of the North Pacific. Yet just in case, she knew, plans were already being made to take what was learned today for use against China in the future. What did it matter if a person like Webber did the right thing, if the system never would?

The young commander who had summoned Cory and Webber escorted them to one of the front consoles in the forward section, just to the left of the three large wall screens. She indicated the chair for Cory and helped her slip on a small headset. Webber took the chair beside her.

On one of the console screens, Cory saw a countdown timer. It had just reached ten minutes. She heard a buzz of static in her earphone, then realized the lighting had changed in the room. She looked up to see the new images on the three-screen wall display.

The main display on the left side held what she now recognized as an ETEM map of the Philippine Sea, showing the Chinese coastline north from Taiwan, up to the top of the Japanese island of Honshu. But the land areas were off to the left and to the top of the map. Most of the depicted area was a black expanse of nothing—the Pacific Ocean, obviously—broken by a scattering of small colorful triangles, squares, and circles.

Two yellow X's pulsed in the center of the screen, and from their location relative to the Japanese coast, Cory knew they marked the first of Cerenkov's target sites intended to shield the key population centers in China, Korea, and Japan. Cerenkov's Icefire study had predicted that if a large enough nuclear explosion was set off at each site at the same time, then the 300-mile-long section of seafloor that ran between the two sites would collapse approximately eighteen inches into the Ryukyu Trench. And if those explosions were set off at the exact right time—just as the wave approached that section of the trench—then the resulting downward displacement of the water over the collapsing seafloor would act like a sponge to soak up the energy of the wave.

If Anatoly Cerenkov's calculations were correct, and if Cory's measurements were accurate, within ninety seconds of the explosions, a 300-mile-wide section of the wave arc would simply disappear.

Cory heard a familiar voice in her headset. "Dr. Rey? Are you on the circuit?"

"Hi, Major Bailey. You keeping everyone on their toes?"

"They don't need me, Doctor. I've got the President on the other line and he's just given the crews a pep talk you wouldn't believe. Hold on, now, I'm going to put you through to Chief Petty Officer

Braun. She's our Navy interpreter on the *Red Dawn*. She'll give you the blow-by-blow so you can confirm the launch times."

Cory was picking up the lingo. "Copy that, Major. I'm standing by." She caught Webber's attention and pointed to the leftmost wall screen. "Which one's the *Red Dawn?*"

She jerked forward in surprise as someone else leaned close to her and whispered, "Try the triangle." Easing behind her to take a seat on the other side of Webber, Admiral Hector Sweetman smiled at her reaction, brilliant white teeth startling against his dark olive skin. "Sorry, Dr. Rey, I was just sneaking in for a front-row seat."

He nodded to Webber. "Captain. Good to have you aboard." Then he pointed out to Cory and Webber the red triangle midway between the two target sites, about one hundred miles closer to Japan. "That's the *Red Dawn*. The flagship," the admiral said. "Her captain will be coordinating the launches from the *Long March*, on the eastern site, and from the *Soft Wind* on the western site."

Then the admiral pointed to the middle screen. There was a new display there, also a map, but made up of smeared gray and white streaks, very impressionistic. "Now, that's a near-realtime sonar scan, it probably runs about thirty, fifty seconds behind what's actually going on, and it's made up of returns from at least a thousand sonar buoys we've dumped from helicopters out there, our own sub listening net, and active returns from all the ships we have in the area. You can see the *Red Dawn* is that white smear. And left and right of it are the other two."

Cory saw the smears the admiral had indicated. She also saw that the third screen looked like a thermal map of the same area of the ocean, though the temperature zones were long and narrow and didn't seem to make sense. "How about that one?" she asked.

"Well, that's so top-secret you shouldn't even be looking at it," Sweetman said. "But since you're part of the family now, that's ocean surface displacement. In a nutshell, it's a very fine-resolution, synthetic-aperture radar scan. The computer calculates wave movement, then subtracts it to create a mathematically-flat ocean surface. And then the distortions that are left—all those lines and curves— are the upward displacement that a submarine causes when it moves under the water. That's measured in millimeters, but the trails last for hours."

Cory was amazed as she realized that the streaks on the map indicated submarine movements. She guessed there were at least fifty. Though there were no streaks below 20°N. She hoped that that meant the computers weren't able to adjust for the passage of the wave, and *not* that no submarine had survived it.

"No wonder the Navy always know where every sub is," she said to the admiral.

"Ah, but the *Navy* discovered that technique by accident. Some meteorologists didn't understand what they were seeing when they analyzed high-resolution SAR data from a satellite mapping waves and currents. When they asked the Navy for advice, someone smart over in Interpretation realized the satellite was picking up our subs and the Soviets'. I believe then the Navy made the university shut the satellite down, by claiming an attitude thruster had malfunctioned."

"But they've been broadcasting SAR images of the ocean on all the news channels to show the wave. Everyone's got the technology now."

"Well, now, Doctor, that's because Navy computers process all the high-resolution data first, and digitally delete the subs. In fact, that's one of the reasons the Navy funds so much weather-imaging research, so we can see the data first. Of course—you didn't hear *any* of this from me."

"Dr. Rey," Major Bailey's voice interrupted, "I am patching you through to CPO Braun."

Cory touched her headset to let the admiral know that she had an incoming call.

A young woman's voice now came in, with the flattened vowels that suggested a Boston origin. "Is this Dr. Rey?"

"Hello, CPO Braun. How's everything where you are?"

"Hectic, ma'am. I got chopped out two hours ago, lowered in a boson's chair and, well, it's my first time on a sub, and I never thought it would be a Chinese one."

Cory could relate to that. "How come it's your first time?"

"Well, ma'am, they needed someone who could translate Chinese and Japanese and English. And . . . almost everyone else at the naval liaison office was out of town for the weekend."

"And you can do all that? Translate those languages?"

"It's sort of what I'm good at, ma'am. I have a knack for it, my mother always said."

Cory held her hand over her microphone, looked over at Webber and Admiral Sweetman, who were deep in conversation. "Why do we need a Japanese interpreter?"

"The Chinese have the nukes," the admiral said, "but the Japanese have detailed seafloor charts for the area. There're Japanese navigators on all those Chinese subs."

Knowing the long history of mutual distrust between the two Asian nations, Cory was struck by the way in which they were working together to respond to the wave crisis. Maybe there would be hope for the world after the wave.

"I think they're ready, Dr. Rey," the young translator said in her ear. "I'm going to be giving you the back-and-forth between the captain—that's Captain Ning—and a Mr. Hito—he's the senior Japanese official aboard. The captain is saying that he is ready to begin the three-minute countdown on his sister ships. He would like you to confirm the timing of the detonations."

Cory remembered Webber's comment. *A director of Earthguard calling in a nuclear strike.*

There were still no storms in the area, no unusual temperature variations, nothing to affect the calculations. The calculations themselves were on the console monitor in front of Cory, set out in cells just like a spreadsheet. Cerenkov's equation ran at the top. Below it were the constantly updated satellite measurements of the wave arc rushing for the target sites, their values refined by the data adjustments derived from the absolute measurements the Russian scientist had bought with his life on the Honolulu runway.

This is it, Professor, Cory thought, then spoke clearly and precisely into her headset's microphone. "CPO Braun, please tell the captain that I have confirmed the timing."

Cory heard the young translator speak in Chinese, then: "Captain Ning says . . . start the three-minute countdown. And he says, Thank you, Dr. Rey."

Cory saw that her own countdown timer was indicating seven minutes until the detonations. The four-minute difference was the travel time for the warheads. "What exactly are those two subs going to be launching?" she asked Admiral Sweetman.

"They haven't been that forthcoming," the admiral said. "We're assuming they'll be CSS-N-5s. What they call the Julang-3 submarine launched missile—Julang! Would you believe it means 'Giant Wave,' of all things? But in a missile launch, they'd have to allow time for the warhead to sink to the right depth before detonating, and they haven't done that, so we think they might be launching nuclear torpedoes. And as far as we know, they don't have those in the two-kiloton range."

Cory nodded her head back at the suits. "Which is why all the spooks, right?"

The admiral grinned. "Very good, Dr. Rey. You've been paying attention."

Webber grinned, too, but said nothing to expose the source of her insight.

Cory turned back to her monitor to make certain that no numbers changed unexpectedly.

The next two minutes were slow, tense, and uneventful. Cory passed the time to find out more about CPO Olivia Braun, discovering she was twenty-one and had never had to work at learning languages. In addition to Chinese, including both the Cantonese and Mandarin dialects, and Japanese, she was fluent in French and Spanish, was understandable in Farsi and German, and could handle basic communications in eight other languages. Pursued by the Navy, along with every other military service and a dozen corporations, CPO Braun had chosen the Navy and she loved her new Japanese posting. And she was coming home for Christmas, to Boston, where she was sure her boyfriend, Ben, was going to ask *the* question.

Cory was just wishing Braun luck when the young woman interrupted her. "Hold a minute, ma'am. The sonar officer is talking to the captain."

As Cory strained to hear what was being said on the *Red Dawn*, she was suddenly aware of Major Bailey's voice on the situation room's speakers. "This is U.S. Space Command. We have a confirmed loss of signal on the *Long March*. I say again—"

Cory felt Webber's hand on her shoulder as he turned her to look at the middle sonar screen. There was a billow of white near the eastern target site. "What is it?"

"An explosion! A fucking explosion!"

Cory heard the background conversations in the situation room pick up in volume. She cupped her hand to her headset earphone. "Olivia? Did you hear that? The sonar display shows an explosion near the *Long March*."

"That's what the sonar officer is saying to Captain Ning. He's not . . . he's not hearing the *Long March* anymore. . . ."

Webber turned to Admiral Sweetman and spoke sharply. "Sir, there's a hostile sub out there! Tell the *Soft Wind* to launch! Tell them to launch now! Get the *Red Dawn* ready to fill in!"

Now CPO Braun was saying something that Cory couldn't hear. "I'm sorry, Olivia, what was that?"

Again the CPO's words were drowned out by a chorus of shocked moans from the situation room. Cory looked up to see another white bloom at the *Soft Wind*'s position.

"They've got the *Soft Wind*," CPO Braun was saying. "They've got both submarines . . . explosions . . . Dr. Rey—the missiles did not launch. The captain wants you to know . . . the missiles did not launch."

"There!" someone shouted from the back. "It's a displacement trace!"

Another voice called out, "But where's the sonar?"

"Mitchell, what's going on?"

"Torpedoes." Webber spoke tersely, eyes fixed on the wall screens. "The two Chinese subs were *taken out*. The surface-displacement data shows torpedo traces, so we know they were down there, but there's no sonar trace."

"Dr. Rey!" CPO Braun's voice blared in Cory's headset. "Captain Ning is preparing to launch two missiles at the target sites . . . he needs an update because . . . because they will impact from the ocean's surface. . . . Mr. Hito says . . . the first subs were supposed to launch torpedoes . . . now we need to calculate the delay before . . . setting off the warheads. . . ."

Cory looked immediately at her console screen. There was no time to recalculate. "Admiral," she said, "we're losing the window!"

But Admiral Sweetman was staring at the sonar screen. "Blast them to hell, someone's got a *stealth* sub out there."

Webber addressed the admiral. "But no one uses radar under water. Stealth doesn't matter. It's impossible to hide from active sonar."

"Do you have another explanation, Captain?"

Cory looked at the countdown. Thirty seconds. Their window was only ninety seconds either way. She didn't have to run the numbers, the missiles couldn't travel from the *Red Dawn* in the time that was left. "We missed it," she said quietly. "There's no second chance."

439

The room fell silent as the rest of the audience realized, as she had, that the mission had failed.

Admiral Sweetman looked at Webber, not Cory. He said only one word. "Tokyo."

Cory understood what the admiral meant. Tokyo's population was over eight million people and its evacuation was going too slowly. When the wave surged into Sagaminada Bay, and then through Uraga Strait to Tokyo Harbor, the Japanese government estimated four million people would still be at risk. Another one and a half million people would be trapped in Yokohama, so close to Tokyo that the two cities were virtually one.

Because the Chinese and American navies had missed their window, more than five million people were going to die.

"Get Space Command," Admiral Sweetman ordered Cory. "Have them contact the Japanese government. We've got subs in position to try the Taiwanese and Yellow Sea sites next. But tell the Japanese we've lost Honshu."

"No," Cory said, refusing his order.

Admiral Sweetman stared at her.

"There has to be another way," Cory said. "It's not Honshu. It's five million people. We can't give up this fast."

"We're not surrendering, Doctor," the admiral said testily. "We're accepting our losses and moving on. It was a gamble. We all knew it. But we tried."

"We can try again."

"Of course we will. At the other target sites."

"No," Cory said again. Her body thrummed as if she were still in the Nevada Rain.

Admiral Sweetman frowned at Webber as if Cory had suddenly become Webber's problem. He reached for the headset. "*I'll* talk to Space Command."

Cory blocked his move with her hand. "You're not hearing me, Admiral. All this obsessing about data streams and imagery and open channel D—we're being blinded by the *numbers* we're dealing with."

Webber leaned toward her. "Cory, I know you're worried about the people, but—"

"No! I'm worried about the *physics!* We have to take that wave front out."

"You said we couldn't do that. Even Cerenkov said we couldn't do that. It's too big."

"There's a way, Mitchell. One hole. One hole just big enough for Tokyo to slip through it."

She locked eyes with Admiral Sweetman. "What do they have on that submarine?"

When he didn't respond at once, she stood up suddenly, and turned to face the roomful of strangers. She raised her voice. "Anyone here know what the weapon load of the *Red Dawn* is?"

In the suddenly silent room, a hesitant voice answered, "Um, a battery of twelve Julang-3s. Single warhead. Two- to three-megaton range."

Cory did the math in her head, rapidly estimating what thirty-six megatons could do. From the corner of her eye, she saw Webber put out a hand to restrain the admiral from interfering with her.

"Okay, people, then here's the plan. We're going to launch those missiles in a spread. Can the sub handle multiple launches?"

"Yes, ma'am," someone shouted back.

"All twelve, in the air at the same time," Cory said decisively. "Two-mile separation. That's a twenty-four-mile gap we can blow open in the arc."

Still standing, she turned back to her console, leaning down to swiftly input the numbers in a blur of motion, without conscious thought. The speed and direction of the wave, the GPS coordinates of Sagaminada Bay. In less than a minute she had the missile-spread solution. Unproven, unchecked, but that didn't matter.

"This is going to work," Cory said, not looking at either the admiral or Webber, neither of whom had made a move to stop her. *This is how combat must feel to Webber.* She knew what she had to do, and she knew she would do it.

Cory held her hand to her headset. "Olivia, are you still there?"

"Yes, ma'am." The voice that came back was weak, but she was still there.

"Are you with Captain Ning and Mr. Hito?"

"Yes, ma'am."

"Tell them I have new firing instructions. Tell them if they follow these instructions they will prevent the wave from reaching central Honshu." Cory waited. The situation room was silent, watching, waiting.

"They're standing by for the new instructions, ma'am."

Cory looked up. "Can someone put this on the room speakers?"

There was a squeal of static, then Cory took off her headset. "You still there?"

"Still here," Olivia said. Her young voice now filled the silent situation room. "That wave . . . it's almost right on top of us, isn't it?"

"Ten minutes, Olivia." Cory spoke quickly. "It's ten minutes away. So we've got to make this fast. I'm going to read you the coordinates the captain must set into his missiles. Are you ready?"

Olivia said she was. Cory read out the twelve sets of GPS readings. The Global Positioning Satellite system was so good, even the Chinese Navy used it.

"Um, ma'am, Mr. Hito . . . he says that these coordinates are right above us . . . he says—"

"I *know* what the coordinates are, Olivia." Cory's concentration was fierce. "You tell Mr. Hito there are still *five million* people in Tokyo. They won't be able to get out. *Tell him.*"

Olivia Braun's tremulous voice spoke in Japanese from the overhead speakers.

There was no response.

"Did you tell him?" Cory asked.

"They're talking, ma'am. Captain Ning and Mr. Hito . . . I can't hear them . . . I . . . what's that? Ma'am, they *are* programming the missiles with the coordinates you gave. Oh, God . . ." CPO Braun broke off with a gasp. "I'm sorry, ma'am. I'm . . ."

"I know," Cory said. And she did.

Just then the admiral cleared his throat, spoke up. "CPO Braun, this is Admiral Sweetman. I . . . I want to tell you that I believe you are doing a splendid job there today."

"Thank—thank you, sir."

"And because of what you are about to do, millions of lives will be saved. I want you to know that."

"I do, sir. I am . . . I love the Navy, sir."

Cory looked away from the admiral as the muscles worked in his jaw.

"Chief Petty Officer Braun?" the admiral asked.

"Yes, sir?"

"Do you believe in God?"

"I do today, sir."

"So do I. God bless you, child."

Cory heard more voices then, in Chinese and Japanese, rapid, but professional. Then CPO Braun spoke again.

"Captain Ning says . . ." The young voice paused, then seemed to gather strength and resolve. "The captain says the missiles are now on a thirty-second countdown, they will launch in staggered pairs at ten-second intervals, with simultaneous detonation to follow thirty seconds after the final launch. He is proud to serve the People's Army and to offer this aid to his Japanese brothers."

More talking in Chinese and Japanese followed. Then Cory was sure she even heard someone on the submarine *laugh*.

"And now . . . now Mr. Hito extends his thanks to the government of the People's Republic of China for their efforts on behalf of his countrymen. He hopes what they do today—" Braun's voice halted as a thud came over the speakers. "I'm sorry . . . that was . . . the first pair of missiles has launched. Ah, Mr. Hito hopes that what we all do here today will—" Another thud. "—will serve as an example of . . . Dr. Rey, I'm frightened. . . ." Another thud.

Cory sat down at her console. There was a microphone there. She spoke into it, softly. "I know. I am, too."

"I was going home for Christmas." Another thud.

"You told me. I'll call Ben."

"I've never even been on a submarine before. I wasn't supposed to be here." Thud.

"Olivia, if I could do it, I'd be there now instead of you." The last missiles launched. Thirty seconds.

"Would you?"

"Yes, I would. I'd be just as scared. But . . . I'd be doing my job, like you. Keeping my world safe."

"Are you Navy, Dr. Rey?"

"Well, like Admiral Sweetman said, I'm part of the family."

"Do you have someone special, like I have Ben?"

Cory didn't look at the countdown timer. She didn't want to know.

"No. Not for a while. . . ."

"My mother always said no one really wants to be alone. She always told—"

Silence filled the room.

Major Bailey announced, "We have confirmed loss of signal on the *Red Dawn*."

Cory looked up as a SAR feed replaced the ETEM map. A huge

cloud of something appeared along one short segment of the wave's arc.

The room was silent. Cory shivered with remembered cold. She wondered what it was that Chief Petty Officer Olivia Braun's mother always told her about why no one should be alone.

Then a few people clapped, one or two cheered, then stopped as within a minute, the wave moved far enough to show that it had been broken in two.

Cory traced the route with her eye. Honshu was safe. She had not failed. But it had taken thirty-six megatons of nuclear explosion to flatten one small arc. And CPO Braun's submarine.

"I would have been there instead of her, if I could," Cory said quietly to Webber, still beside her at her console. "And so would Johnny."

Webber's eyes met hers. Cory saw in them what she knew was in hers.

She finally understood Webber's "deal."

Five million lives in exchange for Olivia Braun.

One life in exchange for Johnny Rey.

It had taken Mitch Webber to make her understand. That Johnny hadn't died for *him*. Johnny had died for *her*.

And the dying wasn't over.

"There's another sub out there, isn't there?" she asked. "Waiting for whoever tries to save the West Coast."

Webber nodded. "There's another sub."

California had two hours left.

EVENT PLUS 39 HOURS

The Japanese island of Honshu was spared, and with it Tokyo-Yokohama. But the death toll in Japan was still more than two million. Many had not believed the reports of the wave coming from the west. Many never left their homes.

At the southernmost tip of the Ryukyu Trench, at the second Cerenkov target site, a nuclear torpedo fired from an aging Han-class submarine failed to detonate. The single torpedo that did function properly caused a slight subsidence in the seafloor, but the wave hit Taiwan at 240 mph, with crests recorded at 800 feet. Still, after decades of preparing for an invasion from the mainland, Taiwan's coastal-evacuation plans had been flawless. Casualties were less than 1,000. In the days that followed, the government would politely decline the offer of relief from the PRC.

Where the Yellow Sea was to have been protected, at the third Cerenkov site, the Chinese subs, the Mao Zedong and the Wu Ch'i, the newest of the Tzu class, never made contact with SPACECOM. Something unseen had lain in wait for them as well.

Thus the wave passed the Ryukyu Trench unimpeded, and funneled into the Yellow Sea where its energy was even more concentrated. In seventy-two minutes, any thought of future conflict between the Koreas became a fleeting dream as apocalyptic floods destroyed all arable land on the interior coast of the Korean peninsula. In some places, the wave deposited crop-destroying salt water up to twenty miles inland.

But for all the coastal damage wreaked on China herself, Beijing remained untouched. Total deaths in that country would later be estimated at 600,000, less than 0.05% of a population of 1.3 billion. As her generals had anticipated, the response of China was like that of a tiger shaking off a flea. Though tragedy and economic loss pounded China's shores, the assault of the wave, when considered from the perspective of 5,000 years of unbroken civilization, left their country undiminished.

The one general who had been captured when the coup had collapsed was executed before the wave even struck, and never saw how right, and how wrong, he and his co-conspirators had been. The purging of the PLA would last another year, as all those involved were uncovered. The fifth general officially would remain at large, the circumstances of his fate never made part of the public record.

In the ocean to the east, the wave continued uninterrupted. At the widest reach of the wave's arc, weakening fragments brought high surfs to Mexico. Damage was extensive, casualties were few. In the long run, the building boom would improve the Mexican economy.

But when the wave reached Baja California, the long, slender peninsula of Mexico that extended south of California, the wave was not a weakened fragment.

There, with all the power of the Ice Shelf collapse still pent up within it, the soliton continued.

Two hundred feet high. Two hundred miles an hour. The wave discovered the shoals of North America, and like a predator scenting prey, it quickened its pace.

The pressure of that mountain of water sped up the coast through the ocean, and where the continental shelf sloped up to meet it, energy was also transferred into solid ground.

There were fault lines ahead. There were ancient pools of oil, trapped in fragile strata.

Amplified in the oscillations of the wave's advance, now seismic waves rushed forward as all of those faults began to feel the power of the wave before it even neared them. In the language of geologists, the ambient stress field of the coastal rock system increased dramatically. Rock bursts—the sudden and violent failure of solid strata—were inevitable.

Thus the oil pools cracked and seeped, and the liberated oil rose through the water.

Now the wave scooped up the oil as it had the mass of lighter air in Hawaii, sucking it up in the drawback, then pushing it forward as well.

The scattered oil slicks off the coast of Baja grew to become pockets. The pockets of oil became lakes as the northward-racing wave carved the shore in its path, tossing and shattering wooden docks, metal cars, and propane tanks from winter homes as if they were seeds to be scattered to the wind.

And then the odds that a Russian scientist had calculated more than twenty years ago finally played out.

In the midst of the madly churning cyclone of debris, metal met metal and there came a spark. Not once, but hundreds, thousands of times.

And when the sparks found the oil, the ice of the fallen Shelf finally met its opposite.

What the scientist had conceived was now fully born.

It was no longer a wave that swept up toward America.

It was Icefire.

FOURTEEN

HUNTER THREE FIVE/SOCORRO FRACTURE ZONE

Mitch Webber closed his eyes and saw the Ice, wind-smeared in an early summer blizzard of loose snow. He felt the helicopter pitch and bank, pushing him on through the night. But the roar of the engines was not the steady thrum of a UH-N1 Iroquois.

He opened his eyes and saw the Pacific, one hundred miles south of San Diego—forty hours and nine thousand miles from where the race had started. Twelve minutes from where it would end.

This helicopter was not orange for survival. It was sea gray for ocean combat. A Kaman SH-2G Seasprite. Subhunter. Subkiller.

And as Webber had known and Webber had said, there *was* another sub out there, waiting to annihilate the Navy's last-ditch effort to stop the wave from reaching San Diego and Los Angeles.

Webber had seen the latest projections on CNN. If the wave could not be stopped, three million would die, because the West Coast cities had not been cleared. San Diego would be buried under thirty feet of silt. San Clemente and Catalina would be scoured to bare rock. Encinitas, Oceanside, Huntington Beach, wiped from the coast and the map. Then Long Beach, with its southward-facing promontory, would concentrate the wave into a 1,200-foot monster that would leave no structure standing for a mile from the shore.

And then Los Angeles. A twenty-foot-high seawall of water moving straight into and across the basin for almost five miles.

Already, local traffic helicopters showed the L.A. freeways frozen with cars. People were even trying to escape on foot, because it was faster. But when the wave came, only 100 minutes away now, no one would be able to run fast enough.

The Air Force had wanted to ready their B-2 bombers, to drop a systematic barrage of strategic nuclear weapons across the face of the wave, to achieve what the *Red Dawn* had achieved. But the President had rejected that plan when DOD meteorologists had shown that clouds of radioactive water vapor would travel hundreds of miles inland.

Webber's eyes blurred. He shook his head in his heavy flight helmet, watching the display screen of the ASQ-81 magnetic anomaly detector. But the MAD was not expected to work. None of the detection devices on the eighteen Antisubmarine Warfare Seasprites covering the Socorro Fracture Zone were expected to work.

The People's Liberation Army had explained why.

They called it *Sun Wukong*. The Monkey King. The hero of *Journey to the West*, a favored Chinese novel. The Monkey King could pull out a handful of his own fur, and each hair would be transformed into a monkey warrior, ready to do his bidding. The PLA said it was how their scientists had come to refer to nanotechnology.

Somewhere below Webber was a Chinese submarine unlike any sub ever deployed. Its radical disk shape, a counterintuitive departure from the simplicity of the standard cylindrical design, had been sculpted not for speed, but for stealth. Its height was only thirteen feet, its width thirty-seven, and its hull was composed of layers of carbon-fiber composite plates, covered in turn with anechoic rubber tiles, and lastly by a conductive plastic mesh which supported what USN advanced-concept designers called the Big DAADY—a Dynamic Antinoise/Acoustic Decoupling system.

The Chinese technicians who had just provided the specifications for the Sun Wukong-class stealth subs had taken justifiable pride in their creation. For even now that the U.S. Navy knew exactly what to look for near the first North American Cerenkov target site, there was no guarantee that they could actually find it.

Literally no metal was used in the construction of the Sun Wukong-class subs. Engine parts were ceramic. Computer command and control systems, fiber-optic. Only the warheads of the tactical nuclear missiles and torpedoes they carried could possibly register on a magnetic anomaly detector. And even then only if the helicopter or ship using the device happened to pass directly over the sub.

The Sun Wukong-class were even more silent in operation than the latest American Sea Wolf subs. The Sea Wolf-class subs were 353 feet in length, 40 feet across the beam, carried crews of 134, yet radiated no more sound energy than a 10-watt electric lightbulb. The Sun Wukongs each had a crew of ten, and a single deck isolated from the hull by plastic springs and rubber pads. The propellers that drove the craft were internal, and antinoise sensors on the thruster outlets measured any stray sound produced within and then generated an opposite sound that canceled the offending noise at once. The principle was the same as the earphones worn by travelers to blank out the constant drone of an airplane.

Angled fins on a Sun Wukong's dorsal surface created interference patterns in the water overhead. When the stealth sub moved forward, after fifty feet the water it had displaced spread out so far to port and starboard that it created a pattern America's surface-displacement scanning satellites had not been programmed to find.

There was only one other method of submarine detection available: active sonar—a deliberate noise generated by a buoy or another sub or ship, a noise that propagated through the water and then was reflected back by whatever it hit, just as radar waves were reflected from objects in the air. But as stealth fighters and bombers had shown, radar waves could be scattered and absorbed.

Now, so could sonar. But only by the Chinese stealth subs.

The Sun Wukong-class subs were covered by 860 one-inch-long carbon filaments per square inch, which all sprang to life whenever they were touched by a sonar signal. The filaments of the Dynamic Antinoise/Acoustic Decoupling system moved in response to a magnetic field generated in the conductive plastic mesh to which they were attached.

These were the hairs of the Monkey King. More than 180 million microscopic soldiers standing ready to defend their ruler.

The movement of the filaments was triggered by sound itself. Instantly reconfiguring at the proper angles in reaction to the frequency of the sonar ping that reached them, the filaments increased the surface area of the sub being illuminated by the sound by a factor of more than one thousand—reducing the strength of the sonar return by the same amount. In addition, most of the sound waves that reached the sub's filament cover were not reflected directly back to their transmitting source. Instead, they rebounded back and forth between the carbon filaments like a beam of light that has been reflected from a long series of mirrors. By the time the sound waves finally escaped the sub's beard of acoustical whiskers, most of them were too faint to be perceived by whatever equipment had sent them.

Those signals that were reflected were little more than the weak returns sonar operators had come to associate with scattering layers of microscopic organisms that banded the sea in horizontal layers, or waving kelp beds, or even loose silt on the ocean bottom. If the stealth sub was in motion when active sonar was used, a careful operator would have to scan the same swath of sea many times before detecting something as unlikely as a moving kelp bed. And even if such an unusual return was noted, the logical explanation would be that the return was produced by sound reflections from shifting currents of water at different temperatures. But if the stealth sub remained motionless near the seafloor, it was impossible to detect.

Thus the Sun Wukong submarines could not be heard, had almost no magnetic signature, disguised their displacement signatures, and did not reflect sonar in any useful amount.

They were the greatest achievement of Chinese naval engineering. And the American technicians who received the specs ruefully recognized most of the systems as having first been invented in their own country.

China declined to say why they had built such a craft. Three such craft, to be precise. But in a personal message to the President, the Chinese Premier had admitted that six months ago, all three Sun Wukong subs had disappeared from their top-secret base. Even the People's Liberation Army Navy had been unable to find them. Until the destruction of the Long March and the Soft Wind, and the gallant sacrifice of the Red Dawn.

Chinese observers of the failed attempts to stop the wave deduced that there was only one explanation for the mysterious disappearance of the three Sun Wukong-class submarines. Those who had unleashed Icefire had known the wave could be stopped, and so they had prepared a backup response that had involved "borrowing" the three submarines. The rebel Chinese generals stationed two of the Sun Wukongs on the Ryukyu trench, to ensure that Japan and China would be struck by the wave. Japan, so an enemy would be diminished, and China, so the world would not suspect her involvement.

Clearly, the third Sun Wukong would have been stationed off the West Coast of America. Any submarines dispatched to trigger the subsidence zone there were at risk.

The China's Premier had wished America's President luck, and then ordered his country's navy to give up its plans for its invincible weapon.

Mitch Webber had attended the briefing in which the Chinese stealth subs' capabilities were described. And as the Navy personnel had absorbed the ramifications of that technology in thoughtful silence, it was Cory Rey who first saw the weakness. Webber had felt as proud as if he'd been her teacher, and she his gifted student.

"So if this stealth sub is out there, you can see it once it fires its torpedoes, right?" she had asked.

A man in a suit had turned to her and said dismissively, "By then it's too late."

"Not if you get it to fire *early*."

An instant debate had broken out in response to Cory's solution. Webber had immediately taken on the role of the stealth-sub commander in the role-playing strategy session that followed.

The American subs could not fire their weapons at the Cerenkov target sites until a certain number of minutes before the wave was to arrive—a number which could only be determined in the last few minutes of the wave's approach. If the stealth sub fired at the American subs too early, it would give its position away. Then the American subs could take it out and afterward fire at their target sites, to complete their mission. Thus, Webber concluded, the Chinese stealth sub had to operate under the same tight time limits as the Americans. To fulfill its mission, it had to fire in a window of limited opportunity.

The question then became how to expand the time window, to make the stealth sub reveal its location prematurely.

The solution to this was so obvious that at least ten people had shouted it out at once.

So now, below Mitch Webber and the other ASW Seasprites, in addition to the Chinese stealth sub, the USS *Sea Wolf*, and the USS *Connecticut*, there were two Mk 70 Captor mines.

The Captors were, in effect, portable torpedo tubes. In the past hour, they had been deployed by the *Sea Wolf* and the *Connecticut*, each on a high-speed run twenty miles from their target sites on the offshore Socorro Fracture Zone that would be the last line of defense for San Diego and Los Angeles. The subs had made no attempt to disguise their presence, but the sound signature they created had been intended to disguise the dropping of the Captors.

Now, the Mark 48 ADCAP—advanced capabilities—torpedoes rested near the sea bottom, each one miles from the subs that would control them, waiting for the command to fire.

After the deployment, the *Sea Wolf* and the *Connecticut* had gone to silent running. The Captors were located within a likely radius the subs might have traversed. When they fired, whoever was hidden in the sea, watching, could logically assume that each Captor firing marked the location of an American sub.

High above the target zone, Mitch Webber's Seasprite, F-35, completed its search grid and banked to begin another. The pilot, Admiral Hector Sweetman, a naval aviator who had never enjoyed having to fly a desk, looked over at his passenger. "This'll be the last one, Captain."

Webber looked at his two watches. The wave was ten minutes away. "One way or another," he said.

Then there was a crackle on his helmet speakers. The voice that came through was strong and confident, the voice of a veteran Navy flier. "Hunter Three Five, this is Hunter Four Two, do you copy? Over."

Webber grinned. Forty hours and a hundred years had brought changes he had never thought possible. "This is Hunter Three Five. Hello, Cory, I copy. Over."

"We've got the wave sighted, Mitchell, and the satellite shots were right. The goddamn thing's on fucking fire."

HUNTER FOUR TWO/SOUTH OF THE SOCORRO FRACTURE ZONE

There was no way Cory Rey was going to sit out the last assault on the Icefire wave. She had heard the dark conversations in the corridors and the briefing room of Ballast Point. The U.S. Navy had lost more than half its underway assets in the past two days. The *Nimitz* was gone, crushed by the wave 200 miles from Kingman

Reef. The *Thorn, Fitzgerald*, and *Paul F. Foster* had been abandoned near the Phoenix Islands and were destroyed in seconds.

And the traffic jams that immobilized San Diego had made it almost impossible for the crews who had been called back from their Thanksgiving leave to return to base. Most of the ones who made it arrived on motorcycles or just walked back.

At the end of the last briefing, Cory had pushed her way up through the crowd surrounding Admiral Sweetman and told him bluntly, within Webber's amused hearing, that he could use her help. To make the critical timing work on the strategy he had developed, he was going to need one field observer to give constant updates on the wave's speed.

"I can handle Doppler ranging," Cory said, "and I'm very familiar with helos. I recommend you put me on the observation helo, so you can free up one of your people for an ASW sortie."

As Webber had sprinted out to join a flight group preparing for immediate takeoff, Admiral Sweetman told Cory she'd just been drafted, assigned her a pilot, then hurried off to active duty, as well.

Now she was in a Seasprite SH-2F, an older version of the enduring craft, outfitted for rescue work, hanging over open water as the wave raced for her at 200 miles an hour. The Seasprite could only reach a speed of 170, so when they started to move, they wouldn't stay ahead of it for long. But her pilot, Captain Metcalf, told her the helicopter also had a service ceiling of more than three miles. In the air, at least, the wave would be easy to avoid.

The Seasprite hovered, sending out its radar signals and receiving them back from the wave, allowing the onboard computer to perform the critical calculations. And for all the horror the wave had brought to the world, for all the nightmares it would inspire in the years ahead as those who survived it remembered its coming, Cory Rey looked upon the wave and was in awe.

The night sky was red with it, the stars eclipsed. The burning oil caught in its trough made it look as if the Earth itself had split in two and Cory could see into its core.

It was like watching the surface of the sun, like seeing alien moons cracked by glowing magma. Streaks of flame raced across the surface of the wave in starts and flashes like the sparks that fired in the neurons and synapses of an unimaginable planetary brain.

It was alive to her. A force of nature that even she could not comprehend.

And for just one fleeting visceral moment, a moment that did not admit knowledge of the ruin of countries and the deaths of millions, a moment that simply existed in the most primitive depths of her mind, Cory Rey looked upon the wave and in that moment it was a thing of *wonder*.

But the moment passed and she knew her role in what must happen next.

On the screen before her, where the Cerenkov equation, the satellite images, and the Doppler readings from her own helo's radar combined and were reworked according to her programming, she had four minutes before the wave would reach the target fracture zone.

She had already rehearsed her lines with her pilot. None of the Seasprites in the search for the Chinese sub were to use encryption for their transmissions. None were to narrowcast their contacts back and forth. Because someone else would be listening to them. The whole plan depended on that happening.

"Hunter Three Five," Cory said, "this is the Active Forge countdown, starting at two minutes on my mark . . . *mark*. Over."

"Active Forge countdown under way," Webber replied. "Over."

Cory turned to her pilot and gave him a thumbs-up. He nodded and the helicopter wheeled about, then sped away. The scalding glow of the wave flashed past the windscreen, then vanished.

But Cory knew it was out there. She could feel it reaching out to her. Reaching out to pull her into the deepest crevasse of all.

And it was gaining on her.

FIFTEEN

HUNTER THREE FIVE/SOCORRO FRACTURE ZONE

"This is Hunter Three Five to all Hunters," Webber said. "We are at one minute on the Active Forge countdown. All Hunters climb to two thousand feet and hold until the wave has collapsed. Acknowledge to Home Base. Over."

Webber stared out at the ocean. Moonlight sliced across rough water, but the Seasprite's altitude didn't change. Half the ASW helos would be climbing now, in case their flight pattern was being monitored by another hostile station. But the others would hold their courses in their search grids, ready to act.

Webber's Seasprite was twenty miles to the south of the target site closest to shore. The topographic maps of the area had shown a series of deep trenches in which a sub might escape the overpressure of the wave's passage. Webber had assumed the mind-set of the stealth-sub commander as he had debated the strategies with the others in the briefing room. He now assumed that mind-set again as he saw this particular region of the seafloor. If he were in a Sun Wukong-class sub, he would be somewhere below, waiting for his chance to fire and protect the wave.

"We're at thirty seconds to launch," Webber's pilot, Admiral Sweetman, announced, playing his part of the diversion as they'd rehearsed. "All Hunters stand by for Trigger Launch. Looks like he's not out there, boys."

456

Webber studied the sonar image being transmitted from the EC-135 that circled at 20,000 feet, acting as the central station for the thousands of sonar buoys that had been dropped over the target sites, as it gathered all their separate returns and combined them into an overall theater map. There was nothing moving on the ocean floor.

Webber took over the countdown, stating each number clearly. Finally, all the planning, all the attempts, and the lives they had cost, came down to three words. ". . . two . . . one . . . *launch*."

In less than a second, the sonar screen showed a disturbance as one of the Captor mines launched its Mark 48 ADCAP torpedo toward the target site. The ADCAP wasn't nuclear-tipped. If it reached the target site, Webber knew, its detonation would have no effect on the wave. But the ADCAP was not intended to reach its destination.

Four seconds later, a new disturbance appeared on the screen. It was ten miles to the south, at the edge of a deep canyon. The smear of an accelerating torpedo, coming out of nowhere, launched by nothing that was visible to sonar.

"*Contact!*" Bailey's voice echoed through Webber's helmet speakers, and those of every other Seasprite crew member on the line. From her underground stronghold in Cheyenne Mountain, Major Wilhemina Bailey was coordinating the flow of satellite information to the EC-135.

As the first sonar smear angled to track the ADCAP, a second smear flashed onto the screen, bearing in on the Captor position.

"We got him!" Webber said.

The plan had worked perfectly. The commander of the Sun Wukong sub had been waiting for all of them to make him a gift of the target-site launch. So close to the wave's arrival, he had intercepted the Navy's calculations and assumed, as the Icefire strike force had anticipated, that the ADCAP launch was the firing of a nuclear torpedo from the *Sea Wolf* or the *Connecticut*. Either way, the stealth-sub commander had targeted the ADCAP and its launch position. Right now, for these few seconds, he would believe that he was about to take out both the explosive charge intended for the target site and the only American sub within range that could respond in time to stop the wave. For these few seconds, the Sun Wukong commander would think he had won.

But only for a few seconds.

Webber immediately switched frequencies and activated full encryption as he read the GPS location signature Bailey was transmitting directly to the sonar screen. "All Hunters, all Hunters, we have a positive bearing at . . . GPS thirty fifteen six north, one seventeen fiver fiver west. Immediate strike! Immediate strike! Alpha and Bravo, we are now on *Latent* Forge countdown, repeat *Latent* Forge on my mark . . . mark!"

Admiral Sweetman pulled Webber's Seasprite into a sharp turn and throttled her up to full speed. There were two Mk 46 homing torpedoes on the helo and Webber intended to launch both, if only to pulverize the debris of the Chinese sub. Hunter Three Five should reach the stealth sub's position just about the time the *Sea Wolf* and the *Connecticut*—Alpha and Bravo—launched their POP-DOWN Tomahawks at the target sites. Because all the information Webber had given over the open channel had been false. The wave would be arriving over the fracture zone in *six* minutes, not one. And if Cerenkov's energy-sapping equation and Cory's calculations were right, that's where it would end.

Webber couldn't resist the moment of victory. He switched back to the open frequency as he watched the Chinese torpedoes close in on the decoy ADCAP and the Captor. The hostile's torpedo launched at the Captor would probably circle until it ran out of fuel because its homing sonar would find no target anywhere near the coordinates it had been sent to.

"Hunter Four Two, this is Hunter Three Five, do you copy? Over."

Cory's voice came back, her words showing she knew enough not to give away any information until there had been a confirmed kill on the Chinese sub. "This is Hunter Four Two. Captain Metcalf's being a drag. He says we can't do a victory roll in one of these crates. Over."

Webber laughed. He and Cory had won. Almost, at least. "Tell you what, Hunter Four Two, I know a hangar out at Groom Lake where they've got this helicopter called a Comanche. We can do loop-the-loops till your eyes fall out and then fly sideways."

Webber heard Cory laugh back. It was a good sound. They were almost home.

Then there was a crackle of static and another voice broke into the circuit. A voice just as familiar as Cory's. A voice, Webber knew, he had expected to hear again. Though not here. Not only must the Chinese generals have had access to the Chinese equivalent of a Harrier, some type of hypersonic transport must have been available to them as well.

"Happy trails, cowboy," Nick Young said. "If I were you, I'd be getting the hell out of Dodge about now."

Webber saw Admiral Sweetman's questioning look, but he shook his head. There would be time for explanations later.

"Thanks, *pal*," Webber radioed back on the open channel, refusing to reveal how surprised he was. "But you and I've got unfinished business." As far as he was concerned, Nick Young, his best friend, the traitor who had left him to die on the Ice, had less than six minutes to live. And this time, Webber would fire the first and last shot.

HUNTER FOUR TWO/SOUTH OF THE SOCORRO FRACTURE ZONE

Cory's face creased in puzzlement. "Hey, Mitchell, who's that on the circuit?"

The new voice seemed amused. "Is that the infamous Dr. Corazon Rey?"

"Copy that," Cory said. "Who's this?"

"Nick."

"Oh, my God."

"Close enough," Young said. "I've got to tell you, though, you sure twisted up my good buddy. He bitched about you for two years. Drove me nuts."

"He said you were his friend."

"We've all got our crosses to bear. Right, cowboy?" Then Young chuckled. "Oops. Looks like you just lost your torpedo."

Cory looked at her display screen with the sonar theater map transmitted from the EC-135. It showed the familiar bloom of an underwater explosion where the torpedo launched from the stealth sub had hit the Mk 48 decoy torpedo.

"You can't stop it, Mitch. It's the wave of the future."

"Why, Nick?"

Cory understood that Webber's question was in shorthand, just the tip of a question he had asked before.

"I'm here for my country, same as you."

"Two big problems, Nick. First one is, your country isn't here for you. Your generals, they're being rounded up. At least three of them are dead. As far as your connection to it all, I'm putting my money on Wei Jincheng. I'd say there's a family resemblance. How about you? You going to miss your uncle Jincheng? Or cousin Jincheng? Or—"

The sudden emotion in Young's voice told Cory that Webber was on to something. "Fuck you," Young said.

Webber didn't let up. "Better check your second torpedo. Has it found a target yet?"

In her Seasprite SH-2F, Cory watched the sonar map. The trace of the second torpedo was curling into a circle. Over the open channel, Webber's voice was harsh. "Trust me, *cowboy. That's* what they call the last roundup."

Another bloom appeared on the sonar screen. Bailey's voice came over the secure channel.

"U.S. Space Command has confirmed launches of two POP-DOWN Tomahawk cruise missiles, from Alpha and Bravo. Let's hear it for the good guys."

Cory checked her time readouts. The Tomahawk she could see on her screen was two minutes from its target site in the fracture zone. The wave was four minutes, thirty seconds away.

It was almost over.

THE *SUN TZU*/SOCORRO FRACTURE ZONE

Nick Young stared at the sonar traces smeared across the liquid-crystal display screen of his command console. He refused to believe what he saw. When had Mitch Webber ever been on time for anything? And when had he ever been *early*?

"Colonel Wei," the diving officer said urgently. "We must change position at once."

Young understood the man's reasoning. The *Sun Tzu*'s torpedoes weren't stealthy. The Hunters above had undoubtedly marked their point of origin, and knew that the *Sun Tzu* would be at that location. The helicopters would be launching their torpedoes within seconds. But Young said, "No. We hold position here. The torpedoes from those helicopters will not be able to find us if we remain motionless. If we move, there is so much sonar out there, they are bound to notice a background disturbance."

Young looked back to see how his crew were holding up. It had been a given that if the *Sun Tzu* were forced to fire, the Americans would know their location. And the crew knew how vulnerable their remarkable submarine was once it was stripped of its cloak of invisibility. The only hope they had had of escaping destruction was if the wave had come immediately after their torpedoes had been fired.

But Webber, the true-blue American hero, had done the one thing Young had never expected of him. He had lied. Active Forge countdown, indeed.

The sonar officer called over from his station. "Colonel Wei, I hear missile launches. Two missile launches."

Young caught his breath in rage and made a fist, even though he knew there was nothing he could strike. The plastic control consoles were too fragile.

"Target the launch points," he said. "Fire torpedoes at will."

The diving officer grew even more concerned. Firing torpedoes at the American submarines that had launched against the target sites was only intended to help add to the confusion in the final moments before the wave came, to provide an extra chance that the *Sun Tzu* might successfully hide. Under present conditions, Young knew, his order would seem a senseless, and risky, maneuver.

"Colonel," the diving officer said, "that is unnecessary. Launching more torpedoes can only tell them that we have not moved from our position."

Young couldn't remain sitting at his station any longer. He was a battlefield warrior, not a sub commander. He rose to his feet and shouted at the diving officer. "It doesn't matter anymore! They have us! Fire the torpedoes and arm the missiles!"

The weapons officer looked up from his console. "Missiles, sir?" They were nuclear-tipped, modified Julangs, 2.5 megatons each."

"Set them for airburst directly over the target sites," Young said. "Maybe we can knock down the Americans."

The weapons officer wiped the sweat from his face and turned back to his console, hands trembling.

The diving officer leaned closer to Young, hissing into his ear. "We'll never be able to launch in time to hit the American missiles."

Young grasped the officer's collar with both hands crossed at the wrist. A simple twist, and the man would be unconscious, unmindful of his own death. But Young refused to show him that small mercy.

"I don't care about the American *missiles*," Young said. "I want the American. I want Mitch Webber."

HUNTER THREE FIVE/SOCORRO FRACTURE ZONE

"He's the one, isn't he?" Sweetman said.

Webber knew what the admiral meant, watched the sonar display. "Not for much longer."

One after the other, two torpedo traces had appeared three miles west of Young's position. Another Seasprite had dropped its homing torpedoes, beating Webber to the punch. The Chinese techs had reluctantly explained that the Sun Wukongs had limited maneuverability. Their strength lay only in their ability to hide. Once found, they ceased to be weapons of war. They were only targets.

Webber knew the homing torpedoes would not be able to get a sonar lock on Young's sub. But they were equipped with Block III GPS receivers and were set to explode when they reached Young's last recorded location. Webber knew the disk-shaped sub would not be able to move away fast enough to escape damage. The same microfilaments that allowed it to scatter and absorb sonar also dramatically increased its drag. Nick Young was finished.

Then Webber saw the plume of another impact on the screen. The POPDOWN Tomahawk launched from the *Connecticut* had reached the target site and hit the water. Designed to shed its aerodynamic outer shell and continue down as a torpedo, the newest Tomahawk in America's arsenal had less than thirty seconds to impact. If all went as planned, 300 miles to the west, an identical Tomahawk was thirty seconds from target site at the other end of the fracture zone.

As the sky over the coast of San Diego began to glow with the approach of the wall of liquid fire, Admiral Sweetman pushed the Seasprite into a power climb. Webber cupped his hand to his flight helmet's mike to be sure his former best friend heard every word he had to say. "Time's up, Nick. You lose."

"Never." And that was the last word Nick Young said.

The two-kiloton Tomahawk warhead ignited.

EVENT PLUS 40 HOURS

The wave was six miles from the Socorro Fracture Zone off San Diego when both W-80 warheads detonated 164 feet above the seafloor, 300 miles apart.

The first pressure waves to hit the fault came from the fireballs themselves. Pushing out with supersonic, instantaneous spheres of steam, those quick punches awakened the fault and they hammered at the fault like a pair of 500-foot-wide sledgehammers.

The second set of pressure waves to hit the fault were transmitted by the water that reacted to the fireballs' force. These traveled toward each other at 3,400 mph along the fault channel as they made the fracture zone ripple.

And then, before the fracture zone snapped back into its stable configuration, a third set of pressure waves, those traveling through the seafloor, set up harmonics the fracture could not withstand.

Rock lost strength. Strata lost cohesion. The pressure waves confused the system of tension that had held the fracture zone stable for more than 350 years. Then gravity took over, and for thirteen seconds, it became the most powerful force to act upon the fracture zone.

The physics were simple. The seafloor collapsed. It could do nothing else.

One hundred and sixty square miles of it dropped, on average more than thirty-six inches. In some places, the seafloor dropped more than ten feet.

The water above followed the seafloor down.

Then, above that region of seafloor, the surface of the ocean suddenly deformed, drawn downward, as it formed a trough.

At the same time, from the south, the hungry wave came, sucking up the water before it, to fuel its moving mass.

But when it reached the depression caused by the Socorro collapse, the wave suddenly ran out of fuel. There was insufficient water to feed the wave.

The energy of the wave now had nowhere to go, and so it was transformed again—from the potential energy of the 200-foot, 200-mph soliton to the kinetic energy of a wave of water that climbed to 1,100 feet in ten seconds. Like a runner skidding to a stop, the wave staggered, then overbalanced, growing too big to support itself.

Its momentum shattered, it was no longer a soliton that would never lose energy.

The speeding water fell, with each second, losing energy.

The water now rushed into the trough before it, like rainwater spilling into a gutter.

The perfect sine wave had collapsed, and its energy was now consumed by its efforts to fill the depression that had been caused by the seafloor's collapse. One collapse had equaled another.

For one 300-mile-long arc of the wave front, Icefire had been defeated. San Diego, San Clemente, Catalina, Encinitas, Oceanside, Huntington Beach, Long Beach, and Los Angeles had all been spared. From National City to San Luis Obispo, no monstrous wave, no moving wall of fire would strike the coast of California.

Other submarines waited farther north, by additional Cerenkov target sites. The technique had been proven now, and there would be no more stealth subs lurking behind a shield of sonar invisibility.

The equation had been right.

The calculations had been right.

In fact, there had been only one small miscalculation.

When the W-80 warhead exploded over the target site, twenty miles away from the Sun Wukong-class submarine, the explosion triggered an electromagnetic pulse.

The salt water transmitted that pulse with great efficiency.

Within one second, the control circuits of the torpedoes launched against the hostile stealth sub were wiped clean.

The wave had died.

But the enemy still lived.

SIXTEEN

THE *SUN TZU*/SOCORRO FRACTURE ZONE

The weapons control officer was too slow, too frightened, and Nick Young pulled him from his chair, then began to input the missile release codes himself.

The rest of the crew were frozen in position, heads upturned, listening to the maddening whine of the American torpedoes as they closed in.

Webber's voice sputtered from the control room speakers. "Time's up, Nick. You lose."

But Webber knew nothing about time. "Never," Young answered.

And then another sound eclipsed the torpedoes'—a detonation so powerful that Young was thrown to the deck, ears ringing, with no doubt as to what had just happened. But at least the craft was shielded against EMP. At least he still had a few more seconds in which to fight.

"Diving officer! Take us off the bottom!" he shouted. "Everyone else, brace yourself!"

The *Sun Tzu*'s deck pitched as it moved up. Young knew that a shock wave was approaching from the detonation over the nearest target site. If it hit the *Sun Tzu* while the submarine was still close to the bottom, the *Sun Tzu* could be split open on rocks or its sonar-absorbing blanket hopelessly mired in silt.

"Faster!" he commanded as the submarine creaked and groaned with the rapid pressure change.

And then it was too late.

The *Sun Tzu* reared up, spun once, then was plunged into darkness as its internal power failed.

Young rolled down the now almost-vertical deck, slammed into another crewman, then fell away again as the *Sun Tzu* revolved like a wheel.

He heard screams, saw sparks flash, and as if in a dream, in the afterimage of those brilliant strobes of light, saw the towering buttes of Arizona, could almost hear the hoofbeats of—

The *Sun Tzu* thudded to a stop. Emergency lights flickered on. Someone was moaning.

He tried to push himself up but his right arm wouldn't work. He stared at it, as if it belonged to someone else. A jagged-edged bone had ripped through his skin at the elbow. He felt nothing. Pain had no more meaning. The blood that ran from him was only an abstraction.

All that mattered was the sound.

The sound of rushing water.

A vibration began and Young recognized it as the last manifestation of the nuclear blast.

The seismic disturbance had begun. The Socorro Fracture Zone would be collapsing, taking the Icefire wave with it.

The *Sun Tzu* trembled like a plaything in the hands of the gods. Then it shifted again, slipped sideways, and floated down, completely out of Young's control.

Young pictured the sonar map of the narrow canyon the submarine had rested beside. He knew that was where he was now, descending. If the sub reached the ledge at 550 feet, then perhaps it would survive. But if it missed the ledge and kept falling, then even if the *Sun Tzu* had been intact, it would never survive the pressure long enough to reach bottom. Without metal, the craft was indetectable. But it was also weak.

One of the crewmen was sobbing. Part of Young understood that fear. Part of him never could. Those two halves, always at war within him, now joined in uneasy truce by the imperative for revenge.

Then, with another violent jolt and scream from the overstressed hull, the *Sun Tzu* stopped falling. It had landed stern-down on the canyon's ledge.

Young braced himself on the central helm console. The deck was at a forty-degree angle. Water sprayed everywhere in high-pressure jets. But some of the consoles were flickering back to life.

Without using his right arm, he climbed sideways to the weapons console. Two control surfaces were lit.

With his left arm, he wiped a spray of salt water from the controls, squinting at the readings they displayed.

Then he smiled.

Though he had no memory of it, he had entered the complete code sequence *before* the detonation had occurred.

The Julang missiles were armed.

Young glanced down the deck to see water rising up from the crew cabin. Four or five of his crew were floating in it, unmoving. He had no idea where the others were. He didn't care.

The *Sun Tzu* was dying, but it was not dead yet.

And Mitch Webber was still alive somewhere overhead.

HUNTER THREE FIVE/SOCORRO FRACTURE ZONE

This was the moment to cheer, and the open channels erupted with triumphant shouts and the thunder of applause back in the Ballast Point situation room.

"We have achieved an ex-wave!" Major Bailey of SPACECOM proclaimed. "TOPEX/POSEIDON shows the forward motion has slowed over the full three-hundred-mile arc! Looks like we're going to get some breakers south of L.A., but that first segment of the wave is outta there!"

Webber punched the air with his fist, then looked over at Admiral Sweetman and saw the same emotions of joy and success and relief.

"We earned our pay today," Sweetman said with deep satisfaction.

Webber switched from the cheers on the open channel to the relative calm of the secure channel. "Hunter Four Two, this is Hunter Three Five. First-rate job, Cory. The admiral plans to hire you and fire me. Over."

He waited, wondering what insult she would inflict on him for the compliment.

No comeback.

He tried again. "Hunter Four Two, this is Hunter Three Five. Do you copy? Over."

This time, there was an answer. But not the one he expected.

It was Major Bailey at SPACECOM. "Captain Webber, we've got a mayday on Hunter Four Two. Her last position was right over that wave!"

OPEN OCEAN/SOCORRO FRACTURE ZONE

The wave had collapsed, but it had not collapsed uniformly.

Where the change in seafloor elevation had been uneven, different parts of the wave had fallen at different speeds. Sometimes, two columns of water had fallen together and canceled each other out. Sometimes, two columns of water had fallen out of phase with each other, and enormous backsplashes had resulted.

The last of the fire and the last of the debris rode some of those backsplashes high into the night.

Hunter Four Two had been holding at 2,000 feet, as it observed the wave die. Cory had witnessed the fountains of flames that rose up from the wave.

Then, with a terrible *twang*, the Seasprite had shuddered. The rotor seemed to speed up as the craft began to spin.

Cory could only grip her seat as Captain Metcalf, her pilot, fought the controls.

"Mayday mayday mayday—this is Hunter Four Two in uncontrolled descent! We have been hit by debris. A blade's delaminated! We're going in! Mayday mayday mayday!"

The world spun in a blur round her and Cory was surprised by how unafraid she felt. Since the crevasse and the wave, she had, all along it seemed now, been expecting this.

"We gotta ditch!" Captain Metcalf shouted as the engines began to whine. Flashing red lights sparkled across the control console. Through the windows, Cory could see far below pockets of flame still burning themselves out on the water. "Pull back on the door handle!" Metcalf yelled.

Cory did as she was told, grabbing the leverlike handle and yanking it back.

Instantly, the cabin filled with a swirl of cold air that carried the stench of the sea and of burning oil.

"Don't jump till I say you jump!" Metcalf warned. "And don't pull the cord on the life vest till you're in the water! Understand?!"

"Yes!" Cory shouted back.

The fires in the water were growing larger as their craft spiraled down lower and lower. Captain Metcalf struggled with the controls like a rodeo rider trying to ride a bull. "She's out of control! I can't hold her steady! Get ready to go!"

Cory had no expectations of what it would be like to leave a spinning helicopter in flight. She put one hand on the open door frame. Watched the fires below tunnel round her, reaching upward, leaping closer with each disorienting revolution of the craft.

"Two hundred feet! When I say go!"

Cory had no clue how she should do this.

"One fifty!"

She could work the life vest. She remembered they'd told her it held a battery that seawater would turn on.

"One hundred!"

The battery could power a light and a radio transmitter.

"Fifty . . . this is it!"

But Cory still didn't know what she was supposed to do.

Then Captain Metcalf punched her in the chest and her seat belt and shoulder harnesses popped free, as the toplike motion of the Seasprite hurled her out the open door. And, for the longest moment of her life, she finally made that long-desired jump between the house and the garage.

Nothing had changed.

She wasn't going to make it.

HUNTER THREE FIVE

Hunter Three Five sped toward the rivers of fire that stretched across the open sea. Webber stared hard ahead as he looked to see if any of the fires came from Hunter Four Two.

Bailey relayed GPS coordinates to Admiral Sweetman. Webber saw the running lights of other Seasprites converging on the same spot.

And then the radio hissed. "Still there, cowboy?" Young coughed. "If you are, it won't be for long."

"Shut up and die!" Webber growled. "We stopped the wave. You're finished."

"I've still got my nukes," Young said. The whispery breath of rushing water blurred the sound of Young's transmission. "And from the strength of your signal, I'd say you were . . . in range."

OPEN OCEAN

Cory rolled in liquid, cold darkness, blind, confused, one hand reaching for her life vest's cord on instinct alone. She heard a distant muffled rush of air, then felt herself tugged upward, and her head splashed free of the water.

Above her, she could see Hunter Four Two spin drunkenly away. The angle of its whirling blades was almost forty-five degrees. Her gaze followed the arc of the Seasprite, saw its blades slice into the water, and tip the craft forward, onto its side, into a blazing lake of oil.

Hunter Four Two exploded before it had even stopped moving.

Bobbing in the swells, Cory stared numbly as the fireball billowed skyward from the scattered wreckage.

Small particles of debris rained down into the water around her. She could see them hit in the flashing light from the shoulder of her vest.

The fireball faded, its thunder a memory. Now all she could hear was the hissing, burning oil that began to collect and pool around her.

The cold thickness of the vest around her neck forced her head back and she gazed up into the sky. Dawn was coming. But the water was cold and she knew she wouldn't live to see it.

HUNTER THREE FIVE

Webber adjusted the sonar scan. Swearing, he forced it to expand past the point of clarity so he could see the area immediately around him.

"There!" he said as he jabbed his finger at the screen. "That's him!"

The sonar return was a wide, white circle, splotchy, low-resolution. To Webber, the white circle could be the Sun Wukong on its side on a ledge halfway down a canyon. For sonar to be able to see it meant that the stealth sub's DAADY was no longer working or had been ripped from the hull. Whatever had happened to it, the Sun Wukong was in trouble. But not enough trouble.

"We've got to launch the torpedoes!" Webber said.

Sweetman pointed out to port. "Over there! Flashing light!"

Webber turned sharply to see it. A mile away. The emergency beacon from a life vest. But there was only one. Who had made the ditch? Cory? Or her pilot?

But Nick Young was below them. And his sub still carried nuclear missiles. He could reach shore from here. He could reach San Diego. And from the very beginning, Webber's mission had been clear.

He was there to stop the nukes.

The mission could not fail.

No matter the cost.

Please, God, Cory, understand.

Admiral Sweetman swung the chopper toward the flashing light.

"No!" Webber said, his voice tight in his throat. "If he's got nukes down there, we have to take him out!"

Sweetman's eyes met Webber's in silent sympathy; then the admiral turned the craft around, and the Seasprite circled back to head for the sonar image of the dying Chinese sub. Webber watched the flashing light bob up and down, then disappear into choppy waves and burning oil slick.

Whoever had survived the crash was on his—or her—own.

THE *SUN TZU*

Nick Young felt the freezing ocean swirl around his feet. But he ignored it. It was a small price to pay for what he would do next.

"From out of the dust," he said into his microphone tube as he enabled the missile launch sequence.

He heard sonar pings all around him as the Seasprites dropped their active arrays, desperately trying to find him.

"A galloping horse with the speed of light," Young crooned, in an almost incoherent singsong. He knew now that he was the ulti-

471

mate Lone Ranger, the ultimate masked man. It all seemed so clear now. And the Julangs would be his ultimate silver bullets.

He pressed the control that would open the first missile hatch. The *Sun Tzu* shook as a cascade of compressed air bubbled up from it. But all the status lights turned red—the sign of proper operation in the PRC.

"And a hearty Hi-yo Silver," Young whispered.

He pressed the button that began the launch.

The *Sun Tzu* shook again. But the submarine didn't change position.

Young gripped the console with his left hand. He pictured the rush of compressed air that would shoot the missile out until it was far enough away for its main engine to ignite.

He closed his eyes as he imagined seeing it leap from the launch tube.

That was something Webber had always said he wasn't good at. That he could only imagine the terrain in two dimensions, not three.

But Young saw in all dimensions now.

He saw the missile leaving, not straight up, because the *Sun Tzu* was angled. So it would travel sideways at first.

Sideways . . .

The canyon wall.

Nick Young opened his eyes as he pictured the inevitable course of the nuclear-tipped missile in three dimensions.

In that last moment, he did the American thing.

He laughed.

HUNTER THREE FIVE

Even as Webber prepared himself for the sight of a sub-launched nuclear missile leaving the water and heading for shore, he realized that because the sub was on its side, Nick Young had just fired his weapon toward the wall of the underwater canyon. That meant—

"Swing left! Swing left!" he shouted.

Admiral Sweetman spun the helo around and tore off to port.

"Find that light . . . that light . . ."

The sonar screen flashed white as every return was obliterated by a sudden explosion.

The Seasprite shot forward, skimming over the water, darting through the fire that lay upon it.

Webber looked in the outside mirror.

He saw the ocean glow as a fireball emerged from it, displacing a column of water hundreds of feet high.

And from the center of that column, there came a wave.

It was heading where the flashing light had last been seen.

OPEN OCEAN

Cory was slammed from behind as the explosion's shock wave passed her by. For a moment, her lungs could not fill with air, as if someone had just pounded her heavily on the back. Seawater rushed into her mouth.

She coughed up salty water. Her ears rang from the impact. Light flashed, bounced across the dark surface of the water between the pools of flame. The swells swung her around.

She saw the wave. Smaller, but still fast enough and high enough to crush her just the same.

"Johnny," she cried out, but she couldn't even hear her own voice.

Suddenly the water flattened all around her. She felt a strong wind press down and then begin to draw back, and pull her with it. The wave was almost upon her. Cory looked away. She didn't want to see the wave. She'd seen enough. The wave had won. She looked up instead to the dawn.

And saw Mitch Webber three feet above her, reaching down for her hand.

There was no time for the winch, no time for anything else. Webber had already released his restraints, popped the door, then moved forward, one hand gripping the helicopter's door frame. He hooked his feet around the bottom of his seat; his other hand reached down as Sweetman sharply angled the helo and its rotors kicked up a spray of water.

Only seconds from Cory, the tsunami caused by the detonation of Nick Young's underwater missile rolled forward to claim her.

Webber felt his hand make contact with Cory's. He grabbed it and shouted at Sweetman, *"GO! GO! GO!"*

The Seasprite pulled up and away from the water with such power that Webber slid forward, his feet losing their purchase, until his only support was his hand on the door frame.

Cory's small body trailed water, almost doubled in weight by the water filling her boots and her jumpsuit. Webber's hand on the door frame was numb with cold. The Seasprite screamed as it climbed 200 feet and the wave rushed at them until the very crest of it sprayed around Cory's boots.

The Seasprite rocked and bucked in the backdraft caused by the wave's passage. Webber's hand began to slide off the door frame.

Webber stared down into Cory's eyes. They were open, accepting.

But he made his choice.

He would not let go.

He would not let her go.

Cory looked up into Webber's eyes and saw his intent. She saw his fingers tight on the door frame, all that was between them and the ocean, 200 feet down.

She wouldn't let him do it.

Not after all she had seen. All she had learned. All that he had made her understand.

She knew the deal now. He had taught her the lesson.

Her life for his.

She let go of his hand.

But he didn't let go of hers.

In a timeless eternity of horror, she saw Webber's fingers slip from the door frame of the Seasprite.

Then, knowing he had chosen to die for her, knowing she had killed him, Cory dropped away from the aircraft, Webber's hand still locked around her wrist.

Together, they fell to the ocean.

All of five feet.

As Webber had lost purchase, Admiral Sweetman had swiftly dropped altitude, returning them to safety once the tsunami had passed. And because of her life vest, Cory's head didn't even go underwater. Webber's did. She used his death-lock grip on her wrist to yank him up to the surface. Then she pulled on his life vest cord and the vest puffed up around him.

Cory was shaking so hard she couldn't speak. As she saw Webber's lips turn blue, she realized he'd not be saying anything much either.

As the gentle swells bore them up and down, the rescue Seasprite above them lowered its winch. And all Cory and Mitchell could do was float together, hands still joined, in uncharacteristic, peaceful, silence.

The sun rose higher in the sky.

It was dawn.

SEVENTEEN

CRYSTAL CITY, WASHINGTON, D.C.

Charles Quincy Abbott, general no longer, stood at the front gate of his house. The house was red brick. Solid. Built in the twenties. Dusted with snow now. Summer's flowers gone.

Automatically, he checked his watch. Forty-nine hours, sixteen minutes, and twenty seconds since he had formed his Crisis Action Team in the National Military Command Center. He pressed the tiny button that would stop the counter. Read the numbers again. Then pressed the button that reset them. 00:00:00.

He pushed the gate open and walked up the path.

The front door wasn't locked.

He would have to speak to his wife about that.

Then he remembered that she had said something in one of her messages about an emergency. Maybe he should have been back earlier. But he had been listening to the news in the car, as his driver took him round the Mall, over and over. That insufferable man from Motorola, Clifton something or other, who had never accomplished anything, had been bleating to reporters about how the Pentagon had tried to block all the news coming out of Antarctica. Clifton was enjoying his fifteen minutes of fame. The President, too. He had called for an inquiry into DOD operations, to find out why the country hadn't responded more quickly to the wave. Abbott could tell him. But he wouldn't. The President didn't deserve to know.

Abbott kicked the snow off his shoes, stepped through the door, and closed it behind him. There was a note from his son Sam on the front hall table, but he didn't read it.

It was still there, untouched, a few days later when the ambulance came because of the neighbors' complaints.

The house was empty after that. In a way, it always had been.

CHEYENNE MOUNTAIN, COLORADO

The three-foot-thick blast doors opened and Major Bailey squinted into the white glare of sunshine. She had been in the ESC for less than three days, but it had felt like a year.

Beside her in the personnel bus, Commander Huber rubbed at his eyes as well. Then he looked at the message slip again.

His sister had been calling him for the past twenty-four hours, unable to get through the switchboard, wondering how he was. She was at an astronomy conference in the Canary Islands, almost a third of the world away from her home in Hawaii.

Bailey had been happy to see the flush of relief on Huber's face as he had seen that message. Bailey had felt the same way when she had spoken to her family in Palm Springs.

The small bus stopped by the main parking lot. Bailey sighed as she got to her feet. Huber stood up beside her, followed her off.

They stood together beneath the brilliant blue Colorado sky. The parking lot had been freshly plowed. The day looked new.

Bailey could think of nothing except getting some sleep, but her first stop was going to have to be the airport to get wait-listed on a flight to Palm Springs. Yet she found it difficult to walk off and leave Huber as if it were just another ordinary shift that had come to an end.

Huber seemed to be hesitating, too.

Then he said, "I'm thinking of leaving the Air Force."

He looked at her, gave her that easy smile.

Bailey tried not to think what she was thinking. "What . . . what would you do?"

Huber ran a hand back and forth over his short-cropped red hair so that Bailey knew she wasn't getting the whole answer. Not yet at least.

"Don't know," he said. "Maybe we could talk about it over dinner?"

Bailey knew she had the silliest grin of her life spread over her face. Maybe it was because of the President, or because she personally had shut down the Pentagon's communications system, or because she had helped save millions of lives.

And maybe it was because of something else. Someone else.

"How about breakfast?" she said.

They ended up flying to Palm Springs together.

SAN DIEGO NAVAL STATION

Webber slept for twenty-two hours, and when he woke up in the infirmary, there had been a note from Admiral Sweetman assigning him to quarters on the base. The debriefing sessions were expected to take at least two weeks. Probably more.

Sweetman had also included news updates. Of the other eight wave arcs that had been targeted, seven had been collapsed as planned. The eighth attempt had been mistimed and the wave had burst into the Gulf of Anadyr, up where Russia almost joins Alaska. The region had had more than enough time to evacuate, so there had been no human casualties.

Now there were rebound waves circulating in the Pacific, and higher than usual swells were spreading into the Atlantic and the Indian Ocean. But that was all. The worst was over.

Webber pulled on a thick navy cable-knit sweater over his gray sweat suit and stepped out into the infirmary grounds and the California sunshine. He decided it would be a long time before he felt warm again.

Cory was there, sitting on a picnic table. She wore a white cotton shirt and rolled-up jeans, bare ankles in the sun. Webber sat down beside her so they could both look out to the ocean.

"What's that?" Webber asked.

Cory had a small scrap of paper. She was holding it carefully. It looked like an envelope with something written on it in pencil. It had been soaked, then dried out.

"The cadet," Cory said. "He gave me a letter. I put it in a plastic bag but . . ." She showed the envelope to Webber. The water had ruined it. The writing was illegible. Webber could see that Cory was upset by the damage. "It sort of makes it seem as if it never happened, you know. All those people just . . . disappeared."

Webber took the envelope from her and smoothed it out on his knee. "Think of all the people who didn't. Because of you."

"And you."

Side by side, they stared out at the sea for a long time without speaking. After a while, Cory asked if he could remember them ever spending this much time together without having an argument.

"Maybe we don't have anything important left to argue about," Webber said.

Her hand sought his. "We'll think of something."

EVENT PLUS 10 YEARS

For a few years, the winters were warmer. For a few, they were colder. No one ever won the debate that the climate fluctuations that followed were due to the Icefire wave, or that they would have occurred anyway. After the first ten years, only the scholars cared.

Some Pacific islands disappeared as completely as Atlantis. The Big Island of Hawaii remained, but its single live volcano, now the largest on the planet, made it too dangerous a site for human habitation, and its fifteen thousand survivors were resettled. Most chose inland states.

After the underwater detonation of more than 100 megatons of nuclear explosives, the biologists were at first relieved at how little long-term disruption appeared in the food web of the Pacific. The Earth appeared to be more resilient than they had expected. Then the biologists grew concerned because that resiliency might make the idea of nuclear war more acceptable.

The first Thanksgiving after Icefire was celebrated in all the countries of the Pacific Rim. Within five years, it was celebrated around the world as a truly international holiday. In most places, it became traditional to scatter flowers on the water, and remember.

China and Japan resolved some long-standing differences, but not others. They were no closer, yet their relations were conducted with greater respect.

China and the United States did not go to war, though they sel-

dom agreed on any substantive international issue. The differences between a culture 5,000 years old and one less than 250 would always be profound, though wisdom and patience were qualities that transcended borders on both sides.

There was a minor economic slowdown in the Western world, but again, in the long run, it might have happened anyway.

All of it might have happened anyway.

McMurdo Station was rebuilt and reopened the next austral summer. Within two years, it again operated year-round. At the new Elizabeth Germer Science Facility, scientists studied the rapid reestablishment of the Ice Shelf over the Ross Sea. It was growing much more quickly than anyone had predicted.

The Ice was unmindful of the attention.

The soldiers had come. The soldiers had gone.

But the Ice remained.

Stable and unchanging once again.

Waiting.

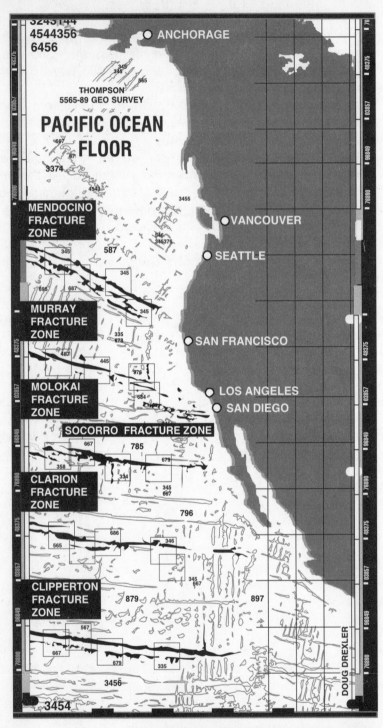

**WESTERN SEABOARD FRACTURE
ZONES AND THRUST FAULTS**

ACKNOWLEDGMENTS

John Morgan and Mike Finnell of Renfield Productions, the first to hear the *Icefire* story, whose enthusiasm and encouragement made this book possible.

Richard Bangs of *Mungo Park*, the Microsoft Network's online adventure travel magazine, for inviting us to travel anywhere in the world as part of the magazine's WildLit program.

The Mountain Travel*Sobek adventure travel company, expedition leader Jonathan Chester, the staff, crew, and passengers of the *Professor Multanovsky*, and Kim Brown of *Mungo Park*, for getting us to Antarctica—and more importantly, bringing us back.

Our editor, John Ordover, and Scott Shannon, Gina Centrello, and all at Pocket who do the hard work after we have all the fun.

Our agent, Martin Shapiro, for his guidance, support, and all the new challenges he has brought us.

Neal Moritz, Charles Pogue, and Sanford Panitch, for their invaluable insights and advice.

Doug Drexler for his exceptional maps.

For technical background, we are indebted to Dave Bresnahan, National Science Foundation Office of Polar Programs, Lieutenant Mel Schuermann and Petty Officer 2nd Class Bill Danzi, Navy Office of Information, West, Penny Juday, and many others. As they read the use to which we have put their much-appreciated contributions, we trust they will remember this is a work of fiction.

The use of nuclear explosives to accelerate the flow of ice from

Antarctica was first proposed by Hugh Auchincloss Brown in 1948, though for reasons other than warfare.

In the February 21, 1997 edition of *Science*, Charles R. Bentley, a researcher with the Geophysical and Polar Research Center, University of Wisconsin, states that the possibility of a rapid, worldwide rise in sea level caused by the collapse of the West Antarctic ice sheet is "a question of widespread interest, great societal import, and considerable controversy." He concludes that, at this time in its history, the WAIS is stable, and only an induced collapse could have such an effect on sea levels.

In light of this, government study of the possibility of a deliberate attempt to collapse the WAIS seems to be a wise precaution. Thus, in our research we were not surprised to discover two references to a study undertaken in the 1960s by the Institute for Defense Analyses in Washington, D.C. Reportedly, the study examined the possibility of terrorist use of nuclear weapons to speed the flow of ice from Antarctica, in order to trigger massive tsunamis and global devastation.

However, in 1997, the IDA would not confirm that any such study had ever been undertaken or published by them. Which means, as Cory Rey might put it, either the government knows nothing about the Icefire scenario, or the government knows too much.

J&G Reeves-Stevens
Los Angeles, June 1998
pacshield@aol.com

7/98

**PLEASE DO NOT REMOVE
DATE DUE CARD FROM POCKET**

By returning material on date due, you will help
us save the cost of postage for overdue notices.
We hope you enjoy the library. Come again and
bring your friends!

FALMOUTH PUBLIC LIBRARY
Falmouth, Mass. 02540-2895
508-457-2555